THE MALEVOLENT EIGHT

Also by Sebastien de Castell

THE MALEVOLENT EIGHT

SEBASTIEN DE CASTELL

Jo Fletcher
BOOKS

First published in Great Britain in 2025 by

Jo Fletcher
BOOKS

Jo Fletcher Books
An imprint of
Quercus Editions Limited
Carmelite House
50 Victoria Embankment
London EC4Y 0DZ

An Hachette UK company

The authorised representative in the EEA is Hachette Ireland,
8 Castlecourt Centre, Dublin 15, D15 XTP3, Ireland (email: info@hbgi.ie)

A CIP catalogue record for this book is available
from the British Library

HB ISBN 978-1-52944-091-1
TPB ISBN 978-1-52944-092-8
EBOOK ISBN 978-1-52944-094-2

This book is a work of fiction. Names, characters,
businesses, organisations, places and events are
either the product of the author's imagination
or are used fictitiously. Any resemblance to
actual persons, living or dead, events or
locales is entirely coincidental.

1

Typeset by CC Book Production
Printed and bound in Great Britain by Clays Ltd, Elcograf S.p.A

Papers used by Jo Fletcher Books are from well-managed forests
and other responsible sources.

For Jon Wood, my inestimable literary agent, without whom *The Malevolent Seven* might never have seen publication. More sensible minds insisted a novel about a bunch of emotionally damaged anti-heroes blowing stuff up and swearing all the time was hardly the stuff of grand literary aspirations.

We sure proved them wrong, didn't we, Jon?

Jon?

Contents

Contents

The Twelve Esoteric Realms

Wonderists draw their abilities through momentary breaches between their own plane of reality and an adjacent one whose physical laws are different from their own. Each wonderist is attuned to a single realm whose properties determine the nature of their magic. Scholars have catalogued the twelve planes of reality conducive to wonderism.

Symbol	Realm	Esoteric Nature
	Tempestoral	A realm of endless mystical storms which can be channelled into near-limitless forms of combustion and explosions. Thunderers are basically walking, talking natural disasters.
	Auroral	The Lords Celestine grant to their goody-two-shoes followers blessings in the form of various defences against enemies and a predilection for smiting people.
	Infernal	The power of the Lords Devilish is sometimes granted to ethically challenged wonderists by even more ethically dubious Diabolic Contractualists. Infernalism is the magic of manipulation and perversion. But hey, some of your best friends are perverts.
	Sonoral	The sphere of vibrational control and amplification. Echoists can make even the most awkward of valedictory speeches into rousing clarion calls which can stir armies into battle. If that's the sort of thing you're into.

 **Luxoral**

The domain of light. Luminists are unequalled at constructing illusions and entertaining at children's parties.

 **Floranistic**

The realm of plant transmogrification. Florinists can cover their skin in iron-hard bark or bring a tree to life. Basically, they're like snooty gardeners.

 **Portalistic**

Through this arcane nether-space, wonderists attuned to Portalism can construct keys enabling them to open doors to faraway places: good for fleeing a crime scene, outstanding for avoiding traffic.

 **Totemic**

The domain of animal symbolism. By attuning themselves to a particular type of animal, totemists gain various abilities and spells aligned with that animal's nature. Avoid dating totemists unless you like finding bits of fur everywhere.

 **Abyssal**

The Abyssal plane is an eternal void that cosmists wrap around their physical forms, making them the deadliest of all wonderists – unless they get depressed and collapse in on themselves.

 **Fortunal**

A realm where probability itself is a form of matter which can be manipulated by chancers to alter the odds in their favour. Do not play cards with Fortunal mages.

 **Sanguinal**

Technically, blood magic comes from the wild magic of the Mortal realm itself, so it's a bit ironic that sanguinalists are inevitably driven to exsanguinate their fellow mortals.

 **Pandoral**

Little is known about this bizarre realm other than the fact that those attuned to it can unleash chaos into the world around them. Still, if it's a choice between dating a rat mage or a pandoralist . . .

The Auroral Hierarchy

While the full nature of the Auroral Hierarchy remains a mystery to scholars of the Mortal realm, encounters with various Auroral beings do occur with regrettable frequency.

The Auroral Sovereign
The ultimate authority and benevolent ruler of the universe – or they would be if any such being existed. Seriously, the Auroral Sovereign is an entirely made-up figurehead invoked by the other members of the Auroral Hierarchy when they want to justify whatever they were planning to do anyway.

The Lords Celestine
The Lords Celestine are all too real, alas. These twelve 'heavenly beings' are each supposed to embody a specific virtue. They like to meddle in Mortal affairs while pretending they're not. In case you're wondering, Decency and Reasonableness are not Celestine virtues.

Angelics
Various beings created by the Lords Celestine to carry out their glorious design upon the Mortal realm. While the full range of angelic types is too numerous to list, the most common ones encountered are Angelic Emissaries, who are heralds able to shapeshift into whichever form will most entice Mortal rulers to side with the Lords Celestine, and Angelic Valiants, who are like smug mob enforcers, only much better looking.

Glorians

Human agents of the Lords Celestine blessed with various abilities, to be used only in the service of their mission (but nobody minds a little extra smiting now and then). There are numerous types of Glorians, including Justiciars, who enforce Auroral Edicts on the Mortal realm, Ardentors, who 'improve' their fellow Mortals (usually with smiting), Parevals, who ride around on silvery-coated steeds doing . . . well, no one is quite sure what the point of the Parevals is supposed to be, but they sure are pretty to look at.

Sublimes

Young, beautiful innocents raised in monastic institutions to give themselves utterly to whomever their religious leaders deem suitable. They don't even get any supernatural blessings.

The Infernal Hierarchy

The Infernals aren't precisely 'evil'; they're more like a bunch of immortal teenagers obsessed with convincing other beings to experience every sensation imaginable. You know, like self-righteous drug dealers.

The Lords Devilish

These are the thirteen rulers of the Infernal realm, each embodying a different 'experiential imperative', such as Spite, Avarice and Gluttony. A more universal term by which to understand the Lords Devilish is 'fuckwits'.

Diabolics

These are the diplomats and deal-makers of the Infernal realm. Acting as con men and carnival barkers, Diabolic Contractualists are always on the lookout for morons to recruit into their schemes. Moral compromise is a virtue as far as Diabolics are concerned, which makes them rather like horned politicians.

Demoniacs

When one imagines a 'demon', one is usually envisioning a demoniac: the fanged, growling, drooling thugs, warriors and assassins of the Infernal Realm. The Lords Devilish use them to wage war – mostly on one another.

Ferocials

Technically, these are a type of lesser Devilish, but the Lords Devilish would prefer you think of them as breeding experiments gone wrong.

Infernalists

These are mortal wonderists who make trades with Diabolic Contractualists in exchange for Infernal spells, which usually manifest as sigils imprinted with unsightly charring of the skin, each one representing a fractional sacrifice of the Infernalist's soul. Nice guys to have a beer with.

Profanes

Mortal apostates of the Aurorals whom the Diabolic Contractualists occasionally manage to recruit on the basis of moral outrage rather than trading for actual spells. Another word for Profanes is 'suckers'.

The Damned

These are the hollowed-out spirits of those who've made one too many deals with Diabolic Contractualists and are now subject to the whims of the Lords Devilish. Eternity is a long time to spend contemplating one's failure to read the fine print.

CHAPTER 1

Epitaph

Can you hear it yet? A sound so subtle your heart mistakes it for the first blush of dawn before the sun kisses the darkness from the horizon.

Or maybe it's more like the innocent joy of a puppy licking your face. What? You don't like puppies licking your face? Fine, it's a cat. Imagine a sound that reminds you of a furry kitty-cat head nuzzling your cheek. Can we get down to business now?

Envision a blanket of golden sand beneath your feet. Look down and watch the breeze sending thousands of perfect crystalline grains skipping across a pristine desert, dancing to unheard rhythms. It's in your body now, this song that slips past the ears to echo deep in your bones. Lyrics written in a language never before spoken in this land whisper a thousand nuanced meanings that will thrum for ever inside your heart.

What shall we call this immaculate love song, this clarion call to the soul? Some have named it the Ballad of the Celestines, others, the Sublime Symphony.

Me? I call it the sound of angels being tortured to death.

'Well, fuck me,' Corrigan said, collapsing the three brass tubes of his spyglass and tucking the device into the bandolier across his chest. Sparks of indigo magic tickled the braids of his beard, illuminating his onyx-black skin and the unpleasant gleam in his grin. 'That's some nasty devilry right there.'

When a Tempestoral mage refers to something as 'nasty', you can skip right past words like 'terrifying' or 'horrific' and jump right to—

'Obscene,' Galass murmured. Pale arms crossed over the sleeveless silver gown she'd worn when she was still a Sublime: one of the Mortal handmaidens of the Aurorals. It wasn't the chill desert air making the slender seventeen-year-old shiver, and lacking Corrigan's spyglass, she hadn't yet seen the atrocities unfolding a quarter of a mile down the road from us. But Galass was a blood mage, a sanguinalist, if you want to get technical about it; her mystical attunement to the flow of life here in the Mortal realm left her particularly sensitive to death and torment. The tresses of her hair, usually a dark brown, turned scarlet as they began to weave and whirl in the air like asps waiting to strike – never a good omen with blood mages, who tend to be borderline lunatics at the best of times.

'We've seen worse,' said Alice, adding that derisive snort she used as punctuation when addressing . . . well, pretty much everybody. The demoniac unwound the silver ribbon of her whip-sword in preparation for the mayhem awaiting us down the road. Despite being a denizen of the Infernal realm herself, Alice had been initiated into the rites of the Glorian Justiciars, making her the first and only demoniac to become a pompous, moralising prat. The bat wings that sprouted from her back – utterly useless on this plane of reality – flapped in anticipation of eviscerating her fellow Infernals.

'Leave the child be,' Shame admonished Alice with her customary patronising seen-it-all-before sigh. Shame never mean to be rude; it was just, as a former Angelic Emissary, she was roughly seven thousand years older than the rest of us. Shame and Alice never got along, despite both of them being traitors to their own realms. There's nothing funnier than watching an ancient apostate angelic arguing theology with a teenaged demoniac desperately trying to prove herself as a Paladin Justiciar. Well, it's funny until someone loses an eye. Or a soul.

'Everybody keep your pants on,' I said, not that anyone in this motley band of wonderists ever took my commands seriously. I pinched the tip of my forefinger against my thumb to form a loop, held it up to my right eye and whispered an apparently innocuous invocation that was far more despicable than the Infernal spells I used to cast before I'd become attuned to a much more dangerous mystical realm. Inside the circle formed by my thumb and forefinger, the empty air warped and quivered, defying the laws of physics to collapse the distance between us and the outskirts of a small town once called Pleasance and now . . . well, it hardly mattered what anyone called it any more. What was important was that I could now clearly see a contingent of low-level Infernal infantry putting the finishing touches on a singularly gruesome gallows.

Atop the platform, four Angelic Valiants – picture heroic, golden-skinned Auroral warriors deployed to smite the unworthy on behalf of the Lords Celestine – were screaming in helpless, transcendent harmonies. Around their necks hung nooses made of three-foot-long centipedes whose twitching stingers continually pierced their heavenly flesh. The unspeakable agony was tearing the Auroral Melody from their throats, and unlike my companions, I was familiar with the particular words being sung. The captives weren't pleading for the Lords Celestine to rescue them; they were begging for oblivion.

'How fare the noble townsfolk, Brother Cade?' asked Aradeus in a voice exactly as smooth and pompous as that sentence suggests. Rat mages, being annoying, unconscionably handsome fops who think 'swashbuckling' is a valid lifestyle, refer to almost everyone as 'noble'. Aradeus Mozen was as decent and valorous as he appeared, which made it hard for me to trust him with a mission like the one we were about to undertake.

'The townsfolk are fine,' I reassured him. 'Getting nobler by the minute.' Actually, the good citizens of Pleasance weren't doing anything other than standing there in mute horror, witnessing the morbid performance unfolding before them. 'The demoniacs aren't interested in executing humans. The Lords Devilish probably orchestrated this little show to convince the townies to switch sides.'

The Lords Celestine and Lords Devilish had been plotting this 'Great Crusade' against each other for millennia, and ever since they'd found a way to enter the Mortal realm, they'd set about recruiting us humans to serve as cannon fodder in their no-holds-barred fight against one another. Their emissaries were going from one town to the next, offering the residents mystically erected temples and palaces. Of course, when bribery failed, they resorted to more brutal means of persuasion.

There was no one standing ready to pull the lever that would open the trapdoors beneath the angelics' feet, finally allowing them to die. No, the demoniacs in their macabre military garb were too busy cheering and dancing around the gallows. I squeezed my thumb and forefinger tighter to focus my unnatural lens on a tall, leathery-white-skinned diabolic whose twin sets of ram and goat horns marked him as a mid-level Infernal Schemelord. Looking smugly pleased with the unfolding theatrics, the Schemelord was gathering golden tears from his captives into slender silver champagne flutes, which he passed one by one to his lower-ranked subjugators so they could toast this latest victory of the Lords Devilish against the Lords Celestine. Off to one side of the gallows, a demoniac Hellion – kind of like a sergeant only more prone to eating anyone who irritates them – was gleefully pounding a sign into the sand. The sign read, 'Infernal Territory. Aurorals Will Be Fined.'

You've got to appreciate the sense of humour.

'Well, oh mighty coven leader?' Corrigan asked, jostling me with his elbow. The big thunderer was spoiling for a fight and resented having to wait for me to give the order. 'Are we butchering some Infernals or not?' He gestured to the final member of our unhallowed company. 'Temper's getting bored.'

'Temper' was what we called the seven-foot-tall furry— No, you know what? Better I leave that malicious monstrosity to introduce himself in his own inimitable style. Corrigan did have a point, though: if we waited too long to let Temper start killing things, he might reevaluate his position on whether we were friends or food.

'Okay, fine,' I agreed, mentally putting the finishing touches on my brilliant peace plan.

'About fucking time,' Corrigan muttered, stomping across the desert sands towards the gallows. The rest of us had to run to catch up with him before delivering what passes for a rallying cry amongst our little band of lunatic wonderists: 'Peace at any price, no matter how many dumb fucks we have to kill!'

I know, needs work.

Pity the confused folk of the tragically named town of Pleasance; they were probably praying for a squadron of Glorian cavalry to come charging in on magnificent white steeds, their golden hooves barely touching the ground. What they got instead were seven emotionally unstable mercenary mages with unpredictable powers and severely compromised moral compasses.

What they got was the Malevolent Seven.

CHAPTER 2

Diplomacy

The rising sun at our backs sent our shadows stretching out before us like grim heralds as seven of the deadliest wonderists ever to wield magic strode towards the gallows. Well, six of us strode. One of us hopped. I'll get to him in a minute.

The repugnant mechanics of angelic torture ground to a halt once the Infernal soldiers became aware of our approach. More than three dozen demoniac Hellions, Burrowmancers and Subjugators froze in contorted poses of gleeful dancing. The wailing of the captive Angelic Valiants quietened, leaving behind the aching memory of an Auroral melody that had once thrummed in my own heart. As for the townsfolk, they just stood there, watching and wondering what new misery was coming into their lives. The grimy stone walls of the settlement behind them were so weatherworn that a single decent catapult shot would have tumbled them to the ground – yet near the centre of town were spires of gleaming marble and alabaster rising up to kiss the sky.

Such beneficent architectural gifts had become common in the six months since the Lords Celestine and Lords Devilish had passed through the gates left behind by the Pandoral wonderists whose invasion plot we seven had foiled, only to discover we'd been played by the Aurorals and Infernals. The temporary truce was over and now both sides were intent on claiming as much of the Mortal realm as possible before they finally settled down to the mass slaughter of their Great Crusade. The fact that a troop of demoniacs had seen fit to capture and torture a squad of Angelic Valiants meant war was getting closer – the very war Corrigan, Galass, Shame, Aradeus, Alice and I – along with Temper, assuming he understood any of it – had sworn to avert.

'Kneel,' the four-horned Schemelord commanded. The demoniac looked rather dashing in his bronze uniform, though it wasn't so much a uniform as a gooey orange oil Infernal soldiers dunked themselves in which hardened into a type of flexible lacquer armour impervious to most weapons.

Which is different from being impervious to *all* weapons.

An ear-splitting thunderclap accompanied the bolt of indigo lightning that tore through the Schemelord's chest. It left behind a hole big enough to see his terrified subordinates cowering behind him. The confused Schemelord, not yet aware he was dead, reached up a hand so his fingers might trace the curve of one of his ram's horns, something they generally do when trying to puzzle out a particularly thorny problem, like, *Why is there a hole in my chest?* I found the gesture oddly human in a way that pricked at my conscience. Fortunately, I'd taught my conscience to shut the hells up long ago.

Corrigan's spell hadn't quite finished, so the rest of us stood and watched as the last sparks of his Tempestoral obliteration spell dissolved that impressive oil-lacquer armour into blackened ooze and Infernal flesh into ashes which blew away in the gentle breeze.

'Speech?' Corrigan asked.

According to all the literature on ethical warfare we'd consulted these past months, it's considered good manners to make at least a token effort at diplomacy.

'The laws of armed conflict demand an overture,' Alice reminded me sternly, as if I hadn't been a Glorian Justiciar long before my former mentor – a crazy old bat named Hazidan Rosh – had decided to indoctrinate a demoniac into an Auroral order, and one which no longer existed because the Justiciars were almost all dead. With her long silvery hair and bluish leathery skin engraved with the esoteric markings of her lineage, Alice looked as if she should be taking the dead Schemelord's place rather than giving me grief about the proper etiquette for wiping out enemy troops. Like generations of petulant teenagers before her, she crossed her arms and declared, 'I will not fight until the speech has been given.'

The Infernal troops, having decided that their commander's death had not, in fact, been some sort of practical joke, were now being formed into attack lines by a demoniac Subjugator who had quickly promoted herself to acting Schemelord.

'Cade?' Corrigan asked with rare deference.

'Yeah?'

'Can I give the speech this time?'

'That depends. Do you think you can deliver a diplomatic overture without making reference to your genitals?'

A look of long-suffering patience darkened the thunderer's already onyx-black features. 'That was *one* time, and it was only a practise run. I needed a word to rhyme with "massive cock".'

'That's not how rhymes work,' I reminded him. 'Also, that "practise" speech went on for half an hour. You'd think someone whose magic revolves around sudden explosions could get to the point expeditiously.'

Aradeus drew his rapier, plastering one of his dozen or so debonair smiles on his lips. 'Those Hellions look better organised than other Infernals we've fought,' he warned. Dressed all in grey, with paradoxically youthful collar-length grey hair, neatly trimmed beard and whiskery moustache, Aradeus Mozen cut a fabulously dashing figure. He pointed his sword at the enemy as if awaiting permission to challenge them – all of them – to a duel. 'I do believe there might be a pair of Malefic Blademasters among their number.'

The subjugator who'd taken the reins of command was tall, with a septet of short curved horns protruding in a circle around her hairless skull, which made her look as if she were wearing a crown. I supposed that qualifies a diabolic for rule as much as any formal leadership training.

'Your suffering will be the stuff of nightmares,' she hissed at us. 'You will join the angelics in the myriad agonies await—'

Alice interrupted. 'The moron is right,' she said to Corrigan. The moron to whom she was referring was me. 'Your speeches go on for even longer than the Fallen One's.'

'*Fallen One*' is Alice's pet name for me on account of my having abandoned the Order of Glorian Justiciars.

She jabbed a finger at Corrigan's chest. 'Furthermore, you appear incapable of uttering so much as a stanza without dropping your trousers.'

'Pantaloons,' Corrigan corrected, hastily refastening the belt around his waist to cinch the blowsy, purple-striped leggings that he had been about to let fall. Given how quickly the temperature rose around him whenever he hurled bolts of aetherial thunder at his enemies, I suppose it was understandable that he preferred a little air circulation to keep from getting hot and sticky down there.

Shame tapped my shoulder. 'The demoniac artillerists appear to be arming some sort of weapon.'

I tried not to flinch. There's something unnerving about being touched by someone who can sculpt your flesh any way she chooses and has no real attachment to humanity. Having been created as an Angelic Emissary, her own form was perpetually mutable. To her, the physical world was little more than an ever-changing set of arbitrary circumstances to which she adapted herself as needed. Ever since we'd freed her from the brothel ship to which the Lords Celestine had consigned her to curry favour with a local prince, which gave a whole new meaning to the term 'all-loving', Shame had chosen to spend most of her time in the form of a heavyset, plain-faced middle-aged woman. She claimed this made her invisible to most humans, which pleased her no end. At the moment, however, she had adopted the form of an over-muscled armoured rhinoceros on two legs, with crab pincers at the end of her tree-trunk-thick wrists – a wise choice given the Infernal scarab currently aimed in our direction.

One might have expected the Infernals and Aurorals to use more classical weaponry, like flaming longswords and tridents with poisonous tines – although, the Infernals *did* employ such tridents and they're rather clever, actually, made from a trio of poisonous snakes, each snakebite delivering a different venom— All right, fine. Fascinating as that particular piece of military cryptozoology might be, the weapon about to be deployed against us right at this minute was of an entirely different order of magnitude.

The scarab, a four-foot-long blue-carapaced beetle, was being jammed arse-first into the barrel of a large cannon whose only function was to generate initial velocity, as the scarab had its own wings and would fly to its target regardless of any inaccuracies in aiming. The Scarabist who'd no doubt raised the creature from birth was currently whispering into what passed for its ear, telling it who to attack and how spectacularly gruesome to make the victim's demise. That's kind of a theme with Infernals: these guys really like putting on a show.

So do we, as it happens.

'Galass,' I asked, 'does that thing bleed?'

I could tell from the tightness at the corners of her eyes and mouth that she'd been anticipating the question. Trained as a Glorian Sublime since childhood, she'd been raised to believe that spiritual fulfilment came only from giving oneself utterly to whomever the local Glorian Ardentor gifted her. If you're starting to think that the Lords Celestine employ this particular brand of diplomacy more often than is theologically sound, re-read your copy of the Seventeen Hundred and Seventy-Seven Auroral Edicts. I'm telling you, whoring oneself out for God comes up *a lot*.

You'd expect a Sublime to be demure and submissive, but from the moment an Ascendant Prince had tried to reward me with Galass in gratitude for a particularly bombastic piece of destruction Corrigan and I had perpetrated against his enemies, she had proven to be rude – and worse, prone to picking philosophical fights with me. Having someone argue that trying to give them their freedom is an insult to their religious devotion gets really old, really fast. Oddly, the subsequent Infernal pact made on her behalf that turned Galass into a blood mage smoothed out some of those rough edges. I suppose that's what comes of constantly trying to restrain yourself from exsanguinating every living being with whom you come in contact. Galass was utterly determined never to descend into the madness that was endemic to blood magic, which was why the spell I was asking from her bordered on cruelty.

The seven of us – well, six, because we really weren't sure what Temper wanted out of all this – had sworn to do whatever it took to prevent this war between the Infernals and Aurorals. Seeing the anguish she was trying to hide behind the determined expression on her face, I wavered. 'Listen, if it's too much—'

Galass cut me off, raising one arm to point towards the scarab. Her fingertips twitched as her attunement to the flow of life sought out whatever it was that enabled the Infernal beetle to exist on the Mortal plane. 'It's not blood, exactly,' she murmured, 'but I can work with it.'

'What about the speech, though?' Corrigan asked. 'That's my favourite part.'

Aradeus, eyes gleaming grey with the tactical perception afforded rat totemists, reminded us of concerns more pressing even than Corrigan's hurt feelings at not being chosen to lead our coven.

'The new Schemelord appears to be initiating a cunning plan for our capture. Those Hellion front lines are preparing to flank us,' Aradeus warned, 'while the rest of the infantry are preparing more conventional cannon – oh look! The Scarabist intends to unleash his lovingly nurtured beast upon us while the other troops encircle us to prevent our escape. I grant there's nothing particularly clever there, but I suspect their bosses will be pleased with the result.'

'The new Schemelord is also positioning herself to get a better view of the scarab devouring us,' I added. 'Sorry, Corrigan. Looks like neither of us gets to give the big speech. Maybe if you'd prepared one as short as your—?'

Corrigan's thick fingers clamped down on my shoulder and for an instant, I thought we were going to have the conversation we'd been avoiding these past three months on the subject of who was best qualified to lead our little band of psychotic pacifists, and why I kept acting like the obvious answer was me. 'It's not for me,' he whispered. 'It's Temper. I think he's feeling a bit left out lately. Maybe if we let him give the speech . . . ?'

I looked back over my shoulder at the unnerving otherworldly creature whose twitching— No, it's better when you see him in action.

'"Temper" does not speak,' Alice reminded Corrigan. 'This is because "Temper" is not a person. It is a fucking ka—'

'Fire!' bellowed the recently elevated Schemelord to her Scarabist.

Smoke and flame erupted from the barrel of the cannon as it hurled the massive blue-carapaced bug at us. For a second, I wondered if Corrigan and I had bickered ourselves into an early grave, but just as suddenly, the Infernal beast halted in mid-air, coming to a stop five feet from Galass' outstretched hand. Slowly, the scarab turned on its axis, spindly insect limbs darting out at its captor in futile rage.

'This is sadistic,' Galass said quietly as she stepped closer to the scarab.

'It's an Infernal weapon,' I reminded her. 'Sadism is the *entire* point of its creation.'

She shook her head, ignoring the hissing and spitting of the deadly creature bound by her control over its life fluids. 'You don't understand. The scarab isn't just acting out of instinct. This one was specially selected from among its siblings for the joy it takes in causing pain.' Galass turned to me, her scarlet tresses weaving in a manner I always take as subconscious resentment at the moral quagmires I kept drawing her into. 'Why would *anyone* put so much effort into creating a living being that takes pleasure in the suffering of others? Isn't the sole point of a weapon to kill efficiently?'

In fact, the answer was a bit more complicated than, '*Because the Lords Devilish are a bunch of cruel shitbags who get off on torturing anyone who opposes them.*' Mortals like us, being prone to thinking in absolutes, struggle to appreciate that Infernals aren't actually 'evil' – not in the way most of us define the term – any more than the Aurorals are entirely 'good'. The essence of the Infernal dogma boils down to *experience*: the belief that one must savour *every* sensation, *every* emotion, *every* part of what it means *to exist*.

Self-restraint is no virtue to an Infernal: it's a sin. Demoniacs, malefics, diabolics and the rest don't just eat, they *devour*. They don't walk or run, they dance and whirl and race. When they make love, it's in search of the most transcendent pleasure, and when they make war, they don't simply kill their enemies; they obliterate them in the most horrific ways imaginable.

'The Lords Devilish are shitbags,' Alice replied tersely, cracking her whip-sword in the air to emphasise her disdain. The two of us had debated this point many times; she vehemently disagreed with my perhaps rosy assessment of her fellow Infernals.

The recently promoted Schemelord, having witnessed us taking control of the scarab, was busily revising her attack plans, no doubt concocting something even more macabre. Like I said before,

Infernals don't rush blindly into battle. Mere death isn't enough to get poets composing 47-verse laments to the true horror of your demise.

'The optimal time to strike is now,' Aradeus observed. 'While the Schemelord wastes her advantage concocting ways to make a truly memorable end to us, we can throw off their rhythm and gain the upper hand.'

Aradeus might actually have made a good leader for our coven. He was cunning, yet kind; idealistic, yet sensible. Alas, not even Galass credited him with the ruthlessness it would take to prevent this war. 'Peace at any price' was our motto, which is why we were willing to kill as many people as it took to get the job done.

Still, when seeking to avert a cataclysmic crusade between two despotic supernatural armies who've been waiting for countless millennia to finally unleash their hate upon one another, not to mention any innocent bystanders who get in the way, who's to say diplomacy can't win the day?

'You do it,' I said to Galass.

She was still mesmerised by the hideous four-foot-long scarab floating in front of her face. 'Hmm?'

'The speech. You give it.'

Now she turned. '*Me?* I've never even practised "the speech". It was always supposed to be you or Corrigan or Alice. What do you expect me to say?'

'I don't know, but we're trying to stop a war that threatens humanity and yours is the only form of wonderism born of the Mortal realm. You're attuned to the wild magic of life itself. That's got to mean something.'

'Indeed!' Aradeus exclaimed. He was never one to let a sappy sentiment go by without horning in on the action. 'Yours, my lady Galass, is the voice these troubled lands most need to hear: yours, the words left too long unuttered. Speak you now on behalf of our noble cause and share with these otherworldly belligerents the infinite wisdom and compassion we battered souls all sense resides in your heart.'

See what I mean about rat mages? The prick even managed to turn coaxing a speech out of someone else into its own speech.

Galass hesitated, her gaze travelling from the Infernals to the four Angelic Valiants noosed to the gallows, to the townsfolk beyond. I wondered if her attunement allowed her to peer into their hearts. Probably not, I decided, since hearts are muscles with no actual emotional or spiritual significance. No one knows precisely how blood magic works, because those attuned to it never live long enough to find out. Watching Galass, however, I could see she was intuiting precisely what her disparate audience needed to hear.

She began quietly, no unnecessary shouting or forced passion, unlike Corrigan. 'We are seven wonderists of no particular repute,' she started. 'We wear no crowns, hold no insignia of rank. We possess neither the authority nor the right to speak for the peoples of this world, and yet we stand before you as uncommissioned emissaries of the Mortal realm, bearing this message for your masters. *Desist from this place.* If your continued existence holds any attraction for you, abandon the path upon which you have set yourselves. Turn away from the innocents you bribe, cajole and blackmail to your cause.' Her voice deepened, becoming louder, as if she meant her words to echo from the mountain range that ringed the desert. 'This world is not a board upon which you and your opponents may play your childish games. Humanity will not be reduced to toy soldiers for you to move from one square to the next. Take your Great Crusade back to your own demesnes if you must – argue over boundary lines on ancient maps and concoct such devious battle plans as feed your arrogance. Raze forests and fields, obliterate cities and temples, eradicate the cultures of your own domains. But heed these words, you would-be conquerors: from this day onwards, when you step upon the soil of this realm, you find yourself in' – a wry smile came to her lips – 'Malevolent territory.'

'Damn,' Corrigan muttered next to me. 'Why can't you give speeches like that?'

She was no longer that traumatised young Sublime I'd met in Ascendant Lucien's war camp. With her right hand extended, she made a fist. It looked as if the scarab were collapsing in on itself. Then she suddenly spread her fingers wide – and the creature exploded into thousands upon thousands of glittering shards of iridescent shell and gobs of sickly yellow blood that splattered over the demoniacs surrounding us.

'Desist, you petulant children masquerading as warriors,' she said, 'else we seven shall henceforth Fuck. Your. Shit. Up.'

Peace at any price, I thought proudly.

The sizzle of Corrigan's thunder joined the crack of Alice's whip-sword and the eerier sounds accompanying the rest of our respective magics. I offered a silent apology to whichever spirit of decency might be questioning the ethics of seven wonderists trying to stop a war by engaging in rampant bloodshed. Well, those spirits could go ahead and close their eyes if they were squeamish, because peace was a dirty business, especially now. The gallants of long ago had left the rest of us with a world unprotected from the supernatural sons-of-bitches presently fighting over it. Corrigan had named us 'The Malevolent Seven' and that's what we'd become. Maybe we weren't the kind of heroes the world deserved, but we were the ones it got, and we sure as shit weren't going to save it by pretending to be the good guys.

And now, without further ado, let me to introduce you to Temper.

CHAPTER 3

Temper

The story of how the creature Corrigan had affectionately dubbed 'Temper' came to join our coven is somewhat ... tangled, not least because confessing my own part in the beast's existence would almost certainly get me killed – likely by Corrigan himself. Nonetheless, as our mission was, as we say in the peace-making business, to *make an impression* upon the Infernals and Aurorals, there was no question that Temper was perfectly suited to that endeavour.

'By the Auroral Sovereign's Tears ...' Shame swore as she watched him in action. It takes a lot to shock an Angelic Emissary who's witnessed the darkest depravities of the Mortal realm.

'By the Sovereign's Tears, indeed,' I agreed.

It had been a long time since last I'd uttered that oath. Doing so now set the tip of my tongue to tingling, an uncomfortable reminder that no matter how hard you might try to turn your back on your training, the instincts beaten into you always remain.

But to get back to Temper ...

Picture a seven-foot-tall tawny rabbit, but shorten the ears. Shorter – no, stop, that's too short. It's not a fucking hamster. Aim for something like the ears of a red fox, or maybe a bat. Okay, now, the tail: neither fluffy nor round, not rabbity at all, more long and thick, tapering towards the end. Oh, and imagine the beast launching itself with haunches powerful enough to send it leaping ten feet in the air and twenty-five feet towards you so that it can wrap that muscular tail around your neck and secure you tight so it can punch you into oblivion with paws quite capable of pulverising bone and rending flesh into a bloody pulp.

In retrospect, picturing a rabbit probably wasn't a useful starting point. What I *can* tell you is that, according to the sole text I've found in the months since Temper's arrival on the Mortal plane, scholars of cryptozoology believe his species derived from an especially violent, unhinged plane of existence where they were known as 'kan-gar-oos'.

Kangaroos.

Even the name sounds ominous.

That's not even the worst part. See, most creatures can't survive in realms beyond the ones where they emerged naturally, and when they *do* survive, there tend to be . . . side-effects.

'*Must* he do that with the bodies?' Alice complained, swinging her whip-sword in a wide arc at the enthusiastic bronze-lacquered pair of Hellions lunging for her. Before the blow could land, the silver ribbon of her blade split apart into thirteen segments, scattering past the heads of her opponents. The demoniacs grinned as they advanced upon what they naïvely believed to be an unarmed traitor to their cause. They were still wearing those grins as the shards of Alice's whip-sword first slowed in mid-air, then darted back to rejoin the hilt by way of first slicing through the Hellions' skulls.

Mind, even that disgusting piece of gratuitous butchery couldn't hold a candle to the gruesome spectacle of Temper, his tail wrapped around the neck of an Artillerist he'd punched to death moments before, lapping up the blood pouring out from the wreckage of the demoniac's face.

Yep, our latest recruit wasn't merely a savage, remorseless kangaroo. He was a fucking *vampire* kangaroo, who made it his business to messily imbibe the blood of his enemies. And business round here was plentiful.

'Watch your own tail, Cade,' Corrigan warned as he blasted a trio of demoniac Mortarists creeping up behind me with shrapnel lanterns. The Mortarists ended up being the ones decapitated when a bolt of Tempestoral lightning sent them to whatever passes for their ancestors' warm bosom.

With typical thunderer recklessness, Corrigan's Tempestoral eruption had also set off the lanterns – I would've been torn to shreds by the shrapnel, had it not been for Aradeus' totemic quivering spell, which enabled his rapier to *literally* bat every single shard of steel and bone out of the air before they reached me.

Rat mages are *such* show-offs.

'Will you be fighting any of your own battles, Fallen One?' Alice asked, her whip-sword now moving with devastating speed as it decapitated one enemy after another.

'The rest of you appear to be doing just fine without me,' I said. 'Besides, someone needs to keep an eye on the prize.'

I had no idea what that meant in the context of a chaotic massacre of otherworldly invaders, but Alice was contenting herself with eviscerating yet more of her fellow demoniacs. I did cast a few spells here and there, ones that looked enough like chancer magic – that's a form of wonderism derived from the Fortunal plane of existence, where the physical laws allow for the alteration of probabilities – to avoid suspicion amongst my friends.

Every wonderist draws their spells from whichever plane of reality they're naturally attuned. As a young man, my magic had come from Auroralism, which manifests as blessings conferred by the Lords Celestine. After I'd booted myself from their ranks, the only other attunement I could manage was to the Infernal realm, where spells are bartered for services negotiated by a diabolic representative of the Lords Devilish. If neither of those sound like appealing ways to acquire magic, it's as Corrigan always says: 'You can pick your friends and you can pick your nose, but nobody gets to pick their fucking mystical attunement.'

I've never been entirely sure that's the right punchline for that particular saying.

Six months ago, an opportunity came along – one that very few wonderists in history ever got and almost all would've killed for – the chance to alter my attunement using a device ponderously named 'The Empyrean Physio-Thaumaturgical Device of Attunal Transmutation'. Seriously. You can see why we in the business call it the *Apparatus*. Regardless of appellation, that coffin-shaped relic is the only known means of choosing one's attunement. Corrigan, knowing my propensity for relying on luck, assumed I'd attuned myself to the Fortunal realm. He'd guessed wrong.

Inside the ruins of a massive stone fortress racked by magical forces more chaotic and dangerous than any we'd ever encountered, we'd witnessed the culmination of an unbelievably nasty conspiracy by the Lords Celestine and Lords Devilish to create a set of gates that, for the first time in recorded history, would allow their respective armies to enter the Mortal realm. Here, the long-prophesied cata-clysmic war between them would at last come to pass. Given the low probability of our surviving such a war, I'd used the Apparatus to give myself a far less . . . whimsical attunement.

Alice was the most suspicious of me, mostly on account of me having abandoned my role as a Glorian Justiciar. She had devoted herself to just such a calling, despite the fact that *no way* was any demoniac *ever* going to be inducted into the order. Deep down, she must have known that Hazidan Rosh, the greatest and also most rebellious Justiciar who'd ever lived, had put her on a completely futile path. And yet . . . Alice couldn't give up her pursuit of that impossible dream.

'I've got my eye on you, Fallen One,' she warned me, laying low a demoniac Burrowmancer who'd somehow convinced himself that one of those creepy three-foot-long centipedes they'd used on the angelics could get around her whip-sword.

Alice's blade sliced through both soldier and centipede with ease.

You could admit to her what you did, I tried to convince myself. *You could tell all of them why you chose a form of magic so inherently dangerous that someday soon, you'll likely become as big a threat as the Aurorals and Infernals together. Come on, Cade, just spit it out. Make them see why what you did wasn't* reckless but necessary: *an act of sublime self-sacrifice for which, really, they should be applauding you.*

Yeah. That was never going to fly. Alice would definitely try to kill me when she found out. Corrigan would attempt to stop her, of course; my best friend would surely consider it his own personal duty to carry the pain and blast me out of existence himself.

'Cade, are you all right?' asked Shame, coming to my side. Looked like there were some demoniac trident fighters there after all, as I recognised the viscous remains of their internal organs she was wiping off her fingers. Angelic Emissaries, once freed from the laws imprinted upon their spirits by the Lords Celestine, can learn to unleash their flesh-sculpting powers upon bodies besides their own. It may not be the most painful way to die, but it's definitely the gooiest. 'I can sense your desire for the violence to end,' she announced. 'Why aren't you calling for a ceasefire?'

That's the other problem with Angelic Emissaries. The Lords Celestine created them to embody the physical ideals most prized by those with whom they came into contact, and that was mostly to present diplomatic entreaties. That in turn required an instinct- ual awareness of the desires of those they were sent to persuade. Although Shame had left the service of the Celestines, the yearnings of those around her still tugged at her transmutational abilities. I guess my particular yearnings were currently tugging hardest, because she'd shed her walking rhinoceros guise and was now a woman near to my own age, the same black hair and even a matching dent in her nose where mine had been broken by my fellow Glorian Justiciars shortly after I'd announced my departure from the order. The woman standing before me now could have passed for the sister I'd never had – and until this moment, had never realised how badly I wished were real.

'We came to deliver the Lords Devilish a message,' I reminded her, searching for some sign of forgiveness in her eyes and disgusted with us both when I found it there.

Is this you finally trying to connect with humanity, Shame? I wondered silently. *Or is it more proof that you'll never understand us at all?*

I turned to Galass, who until now had turned her sanguinalist abilities only on the living weapons wielded by the Infernal troops. Blood mages, counter to what most people think, aren't cackling warlocks spreading death wherever they go. In fact, it's quite the opposite: their magic attunes them to the natural ebb and flow of life itself.

That's why my next request was so unforgivable. 'Finish them off,' I told her.

Demoniac soldiers, whether Hellions, Burrowmancers, Mortarists, Subjugators or Schemelords, come armed with plenty of their own spells. Throughout the battle, their Infernal shields had protected them from magics that manifested *inside* the target, but Corrigan, Alice, Shame, Aradeus and Temper now had them on the ropes. I might have given up my attunement to the Infernal realm, but I could still perceive the esoteric frequencies of their spells, which was how I knew their shields had begun to collapse enough for Galass to employ the most innate and intrusive ability of her sanguinalist magic. I wished there were some other way, but the Lords Devilish don't care about a few soldiers killed here or there, and they certainly don't give a shit about how many get taken captive.

'Do it,' I ordered her.

Young she might be, but Galass isn't the sort of person to take commands, especially from me. Nonetheless, she'd understood the job when she'd signed up for it. Furrowing her brow, she extended both her arms and gave her body free reign to unleash the spell it so badly craved and which she, very much to her credit, fought so hard to deny it.

At first the magic manifested as little more than a hazing in the air between Galass and the demoniacs. Unlike human blood, the life-fluid of Infernals comes in all sorts of colours. It began to look like a rainstorm had appeared from a cloudless sky, the drops blown by a dozen different winds in a dozen different directions. Her silver gown was quickly showered in the myriad hues of blood seeping from the increasingly ashen flesh of the Infernal troops.

'Void take me, that's disgusting,' Corrigan swore. He clamped a hand over his mouth and nose to keep the blood splatters flying towards Galass from getting inside him. 'Temper, close your muzzle. You're being gross.'

The kangaroo ignored the admonishment and kept hopping up and down in the air, jaws open wide to catch every droplet of demoniac blood. Try painting *that* image on a portrait of seven heroic mages out to save the world.

Our enemies slumped one by one to the ground, their leathery skin engraved with the intricate symbols of their respective lineages turning paler as they died what must have felt to them a depressingly Mortal sort of death.

When it was over, I knelt by Galass, holding her hair as she vomited onto the desert sand. Her crimson tresses whipped out at me, the tips jabbing at my hands and arms. I ignored both them and the uncomfortable intimacy. I noticed neither Alice nor Shame were volunteering to take my place.

'I'm okay,' Galass said at last, trying to mask a sob. 'I . . . I understand why it has to be this way.'

'A grim duty,' Aradeus said, keeping a respectful distance. 'Take solace, Lady Galass, in the lives that will be saved by this unfortunate yet necessary violence, and trust in Brother Cade's virtuous leadership of our coven.'

Why did the damned rat mage have to make me sound gallant right when I was about to commit an even more heinous act?

You wanted to save the world, I reminded myself. *Now be a hero: go and kill some angels.*

CHAPTER 4

Balancing the Scales

I waited until Galass was done voiding her guts along with the remains of her conscience before walking to the gallows and ascending the hastily assembled wooden stairs. The centipede nooses slowly strangling the angelics tried to attack me as I unwound them from their victims' necks, but the curse I quietly cast upon them warped their aggressive instincts into something more akin to those of house cats curling up on a warm lap. Several of the centipedes began nuzzling my hands, which was more unnerving than when they were trying to stab me with their stingers. Even that, however, couldn't compare to the stomach-churning enthusiasm of the Angelic Valiants I was freeing.

'Bless you!' they cried out in splendiferous harmony. The four of them, Auroral warriors of surpassing might, launched into a new song, no longer a lament but a triumphal anthem heralding the inevitable victory of the Lords Celestine.

'Mind keeping it down?' I asked, setting aside the last of the centipedes. The confused creature slithered down the steps of the gallows and into the desert in search of a life in this realm that had neither given birth to it nor had any place for it. There was an omen in there somewhere.

'Rejoice, all of you!' the tallest of the Valiants commanded the awestruck townsfolk below. He spread his arms wide as he shared the good news. 'Today's battle foretells of greater triumphs to come! No longer are you the wretched inhabitants of a forgotten town. Henceforth this pitiable settlement takes its rightful place as one small part of a magnificent, boundless city that will soon encompass this entire world. Arise, citizens of New Celestine!'

'They're already standing,' I muttered, though it hardly mattered; Valiants have no measurable sense of humour.

Corrigan, joining me atop the gallows, shot me a questioning look. The next step in my cunning plan was apparently pushing even his ethical limits. Hells, the damned kangaroo was looking squeamish too.

This is the job, I told myself. *You're the only person alive who's been attuned to both the Auroral and Infernal realms. No one else understands the cycle of never-ending carnage the Lords Celestine and Lords Devilish will unleash on our realm if they're allowed to turn it into their personal battlefield.*

'I need a favour,' I said to the leader of the angelics. 'You know, as payment for rescuing you after you got your arses handed to you by a gang of demoniac grunts?'

The valiant frowned at my crass interruption of what would no doubt have become a rousing tale of Auroral supremacy once filtered through angelic oratory. 'Righteousness is its own reward,' he reminded me, 'lest its lustre be tarnished by personal desires. You should know this, Cade Ombra, for are you not the last Glorian Justiciar?'

In theory, that was true. The other Justiciars were all dead and Alice didn't count, since she'd never been formally inducted into the order and was, from a species perspective at least, ineligible to join. Fidelity, Dignity and the rest of my former comrades had been slain by the Seven Brothers, who left their still-living decapitated heads for me to find shortly before the brothers transformed themselves into living gates through which their Pandoral patrons had intended to invade the Mortal realm. Corrigan, Shame, Alice, Galass, Aradeus and I had risked our lives and defeated the brothers to prevent that conquest – only as soon as we'd triumphed, we'd discovered that our entire mission had been a ruse perpetrated by an innocent-looking – and totally evil – eleven-year-old boy named Fidick. He'd refashioned those same gates and allowed the Aurorals and Infernals into our realm so they could fight their long-foretold Great Crusade against one another, using Mortals for cannon fodder. If I ever met Fidick again, I was going to let Temper eat him, from his pretty little toes up.

'Honoured Valiant,' I began with a formal bow, 'on my honour as a Glorian Justiciar, 'tis a righteous message that I beseech you deliver unto the Lords Celestine.'

The quartet of angelics went ominously silent. Without my former tether to the Auroral Song I could no longer hear what they were saying, but the familiar buzzing in my ears suggested they were at least debating the issue.

When they were done, their leader honoured me with a smile he clearly thought should make me swoon. 'Exult in our gift,' he sang. You learn to ignore that after a while. 'Through us, the Lords Celestine have deigned to hear your plea. Speak, Justiciar Cade, and know that your words are being heard by those whose every breath is revelation.'

Glowing golden fingers appeared upon the shoulders of each of the Valiants: the famed guiding hand of the Lords Celestine – and proof that the smug bastards really were listening. The Valiants shimmered as they hummed in quiet harmony. Always nice to have a heavenly orchestra accompanying your entreaty.

'Cool, thanks.' I still wasn't sure how best to convince a group of self-appointed divine beings to reconsider the holy war they'd been waiting to prosecute for thousands of years, but in precarious diplomatic situations, I find plain-spoken humility works best.

I knelt before the quartet of Angelic Valiants. 'How shall I put this?' I began. 'You and your bosses sometimes have trouble recognising sarcasm, irony or, you know, expressions of free will, so I'll speak in short sentences and try to be as literal as possible. You remember the warning we gave those Infernals right before we blew them all up?'

The angelics were staring at me. I think they'd just worked out I'd insulted them.

I ignored their shocked faces and carried on, 'Well, that goes double for the Lords Celestine. Tell all twelve of those arrogant pricks that it's time to pack their bags and fuck off back to the Auroral demesne. Find some other plane of reality to prosecute their prophesied pissing contest. Galass told them and I am telling you: effective *immediately*, the Mortal plane is closed for business.'

I looked up so the nearest valiant could hit me with the infamous Auroral Glare and see how little it bothered me. 'Think you can remember all that? Or should I write it down?'

That flawless upper lip curled and I felt the faint whoosh of air as he gathered unto himself the blessings of the Lord Celestines in preparation for smiting me. Unfortunately for him, I'd had enough being smited for one lifetime and was about to smite the smug off *his* face when the Valiant behind him suddenly spoke.

'Well, darn, Cade, that doesn't sound friendly at all,' she said.

Well, darn, Cade? Was that a hint of a drawl?

There were two problems right there: first, angelics don't talk with a drawl, and second, they don't use slang like 'darn'. I didn't waste time wondering why they hadn't referred to me by my former Justiciar name, just enjoyed the respite.

I jumped to my feet and backed away, preparing to hurl the nastiest spell in my current arsenal at her, even though that risked revealing my true attunement and some very tough questions – when a third curious development revealed itself.

'The hand!' cried the leader of the Valiants, pointing.

The glowing aetherial fingers upon his comrade's shoulder had begun to smoulder an ugly red. I didn't know they could do that.

28

The Celestine on the other end of that hand was certainly trying to pull away, but was now ensnared.

'What foul magics assail you, Sister?' the Valiants' leader asked sternly, as if it were her fault.

'*Sister?*' she asked, lending the word an amused melancholy. 'How can we who were never born claim kinship with one another? No mother's womb held us, "Brother". We were merely ... *fashioned* by the Lords Celestine, destined to be servants without souls, our dooms forever etched in the emptiness of our creation.'

'Blasphemy!' declared another valiant, casting a scathing eye at me. 'What Infernal perversion have you wrought, Fallen One?'

I *really* hate it when people call me that.

'Hey, don't pin this on me, friend. I'm just enjoying the show.'

The once-golden hand of the Celestine was now aflame, the fingers spasming in what appeared to be a futile and agonising bid for release.

'Really, Cade?' the possessed Valiant asked. 'You always did strike me as something of an idealist.' An amused smile came to her lips. 'Only an idealist would be so arrogant as to presume he could stop a war foretold millennia before his birth and destined to last epochs after his death.'

'Arrogant? I'm humble as a bumblebee and I've never been partial to prophecies. Who the fuck are you?'

One corner of the Valiant's mouth rose. 'A prophet, of course. Care to have your fortune told?'

I glanced back at Alice and Aradeus to make sure they were ready for a fight. Corrigan and Shame had already expended a great deal of their magic against the Infernals, and Galass could barely stand. As for Temper, well, you know: bloodthirsty kangaroo. I reached into the pocket of my azure coat and fished out the smallest silver coin I had – it also made a decent conduit for spells – and tossed it at the feet of the possessed angelic. 'Okay, lady. Tell me my future.'

Her initial silence made me wonder if the Lord Celestine with the burning fingers was trying to reestablish control over his minion – until the hand withered to wisps of grey and crimson smoke, leaving behind only a small pile of ashes on the angelic's shoulder, which she promptly brushed away. 'That's better. Those Lords Celestine really need to get a sense of humour. Now, as for you, Cade – you and your . . . what are you called again?'

'The Malevolent Seven,' Aradeus said – and yes, of course he bowed.

'The Malevolent *fucking* Seven,' Corrigan corrected.

The angelic chuckled. It was a pleasant laugh, although for some reason it felt to me kind of like church bells tolling my imminent demise. 'Well, my magnificent new friends, my prediction is that you'll all live long, happy lives . . . so long as you learn to mind your own fucking business.' Absently, she gestured to the other three Valiants. 'Leave these numbskulls to their war. Trust me, it'll be better for all of us in the long run.'

'Sure. No problem.' I raised my right hand. 'On behalf of the Malevolent Seven, we hereby swear and avow to cease any and all interference in the war between the Aurorals and Infernals.' I made a show of looking around the gallows. 'If anyone's got a pen, I'm happy to put it in writing.'

The possessed angelic laughed again. 'You know, you're funnier than you were back then.'

'Back when?'

Golden curls danced across perfect rose-tinted cheekbones as she shook her head. 'Ah, ah, ah. It's ungentlemanly to expect a girl to reveal all her secrets on the first date, Cade. You'll have to guess.'

'How about a hint?'

She favoured me with a smile which was not at all angelic. 'Fine, one hint. If you want to know when we first met, go and ask your old—'

The leader of the Valiants was clearly getting bored. 'Enough!'

he bellowed, drawing a glowing sword from a scabbard that hadn't been at his waist until that very moment. 'Whatever ruse the two of you are attempting, this blasphemy ends *now*!'

Fucking moron, I swore silently. *Just like a valiant to completely botch an interrogation.*

'A ruse?' the possessed angelic asked. 'Destiny isn't trickery, you silly boy. It's inevitability. It's preordained.' To me she asked, 'Did you know that another word for destiny is doom? Here's an interesting fact that all those theologians somehow failed to include in their religious texts that claim to reveal the natural order of the universe: every sentient being creates three dooms for themselves. With each decision we make, we bring ourselves closer to one of those three endings.' She tapped her chest. 'This pretty little angelic here? Even without a proper soul she's still got three different destinies awaiting her. Poetic, don't you think?'

'I prefer erotic poetry,' Corrigan put in.

The possessed angelic shot him a saucy grin and cocked her hip suggestively. 'Too bad death by excessive orgasm is only one of your three dooms then, handsome. The other two . . . well, I don't want to spoil the surprise. Maybe if you're especially nice to me I'll let you pick which of them comes true.'

That was either an entirely inappropriate proposition to make in the middle of a stand-off, or a claim to a kind of power unheard of in any esoteric realm I'd ever encountered. 'I'm pretty sure that's not how destiny works,' I broke in, in an attempt to goad whoever was possessing the angelic.

'Oh? Shall we test that theory?' Her hand dropped to her side, fingers weaving idly as if she were recalling an old song. 'How about, instead of waiting to discover which doom awaits this particular angelic, we simply choose one and bring it to the here and now?'

A shadow began to form on the wooden planks beneath her feet. I glanced eastwards, confirming that the angle of the sun was entirely wrong for casting shadows upon the gallows.

Another of the Valiants pointed. 'Why . . . why is the shape contorted like that?'

'Haven't you been listening?' the possessed angelic asked. 'That's one of her three dooms. Six hundred years from now, she goes mad with grief and attacks a fellow Valiant, only to be slain by a sword through her stomach. Angelics being such useless creatures, my question is, why wait?'

Without warning, she'd spun on her heel and was extending both palms to the sky. Golden talons long as curved daggers burst from her fingertips as she drove them into the other Valiant's eyes. He screamed in agony, limbs twitching until they lost all strength. She held him upright, the fingers of one hand still embedded into his eye sockets.

'Now, you . . .' She gestured with her free hand to the leader of the Valiants. 'Well, not you specifically, since you were never going to live another six hundred years. No, you'll be dead in about two minutes. But for now, go ahead and take the place of the Glorian Justiciar who executes her. He draws a blade just like the one you're holding. Now listen – this part's important – as he stabs her in the belly, he shouts in righteous fury—'

'May the Void take you, traitor!' the leader of the Valiants bellowed as he impaled the angelic he'd called 'sister' only moments before.

Back when I rode with the Glorian Justiciars, I'd witnessed the damage Celestine-blessed blades inflicted on everyday, run-of-the-mill psychopathic wonderists on a rampage. The weapons burn with fiery golden curses meant to purge the opponent of their sins – which is bad enough. In practice, it's rather more gruesome: the sin *literally* burns through the unfortunate victim, melting their flesh like candle wax until it drips from their bones.

What I'd never seen was the result when one angelic Valiant stabs another with a 'blessed' sword.

'What . . . what is happening to her?' asked Galass, looking nauseous. 'It's as if her skin is—'

When a blood mage is too horrified to finish a sentence, you know it's got to be pretty bad.

Angelics are forged from raw ecclesiasm, the stuff of consciousness which, according to Corrigan, screwed up what would've been a perfectly peaceful universe by bringing sentience into being. In the case of angelics, that ecclesiasm was purified by the Lords Celestine, making these beings incapable of sinful acts in body and mind, since their every thought is bounded by the twelve Celestine Virtues of humility, justice, abnegation, rationality and so on.

The angelic being without sin, the golden blade *should* have passed cleanly through without leaving so much as an unsightly scab – except, this *particular* angelic had been possessed. We'll have to ignore the fact that possession should have been impossible, since Valiants are perpetually attuned to the Auroral Song. Anyway, whichever power had enabled the wonderist possessing her to burn away the guiding hand of a Lord Celestine was now waging spiritual war against the angelic's own nature.

As the lead Valiant's sword pierced the chest, droplets of melting flesh sloughed from skin and muscle, only to then slither back like hissing snakes. The Auroral blessings were tearing through what they perceived as the sin permeating the angelic's very bones: skin crackled like paper dropped in the hearth, sinew sizzled into ashes and one by one her exposed ribs popped open like fingers being pried apart. I hadn't known until then that angelics had hearts, or that they looked like flowers, the petals unfolding as they died, revealing a delicate golden butterfly whose wings burned away into nothingness before the last grey flakes drifted down to the ground. And all the while, the dying Valiant was smiling at me.

'We'll see each other again,' said the wonderist as the Valiant's tongue was turning to ash inside a pale jaw no longer clad in once-flawless skin. 'Three more times before my bosses order me to kill you.'

One benefit of having witnessed any number of atrocities in my relatively brief career as a wonderist was learning not to waste time on disgust or despair. 'What bosses?' I asked quickly. 'Who are you working for? What do they wa—?'

'They want peace, Cade,' she replied as the ruined body she'd possessed slumped down to the wooden platform, perfectly filling the contorted, unnatural shadow waiting for it. 'Just not the peace you were hoping for.'

CHAPTER 5

Self-Defence

'Spirits of decency!' Galass cried, rushing over. She wasn't concerned with me, of course, only the dead angelic. She was the only one to bother; unlike Corrigan, Shame, Aradeus, Alice and even Temper, she hadn't worked out that the butchery wasn't quite done yet. But Galass was young and still determined to make the world a place worth saving, even if she had to bend it into shape with her bare hands.

'Cade, what just happened here?'

'I don't know.' I might as well have plastered a villainous leer on my lips and declared, '*Why, it's all part of my evil plan, of course!*'

'*You!*' screamed the leader of the Valiants predictably, still staring aghast at the golden blood of his comrade staining his blade. 'This was some Infernal trick of yours!'

'Hey, arsehole,' Corrigan said, keeping one fist behind his back to hide the indigo sparks erupting across his knuckles. He too had had plenty of experience with supernatural beings convinced of their own holiness. 'Have you *already* forgotten that we just took out an entire troop of *actual* Infernals to save your increasingly worthless existence?'

'All part of your ruse, thunderer,' accused the Valiant. His remaining comrade indicated his agreement with that preposterous conjecture by drawing his own sword.

35

'Whoa,' I said evenly. For Galass' sake, I was determined to give diplomacy one final attempt. 'Whoever possessed your fellow angelic clearly wants us to fight. Did you not hear what she said about letting the war unfold? The Lords Celestine are being set up, so maybe the Lords Devilish are too. We need to figure out who's behind ...'

I let that futile entreaty die unfinished. The identical looks on the faces of the two Valiants made it painfully obvious that some calamities really *are* inevitable.

'Seven deaths, each bloodier than the last, will you and your foul coven die at our hands!' declared the leader as he raised his now-flaming sword.

'As it is spoken, so shall it be!' cheered his fellow paragon of Auroral forbearance.

'Oh, come on, man,' I said. I really shouldn't have been so astounded at how genuinely convinced these two morons were, not only of their righteousness, but that the great Auroral Sovereign – who doesn't exist, by the way – was going to grant them victory. 'Can't you guys see this is all part of some—? Ah, forget it. You know what? *This* is why I became a mercenary war mage instead of a diplomat.'

With that, I stepped back, giving Corrigan free rein to blast the living shit out of the remaining Angelic Valiants. Normally, their Auroral blessings would remake their physical forms faster than any Tempestoral bolts could tear them apart, but Galass was using her sanguinalist abilities to prevent their angelic blood from spreading the healing blessing, while Shame was disrupting the transmutation of their angelic flesh. It was weird as shit, watching the battle as the bodies of the two Valiants fluctuated back and forth between destruction and resurrection.

The stalemate ended only when Alice decapitated both Valiants with a single slash of her whip-sword.

How the hells are we going to stop a war between two unimaginably powerful armies led by hierarchies of zealots, neither of whom can be dissuaded from believing that their own victory is inevitable?

The two golden heads tumbled to the wooden platform and went rolling along the planks to stop at my feet. One of the many creepy things about angelics is that even beheaded, their mouths can always whisper final maledictions against you. We weren't worried, though; we were already on the Celestines' shit list.

I decided a moment of silence was in order at the passing of the angelic warriors, mostly because I needed a minute to stop my hands shaking.

Of course, not everyone shared my delicate disposition.

'Temper, stop that!'

The kangaroo completely ignored me. He'd snatched up one of the severed heads and was eagerly slurping the golden blood from the neck.

This is why smart people don't accidentally summon vampiric beasts from savage realms and then recruit them into their covens just because a certain Tempestoral idiot insists, 'We're called the Malevolent Seven, Cade. Seven. Not six.'

'You look frightened, child,' Shame told me.

'I am.'

'No, you do not understand. I can always sense your fear, your anxieties, your worry that you have set us on the wrong path.' She reached up with a finger and pushed at one corner of my mouth as if to try and force a smile. 'Usually, you hide it from the others.'

What do you expect? The whole world's going mad – madder, I should say, and now there's a new player on the board with powers I can't explain who is apparently convinced we have a shared history that I can't remember.

'Hey, you want to see something funny?' Corrigan asked, giggling like a schoolboy and pointing to the sands below the gallows.

Temper was hopping clumsily in a circle, a massive grin on his blood-soaked muzzle, playing toss with the head.

'What ails our prancing comrade?' Aradeus asked.

Shame peered over the edge of the gallows. 'The beast appears . . . *is he drunk?*'

'Auroral blood,' Alice explained, failing to hide the fact that she was licking her own lips. 'Some find the taste . . . inebriating.'

As if our misbegotten coven wasn't creepy enough, I thought.

'Aw, I think it's cute,' Corrigan said.

One day, we were going to wake up in the middle of the night to find Temper draining all our blood, at which point I was definitely going to tell Corrigan, '*I told you so.*'

Until then, I had more pressing concerns, starting with figuring out who had the power to possess an angelic Valiant, to scorch the aethereal hand of a Lord Celestine and then to enact one of the most unpleasant murder-suicides I'd ever witnessed. Oh, and let's not forget she'd threatened to do likewise to all of us unless we allowed the Great Crusade between the Aurorals and Infernals to sweep unhindered across the entire Mortal realm.

First, we had to round up the kangaroo before he passed out from his whirling, drunken dance.

Oh, and deal with the townsfolk, who'd finally started moving. A woman who looked to be in her forties stepped forward. She was modestly dressed, but her air of effortless authority told me she was probably the town mayor.

'Why'd you go kill them angels?' she asked.

'Self-defence.'

The mayor grabbed my arm. 'Our town *chose* to side with the Lords Celestine.' She turned me around and pointed to the gleaming alabaster spires that were already crumbling as the Auroral will faded from the settlement. 'They promised us a shining city – every home a palace – no more need for us to toil in the fields or drudge for money.'

The indignant outrage might have been more convincing if I'd believed the mayor was as big a rube as she pretended to be. 'And in exchange?' I asked her. 'All you had to promise was your souls and those of your children, right? A thousand generations of your descendants, condemned to serve as foot soldiers in their endless Crusade?'

She did a passable job of hiding her embarrassment. 'We . . . We thought . . . When you showed up here, fighting those demons so fierce and all, we figured you for heroes.'

Since no one else was bothering to help Corrigan carry Temper, I went over and grabbed one of the unconscious kangaroo's arms and slung it over my shoulder. 'We're trying to be heroes,' I admitted, following the others back into the desert, where our horses were likely praying to whatever horsey gods exist that the seven of us weren't returning so they wouldn't have to deal with Temper looking at them funny all the time. 'We're just not very good at it yet.'

CHAPTER 6

The Hero Business

We did a lot of blowing stuff up over the next few weeks, riding down dusty dirt paths and well-kept cobbled roads to find quiet backwoods villages, boring one-horse towns or heaving overcrowded cities . . . Wherever the emissaries of the Lords Celestine or Lords Devilish had managed to convince the locals to sign a pact, we'd come along and convince them to tear it up. Sometimes persuasion and logic got the job done; other times, we'd get chased out of town by an unexpectedly well-armed mob. We could've fought back, except for that whole 'not killing the Mortals' thing. Hells, most of the time, our only injuries came from trying to restrain either Corrigan or Temper from blasting our pursuers to death or drinking their blood. Fortunately, one of those two hotheads was usually sane enough to help us talk the other one down from going berserk. There's something unsettling about witnessing a vampire kangaroo patting the cheek of an enraged thunderer while cooing soothingly . . . actually, it was worse when Corrigan tried to calm Temper down, which involved a lot of weeping and hugging and recounting of childhood traumas that the big brute had never even revealed to me before.

'You wouldn't understand,' Corrigan had insisted one night when I'd confronted him privately about the matter – we were supposed to be best friends, after all, even though neither of us had much conception of what that meant.

'You think *my* childhood wasn't traumatic?' I asked indignantly. 'Or Galass? Or Alice? We're wonderists, for fuck's sake – trauma's practically the only requirement for any sort of mystical attunement! I'll bet even Aradeus got locked in a root cellar by his parents or touched inappropriately by some close relative when he was a kid.'

Corrigan ignored my tirades. Those nights when we were too far away or too unwelcome to find lodgings, he'd huddle with the kangaroo having deep heart-to-heart chats with a beast who didn't even speak our language – or any other language that didn't involve grunts, growls or the occasional hiss that preceded Temper ripping out the throat of the nearest angelic or demoniac before draining them of blood.

'That can't be healthy,' Aradeus observed in the aftermath of our attack on an Auroral recruitment camp. 'One would expect a vampiric being to become more robust with the consumption of blood, yet our comrade is looking increasingly bloated and sickly after these bouts of gluttony.'

'Constipated is more likely,' Alice said dismissively. She wasn't especially fond of Temper, who was much too like the mystically engineered beasts of her own realm. 'Look how he bears down on his haunches, clenching his teeth afterwards.'

Corrigan, looming behind us in a distinctly threatening manner, said, 'Nobody fucking laugh, understand?'

Whenever Temper went into one of these post-gorging fits – which really did look like someone experiencing overwhelming constipation – he'd end with a single bound in the air, as high as his powerful hind legs would carry him, and land on his face, where he'd lie unconscious until morning. I swear, keeping a straight face during this performance required more self-discipline than performing a twelve-hour abnegation ritual.

Not even Galass could explain what was going on with Temper's odd behaviour. She tried to link her attunement to the flow of the kangaroo's blood to ease his discomfort, but her hair suddenly turned white and her hand shot away as if she'd been stung. Only after her tresses returned to their normal colour would she tell us that there was a planar breach inside Temper, like a mystical attunement that wasn't able to pierce the veil between realms. That of course led to questions about where he'd come from in the first place, which was my cue to change the subject by going over the tactical plans for our next attack.

We'd drawn a line in the proverbial sand back in the Blastlands, where the Seven Brothers had become unwilling portals to this realm from the Auroral and Infernal demesnes. We'd vowed then that we would do whatever it took to prevent the Great Crusade from engulfing humanity. Most high-minded moralists skip over the ethical implications of such a vow, but Corrigan and I were mercenary war mages, Shame, when an Angelic Emissary, had witnessed the darkest depths of human desire and Alice, a demoniac, had been trained as a Justiciar by the great Hazidan Rosh herself, so we all knew there would be a hefty price for denying the Lords Celestine and Lords Devilish their precious crusade. As for Galass, she'd been raised as an Auroral Sublime, to be offered as a reward to Ascendant Princes doing the work of the Celestines upon the Mortal realm. She knew that *every* war got ugly, and trying to *stop* a war would likely get even uglier.

So we'd set one rule: no attacks on humans, not even if they'd given in to Auroral or Infernal blandishments. We would fight back if they came at us, and not hesitate to kill to save one of our crew, but otherwise, we'd leave Mortal recruits alone. Luckily, angelics and demoniacs alike considered human soldiers far beneath them, so they were generally housed separately. Once we'd given up trying to convince the humans to abandon their newly signed pacts, there was almost always an opportunity to leave a trail of demoniac or angelic corpses to help the locals reconsider the merits of our well-put arguments.

There was one exception to our don't-kill-humans-unless-you-have-to rule: Glorians. Whether they were Justiciars like I'd been, or Ardentors, Parevals, Arbiters or any of the rest, the way I saw it, you accept the supernatural blessings of the Lords Celestine, you take your lumps. The same was true of human wonderists who signed with the Aurorals or Infernals, although those who were still alive after the débâcle with the Seven Brothers up in the Blastlands were pretty much keeping their heads down – which was why I was surprised at the enthusiasm when Aradeus and Galass returned from a scouting mission to a nearby settlement rumoured to have thrown their lot in with the Aurorals.

'My Lady Galass was marvellous!' Aradeus enthused as the two of them entered the room we'd rented above a roadside ale-house; luckily for us, the owner preferred to spend his nights at his lover's cottage. The rat mage began removing a clever little totemist glamour from himself and Galass, grey-gloved hands weaving in the air as he shooed away the odd dust motes into which his spell had manifested. It hadn't altered their appearances, just made it so that others would perceive them as utterly unremarkable, regardless of the situation.

'It was nothing,' Galass said, looking down at her feet and blushing.

'*Nothing?*' Aradeus turned to me. 'Cade, she had a Glorian Pareval eating out of her hand, revealing secrets no amount of torture could ever have loosened from his tongue, all while the golden-garbed fool thought he was correcting *her* on theological discrepancies in the Auroral Edicts!'

'What secrets?' I asked.

Galass waited silently until Aradeus was done banishing his glamour. Despite his unimpeachably gallant nature, the proximity of *anyone's* hands so close to her body tends to make her hair turn scarlet and stabby.

Once he'd finished, she sat on a cot and began, 'The Lords Celestine are beginning to worry about a certain group of wonderists interfering with their war preparations.'

'Damn right!' Corrigan interrupted. His biggest problem with my strategy of making recruitment unprofitable for them had nothing to do with the likelihood of our deaths, just that no one would even notice our efforts. He pounded me on the back. 'Told you it would work,' he said, although he never had. Not once. 'Soon, every Auroral and Infernal will be whispering our names, fearful of the day the Malevolent Seven will descend upon them and kick their arses off the Mortal realm once and for all.'

'The Apocalypse Eight,' Galass said.

Corrigan stopped thumping me on the back. 'What?'

'The Apocalypse Eight,' she repeated. 'Apparently, there's another group of wonderists out there staging sneak attacks on hidden Auroral and Infernal spies and scouts, binding them up and dropping them on their enemies' doorstep.'

Spy-hunters? I wondered silently. Every army has squads devoted to chasing down enemy scouts and rooting out spies, but unlike sabotage operations, this wasn't something they farmed out to mercenaries.

'The Aurorals and Infernals both believe this shadowy coven is working for the other side,' Aradeus continued. 'It's causing quite a stir among their respective leaderships, who have been working hard to keep these unusual events secret. Cade, do you suppose our rebellion is inspiring other wonderists to take up the cause?'

'Absolutely not!' Corrigan thundered, figuratively and literally, indigo flames flickering up and down the braids of his beard. 'First of all, "The Apocalypse Eight" is a stupid name. Second of all . . . well, that should be enough.'

'Keep it together, would you?' I told him.

Temper hopped over and patted Corrigan on the head before resting his muzzle on the big man's shoulder.

'You're right,' Corrigan said – although not to me. 'I shouldn't take these things so personally.'

Anyone referring to me as the 'leader' of this coven probably meant it ironically.

'Any word on the attunements of this coven?' I asked Galass and Aradeus. 'Could the wonderist who took control of the angelic Valiant have been one of them trying to screw with us?'

Galass shook her head. 'We didn't get any specifics – not even descriptions of their appearance, except that they go around wearing uniforms, almost like some sort of military order.'

Temper growled.

Corrigan reached up and stroked the kangaroo's ears. 'It's all right, my friend. She didn't mean to hurt my feelings.'

I sighed to myself. *I'm pretty sure one of my three dooms is going to involve being eaten by a vampire kangaroo because I didn't let Corrigan buy us all matching uniforms.*

I turned to Alice and Shame. Neither had spoken yet, which was usually because they didn't much care about mundane matters like rival gangs of wonderists or where the next slaughter of their respective former allies would take place. They were staring at each other, and not with their usual animosity.

'What is it?' I asked.

They hesitated, both tried to speak at once, and finally, Alice gestured for Shame to go first.

'The prophecies speak of a time called the Choosing Hour, when every soul must take a side before the war begins,' Shame began. 'However, within the Auroral hierarchy, there has always been an unspoken concern that the Lords Celestine are too eager to launch the Great Crusade.'

'It is the same among the Infernals,' Alice agreed. 'Among us, this period is called the Setting of the Board.'

And you don't start the game until every piece is in place . . . unless the players are too keen to get started.

'So while we're trying to keep the Aurorals and Infernals from completing their military and spiritual preparations, you think this other group of wonderists, this' – I glanced at Corrigan, who wasn't looking at me, then caught Temper's glare and continued more cautiously – 'these irrelevant pricks who are in no way a proper coven and no doubt have very poor taste in attire . . . you think they might be trying to *accelerate* the war? Like some sort of doomsday cult?'

'They've chosen to call themselves the "*Apocalypse* Eight",' Alice said, ignoring the simultaneous glares from Corrigan and Temper. 'If chaos is their intention, they have chosen a subtle yet effective strategy. Despite whatever injunctions the prophecies surrounding the Great Crusade might place on either side, if the Lords Devilish believe their opponents have already begun to fight in earnest, they may well declare war prematurely.'

You wouldn't think of supposedly immortal beings as impulsive, but my experiences with the twelve Lords Celestine and, indirectly, the thirteen Lords Devilish through my interactions with a diabolic agent named Tenebris, who used to sell me Infernal spells, had taught me that both pantheons were prone to recklessness. I couldn't help but recall how quickly the Angelic Valiants atop that gallows had lost their shit when their possessed comrade turned on them.

'That Glorian Pareval who told you about captured Infernal spies and scouts being dumped on their doorstep,' I began, turning to Aradeus and Galass. '*Which* doorstep did the last ones turn up on?'

'A secret prison,' Galass said, frowning. 'The Pareval wouldn't—'

'That's not possible, I interrupted. 'The Auroral Edicts prohibit confinement as a punishment because the mortal realm is inherently corrupting to the spirit. When I was a Justiciar, if the verdict we rendered wasn't execution or exile, the offender's community was expected to enact retributions that nonetheless reintegrated them into society.'

'That's one of the things that had the Pareval so wound up,' Galass continued, starting to pace the attic. 'No one outside the upper echelons of the Auroral Hierarchy is even supposed to know this one's been built, so how would this coven know to leave the captured spies there?'

A secret Auroral prison . . . A strange anxiety was creeping through me. It wasn't just the abrogation of the supposedly unyielding legal principles I'd had drummed into me as a Justiciar, but that *something* was itching at the back of my skull, something I couldn't yet put my finger on.

'I don't suppose either of you know the location?' I asked.

'Alas, no,' Aradeus replied, then sparked one of his mischievous swashbuckler smiles. Reaching into the pocket of his long grey coat, he took out a sleepy-eyed rat. 'However, mine is an innately collaborative form of magic, which can enable my noble little comrades to commune through the Totemic plane. Tell me, Brother Cade, have you ever heard of a prison without rats?'

CHAPTER 7

Nice Wars

'Have I mentioned how stupid this idea is?' Corrigan asked. His arms outstretched, he sent gouts of black and red Tempestoral fire erupting from the centre of his chest to assail the twelve-foot-thick outer walls of the small prison that had been constructed in a forest less than ten miles from a city which had recently signed a pact with the Infernals. No doubt this added to the frustration of the three diabolic spies being interrogated under torture so close to where their comrades were enjoying the manifold pleasures of high society.

Who knew the Aurorals could be such cheeky bastards?

Aradeus' mystical web of rat scouts had eventually found the hidden enclave for us, although it had taken several days, because their beady little eyes had not at first recognised the pristine twelve-sided building as a prison. It was only when they'd conveyed their amusing anecdote about a delightful *secret palace* hidden away from ordinary humans that we'd saddled up our horses and ridden for two weeks to get here.

The pace had been gruelling, but Galass, ever more determined to find ways to use her blood magic that didn't involve killing people, had helped. With guidance from Shame and, surprisingly, Alice, she'd designed a sanguinal spell that reinvigorated our mounts, enabling them to gallop faster and longer than ever before.

Alas, she hadn't yet come up with a spell to improve Corrigan's mood.

'Fucking waste of my talents,' he complained. The rippling flow of Tempestoral lava sizzled as it struck the walls, slowly spreading across the surfaces, fissuring the stone and crumbling the mortar at a pace that did nothing to shorten his list of grievances. His hair and beard were already drenched in sweat: burning through Auroral-blessed stone is nobody's idea of a good time.

We could hear the prison guards massing on the other side of the walls, preparing to rush through the gates. Not that they needed to bother, since we were making them a much larger opening.

'We had a perfectly sensible strategy,' Corrigan grumbled as huge chunks of once-flawless stone crumbled away. 'We go into an Infernal-aligned town, kick the shit out of their troops, deliver a speech to the townsfolk about the perils of selling out their children's children's children's future to a bunch of warmongering immortal fuck-sticks, then find supper and a nice brothel.'

'It was a good plan,' I agreed.

Corrigan wasn't finished. 'Then the next week, we pick an Auroral town and kick *their* arses. Spread the love, as it were. Peace in our time.'

'Forgive my confusion, Brother Corrigan,' said Aradeus, drawing his rapier and, passing a fingertip along the edge, imbuing the blade with an evasion spell that would make it near-impossible to parry. 'Are we not about to, as you so eruditely phrased it, "spread the love" to an entire troop of Auroral soldiers?'

'It's *not* the same thing,' Corrigan replied crossly. The muscles in his arms and jaw clenched tighter as he struggled to bring forth more of the lava-like destructive energies from the Tempestoral realm. 'Instead of bedding down in a nice inn after blowing shit up, we're busting *into* a prison in the middle of fucking *nowhere* – so no beds, no brothels, and I *still* won't get to deliver a proper speech.'

'We're here for information on that other coven, remember?' I reminded him, then poked the knife in a little deeper. 'Are you saying you're content to let a bunch of second-rate wonderists run around pretending to be heroes and calling themselves the Apocal—'

'Don't say it,' he warned. 'Don't you fucking say it.'

Galass had doubts about my plan too, for entirely different reasons. 'Why are you so confident the Infernal spies will reveal anything? Or that they're even still alive?' she asked. 'The Glorians don't take prisoners of war, which means the interrogators have either killed their Infernal captives or haven't been able to break them yet. So what makes you think *we* can make them talk?'

The dramatic, thunderous collapse of the fortress walls saved me; giving up any pretence at structural integrity, they crumbled beneath their own weight, unleashing choking clouds of dust. Alice darted in front of me, whispering an incantation under her breath while spinning her whip-sword in an impressive spiral swing. The whirling blades conjured a tornado-like gust that sent the dust cloud pouring away from us and into the faces of the Auroral soldiers rushing to defend their enclave.

'Nice trick,' I complimented her. 'When did you figure that one out?'

'I've been crafting a spell to drive away Corrigan's breath when he gets drunk at night and starts reciting his growing litany of complaints about the lack of restaurants, brothels and other facilities.'

'Clever. I'm impressed wi—'

'Do not seek to curry favour with me, Fallen One. It's your obstinacy which triggers the big brute's tantrums. You should have let him give the speech back in that last Infernal town.'

'Exactly!' Corrigan said. He paused in his assault on the walls to turn to Temper, hopping about impatiently, no doubt eager to get to some good old-fashioned pummelling before the main event, gorging on the blood of the recently deceased. 'You ask me, buddy, *you're* the one who ought to be leading this crew.'

The assault on my leadership qualities didn't bother me half as much as Corrigan thinking Temper understood him.

'You recall he's a kangaroo, right?' I asked. 'Not a totemist somehow attuned to whichever plane of reality produces monstrosities like Temper, but an *actual* kangaroo.'

Never one to be swayed by logic, Corrigan countered, 'That's just your bigotry talking. If you'd bothered to spend more time with him, you'd've figured out that the only reason Temper doesn't talk is because he's a genius and *some* of us lack the cerebral and philosophical capacity to appreciate his brilliance.'

Alice sounded curious now. 'Yet he considers *you* his intellectual equal?'

Ignoring her, the big thunderer gestured elaborately to Temper. 'Go on, boy, show these ignorant heathens a fraction of your peerless mental talents.'

Even Shame was concerned now, although given she currently looked like a bipedal, two-headed alligator, that concern was probably more to do with the fact that Corrigan was embarrassing us in front of her former Auroral compatriots. 'Perhaps we could save this demonstration for *after* we've freed the spies?' she suggested.

'Shut it,' Corrigan said rudely, urging Temper to demonstrate his genius. 'What's six hundred and ninety-six multiplied by nine times the average length of the summer season at the equator divided by the speed of a drop of water falling from the mouth of a south-flying falcon?'

'Corrigan, remember those inner walls you were supposed to be knocking down before the Auroral troops on the other side get their shit together and launch a counter-assault?' I asked.

'Shh,' he replied, although he did resume hurling Tempestoral hell at the fortress. 'Just watch.'

For several seconds, the kangaroo stood there looking confused, as if wondering what he was expected to do. His weight shifted from one hind leg to the other, his ears went back and with one paw he scratched the side of his furry head.

'The animal looks constipated,' Alice observed. 'Is he about to leap up into the air and land on his face again?'

'Don't distract him,' Corrigan warned. 'This is *different*. Surely you can recognise his *concentrating* look?'

Surprisingly, the kangaroo grew still, a placid grin appearing on his muzzle as he leaned down and scratched numbers into the dirt with his front paw.

Aradeus gasped. 'Has he—? Are those—?'

Galass peered closer. 'It looks like he's written . . . forty-two?'

'Behold!' Corrigan declared triumphantly, indigo bolts erupting from his outstretched hands to take the place of his earlier lava spell. He started obliterating the stone with increased fervour. 'My boy's a genius! I bet not one of you even knows the speed a drop of water falls from a south-flying falc—'

'You *idiot*,' I interrupted, 'I may not know the speed of a – whatever the hell you said – but it doesn't take a genius to know it can't possibly be forty-two. Temper's off by tens of thousands, at least.'

As the other walls fell, Corrigan ceased his assault and glanced down at the numbers scrawled in the dirt. 'Still impressive,' he grumbled.

Alice snorted, her bat wings twitching – that's how you know when she's laughing, since nothing approaching mirth ever crosses her lips. 'I can no longer tell which of the two of you, man or beast, is more stupid.'

With impeccable timing, Corrigan and Temper simultaneously pointed at each other.

Leading a crew of mentally deranged and morally compromised

wonderists on a quest to prevent an eternal supernatural war really is more trouble than it's worth sometimes.

I felt a tug on my arm and turned to find Galass staring at me tentatively. The wan expression on her face told me I wasn't going to like what she had to say.

'Cade, these soldiers – they're ordinary humans, not angelics. Most of them aren't even Glorians.'

Ah, shit. I'd assumed any clandestine Auroral enclave would be guarded by high-ranking angelics, or maybe Glorian Justiciars and Parevals. *Does that mean whichever Celestines authorised this prison have been keeping it secret from the rest of the Auroral Hierarchy?*

Even without supernatural oversight, the tiny fortress was impressively garrisoned. I counted more than forty soldiers in gleaming armour bearing pikes and shields.

'Brother Cade, you yourself affirmed this as our coven's one unbreakable rule,' Aradeus said.

I considered reminding him that no rule is unbreakable – to be honest, I hadn't expected this one to last as long as it had. Look, I get that my plan of convincing the Aurorals, Infernals and their respective human recruits of the tragic consequences of war by literally raining bloodcurdling hells on them might not fit with traditional pacifist ideals – but show me a war that was prevented by pacifism and I'll be the first to shackle myself to a post in the middle of a battlefield and go on a hunger strike.

I'd spent almost seven years selling my services as a mercenary wonderist. I'd fought in dozens of armed conflicts and I can attest that every single one of them was a pointless waste of life in service to a cause no one remembered the year after it was over because by then there was some new enemy to fight. My experiences had taught me two important lessons: first, there's no such thing as a just war, and second, armed conflict is best understood as an extension of economics.

Your country is suffering too many bad harvests? Hmm . . . didn't someone from that neighbouring nation once insult the long-dead ancestor of your monarch? About time we avenged that unforgivable slight, don't you think?

Your nobility's overloaded with too many daughters and second sons, all remarkably well-armed and likely to turn to violent thuggery once they figure out there aren't enough estates for them to inherit? No problem: there's a rich land far to the south filled with lush territory and currently occupied by infidels badly in need of a jolly good smiting.

Of course, war isn't guaranteed good for business; it's always a gamble. But watch any addict at the card tables and you'll quickly observe that they're prone to inflating their odds of winning the next hand. So our job, as dutiful crusaders of peace, was to make war an unprofitable business by convincing the gamblers on *both* sides that the next hand would be a loser – for *everyone*.

However, murdering ordinary human beings for the crime of being gullible and getting swept up in the propaganda of a holy war where unknowable beings were promising to transform mere Mortals into legendary heroes was too cold-hearted, even for me.

The Auroral recruits had fought their way through the dust clouds and were forming their shield wall. The whole ensemble was beginning to look like a rather ugly metal hedgehog.

'Corrigan . . .' I began tentatively.

'You know something, Cade? I liked you better when I hated you.'

Loudly, to ensure I'd be heard by the soldiers crouched behind their shaking shields, I declared, 'On my mark, destroy every man, woman and – well, I would hope there wouldn't be children among them, but if so, kill them, too. Leave nothing but corpses for the vultures and blood for the soil.'

To Corrigan, Alice, Shame and Temper particularly, I quietly clarified my statement. 'And by kill *everyone*, I mean, *don't* fucking kill *anybody*, understand?'

They all replied:

'Typical weak-kneed indecision, Fallen One.'

'Huzzah, my captain! Let our blades be merciful and our hearts rejoice!'

'Death delayed is no less inevitable, child.'

'Thank you, Cade.'

'You pussy.'

'Grrrr—' followed by a burp which ended with somebody's severed finger being coughed up.

Buoyed by my comrades' enthusiastic endorsements, I gave the order to attack the defenders, whereupon we proceeded to – very gently and not at all fatally – kick their arses.

It's hard to imagine why there aren't more heroes clamouring for the chance to save the world.

CHAPTER 8

The Break-Out

There's something tiring about *not* killing people. I mean, I've never been particularly inclined to massacre my fellow human beings – or puppy dogs, kittens or even otherworldly vampiric kangaroos, come to think of it – but having specifically to *not* kill your foes? It's completely exhausting.

I'm not saying it's not worth the effort; it's just that having to take out an entire troop with none of them suffering anything worse than concussion? You try it some day.

Oh, and don't forget: soldiers rarely thank you for knocking them unconscious when you could've just killed them. In fact, they're just more likely to attack you again on the way out.

'Still think we should've incinerated those bastards,' Corrigan fumed, wrapping a strip of cloth torn from the leg of his much-prized purple-striped pantaloons around the wound on his arm where a pike had managed to nick him before Shame had clubbed the fellow on the back of his head with her bare fist. Her bare fist at the time was unnaturally large and covered in alligator-green scales, which is why he went down like a lead balloon.

Ignoring Corrigan's complaints – which can be an even more dangerous approach to life than not killing your enemies – I stopped in a narrow passage inside the small fortress. The others piled into my back with what I thought was unnecessary force.

'Aradeus, what are the rats telling you?'

Aradeus held up his gauntleted hand so we could all see the lines tracing themselves along his palm, mapping out the entire building, thanks to a dozen or so of his rat scouts. There are usually a lot more for him to summon, but Aurorals tend to be fastidious about their fortresses, and this one was new into the bargain. 'There,' he said, pointing to a trio of pulsing points behind a dotted line I presumed was a set of iron bars. 'Those will be the captured Infernal spies.' He peered closer at his palm, seeing something in the subtle shifting of the three individual dots that escaped me. 'I believe they've been badly tortured.'

Galass asked again why I thought I would get anything out of three Infernals. Since Aurorals consider confession a prelude to a merciful death rather than an extended sentence, the interrogators had almost certainly failed to break the prisoners – in any case, torture's an ineffective means of eliciting useful information.

'The thing about the Lords Celestine,' I told her, gesturing for Aradeus to take the lead, 'is that they're far more rigid in their theology than the clerics who trained you as a Sublime would ever realise. The Celestines are all stick and no carrot.'

This sparked Shame's interest for once. 'Whereas Infernals are more amenable to reasoned compromise?'

'It's about contracts,' I clarified. 'Diabolics love making deals – they love haggling. Moral compromise is a virtue as far as they're concerned, which makes them a lot easier to deal with than angelics.'

'We may not have much time for negotiation,' Galass warned, her crimson locks beginning to rise and twitch behind her. 'Some of the soldiers are awakening. They're trying to rouse their fellows for a second attack.'

'We'll be done before they get here,' I said hopefully as we rounded the corner into the final passageway shown by Aradeus' rat-mapping spell. 'This isn't my first diabolic negotiation.'

No lanterns or torches illuminated the cell, nor did the aetheric glow imbued into the walls reach past the bars. Fortunately, angelics come with their own light source.

'A little brighter,' I said.

Shame rolled her eyes at me, but a moment later her skin was glistening brightly enough for us to make out three silhouettes hunched on the floor at the back of the cell. Their posture suggested they were in rough shape.

'Barbaric,' Alice muttered, using her blade to cut through the lock in the iron door. 'Such treatment violates all the tenets of Auroral Justice.'

Despite how gleefully perverse our mutual mentor had been, the old bear had been remarkably strict in her interpretation of judicial procedure. 'When you finally meet some *actual* Glorian Justiciars, you might be disappointed in their more flexible interpretation of Auroral Law,' I said.

Alice mumbled something indistinct which I assumed was a discourteous commentary on my own character, as it ended with, 'Fallen One'. I waited until she was done before I stepped in front of the cell door.

'Afternoon, fellows,' I began, offering each of the three diabolic prisoners a reassuring smile. 'I understand you've had a spot of bad luck recently vis-à-vis getting captured, tortured and then interrogated by Auroral troops.'

'Swallow your own tongue and choke on your own feeble flesh, Mortal,' snarled the nearest of the three. His silhouette had the pointy-shouldered, spine-covered look of a ferocial, which is either a sub-family of lesser devilish or one of the descendants of an Infernally engineered demoniac from millennia ago. I can never get the genealogies straight in my head.

'No need for harsh words, my friends, when I come bearing excellent news – well, if I'm honest, I suppose it's more of a "good news, bad news and possibly tolerable news" situation. But let's start with the good.' I swung open the cell door. 'Congratulations. Your confinement at the hands of your sworn enemies is at an end.'

The one closest to the door failed to greet my benevolence with the appropriate gratitude, opting instead to screech an ear-splitting warcry. Oily black tendrils oozed into the air from his ribcage. 'At my command, paralyse the humans,' he ordered his fellow prisoners. 'Three we shall feast upon, to regain our strength. The minds of the remaining four we shall possess and force them to draw away the fortress guards from our avenue of escape—'

'See, I have to stop you there,' I said, 'although it's funny you should bring up possession, because that's kind of why we're— Oh, you're serious about the whole eating-us-and-taking-over-our-thoughts thing?'

I'll admit, it wasn't the worst plan I'd ever heard from a demon. Infernal magic is excellent for manipulating minds. I could see the lesser devilish already awakening a spell called a Widow's Tear from the engraved sigils on his chest, which made me feel a touch nostalgic about my days as an Infernally attuned mercenary.

I stepped back out of the way. 'Okay, I guess we're done with the good news. Corrigan, would you care to convey the bad news?'

'The bad news is, we don't particularly like Infernals.' The blast of Tempestoral fury he unleashed on the lesser devilish was enough to deafen us all. 'Sorry!' he yelled over the ringing in our ears.

Never bring a Tempestoral on a clandestine mission, I reminded myself for the hundredth time.

It took a moment for my vision to clear enough to make out the remaining two Infernals in the cell. One was near the door, the other remained slumped on the floor in the corner. 'I believe you mentioned something about *more* good news,' the standing diabolic said politely.

'Actually, I believe I said, "tolerable news", but let's not quibble over semantics. The bottom line is this: while we're not partial to Infernals invading our world and would rather there were considerably fewer of you, we're not overly fussed about the occasional diabolic frolicking around the Mortal realm, so long as said diabolic demonstrates basic courtesy and sound judgement.'

'Ah,' drawled the spy. On closer inspection, he looked like a run-of-the-mill demoniac Hellion to me, which was rare for an Infernal in the espionage business. Hellions are more your massacre-the-village breed of Infernal. 'You wish to make a bargain.'

'We are in the market for military information.' I held up a hand to forestall any patriotic objections – and *yes*, Infernals are perfectly capable of patriotic devotion to their people and their cause, so you should be ashamed of your bigoted presumption. 'Nothing tactical – we're not looking for battle plans, or anything like that.'

'Not that your moron Schemelords ever do come up with decent battle plans,' Alice added snidely. I'm not sure what specific lineage of demoniac she comes from, but it's definitely not one of the ones you bring to delicate negotiations.

A rat scurried from the other side of the hall and squeaked up at Aradeus, who said, 'We're short on time, Cade. Of the five best routes out of the fortress, my scouts tell me only one remains unguarded.'

'What *specifically* do you want to know?' asked the spy, understandably keen to come to an agreement quickly.

Of course we wanted information on the coven of wonderists who'd captured him, but it would be so easy to make up an entirely plausible lie.

'Tell me what you know about a form of wonderism that can bring forward a person's destiny to the present.'

The demoniac's eyes began to whirl – well, not *whirl*, exactly: their irises produce these subtle colour shifts when they get excited that make them look as if they're spinning. I wondered if he'd decided I was a sucker who could easily be fooled.

'Ah, destinal magic,' he murmured. 'I am in possession of the answers you seek, but the price will be higher than—'

His body slammed up against the bars, then slid down to the floor. The razor-sharp talon piercing his back was still attached to the severed arm of the lesser devilish Corrigan had killed.

Damn me for a fool. I really should have paid more attention to the third Infernal, the one pretending to be comatose at the back of the cell.

'Let me guess,' I said, working out how best to subdue him, 'you consider it your patriotic duty to die rather than allow one of your comrades to give up any secrets.'

The spy, a Guilish diabolic, judging by his slender form and twin sets of horns, dropped the severed hand before wiping his own on the filthy rags that were all that remained of what must once have been an elegant frock coat. 'Me?' he asked innocently. 'Nah, fuck patriotism. I just figured once you made the deal with this prick you'd kill me to avoid leaving witnesses.'

'We never stipulated that only one of you could leave here alive,' Galass said, horrified. 'You could both have been freed so long as we'd got the information we needed!'

'Really?' asked the diabolic, whose voice was now sounding disturbingly familiar. He stepped over the body of the demoniac he'd killed and into the light Shame was shedding to reveal ivory skin that had been battered black and blue. 'Geez, Cade, you goin' soft in your old age or something?'

It was that snarky, self-satisfied smirk beneath all the seeping wounds and swollen flesh that made me recognise the bastard at last.

Of all the torture joints in all the hidden Auroral enclaves, why did it have to be him?

'Tenebris?' I asked.

My former Infernal agent spread his arms wide, grinning. 'The one and only. Come on, buddy, bring it in.' He grabbed me in an uncomfortably intimate hug. 'How's my best client doing?' Just as quickly, he released me and shot me an appraising look with the scarlet eyes I'd seen so many times behind the aethereal smoke of a spell circle when we were negotiating for spells. 'Not too good, I'm guessing.' He patted my shoulder before adding, 'You look like shit, Cade.'

CHAPTER 9

Strategy

With the help of Aradeus' rodent scouts, we zigged and zagged our way along a maze of narrow passages punctuated by apparently random sets of stairs. Occasionally, we were instructed to just stand still in the middle of a corridor.

'Does this guy let his rats get into the sauce or something?' Tenebris asked, miming someone drinking from a very tiny beer stein.

'They're not *my* rats.' Aradeus corrected him with somewhat less than his usual politeness, making me like him a lot more. 'These rats are sovereign beings, assisting our escape because theirs is the noblest of species and they recognise the urgency of our mission. Daring adventure is in their nature, as is the raw, unbridled heroic instinct that—'

Okay, that cured me.

'Time to go.' Aradeus resumed our labyrinthine escape.

We were about two turns away from a back exit when two guards caught up with us. From the lack of any Glorian glow about them and the desperate way they were clutching their truncheons I could see they were only recruits.

Sparks of Tempestoral magic were already igniting around Corrigan's fist and Alice had her whip-sword out when Galass gave me that look meant to arouse feelings of guilt over the possibility of killing our fellow human beings.

'Let me handle this,' I told Corrigan and Alice. I think I managed not to sigh. Maybe.

'Stay where you are,' one of the guards warned me as I approached. The second one raised his truncheon and reached behind his back to draw a dagger with his other hand.

'That dagger isn't regulation, son,' I informed him. 'You'll wind up digging latrine trenches for the next five years if a Glorian Pareval catches you with a contraband weapon.'

'H-how . . . how would you know?' he asked.

The first guard was getting the look on his face that suggested he was considering what a smart soldier would do in this situation. He'd soon conclude that would be shouting for other guards or trying to delay the eight of us from escaping.

'Strategy,' I said.

'W-what?' he asked, then, because young soldiers hate sounding anxious, said it again, only more forcefully. 'What?'

'Strategy,' I repeated. 'It's the one skill they deny soldiers. They teach you to think tactically, like, for example, "Let's delay these dangerous, magic-wielding infiltrators long enough for the rest of our troops to find us and then we can overwhelm them and win commendations and maybe even a promotion from the Glorian commander." See, that's a *tactic*.'

The second guard attempted a smirk, but just looked constipated. 'Sounds like good advice.'

'No,' I corrected him, 'it's a good *tactic*. The problem is, sometimes good *tactics* make shitty *strategy*.' I gestured to the others. 'Here's what's going to happen. Because I'm a nice guy at heart, one of these lunatics is going to blast the two of you into oblivion. That's nice of me because the alternative is we let the kangaroo have his way with you.'

'K-kan . . . gooro?' asked one of the guards.

64

Temper, helpfully, hopped a little closer, raised his paws like a boxer and showed the guards his fangs.

'Yeah,' I said confirming their suspicions, 'he's a vampire. Honestly, I didn't think they existed. I mean, you hear stories, but this guy?' I patted Temper on the shoulder. 'He loves blood – I mean, fucking *loves* the stuff. Gets it all over his fur and won't even let us clean it off him because he likes to save it for later. You know, as a midnight snack.'

'Y-you're trying to scare us,' the guard on the left said, looking scared.

'Cade,' Aradeus murmured, staring down at the living map drawing and redrawing itself on his palm, 'we have maybe thirty seconds before this path becomes closed to us.'

'Understood.' I turned back to the guards. 'Here are the options, friends. First, you bravely attack us, the kangaroo – *not* kangoo-ro, by the way – kills you in a way that is gruesome and yet somehow embarrassing when your comrades find your corpses, and we escape anyway.'

The second guard mumbled something about duty.

'Exactly!' I said, commending him. 'It's all about duty. Now, your duty as a guard is to stand there and die trying to slow us down. But what about your duty to the Auroral cause? Isn't that the greater duty?'

'Cade,' Aradeus repeated.

'Almost done.' I continued my explanation. 'The *greater* duty isn't served by unnecessary death but by being able to relay vital military intelligence to your commanders. So, here's my deal: you let us by and after we're gone, rough each other up a little – a couple of bruises, maybe. No cuts, mind, they get infected. And in exchange, I'll give you the name of the crew who came and broke out the spy. That'll be far more useful to your commanders than your corpses. You'll be known as the two guys who came face to face with the Malevolent Seven and fought them almost to a standstill, forcing them to flee.'

'You ... you aren't the infamous Apocalypse Eight?' the first guard asked.

'No,' Corrigan corrected angrily, 'we're the Malevolent Seven. *Seven*. Don't they teach you to count in betray-all-of-humanity-by-siding-with-supernatural-invaders school?' He spat on the floor. 'We're trying to build a legend here and people keep confusing us for a bunch of amateurs with a stupid fucking name ...'

I gave the two guards my best Glorian stare – one of them, anyway; there are seven. 'Gentlemen, it's time to choose: tactics, which leaves you dead, or strategy, which serves not only you but the Auroral cause much better.'

The two guards shared a look, dropped their weapons and stepped aside.

Aradeus was already moving back down the hall we'd come. 'That route closed off to us,' he murmured, 'but another has opened. This way.'

'Geez,' Tenebris said, stumbling alongside me. He was looking pretty rough, especially as he'd never struck me as one for resisting torture. 'When did you get all soft, Cade?'

We rounded a corner to find a long straight hallway.

'Probably around the same time you stopped dealing in Infernal spells to mercenary wonderists and took up espionage. Never took you for a spy, Tenebris.'

'Never took you for a pussy.'

'Hah!' Corrigan barked triumphantly. 'That's what I said.'

'Do not say it again,' Alice warned. 'That word is offensive. You should not be referring to female organs as representations of weakness. My own vagina could crush your pathetic phallus to an oozing paste.'

'We call people pricks all the time and you never complain,' Corrigan said. 'How is "pussy" any more offensive?'

'It is hurtful.'

'That makes no sense! How is "prick" acceptable, but "pussy" is—?'

Without pausing in our quick jog down the passage, Alice swung out her fist and punched Corrigan in the nose. 'See? It hurts now, doesn't it?'

The eruption of Tempestoral sparks on his knuckles came and went quickly. I'd been afraid I'd have to hold him back, but Corrigan roared with laughter. 'Outstanding! I must use that. Cade, quick, call me a pussy!'

Have I mentioned that all forms of wonderism are, to some degree, injurious to the mind? On the crazy scale, Tempestoral magic really does turn you into a nutcase.

'There!' Aradeus said, pointing to a door. 'Our scouts caused a furor among the squad sent to guard this door, which has delayed them just long enough for us to make our escape. From there, we need only flee through the breach in the outer wall and into the forest, where we shall easily elude any pursuers.'

'And then,' I said to Tenebris, punctuating the meaningful look I shot him with a squeeze of his bony arm, 'you're going to share every piece of intelligence you've accumulated from your spying.'

The diabolic looked up at me with a sheepish grin.' That's the thing, Cade. I'm *not* a spy. Those Auroral goons picked me up because they refused to believe me when I told them what I actually do these days.'

'Which is?' Galass asked.

Tenebris made a show of straightening the tattered remains of his coat. 'Lady, you are in the presence of the finest restauranteur in the entire Mortal realm.'

'What?' I asked.

His grin widened. 'Seriously, Cade. You've got to try my paella. It's to die for.'

CHAPTER 10

The Perils of Paella

He really *had* become a restauranteur.

The diabolic little fucker had somehow gone from cutting deals for spells with mercenary wonderists on behalf of the Lords Devilish to serving up delicacies to travellers stupid enough to eat in an Infernal restaurant.

'Delicious!' Corrigan declared, pounding a fist on the gleaming azure marble surface of an octagonal table around which the seven of us were seated. The large now-empty paella bowl between us rattled loudly.

This was our first night in the town of Seduction, previously known as Hope's Creek before that name went the way of all discarded dreams. Unlike the people of Pleasance, the townsfolk here had chosen to sign a pact negotiated by my former agent on behalf of the Lords Devilish. This had been, according to Tenebris, part of the deal in exchange for releasing him from military duties.

'I was the big cheese, you understand,' he explained smugly. 'After my – if I might be so humble – genius handling of the whole Pandoral affair – you know, I pretty much single-handedly destroyed the only beings capable of threatening the Lords Devilish and Lords Celestine *and* I arranged for the gates the Pandorals had intended to use to invade the Mortal realm to instead give us and the Aurorals a way here, well, my star was *really* on the rise.'

That a scumbag in rags so recently imprisoned and tortured, barely able to sit on a horse for more than five minutes without passing out, could puff himself up like that was an impressive feat. What Tenebris left out of his self-aggrandising serenade was that it had been *us* – except for Temper, of course, who hadn't arrived here yet – who'd actually defeated the Seven Brothers before they could bring over their Pandoral masters from that chaotic realm. But yeah, Tenebris had tricked us into doing all that, so I suppose he does get the credit.

'They offered me a seat, Cade. A *seat*.'

He meant a seat amongst the Lords Devilish. He was also full of shit.

'No, seriously,' he said, reading my dubious expression. 'The Lords Devilish offered me a place among them.' The flames set the intricate lineage scars on his leathery ivory skin to glowing ominously when he leaned in and whispered conspiratorially, 'You know there can never be more than thirteen Lords Devilish, right?'

'Yeah, and there're thirteen of them because your bosses are so vein they always want there to be one more Lord Devilish than the Aurorals have Lords Celestine. Now, what about this cabal of wonderists who captured you, this so-called "Apocalypse Eight"?'

Tenebris chuckled, ignoring my question. 'Yeah, those Celestines ain't got no sense of humour. My point *is*, that to give me a seat, the Lords Devilish would've had to eliminate one of their own first – which they were going to do. *That's* how big a deal I am to the Infernal hierarchy.'

'*Were*,' I corrected. 'You're a humble restauranteur now, remember? Come on, Tenebris, tell me about the wonderists who captured you.'

He shrugged. 'Didn't see 'em. I got taken by an Auroral binding, though I suppose it could've been an incarcerationalist's spell – I wasn't paying attention then and I'd prefer you not make me relive the torture that came afterwards.' He smiled, stroking the ram's horn on the right side of his skull. He had two little curved goat horns on his forehead too, but he'd always preferred the ram's horns. 'Pleasure is the future, Cade: that's what I had to make the Lords Devilish understand. All this violence and bloodshed, the battle against the Aurorals? It's a waste of time.' He snorted dismissively. 'Those idiot Schemelords running around the Mortal realm with their military intrigues? Most Schemelords I know couldn't find their testicles with both hands and a map.'

'Do Infernals *have* testicles?'

'Not. The. Point.' He shot me a dirty look. 'Geez, Cade. You're an even bigger killjoy than you used to be.'

'I spend more time around Infernals than I used to.'

He jabbed a taloned finger at me. 'Exactly! This is my point. Killing off Aurorals, recruiting humans into our armies so we can hurl them at other humans working for the other side? It's just meaningless. It could go on for ever, without anything getting settled.'

It was weird to hear Tenebris getting uncomfortably close to my own position on these matters. 'But you have a better way?'

'Pleasure!' he announced, spreading his arms wide. 'Sensation. Experience. *Living. That's* the Infernal difference. The Lords Celestine want the monopoly on righteousness and denying physical gratification? Let 'em have it. *We're* the ones offering a meaningful existence in *this* life, not some hypothetical eternity strolling beside some so-called Auroral Sovereign – totally made up, by the way.'

'The Auroral Sovereign is real,' I said with utter sincerity. 'I've met him.'

He's not and I haven't.

Tenebris threw up his hands. 'Whatevs. My point is, the only permanent victory against the Aurorals will come from converting humanity and the other sentient species of this realm to our side.'

'Other sentient species?'

'Yeah. You know, cats, certain breeds of canines, those big weird fish you got in some of your oceans, and . . .' He scratched at his temple. 'You got something called "swirrels" here? Live in trees, eat nuts?'

'Squirrels?'

He clapped his hands together. 'That's the one – swirrels. Apparently they're the highest level of sentience in the Mortal realm. More ecclesiasm in their little left nuts than you have in your whole body. Anyway, you don't convert souls by recruiting them into armies so they and their descendants can die for generations without end. You win them over to your way of thinking, show them the Infernal path to fulfilment.'

I waved away his enthusiastic soliloquy. 'You guys have been tempting humans for ever. There's only so many of us who'll sell our souls for political power or sex with a succubus.'

'Those aren't *ours*, moron. Everybody knows the succubae work for the Aurorals.' He leaned in close again and jerked a thumb at Shame, who was sitting by herself. 'You got one in your crew, in case you hadn't noticed.' He glanced back surreptitiously at the former Angelic Emissary, who was in her customary middle-aged nondescript form. 'Also, she sure did let her looks go. What's the deal with that?'

Chummy banter aside, I was in a pissy mood. All that work breaking into a secret Auroral enclave, risking our necks to not kill any humans and it had all been for nothing. 'The deal is that Shame's beautiful now,' I replied, then leaned closer to whisper, 'and if you try using your infamous manipulation tricks to convince anyone otherwise, your guess is as good as mine which of us beats the shit out of you first.'

Tenebris rolled one eye, which is more creepy than mocking. 'Whatevs. Listen, the fact is, sex and power are overrated – *that's* what I've been trying to get the Lords Devilish to understand. There's more to existence than just slaughtering your enemies and fucking their spouses. It's the little things. The feel of a nice suit' – he mimed stroking a lapel – 'or the smell of fine wine, aged just the right number of years. The melody of a song that isn't a fucking battle hymn. The Great Crusade won't be won with the stench of corpses on a battlefield, it'll be won with—'

'The taste of really good paella?' I suggested.

He grinned, revealing his primary fangs. They were every bit as lethal as Temper's, I noticed. 'See? Now you're getting it.'

I was brought back to our present situation by the sound of Corrigan smashing the empty bowl on the floor and announcing, 'I will obliterate this establishment to ashes if somebody doesn't bring me more!'

Tenebris had, it appeared, come close to perfecting the seductive sensory experience of a truly excellent paella. Every bite was a savoury concoction of rice, a medley of tender salty-sweet seafoods, peppers of at least three different varieties, delicately poached vegetables that softened the flavour just enough to keep your tongue from being overwhelmed by the awe-inspiring, tear-drawing symphony of saffron and spices.

Tenebris clapped and an anxious-looking human waiter promptly appeared bearing another huge bowl, which he placed carefully in the centre of the table before kneeling to sweep up the shards from the floor. There was something telling in the fact that the waiter was more unnerved by us than the diabolic he worked for. Maybe the Infernals paid better wages.

'It's okay, I guess,' I said, sampling the paella and working hard not to let a moan of gastronomic ecstasy pass my own lips. 'Not sure it'll catch on.'

'*Pshaw*,' Tenebris countered now, standing behind Corrigan. He was nattily dressed in a dark blue frock coat that offset his ivory skin nicely. His horns were tipped with silver caps and he'd shadowed his eyes with some sort of bluish kohl. Other than the limp and an occasional wince, Tenebris looked like his old self. 'You know what's *not* going to catch on, Cade? Your stupid peace plan: *that's* what's not going to catch on. In fact, it's going to get you and your friends killed, which is sad for me because I've always considered you and me to be like brothers.'

I let that one pass, because I had more serious problems at hand.

'It is our current approach that concerns me,' Shame announced. She was apparently enjoying the meal, which she was savouring in infinitesimally small mouthfuls. Fuck knows why. Also, she was eating with her fingers rather than using a fork.

'*Savage*,' Alice and Tenebris observed at the same time, then glared at one another with unveiled hatred. Say what you want about Tenebris' sense of honour – and I could say plenty – but the guy was entirely loyal to his people.

'A question,' Aradeus began, because just *asking* wouldn't afford him the dramatic pause he needs for so much as sneezing. 'Given the months we've spent attempting to foil the recruitment efforts of the Auroral and Infernal forces, and despite the intransigence of the Lords Celestine and Lords Devilish which you have so eloquently and frequently articulated, is it wise to shift our focus to pursue an unknown mage of potentially cataclysmic power whose identity we've utterly failed to divine?'

'The rat guy has a point, Cade,' said Tenebris.

'Furthermore,' Aradeus went on, casting a dubious glance at the diabolic, 'given the precariousness of our situation, is it not unwise to discuss the details of your plan so freely in the presence of a Diabolic Contractualist?'

'*Former* Contractualist,' Tenebris corrected. 'Like I keep telling Cade here, I am but a modest restauranteur these days, bringing the pleasures of the Infernal Thrum to the humble masses.' With the claws of his right thumb and forefinger, he proceeded to mime the act of sewing his lips shut, which was exactly as disturbing as it sounds. 'Nothing uttered within the walls of this establishment shall be shared with anyone, not even the Lords Devilish themselves,' he proclaimed.

'Well, if you ask me, you're doing us humble masses a great service,' said Corrigan, brushing bits of rice, peppers and please-don't-tell-me-what-kind-of-meat from his braided beard. 'Look, even Temper appreciates the cuisine, and he usually only eats blood.'

The kangaroo was indeed showing every sign of enjoying the meal, even snarling his fangs at Alice when she slapped his muzzle for trying to stick his entire face in the bowl.

'Nothing like an appreciative audience for one's artistry,' Tenebris said, now looming behind me. 'Good luck finding one for the shit you're stirring, old pal.'

I put down my fork and rose from my chair to face my former provider of Infernal spells. 'Listen, "old pal", nobody here is dumb enough to fall for this "discreet restauranteur" act you're putting on, so why don't you slither back to the sanctum you set up in the back of this stewpit and use whatever influence you have left with your old bosses to find out what they know about this other band of wonderists who managed to capture you and dump you in an Auroral prison nobody on your side even knew about. After that, you might see if one of those half-witted perverts can squeeze their arse out of their throne for long enough to consult with your Infernal spell-concocters, as they might like to know what it would take for a wonderist to make it look as if they were manipulating someone's destiny.'

Bridling, Tenebris snarled, 'How about instead you lick my non-existent testicles? No charge.' He tried to shove me away, but Contractualists rarely engage in fisticuffs, so not only did he manage to miss my chest entirely, he accidentally cut my cheeks with one of his claws.

The wound stung, but it felt shallow, so I ignored it in favour of grabbing the smirking diabolic by his apron and yanking him close enough for our noses to touch. 'Try that again, Tenebris, and I'll remind you why the Lords Devilish used to let you sell me spells at a discount in the first place, because unlike them, I never start a fight unless I know precisely how to finish it.'

Tenebris opened his mouth to speak, but I gave him a shake, just to help him appreciate my displeasure until I was good and ready to send him on his way.

'Paella's getting cold,' Alice pointed out.

I released my former Infernal agent, who made a show of brushing himself off before muttering, 'You know what, Cade? The apocalypse is turning you into a real drag.'

I sat back down, hoping to get one more bite of the damned food, but naturally, the universe – this time in the guise of a vampiric kangaroo – wasn't going to allow that to happen. I shoved Temper's muzzle away from my face. 'Stop licking my cheek, you idiot. I'm not even bleeding.'

The kangaroo snarled, I gave him the finger, the beast's jaws clenched and his mouth worked furiously. At first I wondered if he were about to bite me, but this looked more as if he'd got a strip of leather caught in his fangs or was trying to—

'He's going to speak!' Corrigan shouted, practically weeping with joy. 'I told you he was smart, Cade! Go on, boy, tell us what you—'

For months, Corrigan had been insisting that Temper possessed hidden talents and it was a major flaw in my leadership that I failed to recognise them. Of course, I never failed to remind *him* that the kangaroo had demonstrated no talent for anything except eating people, although I freely admitted he was pretty good at that.

Now, at last, I was proven wrong.

Temper bore down, the impressive muscles of his arms and torso clenching tightly. His mouth opened wide – and he belched, a rumble so deep and continuous that for a moment I would have sworn I could make out words.

When he was finally done and the other patrons had stopped fleeing the restaurant, he sat back on his haunches and smiled at us.

'Welcome to the Malevolent Seven,' I said.

'Got room for one more?' asked the stranger none of us had seen come in who was somehow standing behind the empty seat at our table.

It hadn't occurred to me before, but not all the tables in the restaurant were octagonal. There were at least a couple suited for seven diners.

And yet, Tenebris had seated us at this one.

It's the little details you miss that can get you killed.

CHAPTER 11

The Stranger

She was not like anyone I'd ever seen before, although for the life of me I couldn't say what made her so distinctive. It wasn't her dark skin or the subtly upturned outer corners of her eyes. Corrigan's complexion was a truer black, almost onyx, while the stranger's was more the burnished bronze of the Western Saphirs in their high-towered cities and sprawling garden enclaves. The almond shape of her eyes was more common to the Blastlands from where we'd descended as we'd blazed our trail of mayhem through the small towns the Infernal and Auroral armies had been plundering in their never-ending quest for human recruits.

The woman standing before us holding a tray of brimming pewter beer steins came from none of those places.

You're not from around here, are you, stranger? I thought. I didn't say it out loud because I hate frontier clichés.

Hair almost as dark as mine glistening with some sort of scented oil came tumbling in a cascade of curls past high cheekbones and a firm yet sensuous jawline. There was a leanness to her that spoke of a dancer or fencer's athleticism rather than the bulkier musculature of a soldier or those who labour in fields and factories. Had I been standing next to her, I might have had the advantage of an inch or two.

Everything about her was sleek, from the fitted tan waistcoat over a blousy plum shirt far sturdier than its silky sheen suggested, to the black riding trousers and matching boots. The way she cocked one hip told me she didn't mind the admiring stares she doubtless attracted wherever she went.

None of this set her apart from a thousand other women. Admittedly, the amber irises were unusual, but a discolouration of the eyes is hardly rare among wonderists. And this woman was definitely a mage of some kind.

'Somebody get this boy a canvas and oils,' she said, shooting me a sideways grin as she set each of the eight steins down on the table before tossing the tray behind her to clatter on the floor. 'Happy to pose for a portrait if it'll speed this up.'

'A moment, if you please,' I said.

The accent . . . smooth, refined. Someone who could pass for a native speaker if she was bothered. Her voice lilted at the ends of her vowels, adding an almost musical chime that drew my gaze to her wry smile. Did everyone she smiled at that way assume they must have met her before, I wondered? Or was it just me being mesmerised by her presence?

If the intensity of my scrutiny is leading you to anticipate that this woman was going to play an outsized role in my immediate future, well, sure, that much was obvious. But if you're imagining the two of us falling in love, hand over your prophecy cards and tear up your astrological charts, because your talent for divination has let you down badly. And don't go getting it into your head that she and I are destined to have a night of wild, passionate sex at some point, either. Not. Going. To. Happen. One of my cardinal rules is never to sleep with people who aren't bothering to hide the fact that they intend ruining my life.

Seriously, take a second look at that Cheshire grin on her face and tell me that's not the knowing, enchanting smile of someone who's already figured out she's fated to put me into an early grave.

78

'She has the stink of wonderism about her,' Alice observed, her own cat-like eyes narrowed, and she placed one hand on the bone hilt of her whip-sword. Her upper lip curled, slowly. Demoniacs do that so you catch a glimpse of their fangs. Petulant teenagers, too, I guess. 'Her attunement isn't one I recognise.'

Aradeus casually brushed his fingertips along the whiskers of his moustache, performing a subtle totemist spell particular to his specialisation. That's why all rat mages grow those stupid, wispy moustaches.

'Nor can I discern the plane of reality from whence her powers come,' he said, sufficiently troubled by the fact that, for once, he managed not to leap up from his chair to perform an elaborate bow before pronouncing, 'Though I cannot yet say whether it is a pleasure or an honour to make your acquaintance, radiant lady, I shall eagerly await the hour whence we shall discover which it shall be.'

Ugh. How does he manage to make all that foppish oratory sound so suave?

'Maybe one of us could just *ask* her what kind of wonderism she practises?' Galass suggested, rolling her eyes at the rest of us.

I wasn't the only one staring. Did you notice Corrigan hadn't uttered a word since the woman showed up? Or Temper? The kangaroo was looking almost as entranced as the rest of us.

The stranger settled into the empty chair as if her name had been engraved on the back in glittering gold letters. 'Oh, you know,' she replied vaguely. 'A little of this, a little of that.'

'That is not an answer, child,' Shame observed.

There! I thought, catching the first flicker of animosity in the stranger's eyes. *She doesn't appreciate being called a child. But why? It's hardly an insult compared to what anyone who'd been spying on our conversation has to anticipate will soon come from—*

'Only whores are entitled to be enigmatic,' Corrigan declared with the finality of a judge passing sentence. 'Are you a whore, sweetheart?'

He leaned closer to her. Apparently, thunderers *also* like showing their teeth. 'You're too skinny to be any good at it. Business must be bad. Did you come here in search of a hearty meal or a fat co—?'

'Where I'm from,' the stranger interrupted, saving us all from what would surely have been an extended oration from Corrigan about what he – and no one else – insisted was his finest attribute, 'I'd be called a Spellslinger.'

'That's not a thing,' Corrigan insisted. I guess he didn't appreciate being shot down before being given the chance to demonstrate just how offensive he could be. 'Also, it's a stupid name. *Spell-slinger?* No self-respecting wonderist hurls spells with slings. If they did, I'd be hunting them down and murdering them for denigrating the profession even more than luminists do with their stupid light shows.'

His irritation appeared to be compounded by the beers, which he clearly craved but wouldn't drink because imbibing poison that's literally been handed to you by a mysterious unknown stranger is an embarrassing way for anyone to die.

I figured it was up to me to get answers out of her. Glorian Justiciars practise all sorts of intricate facial expressions and vocal mannerisms designed to induce varying degrees of terror in the suspects they interrogate. I chose the least overtly threatening option, because in my experience it was the most menacing. 'Who – or what – are you?'

She leaned across the table and placed one hand over mine. 'I have been a great many things, Cade Ombra, and lived a hundred lives in only a handful of years.' Her gaze softened, her bottom lip quivered. 'Right now, though, I'm just a girl, sitting in front of a boy, hoping he'll tell her she's the most beautiful, perfect person he's ever met and that, from this moment until his last breath, he'll devote every second of his life to making each day happier than the one before.'

'Gross,' said Alice.

'Ah!' Aradeus exclaimed, slapping a gloved hand to his thigh. 'I understand now. This magnificent lady has come to join our esteemed coven.' He gave me the sort of dashing, I-told-you-so moustachioed smiles for which rat mages are rightly reviled by civilised folk. 'Did I not tell you, Brother Cade? Did I not predict that heroes from across the continent would flock to our banner once word spread of our noble endeavour?'

'Bands of mercenary wonderists don't have banners, Aradeus.'

Well, plenty of covens do strut around with elaborate banners covered in mystical sigils and esoteric heraldry, which does make it convenient when tracking them down after someone's hired you to kill them.

'Besides, we don't *want* anyone else,' Corrigan insisted. 'We've already got those Arsehole Eight or whoever they are horning in on our action. Too many chefs spoil the stew, just like too many co—'

'We need everyone we can get,' Galass retorted. 'Or were you too busy contemplating your genitals while the rest of us were risking our necks in Cade's doomed scheme for stopping the war?'

That hurt.

'Well, you're wrong,' Corrigan declared, standing up as if this somehow added to the authority of his argument. 'Not the part about Cade's plan being awful, obviously. I mean the part about us needing more wonderists.' He jabbed a finger at each of us in turn, counting off as he went before finally ending with himself. 'Seven,' he finished. 'Seven deadly motherfuckers who are going to save the world, which is why we're called the *Malevolent Seven*. Not the *Malevolent Eight*. Not the *Malevolent Nine*. Those names are stupid and I refuse to throw away my life on Cade's idiotic mission if people are going to be giggling at us behind our backs whispering, 'Look, there goes the Malevolent Eight! That's right, they call themselves the *Malevolent Eight*!'

'Got that out of your system?' I asked.

'No. I also want uniforms. Cool ones.' He tapped a finger against his chest. 'With a big number "seven" embroidered in silver thread.'

He sat back down heavily. 'I need a drink. Or a prostitute.' He shot the Spellslinger a sideways glance. 'Not you, honey. A *proper* prostitute with meat on her bones and *without* the gleam in her eye that reminds me of the time my mother tried to strangle me in my crib.'

Corrigan's mother really did attempt to murder her infant son. Several times. The tale of how he survived is quite fascinating. Ask him sometime. Get him drunk first, though, so he can't access his Tempestoral magic. He tends to blow up large land masses when he talks about his childhood.

'I can see how you must put a terrible fear of oblivion into the Auroral and Infernal forces,' the Spellslinger observed. She wasn't an angelic, then, as she was clearly capable of sarcasm.

'Are you one of the other coven of wonderists?' Shame asked. 'Did you come here to brag, child?'

That same flicker of ire sparked in her eyes, but it faded even more quickly this time. 'I'm just passing through. You know, a little business, a little pleasure.' She removed one of the pewter steins from the tray and placing it in front of me, added, 'Mostly, I dropped in to buy my old friend Cade a beer.'

The Infernal concoction inside the pewter container swirled ominously. That didn't necessarily mean it was poisoned; Infernals do like their alcohol to have a little life in it. 'Well,' I began, sliding the beer back across the table to her, 'first, hello. Second, thanks for the beer, and third' – I set my heels against the floorboards and shoved myself back. The legs of the chair screeched along the oak planking in a promisingly threatening fashion. I brought my hand up, my left palm open towards the Spellslinger, my right clenched in a fist as I summoned the first twisting, buzzing energies of my mystical attunement – 'third, I've never met you before, "old friend", and I'm pretty sure you're not the sort of gal a guy forgets.'

Her expression didn't change. According to my old master Hazidan

Rosh, the human face contains forty-three separate muscles. Not one of them so much as twitched.

Think what you want about my track record as a war mage, but nobody – *nobody* – remains that calm in the presence of a wonderist summoning up a spell.

Maybe she's not clever or cunning, I thought, watching her watch me with that placid, knowing expression. *Maybe she's just some insanely hot halfwit who has no idea what magic is, never mind wields any of her own. I mean, Corrigan wasn't wrong: 'Spellslinger' is a stupid term for a wonderist.*

She picked up the beer stein I'd refused and downed its contents in one gulping, distinctly un-dainty swig, then wiped her mouth with her shirtsleeve. 'Guess I can't blame you for not remembering me, Cade. As I recall you had that . . . what's it called again?' She waved her fingers in the air negligently. 'The Celestine Fog or the Auroral Mist or some such thing?'

'The Glorian Haze?' Alice demanded, leaping up from her chair and drawing her whip-sword. 'Cade, what did you do to this wom—?'

'Time to shut your mouth, little girl,' Corrigan said in a pleasant, sing-song voice. Much as he delighted in playing the big, brutish boor, the fact was that Corrigan Blight had one of the finest strategic minds of anyone I'd ever met. Had our mission been to destroy the entire world rather than attempt to save it, he's the one I would've put in charge. Right now, those highly attuned military instincts of his were warning him that our present circumstances were far more volatile than they appeared.

The Glorian Haze.

I still had no memories of the Spellslinger from my days as a Justiciar. That wasn't entirely unexpected: our missions were always infused with the transcendent zeal granted us by the Aurorals. We'd stride the world like demigods in a trance, directed by the guiding hand of a Lord Celestine. In that blissful, righteous state of spiritual certainty, we could perceive every shading of sin around us, even pick out our fugitive from a crowd of thousands on a starless night. And yet the details, the sights, were never truly in focus. The memories became a blur. That's why it's called the Glorian Haze. It's also why the faces of those we imprisoned or executed never haunted our dreams: we simply forgot them and moved on.

What I *did* recall was the fact that Tenebris had seated us around an eight-sided table. Coincidences are rare when dealing with diabolics.

'So, you're a fugitive from the Glorian Justiciars looking for revenge who joined up with a bunch of second-rate wonderists to sell their services to the Infernals?' I asked.

'I prefer to work alone,' the Spellslinger replied, playing with one of her dark, glistening curls in a way that sent a pleasant tingle through me. She dipped a finger in the remains of the ceramic bowl. 'And I hate paella.'

'Heathen,' Corrigan muttered.

'You're telling me the Aurorals hired an ex-con?'

She shook her head. Those damned curls jiggled enticingly as she leaned in close. 'Let's just say, I represent a third party with a vested interest in preserving the natural order of affairs currently unfolding across the Mortal realm.'

'*Natural?*' Galass asked angrily. 'There's nothing "natural" about war.'

The Spellslinger laughed. 'Darling, war is the most natural force in existence. It's the means by which the past gives way to the future.' Her eyes twinkled as she held my gaze and added, 'It's how we settle scores.'

With most wonderists, that sort of idle, companionably delivered comment quickly leads to explosions, aethereal fires and screams of agonising death. The Spellslinger just shook her head in wry amusement as if she couldn't believe I still wasn't getting the joke.

'You know, Cade,' she began, her tone unexpectedly intimate, 'despite everything, I've developed a soft spot for you. I mean, this whole "seven lunatics saving the world" thing you've got going on? It's adorable.' She reached out a hand and pinched my cheek. 'And you're cute as hell.' She rose from her chair and tugged her waistcoat, straightening it. 'That's why I'm giving you a second chance. Stop interfering with the recruitment efforts of the Infernals and the Aurorals. Back away from the edge of this cliff you've run to; it's one wrong move away from collapsing under your feet. Let the Great Crusade unfold, just like fate intended.'

I decided to stay silent. I hate when people make you ask, 'Or else?' The answer's never pleasant.

'Or else?' Shame asked.

Backing towards the door, the Spellslinger spread her arms wide. 'Right now, I'm just the messenger. Once my bosses tire of your meddling – then, sweetheart, my next visit will have a more . . . explosive outcome.'

'Is she talking about sex?' Corrigan asked, turning to me. 'Listen, Brother, you know I rarely interfere in your lack of a love life, but let me find you a nice, plump hooker instead.' He put up his hands. 'Disease-free this time, I promise.'

For the record, there was never a first time. He's thinking about himself.

I followed the Spellslinger's steps to the door, my gaze drawn to her every move. I knew, without a shadow of a doubt, that I'd been mesmerised by her. Just like I also knew it hadn't involved magic or even beauty. She knew something about me – something about *us* – and that gave her a power over me I couldn't explain.

Just before she stepped out into the street, she turned and flashed me that smile of hers one last time. 'The Malevolent Seven,' she said. 'Most darling thing I've ever heard.'

As her footsteps faded, Corrigan said, 'I'll give her this much: that girl knows how to make an entrance *and* an exit.'

'The lady does indeed possess an unmistakable flair about her, does she not?' Aradeus observed.

Galass and Shame were staring thoughtfully at the empty doorway. Even Temper was caught up in the kangaroo equivalent of confounded awe.

Fortunately, one of us proved immune to her charms.

'Are you demented fools going to sit there like rotting vegetables after a wonderist who just declared herself our enemy saunters unharmed out the door?' Alice demanded. Her ire was entirely directed at me. 'What purpose did Hazidan Rosh have for training me as a Justiciar, only to saddle me with cowards who care nothing for justice?' Her whip-sword came crashing down on the table. The azure stone surface shattered, sending plates, cutlery and what was left of the paella scattering all over the floor. 'Tell me, oh great and terrible war mages, is it the Spellslinger's smile or her arse that so ensorcels you?'

'Arse,' Corrigan said before I could stop him.

I rose from my chair. 'Alice is right.'

'Since when?' Corrigan asked. 'I always assumed you'd recruited her because you figured we needed a sulky, ill-tempered mascot.'

Enigmatic warnings and veiled threats are routine in this business. Wonderists on opposite sides of a conflict regularly put on these little performances to put each other off their game. Some might argue the practice saves lives, avoiding catastrophic showdowns by making the enemy reconsider their life choices.

Me? I'd already left behind my old life, twice, in fact, and I didn't anticipate the third attempt was going to end well. So I was done playing by the usual rules.

'Where are you going?' Galass jumped up to stop me.

I shrugged off her grip and stepped out onto the street. 'I'm going to kick that so-called Spellslinger's arse and make her tell me who her bosses are so I can go and kick theirs next.'

I swear, I'm not usually the impulsive one in our group. Three guesses who's usually the one going off half-cocked. Actually, don't bother, because it turned out my sudden reckless streak was far more predictable than I'd expected.

The Spellslinger was waiting for me outside.

The town, on the other hand . . .

CHAPTER 12

Reminiscences of Futures Past

I stepped out of the restaurant and into Armageddon.

Weeks ago, before the folks of Hope's Creek had signed their pact with the Infernals, this place had been a crisscross of narrow footpaths and muddy cart tracks. After the town's rebirth as Seduction, the corps of Demoniac Erectors had littered the soil with burrowing worms that dug deep into the ground, oozing oils which swelled into buildings of gleaming onyx and flagstone streets as magnificent, in their way, as anything the Auroral Engineers could conjure. The promise of palaces, mansions and stores worthy of merchant lords was no lie. Really, if the Lords Devilish and Lords Celestine could have found fulfilment in devoting their efforts to urban improvement projects, everyone would be so much better off.

It was all gone now, though: the black-marble manors, the glittering boulevards . . . all reduced to a charred hellscape. Crumbling ruins as far as the eye could see were interspersed with the bones of desiccated corpses sticking out at all angles from the cracked stones, as though time and cruel fate were slowly swallowing them into oblivion.

'I honestly wasn't sure whether you'd come after me,' the Spellslinger said. The tan waistcoat and the plum silk shirt beneath were the only bright spots of colour among a thousand shades of grey, the only sign of life. 'My employers told me you were impulsive – that you couldn't leave anything alone. They said there's this part of you that knows if you stop racing from one catastrophe to another long enough to think things through, you'll realise that some futures aren't futures at all; they're just histories waiting to be written.'

I glanced around at the devastation she'd wrought in less time than it had taken me to get up from my chair and follow her out of the restaurant. 'This performance art thing you've got going on would be more impressive without the shitty poetry,' I said.

She shook her head. 'It's not a performance, Cade. It's not an illusion or a trick. Some futures aren't foretold, they're already there, just waiting for you to catch up to them.' She kicked at a skeletal hand buried in the ground. The finger bones scattered. 'I just . . . brought this particular one to us.'

The air was stale, like a burned-out house months after the last smouldering embers have died out. I slowed my breathing, closing myself off to the stench even as I opened myself up to my attunement. The breach between planes erupted quicker than usual. I guess that was thanks to the Spellslinger having rid me of any fear of the outcome these particular esoteric energies always seemed to crave. 'Any last words?'

'Last words?' she repeated. Her chuckle was meant to sound light-hearted, but I caught the tinge of something underneath. An ache, maybe. A regret. Only now did I notice among the coal-black ruins at her feet six shadows, contorted, unmoving, save for the way the silhouettes almost quivered in the breeze. 'Funny how your mind works, Cade. It's like those same instincts that blind you to your own destiny somehow figure out what's about to happen before you do.'

Back when I was a Glorian Justiciar, my magic mostly came in the form of Auroral blessings: gifts of mystical armour or visions or really, really cool ways to smite people. When I took up Infernalism, each spell had to be purchased – usually through Tenebris – and then inscribed as an ebony tattoo on my flesh, to be awakened, cast and spent only once. The spells I accessed through this latest attunement were neither bestowed nor bought. Honestly, I wasn't entirely sure how the channelling of the inexplicable physical laws across the breaches I opened worked. All I knew was that this so-called Spellslinger wasn't the only one who could pervert reality and shock the soul.

They say that to a guy with a hammer, every problem looks like a nail. The power I'd allowed into myself in that fortress in the Blastlands when I'd placed myself inside the coffin laughingly called 'the Empyrean Physio-Thaumaturgical Device of Attunal Transmutation' – well, let's just say I came out carrying one seriously nasty hammer.

'Go on,' the Spellslinger said, theatrically bracing herself. 'Hit me.'

I couldn't tell if she was trying to be funny, because my ears were filled with the *clack-clack-clacking* of what sounded like an ever-growing horde of beetles scrabbling over one another in a rush to escape the confines of my being. Their urgency quickly became a need too strong to resist – but then, like the Infernals say, 'Temptation wouldn't be tempting if there wasn't something enticing about it.'

With that piece of dubious ethical philosophy firmly in mind, I let go of all the questions I had for this strange woman, the past she said we shared that I couldn't remember and my qualms about unleashing forces over which my control was at best speculative. Then I blasted her from existence.

Coruscating black waves rippled out of me, becoming an ocean swell that rose up high, cresting far above the two of us before it came crashing down upon the Spellslinger. The flood hardened around her, burying her beneath a mound of pure onyx, only to then explode, unleashing a flock of tiny birds whose talons ripped her apart, one layer at a time. First, they tore away her clothes and skin. Next, muscle, sinew and internal organs unravelled into ribbons that the black birds gobbled up greedily. The bones, they pecked into dust, then scattered away with the beatings of their wings. But there's more to a living being than mere flesh. Several of the birds began catching strands of the Spellslinger's spirit in their beaks. They darted round and round in a counter-clockwise spiral of unmaking, leaving the rest of their flock to shred the last bits of her memories and emotions that had been wrapped around her essence like cloth-of-gold. Stripped of that last protective sheath, her soul became visible to the naked eye: a perfect, living gem free of sin or virtue, formed of pure consciousness. The birds crowded around it, squeezing themselves inside, bloating and swelling until at last what should have been unbreakable exploded into tiny motes of ecclesiasm.

I watched as those last motes of sentience drifted apart, losing the coherence that had, until I came along, constituted all the Spellslinger had been, all that she might have become. Only the devastation remained, along with the six contorted shadows ringing the spot where she'd stood, almost as if they awaited her return.

'What are you supposed to be?' I asked the shadows quietly.

It occurred to me then that my unmaking of the Spellslinger had taken at least a couple of minutes. Yet, I was standing alone out here in the wreckage she'd left behind. Why hadn't any of the others joined me?

'Now *that* was impressive,' said a voice that lacked the benefit of vocal cords, throat or lungs. The sound was coming from other things: the breeze whistling through the empty street, tiny bits of rock and stone crumbling off fallen walls, the trickling of filthy water down uneven ground. 'I mean, I've seen some spellcraft in my time, but— Hold on a second, will you? We can't have a proper conversation with me having to talk this way.'

She remade herself piece by piece, element by element. The floating motes of ecclesiasm returned, whirled around one another as if pulled by the increasing gravity of her will. Her spirit followed, sewing itself back together from recollections and thoughts that, once destroyed, should have been impossible to reassemble. Bones grew from the dust, flesh bloomed from droplets of moisture. Empty air spun itself into cotton, silk and leather that left her clothed exactly as she'd been when first she'd stepped inside the restaurant. The last piece of her remaking was her smile, which shone bright as before, and I would have sworn was meant just for me.

'*What are you?*' I asked.

The Spellslinger tugged on her waistcoat as she had once before. The gesture was so mundane, so . . . *human*, that it frightened me. 'Oh, you know, it's like I told you. I'm just a girl, standing in front of a boy, hoping he'll tell her she's the most beau—'

'What are you, really?'

'Eternal,' she said with a shrug as if it were no big thing, then added, almost as an afterthought, 'For now.'

'That's not what "eternal" means.'

Rather than dispute that, she tugged on her waistcoat once more, frowning. 'Did I get something wrong? The fabric feels tighter for some reason.'

I had no clue what she meant, but I make it a policy never to let people see that I'm in knee-trembling awe of them. 'I think maybe you made your boobs too big.'

Cool as a midnight breeze, I complimented myself.

Hey, you come up with something wittier when you've just committed the foulest form of murder imaginable, only for your victim to come back – not from the dead, by the way: from *non-existence* – and ask you why her waistcoat feels too tight.

The Spellslinger brought her hands up to her chest and gave her breasts a squeeze through the tan fabric. 'You want to hear something weird? I think you might be right.'

I left her to concern herself with her bust while I prepared myself to summon up the esoteric energies of unmaking once more. While legends and fairy-tales tell us that attempting a failed spell a second time is destined to fail again, I live in the real world. Just because a wall doesn't come down when you hit it with a hammer, doesn't mean a few more swings won't get the job done.

'Uh-uh,' she said, wagging a finger at me. 'You took your shot, Cade. Now it's my turn.'

Okay, so: shield spells. Almost every form of mystical attunement affords some kind of protective magic. It's all about figuring out how the—

The heavy heel of Corrigan's boots announced his arrival as he leaped from the doorway of the restaurant down to the broken ground next to me. 'Ah, shit,' he swore. 'Now, this is disappointing.'

'By all that lives . . .' Galass murmured, following close behind. 'Cade, what did you do?'

Notice how everyone just assumes *I* must be the one to blame for everything having been blown to hell?

'Don't get your hair in a tizzy, girl,' Corrigan told her. He gestured dismissively to the devastation. 'This is just luminist magic.' He spat on the ground. 'Illusionists really piss me off. All show, no substance.'

'You're wrong,' said Shame, coming out next. I turned and saw her body had shortened, growing a dozen tentacles with tiny eyes of different colours at the ends which were probing the scene before her. 'This is real.'

'Seriously?' Corrigan asked before turning to me. 'What did you do, Cade?'

Aradeus and Alice joined us. Temper, perhaps wiser than the others, only peeked his furry kangaroo head out from the doorway.

'Come one, come all,' the Spellslinger announced. 'There's plenty of room for everyone.' She pointed first to Corrigan then to a spot on the cracked ground beside her. 'I believe this belongs to you, big man.'

I expected the sizzle of an indigo thunderbolt or a death threat or at least a rude joke. Instead, Corrigan walked right past me to take his place over one of the shadows surrounding the Spellslinger.

'You're dead, obviously,' she informed him, then narrowed her eyes as if trying to recall some forgotten detail. 'Killed by your own thunder, I think.'

'That makes sense,' Corrigan agreed, and then lay down on the ground atop the contorted shadow. 'Like this?'

'One arm across your chest and the right leg more bent,' the Spellslinger told him. 'And, of course . . .' She gestured to his stomach, made a fist and then spread her fingers. 'You know. Boom.'

'Right, right,' Corrigan said, his expression one of sheepish embarrassment. His left arm came up, hand shimmering with the indigo sparks that preceded one of his simpler spells.

'Corrigan, no!' I screamed, but he never heard me. The crack of a breach between our realm and the Tempestoral plane erupted into a deafening thunderclap. A bolt of indigo lightning tore through his torso, leaving behind a blackened, charred hole where his internal organs had been.

'Alice next, I think,' said the Spellslinger.

'Stop,' I said, widening my own breach between this world and the plane of reality whose physical laws made the destructive energies of the Tempestoral realm pale by comparison. But the *clack-clacking* in my mind settled almost instantly to an impotent silence.

'Told you, it's my turn,' the Spellslinger reminded me.

She beckoned to Alice, who approached obediently, though her usual petulant sneer was firmly in place. 'Let me guess,' she said. 'I end up dying by my own blade?'

'Sorry, hon. If it makes you feel any better, you never once wavered in the Justiciar Path. It's an honourable death.' She held her nose. 'Though not a particularly pleasant one.'

I tried to yell for Alice to refuse the unspoken command, but the

94

words tumbled from my mouth as dried leaves that crumbled apart and scattered to the wind.

Alice took her place over the second shadow on the ground. As soon as she removed her whip-sword from its sheath, the silver ribbon split apart into dozens of tiny slivers. She pressed the cross-guard of the now bladeless bone hilt to her chest and squeezed, then screamed as the shards reassembled themselves inside her heart. She fell next to Corrigan, her pose a perfect match for the shadow that gave way for her.

'I believe my death comes next,' Aradeus said, striding past me to find his shadow among the others. 'Corrigan and Alice tend to attack first, but I would not have allowed my other comrades to fall before me.'

The Spellslinger nodded. 'A true swashbuckler to the very end.'

Aradeus drew his rapier, then tossed it away. 'I doubt I would've died by my own blade. Rats are far too cunni—'

'Yes, of course,' the Spellslinger agreed, then leaned over to whisper in his ear. The rat mage paled, but then lay down where his shadow awaited. 'I am ready.'

'No, you aren't,' she said, her voice tinged with sympathy. 'Who could prepare themselves for this?'

Unseen hands began to claw at Aradeus, pummelling his face and body, grabbing hold of his limbs and slowly tearing first skin, then sinew as they stretched him in four directions until at last the bones popped. I don't know why, but I'd always imagined him dying with a defiant smile on his face.

He didn't.

'How are you doing this?' I demanded of the Spellslinger, but my confusion and rage came out as nothing but bits of moss pouring from my mouth.

One by one, I watched them die: Shame, Temper, Galass: passive actors in a gruesome stage play written by a madman and directed by the Spellslinger.

'You can speak now,' she informed me, after Galass had been strangled by the scarlet strands of her own hair.

I've studied the esoteric variations of wonderism more than most scholars of the subject. I first heard the Auroral Song when I was fifteen, when I joined the Glorian Justiciars. Years later, I became a mercenary Infernalist because I couldn't attune myself to any of the other mystical realms. I *know* this business – which is how I knew for certain the Spellslinger was no luminist and none of this was an illusion.

This was *real*.

My friends were dead.

'History,' I murmured, stumbling to where Corrigan and the others had joined a thousand other victims of the devastation all around me. 'History waiting to be written.'

The Spellslinger, this mass-murdering, impossibly powerful mage whose every word, every expression and action indicated she knew me, placed both palms on my chest. 'Get it now?' she asked. One hand reached up, touching my hair. 'The day we met, you were still filled with the Auroral Song, a brave Glorian Justiciar crowned in that glow that gave all of you those lustrous golden locks. Even then, I sensed your true colour was black. Cade Ombra: your last name means shadow, doesn't it?'

'Yes.'

The amber irises brightened. 'But you're no shadow. You're a raven. The gleaming armour and righteous zealotry couldn't hide your feathers from me, Cade Ombra. I saw the raven and knew it would be you who rescued me before the Glorian Magistrate could condemn me for what he referred to as my "crimes of being". But you never came to rescue me, did you, Cade?'

'I . . . I couldn't. I don't remember. The haze, it's—'

She looked down at the corpses arrayed around us. 'Would you like me to rescue them, Cade? Would you like me to rescue *you*?'

'Yes.'

'Tell me I'm a good person. Surely only a good person would go against her employers' wishes to save the friends of a man so determined to interfere in their plans, right?'

'You're a good person,' I said.

'Tell me you love me.'

'I love you.'

'Kiss me like you mean it.'

I kissed her with more passion than I've ever kissed anyone in my life. I kissed her with the desperate intensity of a teenage boy who's convinced he's got to make this one kiss perfect or there will never be another for as long as he lives. I kissed her with all the love I felt for the six people lying dead at my feet.

'That was … nice,' the Spellslinger said as she pulled away. I don't think she was aware of the tears in her eyes. 'Now, one last thing, my raven of shadows. One tiny, insignificant promise before I unwind destiny and give you back your friends.'

Hazidan Rosh, my old master, always said recklessness was both the curse and the blessing I kept bestowing on myself, a never-ending pattern of damnation and redemption that would define my life until death or wisdom freed me from the cycle. But I wasn't stupid, and my impulsiveness hadn't prevented me from becoming the finest investigator the Chief Paladin of the Glorian Justiciars had ever trained.

'I'll stop,' I promised without further prompting from the Spellslinger. 'Bring my friends back and I'll cease any further interference in the war between the Infernals and the Aurorals. Your employers will never hear about me again.'

'Swear to it,' she commanded. 'Give me your oath.'

I dropped to my knees, took her hand and placed her palm against my forehead. 'I swear it.'

She took her hand away, then placed her forefinger under my chin and tilted my head back. 'You can't.'

'What?'

She knelt for a moment so our faces were close. 'You're a fine liar, Cade, but an oath isn't a lie, and nature, despite how it tricks us' – she gestured to the destruction all around us – 'is immutable. That's what you can't comprehend. What's going to happen *is* going to happen. The war between the Aurorals and the Infernals isn't *destiny*, it's *history*, unfolding as it must. You and me, we're the only ones outside that history. Me because . . . well, let's save that story for another time.' She smoothed my hair from my brow. 'You, though . . .' She shook her head. 'What you did to yourself up in that fortress in the Blastlands? Was that impulsive – a moment of reckless insanity? Or did you really choose to make yourself into what you've become?'

'Neither,' I replied, watching her eyes, her mouth, her face, taking in her scent and the breathiness of her voice, everything I could sense about her, and locking it away in the back of my mind. 'I made a bet with the universe.'

She smiled. 'A bet with the universe. I like that.' She rose to her feet and stood a moment in silence, eyes closed. I felt an odd sort of pressure building, as if she were tugging not so much the world around her but its history, tying it to herself like a cloak too heavy and too long for anyone but her to wear. 'I guess we know each other a little better now, don't we?' she asked.

Without waiting for an answer, she walked away from me, down the broken street. I watched her go, the events of the past hour dragging along behind her, pulled away from this place and time like a dirty rug from the floor beneath. The cracks in the road began to mend, the buildings groaned as stone and mortar, marble and plaster shifted back into place. The six bodies the Spellslinger had left behind stood up, dazed, then shook themselves off and came to stand next to me.

'So,' Corrigan asked. 'How fucked are we?'

It took a moment before I could convince my mouth that when next I spoke, actual words would come out instead of dried leaves and my crumbling sense of self. 'Don't worry,' I said. 'It's all going according to plan.'

'That's what I thought,' Corrigan said as he grabbed me by the back of my collar and hauled me alongside him down the still-resurrecting street.

CHAPTER 13

Destiny's Just Another Word for Getting Screwed by the Universe

It's a strange thing to watch a ruined city repair itself before your eyes. Corrigan and I walked side by side along a wide avenue, stepping over chasm-like cracks grunting and groaning as they drew themselves back together, covering themselves like shy lovers with reassembling rocks that moments ago had been blasted shards. On either side of the path, buildings were drawing themselves up from the rubble to their previously proud heights, stitched together with mortar that had been nothing but dust seconds before. Bits of broken marble and alabaster were sliding around like puzzle pieces to form gleaming, seamless façades. With each step we took, the flagstones slid back into place, smoothing and straightening like a carpet being laid out for us.

'What kind of magic can even do this?' Corrigan demanded. He was angry and scared and blaming me for both. 'Who was that lunatic woman and what the fuck did you do to piss her off, Cade?'

Eminently reasonable questions, for which I had no good answers. No doubt the others had concerns of their own, so I supposed I should have been grateful that Corrigan had insisted we take this little stroll by ourselves. Admittedly, my gratitude was muted by the occasions on campaign when he'd suggest a comradely stroll to a wonderist who'd screwed up one too many times. Inevitably, he returned alone. '*Took 'em to a nice farm,*' Corrigan would say later, whilst parcelling out our absent colleague's supplies to the rest of the coven. '*Lots of open space to frolic.*'

If that sounds heartless, well, clearly you haven't been paying attention to all the other times he's blown people up at the drop of a hat. To be fair, though, ours is a precarious business. One wrong move, one ill-chosen spell, one too many *oh-look-Cade's-brought-another-homicidal-immortal-lunatic-into-our-lives* and it's a one-way trip to 'the farm'.

'Tell me this is all some new kind of illusioneering,' Corrigan pleaded, sweeping an arm to encompass the devastation that was slowly, inexorably, reversing itself as the town of Seduction returned to its former – if dubious – glory. 'Actually, I take that back. Better the world's gone mad than the prospect of luminists being taken seriously.'

'It's no illusion,' I told him. 'The Spellslinger isn't drawing spells from the Luxoral realm. I don't think she's attuned to any of the usual ones.'

'Whatever plane of reality she's drawing power from, I wish you'd picked that instead of wasting your one shot with the Apparatus to attune yourself to fucking Fortunal magic.' He ran a few feet ahead and kicked a stone, only to have it veer in mid-air to rejoin its brethren to form the foundation of what soon rose up to become a brothel. 'Fucking unluckiest person I've ever met decides to become a chancer.'

The bones sticking out of the ground slid free of their bonds, clacking into formation and becoming a skeleton onto which charred bits of flesh stretched and smoothed themselves. We watched wisps of gossamer filaments wrapping around the revivifying body of a fair-haired young man, clothing him in the diaphanous toga of his profession. He stood up, confused at first, then offered Corrigan and me an inviting smile. 'Welcome, my would-be lovers.' He pointed to the brothel. 'Three's no crowd in *my* bed . . . or my sister's.'

Corrigan made a sour face. 'Ugh. Why do you young ones always bring up incest like it's some erotic nirvana we all want to experience?'

The reborn prostitute gave us the finger before darting through the door of the still-rising brothel. Nearby, another pile of broken bones and sinew revivified into one of the young man's colleagues, though she was closer to forty and had the wide hips and ample figure Corrigan preferred.

Nice smile, too, I thought as she winked at us.

'Sorry, lass,' Corrigan called to her. 'Much as I'd love to rumpy-pump away the day with you, I'm stuck cleaning up after this moron.'

'Happy to wait outside,' I told him.

Corrigan just kept walking, grumbling at first to himself and then, inevitably, sharing his emotional distress with me. 'Did you see that?' he demanded. 'Perfectly nice whore. Probably putting herself through university on tips. Now you've gone and ruined her educational prospects.'

My patience for casual abuse was wearing thin, partly because I was still holding back my own tremors following my encounter with the Spellslinger. 'Either kill me now or quit your whining, you blustering ox. I didn't ask to be ambushed by a psychotic immortal wonderist with a grudge against me. I didn't ask to watch my friends lie down like sheep and die worse deaths than either of us have seen in gods-know how many wars, just to come back to life and shit all over me!'

The big brute spun on me, the notable absence of indigo sparks around his fists providing no reassurance whatsoever. Corrigan's all muscle, strong and skilled as an arena gladiator, and equally comfortable committing acts of violence with his bare hands as with his Tempestoral spells. '*You're* not the one who died, Cade.' He stared down at his hands. They were trembling. 'You're not the one who . . .' He shuddered. 'You have no idea what it was like.'

'Tell me.'

The ball of his throat bobbed up and down and he swallowed twice, as if he had to force the bile back down before any words could come out. 'When I saw that shadow on the ground and that bitch told me I was already dead, I . . . I didn't even try to resist.' Sparks of red and black began to dance across his knuckles. 'I *knew* it would hurt – I've seen what it's like when I . . . But she was right, Cade. *She was right!* That's how I was supposed to die. That's how I *had* died, only it hadn't happened yet.' He shook his head like a dog with a palsy, the indigo braids whipping back and forth. 'Is she a god, Cade? Did a fucking god just foretell my death? Or did she transport an entire city into the future and then effortlessly bring it all back?'

An answer to that question had begun to form in my mind, bits and pieces of stray thoughts tied together with nothing but instinct and conjecture. The town of Seduction had all but finished its unthinking restoration to how it had been when we'd first arrived here three days ago. The early spring air was clear and crisp. People who'd been dead minutes ago were strolling past us to wherever they'd been headed before the Spellslinger had ushered them to their dooms. And yet I could see the uncertainty in their expressions, the awareness, thankfully already fading, that they had, however briefly, been dead. Soon those memories would unspool so their subconsciouses could weave the traumas into fanciful nightmares, easily dismissed and soon forgotten.

Would Corrigan do likewise? Alice? Shame? Would it be better if I offered up some convoluted theory about momentary distortions and mass delusion?

No, I decided. *We made a deal, the seven of us, to end a war before that war became endless. We all agreed the mission would demand sacrifices of us, and that our own deaths would likely be the least of them.*

I led Corrigan down a boulevard filled with shops, the sidewalks littered with kids pulling handcarts laden with spices and trinkets and whatever else they'd scrounged in search of the busiest spots to sell their wares. 'I don't think the Spellslinger is a god,' I said, watching the hubbub of an ordinary market day unfold. 'And you know as well as I do that no magic allows one to travel through time.'

It's true: the universe might be a chaotic mess, but it doesn't screw around with causality.

'Then *what is she*?' Corrigan asked. 'I mean, aside from a paella-ruining strumpet of strictly average looks and I swear I will fucking murder you if you have sex with her.'

I ignored that jibe, being unsure which outcome I found the most unpleasant. 'She talked about destinies as if they were tangible, somehow. Not so much predictions or prophecies, but ... places. I know this sounds insane, but I think the Spellslinger has the power to somehow summon those places, those destinies, to the here and now.'

I stumbled backwards, a sudden ringing in my left ear and a pain just below my temple. Corrigan had just cuffed me in the side of the head. 'Insane, I can handle. Vague, barely coherent conjectures that sound like lazy teenage poetry really piss me off. So stop being obtuse and tell me what the fuck you mean.'

He had a point, but I doubted I could make him feel any better. I stopped at an intersection. 'Destiny isn't like Fate,' I began. 'It's not a singular proposition.' I pointed to each of the four directions we could take. 'In a sense, destiny is the inevitable outcome of who we are combined with the choices we make. Turn left, and whatever awaits down the road is your destiny. Turn right instead and an entirely different set of events will unfold.'

'Sure, and if we float up to the clouds, birds will peck at our testicles until we get off their turf.'

'Ah, but that's just it, you see?' I pounced on the weirdly apt example. 'What are the chances of two wonderists who lack any spells for ascending to the skies doing so?'

'Zero, obviously.'

I gestured to the boulevard straight ahead. 'The further we walk down this street, the further we get from our friends back at the restaurant. Those outcomes, those *destinies* are hazy, ephemeral.' I pointed to the side street to our right that would lead us back to the others. 'That path isn't just more plausible, it has a sort of . . . *solidity* to it the others don't. Our destinies aren't set in stone, but they're not random, either. They're predictable – inevitable, in a sense.'

Corrigan rubbed at his bearded jaw. 'And this Spellslinger has the ability to . . . how did you put it? *Draw* those destinies to us?'

'Exactly.'

'Wouldn't that make her the most powerful wonderist in existence? What makes you so sure she's *not* a god?'

This part was harder to explain, but I was absolutely positive about it. 'Because she's sad.'

Corrigan barked out a laugh. 'Sad? Oh, well that explains everything! The Spellslinger is *sad*.' He held up a finger to keep me from interrupting. 'You know what? I take it all back. None of this is your fault, it must be mine. If only I'd agreed to bed her like she was clearly hinting, she would've joined our coven – not that I'll ever be okay with "The Malevolent Eight" as a name, mind you. Together, we'd've kicked the arses of the Lords Celestine and Lords Devilish until they agreed to play nice with one another.'

Tempestoral energies gathered around his hands and an instant later, a bolt of red and black calamity tore up a three-foot section of the recently reassembled flagstones in the middle of the intersection.

'Hey!' an elderly woman shouted from a window above a wine

shop. 'What did you do that for, you bloody barbarian? Haven't we got enough trouble with Infernals and Aurorals and who knows what else without a couple of wonderist drifters hurling spells at our streets?'

'Blame destiny,' Corrigan shouted back at her.

'You done yet?' I asked. Sometimes you just have to let him get these things out of his system.

'How do you know?'

'What?'

'About the Spellslinger – about her being sad.'

'It's . . .' I wasn't eager to dissect every subtle clue in the way she talked, those brief flickers between smiles or the way her cocky attitude was ever-so-slightly too consistent. I turned to lock eyes with Corrigan. We'd never talked much about me having been a Glorian Justiciar, someone who hunted down people like us when the Aurorals decided they wanted them either imprisoned or dead. 'I was never the most powerful of the Justiciars. I wasn't the most devout and I sure as hell didn't turn out to be the most loyal. But none of them had my instincts, Corrigan. None of them read people like I could.'

He chewed on that a while, probably because I'd once told him that my first betrayal of the Lords Celestine involved refusing to kill a certain reckless, loud-mouthed Tempestoral mage deemed too dangerous to be allowed to live. 'Well, I suppose I can't fault your taste in friends, at least.' He gave me a punch in the arm that was far more painful than intended, given he followed it with, 'Sorry about smacking you upside the head before.'

'It's okay. You've had a rough day. After all, some crazy woman wrecked your dinner and the paella got cold. Then she convinced some half-witted thunderer to blow a hole in your chest.'

He chuckled at that. 'Damn, that really *was* good paella. You think Tenebris could get his chefs to whip us up some more?'

'Forget it. Paella's for proper villains, not a bunch of milquetoast cry-babies who get their arses handed to them by an opponent so clueless she never once asked to see your cock.'

'Damn straight.' He puffed himself up, needlessly readjusting the bejewelled bands on his thick arms. 'What's the plan, then? Because I don't intend to spend the rest of my almost certainly short life going without decent paella.'

'Simple. We figure out where the Spellslinger's drawing those crazy spells from and who she's working for, whether it's this so-called "Apocalypse Eight" or some other bunch of arseholes. Then we gather the proof that they've played both the Aurorals and the Infernals for fools and get *them* to kill these shadowy warmongers for us, buying us time to diffuse this "Great Crusade" before it engulfs the rest of humanity – all while proving to their respective armies that the Lords Celestine and Lords Devilish are incompetent morons long overdue for dethroning, followed by swift defenestration.'

'Ha!' Corrigan bellowed, thumping a fist against his chest. 'Now *that* sounds like a paella-worthy mission.' He threw his arm around my shoulders, nearly crushing me as we turned right down the side street towards where the others would be waiting for us. 'You know, I feel a bit guilty. When I suggested we take a walk, just the two of us, I was contemplating killing you to keep the Spellslinger off our backs. Nothing personal, you understand, but that chick clearly has a hard-on for you.'

'Why would I take being murdered in cold blood by my best friend personally?'

He nodded. 'Exactly. So, what's our next move?'

As it happened, the first step in my – only slightly adjusted brilliantly masterminded plan – would require uncovering precisely why the Spellslinger had such a . . . hard-on for me. Regrettably, that meant digging into my past as a Glorian Justiciar and therefore I required the metaphysical assistance of a group of people who would be disinclined to do me any favours.

'We need to set up a meeting,' I informed Corrigan as we made our way back to the others – assuming they hadn't come to their senses and abandoned us already.

'A meeting? With whom?'

'My old bosses. We're going to pay a visit to the Lords Celestine.'

CHAPTER 14

Words of Glory

One enters the Presence of the Celestines by stepping inside the Auroral Cathedral through the Gates of Humility. The last part is certainly true, but it leaves out the bit about first *building* the gates – not to mention erecting the whole damned cathedral.

'Remember the good old days, when we used to blow things up for profit rather than constructing shitty pigpens with our bare hands?' Corrigan asked as he pounded an eight-foot-long wooden post into the muddy ground of an abandoned field roughly twelve miles outside of the Infernal town of Seduction. He wiped the sweat from his brow with the back of his hand, which he attempted to dry on the damp, matted hair of his naked chest. 'Also, is there some reason we're not allowed to wear clothes?'

'I thought you liked walking around naked,' I reminded him. '"Got to let the dragon out of his cave now and then, Cade,"' I mimicked in a rendition of his boisterous tone that even I had to admit was atrocious.

'This situation is entirely inappropriate,' said Alice, who was doing an admirable job of using her bat wings to hide various parts of her demoniac anatomy while tying the end of a length of silver ribbon to one of the posts. She unspooled another twelve yards of ribbon and stretched it to the next post.

'An unexpectedly prudish point of view,' Shame observed, obviously amused by her own body, now determinedly heavyset and ageing, various fleshy parts swinging to and fro as she worked. 'One would expect Infernals to be more comfortable with their bodies, given their philosophical predilections for carnality.'

'Says the angelic *whore*,' Alice countered. 'And a typically bigoted response from one whose own species barely think for themselves. *I* am a Paladin Justiciar,' she declared proudly, only to discover that heroic poses caused her wings to flex, which in turn exposed the rest of her body to public scrutiny. 'I hate you all,' she muttered, and went back to tying ribbons to wooden posts.

'I have offended her,' Shame said to me with a sigh. 'Again.'

I watched for a moment as Alice finished knotting a ribbon as if she were strangling someone to death. 'It's not you. Alice was convinced by my old mentor, Hazidan Rosh, the most brilliant, inspiring and utterly perverse human being ever to walk the earth, that even a demoniac could become a Paladin Justiciar if that's what she chose to be.'

'So your mentor deceived her as part of some sort of game or ploy?'

'No,' I replied with more certainty than I had the right to. 'Hazidan was the best of us. The perfect Justiciar. She saw the law as an instrument of restitution, not condemnation. The old woman would fight anyone who denied that redemption was the ultimate proof of free will.'

'But, a moment ago, you claimed she was perverse?'

I smiled, unable, for once, to push back the memories of my years with Hazidan, fighting alongside her, being manipulated into questioning everything and forced to see that the very beliefs I clung to were shackles I was tightening around my own wrists. *That's* why she rebelled against the Celestines and led me to abandon the order. *That's* why she got it into her head to convince an innocent young demoniac that she could become the first in a new order of Justiciars.

Except you're not here to form that order, Master. You're in hell, and I'm stuck here trying to save the world you left behind.

'Hazidan was perverse, indeed,' I said.

Shame was staring at me, watching my eyes, my mouth, as if the fractional movements of the muscles in my face might contain the answers to all her questions about humanity. 'I fear that I will never understand your kind.'

'Do you want to?' I asked.

'I . . .' She hesitated a moment, then, as if confessing to some terrible crime, said, 'I do not wish to be alone for ever,' and walked away from me.

'Give her time,' Aradeus said, taking a break from trimming the branches off our freshly hewn wooden posts. Through what I had to assume was some heretofore unrecorded form of rat magic, he managed to use his rapier to hack off the branches without looking like an idiot. 'However well she hides it, Shame cannot forget the atrocities the boy Fidick, through the vilest of mystical means, forced her to commit on our first mission together.'

What that little pissant kid had done to Shame, forcing her to use her flesh-sculpting abilities to transform a coven of mages called the Seven Brothers into grotesque parodies of humanity, their jaws stretched open wide enough to enable the Lords Celestine and Lords Devilish to walk through their gaping mouths, stepping across distended tongues like red carpets, was a memory I only tolerated when I paired it with the fantasy of finding Fidick again one day and smashing that beatific, flawless face into a paste that I swear I would use to polish my boots with.

Aradeus must've caught my reaction and mistaken it for sympathy because he nodded solemnly. 'That a child who appeared so innocent could prove so callous has left our comrade . . . unsure about what it means to be Mortal. Yet there is no doubt in me that Shame will find her own way to humanity as we all do, through joy, through sorrow, through laughter and, above all else, through love.'

The problem with irreconcilably noble people is that you can't tell whether they actually believe the things they say or whether it's only that they're stupid enough to fall in love with beings incapable of returning those feelings. 'Shame is more than seven thousand years old,' I reminded him. 'Some habits die hard.'

Naturally, he treated this observation as a testament of faith that the enormity of the challenge was proof of its righteousness. 'Indeed!' he declared, resuming his chopping, only to stop again. 'On the subject of ancient Auroral beings, precisely how does one commune with the Lords Celestine by constructing a dodecahedron-shaped pigpen?'

'Yeah!' bellowed Corrigan from the other side of the trenches. 'Enlighten us, oh wise coven leader, why couldn't we just have rented a fucking hovel instead of having to build one ourselves?'

'It's not a pigpen *or* a hovel,' I shouted at my endlessly critical comrades for the umpteenth time. 'We're building a *cathedral*: twelve sides, each twelve yards long. *I'm* not the one who inscribed the Ritual of Celestine Invitation upon the ancient books of Auroral Law, and since bitching about the ceremonial requirements isn't likely to persuade the Lords Celestine to appear any faster, maybe you could all get off my fucking back about it!'

Galass, whose blood magic-infused long locks were vastly more effective in concealing the delicate portions of her anatomy than Alice's wings, paused to scrutinise the posts and ribbons rising up from the outline I'd marked out in the soggy ground. 'But Cade, when the Lords Celestine came through the gates made from the corpses of the Seven Brothers six months ago, you said it was the first time they'd stepped onto the Mortal realm. How can you be sure the ritual will work?'

'Because I've performed it before.'

Everyone stopped and turned to stare at me, making it clear I was going to have to explain something that would lead to even more questions about my past. Questions I'd rather not answer.

Just make sure not to bring up the Celestine of Rationality and you'll be fine, I reminded myself.

'It's like this,' I began, for possibly the only time in my life wishing I had the abilities of a luminist to conjure images out of thin air. 'We're not actually summoning the Celestines themselves, we're entering into the *Presence* of the Lords Celestine. On occasion, those arrogant pricks like to roam the Mortal realm and interfere directly in human affairs. The bodies they conjure for this purpose are, collectively, known as "The Presence".'

'Ah,' Aradeus said, looking excited, 'so when you say we will be entering the *presence* of the Lords Celestine, you are referring to beseeching them to manifest within physical forms more aligned with the natural laws of this world?'

'Exactly. That's wh—'

'Do they fuck humans?' Corrigan asked.

'What?'

He repeated the question, then decided to answer it himself by applying the sort of classical principles of logic that no doubt occupied the thoughts of ancient philosophers. 'You said they liked to "interfere" in the affairs of Mortals. Since they already have angelics and the various orders of Glorians to do most of their interfering for them, the only human activity worth involving themselves in first-hand would be getting in a little rumpy-pumpy.' Corrigan's inferences took on a pedantic tone as he completed his soliloquy whilst demonstrating his preferred version of 'rumpy-pumpy' upon an imaginary partner. 'Thus, we may draw two inexorable conclusions from these unassailable deductions. First, the rulers of the Auroral Hierarchy are far less enlightened than their worshippers believe, and second, Cade fucked a Lord Celestine.'

'What?' Galass asked, shooting me a look suggesting I was some sort of pervert.

'What the thunderer suggests seems ... unlikely,' said Shame.

'Is nothing beneath you, Fallen One?' asked Alice, her voice contemptuous.

'Void take me!' I swore. 'Why are you encouraging this idiot's nonsense? He's never spent even five minutes studying Auroral theology because he's already convinced the centre of the cosmos emanates from his legendarily unimpressive groin!'

Corrigan began wagging his finger at me and singing, 'Cade fucked a Celestine, Cade fucked a Celestine!' which promptly sent Temper into an excited hopping frenzy. Getting both halfwits back to work took nearly half an hour, but with far too much time wasted, we finally resumed our sweaty labours constructing the gods-damned pigpen cathedral so I could give the beings I hated almost as much as the Lords Devilish one more chance to smite me.

'I'm not sure I've ever seen a cathedral with neither walls nor roof and which looks poised to collapse at the first gust of wind,' Aradeus said unhelpfully.

'A gust I'd be happy to provide,' Corrigan added as he trudged along the narrow twelve-yard trench to create a hole for the next post. He did this by blasting the earth with an impressively narrow bolt of Tempestoral fury.

'Dig it again,' I told him. '*With your hands.*'

Another of the rules for the Ritual of Celestine Invitation – in addition to the work being performed 'in a state of profound humility', which meant naked – was that no magic be employed in the construction. Corrigan dropped down to his knees, scooped the earth back into the crater, stomped it down, then began to dig with his hands, shooting me a look that promised a thousand painful acts of retribution. I gestured around, reminding him that he'd have to wait in line when it came time to meting out the punishments he envisioned, for *everybody* was annoyed with the approach I'd chosen for securing a meeting with the twelve Lords Celestine.

'At least you're on my side, right?' I asked Temper.

The kangaroo was the only one of us who was finding the endeavour entertaining. His front paws dug with effortless efficiency, tearing up the twelve-yard-long narrow trenches, which would soon be filled with wine blessed not by any saint or preacher, but by each of us as we expiated ourselves of various sinful thoughts. Every time Temper finished one, he'd leap up into the air with his powerful hind legs, spinning like a dervish, before landing with a thump and beginning on the next.

'That's enough,' I told the kangaroo when he'd finished the twelfth side. 'You're all done.'

He stared down at me, head tilted quizzically, then gave an odd little whining sound.

'You've hurt his feelings,' Corrigan informed me in his annoying 'told-you-so' tone, then directed his next remark at the rest of our coven. 'Not exactly inspiring leadership, if you ask me.'

'The poor fellow does look sad, Cade,' Galass said, piling it on.

'Indeed,' Aradeus added, 'our proud comrade does appear deflated.'

'You have a complaint to register, too?' I asked Alice when I saw her staring at the kangaroo.

The would-be Paladin Justiciar wouldn't meet my eye. 'Perhaps the beast fails to appreciate the motivational value of your constant belittlement.'

Excellent, I thought. *Because worrying about the feelings of a seven-foot-tall vampiric rabbit-rodent thing is definitely top of the list of problems I wanted to think through before sticking my neck on the chopping block in front of the immortal beings who, until recently, had a warrant out for my immediate execution.*

'You did an excellent job digging those trenches,' I told Temper, and when that failed to quell the dirty looks, I patted him on the shoulder. 'Good kangaroo.'

The animal stared down at me, beady black eyes narrowing. I waited for them to turn red, which usually preceded him biting someone's face off and then drinking the blood from the wounds he'd inflicted, but instead, Temper's jaw began opening and closing awkwardly, as if he were trying to dislodge something from the back of his throat.

'He's been doing this more and more,' Galass said, setting aside the pole she'd been planting. Her tresses turned scarlet as she awoke her blood magic, approaching carefully so as not to spook Temper. 'Could this be a sickness caused by prolonged exposure to our realm?'

Corrigan, glaring at me, strode over to join us. 'What's the matter, boy? Did Cade's stupid Fortunal spell screw something up when he found you in th—?'

'Temper's still a kangaroo,' I reminded him. 'Which means he still doesn't speak our language. Or any language, really.'

'The beast appears to be choking on something,' Alice said, though without evincing much concern for his possible death.

The kangaroo's odd masticating had me worried, though. Contrary to what I'd told Corrigan and the others, I hadn't 'happened' upon Temper in a cave out in the Blastlands. His emergence onto this plane of reality had been entirely my fault, and we had no way of knowing whether he could survive here indefinitely. 'Go on, boy, spit it out,' I told him. I started thumping his back, trying to get him to cough out whatever was clogging his throat. 'Shame, get over here – do something!'

Angelic Emissaries don't possess any specific healing magic, but her ability to sculpt the flesh of others might enable her to widen the poor beast's throat before he asphyxiated.

'Stop,' Galass said, standing in Shame's way. The crimson tresses were dancing more wildly now, signalling her sanguinalist abilities were sensing something in the flow of life that the rest of us couldn't perceive. 'Temper isn't choking. He's trying to . . . I think he's attempting to communicate something.'

'I *have* been trying to teach him to speak,' Corrigan admitted. 'Maybe the language lessons are finally paying off?'

'Again,' I reminded them, 'he's not a totemist attuned to some mystical kangaroo realm. He's a fucking kangaroo.' I stared into that open maw ringed with razor-sharp fangs and wondered what my chances were of dislodging whatever he was choking on before he accidentally severed my hand.

Temper's mouth opened even wider and I was about to risk amputation-by-kangaroo-fangs when he moaned something that ended in a grunting cough. 'Mmm . . . uth.'

'What in all the hells?' I asked.

'Mmm . . . uth,' the kangaroo repeated.

'Mouth!' Aradeus exclaimed. 'He wants us to remove something from his mouth—'

'He's in pain,' Corrigan bellowed, trying to push past me. 'We've got to do something before he—'

'Stop!' Galass commanded. 'Listen to him. That's not what he's trying to say.'

Six naked wonderists standing in a muddy field around a seven-foot-tall vaguely rabbit-shaped blood-drinking monstrosity was not how most people would envision humanity's last hope of freedom. *What the hell have I become?* I wondered. *I was a Glorian Justiciar, then a mercenary war mage. I gave up all of that and took on an attunement that's going to get me killed by my own friends when they find out, all so I could be doing this?*

'It's okay,' I told Temper, stroking one of his ears and doing my best to convey a supportive and sympathetic tone to a beast who exsanguinates its many, many victims. 'Don't try to force the words out. Just relax and think . . . think happy thoughts.'

I watched the last shreds of my dignity disappear into the void.

The beast turned to Corrigan, saw the thunderer's big, idiotic grin and said, 'Mmm . . . uth . . . rrr. Mmm . . . uth . . . rrr.'

'Does the animal consider Corrigan to be its mother?' Shame asked. Having shed her role as an Angelic Emissary subject to the emotional desires of others only six months ago, she still wasn't entirely clear on human relationships.

The kangaroo turned to me, then placed his paws on both my shoulders. Powerful jaws working, determination soaking the fur of his forehead in sweat, he locked eyes with me and said, 'Mmmothherr . . . fff—'

'Corrigan?' I asked quietly. 'These "language lessons" of yours – what words have you actually been teach—?'

Temper removed one paw from my shoulder then jabbed it into my chest as he said, 'Motherfucker.'

'You magnificent bastard,' Corrigan bellowed, hurling me aside with one hand as he wiped a tear from his eye with the other. He stood facing the kangaroo a moment, gazing into the beast's eyes before throwing his big arms around him and murmuring, 'I've never felt so proud in my entire life.'

After that, the two of them danced around in a circle shouting 'motherfucker' at each other until both got so dizzy they fell down in the mud, giggling like idiots.

Shame came to stand next to me. 'I was bred to understand love as a form of sacrifice to the highest good. When I was conditioned to become an Emissary, that definition was broadened to encompass various forms of human affiliation, whether romantic, platonic, filial or any of a host of others.'

'And?'

She looked confused. Or possibly nauseous. 'Despite my training, one turn of phrase bandied about by Mortals continued to confuse me. I always presumed it was merely another example of the hyperbole to which humans are prone. Now, though, I wonder . . .' She pointed to Corrigan and Temper, covered in mud and grinning madly, still hurling the same epithet at one another over and over again. 'Cade, is this what is meant by "true love"?'

The answer was obvious to me. 'You bet your motherfucking arse that's love.'

CHAPTER 15

Humility

The work of completing the cathedral was as gruelling as its results were unrewarding: a dodecahedron shaped from twelve inordinately long lengths of ribbon – purchased at a truly exorbitant price, because humans who side with Infernals have an irritating talent for figuring out exactly how badly you want it, even something as completely innocuous as strips of coloured satin – tied between twelve posts in a huge muddy field.

'Hardly looks like a cathedral,' Galass observed.

'The ritual doesn't require us to build a palace,' I began. 'Think of what we're building as more of a . . . welcome mat.'

'And what is a welcome mat?' asked Alice, upper lip already curled in anticipation of my response.

In case I haven't made this clear before, trying to explain the finer points of Glorian esoteric rituals to a group of demoniacs, angelics, former sublimes-turned-blood mages, totemists, Tempestoral mercenaries and fucking vampire kangaroos gets to be a nightmare after a while.

'Look, just follow me and do as I do,' I told them as I handed each a flask of wine. 'We need to symbolically consecrate the twelve sides of the perimeter: so do *not* drink the wine, and just to avoid getting us all blasted to nothingness by immortal extra-dimensional entities who consider themselves gods, let's try to muster up a little sincerity as we do this, okay?'

I ignored the glares and, stepping into the narrow trench between the first set of posts, I unstoppered my flask and let a few drops of wine fall into the dirt. 'I am a sinner against Humility,' I said aloud, contemplating my recent failures in living up to that particular virtue, despite not being particularly fond of it in the first place. 'Allow me to confess.'

'I confess you're a fucking moron,' Corrigan muttered, following behind me. I shot him a look that I hoped conveyed the degree of panic his attitude was instilling in me about our future prospects, until he grudgingly repeated my words and poured a few drops of wine into the trench.

At the second post, I turned to follow the next trench. 'I am a sinner against Chastity,' I said quietly. 'Allow me to confess.'

Honestly, contemplating my offences in this regard was a bit of a struggle. All humility aside, I figured I'd pretty much nailed the whole chastity thing in recent years – but having met the Lord Celestine of Chastity personally, I can attest that that prudish bastard considers even dirty thoughts a violation of his domain, so that helped.

Behind me, Corrigan was sauntering along the trench, repeating the words and then giggling like a twelve-year-old. It would be fair to say his own sins against chastity were manifold. I was *really* hoping Shame, Aradeus and Galass at least would be making up for him in sincerity . . .

And that's how you invite the Presence of the Lords Celestine, friends: build a shitty twelve-sided pigpen and trudge along each side whining about what a sinner you are. Humility, Chastity, Compassion, Generosity . . . I declared myself a sinner in all the Celestine Virtues, even the very last one – the one for which I once swore I would never again ask for forgiveness.

'I am a sinner against Justice,' I intoned, struggling to keep my mind in the correct spiritual alignment. 'Allow me to confess.'

The ritual requires that all parties to the ceremony complete the Walk of Confession before the plea is answered, but as was so often the case with the Celestines, the sacred rules were mostly bullshit. The instant I'd made my last confession, even before Corrigan had opened his own mouth, light and a cascade of pulsing golden rhythms exploded from the centre of our makeshift cathedral, blinding and deafening us. By the time we could see and hear again, the luminescence had dimmed but not departed; nor would it until *they* had.

The twelve rough-hewn posts were now wrapped in pristine marble, swelling and rising up until they were thirty feet high and topped by flames of pure starlight. The silver ribbons dangled from gleaming white walls carved with elaborate reliefs, each depicting one of the twelve virtues.

We walked around our newly erected cathedral, incapable of hiding the awe this towering structure awakened in us. Not even Shame could pretend indifference to the majesty that had taken over this muddy field in the middle of nowhere.

'Wait,' Galass said as we reached the gilded arched entrance through which could be seen the twelve thrones of the Lords Celestine. 'How can you be sure they won't obliterate us the moment we step inside? After all, you did call them "thick-witted morons" obsessed with a "mythical pissing contest" against the Infernals.' She gripped my arm even tighter. 'Cade, you threatened to murder them. Why should they do us any favours now?'

I patted her hand in as patronising a fashion as my trembling fingers could allow and offered up my best Aradeus Mozen impression. 'Nothing to fear, my dear. What steel and spell cannot compel, shall audacity and wit soon propel.'

When that failed to reassure, Shame explained, 'The Lords Celestine represent the twelve highest virtues of the Auroral Song. Petty notions of vengeance over some idle threat uttered by those they would surely deem insignificant Mortals are beneath them.'

'Didn't they condemn you to enslavement on a whoreship for having dared question their plans?' Corrigan asked.

'Yes,' the former angelic conceded, 'but questioning divine will is a far greater sin than mere sedition or murder. So long as Cade doesn't ask the wrong questions, there should be no cause for retaliation.'

'We're all doomed,' muttered Alice, giving me a shove towards the steps to the archway.

It was only then that I realised the flaw in my plan. It wasn't so much that I feared my former masters, or even that I hated them, though both facts were incontrovertible. I'd spent the last several years convincing myself that I didn't miss my life as a Glorian Justiciar, hearing the Auroral Song, being blessed, being . . . *loved*. But I had forgotten to forewarn the others – Corrigan in particular – that when one joins the Glorians, one gives up the mundane appellation of one's birth to be granted a new name more fitting to their vocation.

'Welcome back into our embrace,' the Lord Celestine of Justice said proudly, uttering the name she herself had given years before to an overly idealistic boy with no sense of irony.

I should also have warned Corrigan that it's bad form to burst out laughing in front of the Lords Celestine when entering their mystically conjured cathedral.

'Motherfucker,' Temper added unhelpfully.

CHAPTER 16

The Lords Celestine

The ignorant and ill-educated may imagine the immortal manifestations of the Twelve Auroral Virtues to be flawless golden-skinned figures draped in pristine white togas seated atop intricately carved marble thrones, gazing down in judgement upon worthy and unworthy alike. This is, obviously, a childish oversimplification: the Lords Celestine, even when appearing as Presences upon the Mortal realm, do *not* wear togas. They wear elaborately brocaded coats embroidered in gold, silver and purple threads depicting scenes of moral rectitude. Whenever one speaks, their embroidery comes alive, playing out brief morality tales suited to that Celestine's particular field of virtue. It's distracting as hell.

'Why do you believe you have come to plead before us, Gallantry?' asked the Celestine of Justice.

See what she did there? *Why do* you *believe you have come to plead?* That's because they take it for granted that mere Mortals couldn't possibly know their own minds. To them, we're basically petulant children who act out of instinct, not thought, requiring the guiding hand of the Celestines to achieve even the most basic degree of self-reflection.

This was the third time she'd called me by my Justiciar name, and the third time Corrigan snorted, 'Gallantry!' and elbowed Temper. 'Cade's witch-hunter name was Gallantry! Can you believe it? *Gallantry!*' Whereupon the two equally dim-witted brutes began chortling uncontrollably and highly ill-advisedly.

'Why does this malodorous beast taint this sacred air with its foul stench and discordant mockery?' demanded the Celestine of Courtesy.

That's right: Courtesy is one of the twelve highest virtues. I could explain the spiritual reasoning behind this using incomprehensible algebraic tenets of philosophy, though you still wouldn't understand because you too are an ill-bred beast, at least as far as the Auroral Hierarchy is concerned.

'Hey!' Corrigan said defensively, placing an arm around Temper's shoulders. 'He may be a blood-sucking kangaroo, but he has *feelings*. And he's *not* malodorous—'

'She was referring to you,' I clarified.

Corrigan sniffed his own armpit before conceding, 'Fair enough.'

I prostrated myself before the Celestine of Justice, she being one of the few of these smug bastards I could tolerate genuflecting to without potentially fatal spasms of nausea. 'Celestine Justice, I wish to consult the Glorian Archives.'

When a Justiciar, or any Mortal agent of the Celestines ostentatiously dubbed 'Glorians', acts under the purview of an Auroral Edict, our every move, every sensory perception, every *thought* is recorded, preserved and enshrined in the annals of the Glorian Archives. This is necessary because Mortals operating under the Auroral influence tend to remember nothing about those they've been sent to hunt down, only how brave and righteous they've been in the performance of their duties. So, really no different from most other law enforcement agencies.

'What purpose will reliving the past serve, save to arouse vanity or seek undeserved redemption?' asked the Celestine of Humility with his customary, almost grandfatherly amusement. He was a right prick, that one.

'And why must these errant wonderists appear before us naked?'

asked Chastity. More youthful and slender in appearance, he was a right prick too, with a celestial stick up his butt about nudity. Kind of like a lot of Infernals, though I wouldn't suggest making that comparison to him.

The question, however, was fair enough. The Ritual of Invitation was prescribed by the Celestine of Humility. You might assume Chastity and Humility to be two sides of the same coin, but the truth is quite the opposite: a humble person should never hesitate to debase themselves when pleading for an audience with a higher power; a *chaste* person, on the other hand, has the common decency to cover up their naughty bits in polite society.

'Does not the reliving of such trivial debates diminish any argument we might offer against the Fallen Glorian's request to consult his own past?' asked the Celestine of Rationality. The Presence of Rationality, it has to be said, is unbelievably sexy. She's always been one of my favourite Celestines, despite never having the time of day for a Justiciar like me. Well, except for that one night we had sex inside a conjured cathedral much like this one, but that's another story – which, in retrospect, was probably the fallout from a nasty theological debate she'd had with Chastity. Honestly, I came away from the entire experience feeling somewhat used.

'How long are they going to go on like this?' Galass asked quietly.

'Eternally,' said Shame.

I had failed to warn Corrigan about my stupid Glorian name, I hadn't gagged him to stop him giggling like an idiot every time someone said it aloud and now came my third mistake: I had failed to convince Shame that an apostate Angelic Emissary must never, *ever* speak in front of her former masters.

'Obscenity!' proclaimed the Celestine of Compassion. He was a heavy-set fellow, or at least, that's how he chose to manifest here on the Mortal plane. His jowly cheeks and soft green eyes usually evoked a sense of understanding and forgiveness in those who beheld him. The way he glared at Shame, however, suggested there wasn't a trace of mercy in him. 'You abused the abilities granted to Angelic Emissaries by twisting the physical bodies of the so-called Seven Brothers into grotesque parodies of humanity!'

For the first time since I'd met her, Shame looked as if she were about to stride right up to the Celestine of Compassion and punch his teeth out. I may be no expert on the duties of leadership, according to my so-called friends, but this felt like the right time for me to step in.

'Go ahead,' I told Compassion, standing between Shame and him. 'Pretend it wasn't the twelve of you who groomed the Sublime boy, Fidick, so that when the time was right he would force Shame to perform that particular atrocity so you could enter the Mortal realm.' I jabbed a finger at my old boss sitting three seats to his right. 'But say it to her.'

Compassion didn't take me up on my offer. Perhaps even he felt uncomfortable giving false testimony in front of the Celestine of Justice.

I should've been content with that moral victory, and keeping Shame from getting herself deconsecrated into dust into the bargain, but keeping my mouth shut is one spell I've never mastered.

'That's what I thought,' I said, although it was probably the smug expression I'd failed to keep from my face that caused things to go south from there.

'*You* mock *us*?' demanded the Celestine of Propriety – yes, also one of the twelve highest virtues. In case you're wondering, when first the Auroral Song composed itself and created the Celestine Virtues, neither Decency nor Altruism made the top twelve. Imagine that.

The serene luminescence within the cathedral collapsed into an abyssal darkness that was soon shattered by a tempest brewing above us where the domed ceiling had been. Flames of pure white outrage licked the walls, hissing and spitting like snakes about to strike, while shadows rose up behind them in the shape of shackles and chains from which there would be no release. All around us, heavenly censure and damnation filled the air.

'Now *this* is more like it,' Corrigan said approvingly.

'The abomination will not speak again!' commanded the Celestine of Abnegation. That's 'self-sacrifice' for those who didn't waste half their youth studying Auroral theology.

'Sorry, sorry,' Corrigan said, putting up his hands in apology.

'He was referring to Shame this time,' I clarified.

Former Angelic Emissaries who question their rulers, then, after being consigned to serve as all-you-can-fuck mystical prostitutes aboard pleasure barges, and not only defy their mission but switch sides to the Infernals, are really not supposed to express an opinion when standing once more before their creators. If you're thinking that means only an idiot would have brought one inside a Celestine cathedral in the first place, you'd be wrong.

'The Mortal realm has ever worked according to its own laws,' I said, pleading my case to Rationality. Even in the old days, I never wasted time on Abnegation, who is both a whiny martyr and a right prick. Yes, okay, they're all right pricks, but still. 'Humanity, whether a corruption or a redemption of the Auroral ideals, remains a force of transformation and reconsideration.'

I gestured to Shame, who was showing a distinct lack of that emotion as she glared back at her creators. 'To call an Angelic Emissary an abomination would be to suggest a flaw in her nature, and thus in her creators. Should we not therefore conclude that her apparent defiance of her mission was merely a necessary ... reinterpretation of Divine Will? Does not her adoption of the word Shame reveal both penitence and a desire to one day reunite with the Auroral Sovereign?'

In case you missed that bit, the Auroral Sovereign isn't a real person, but the Celestines insist on pretending there's an invisible holiest-of-holies lending unquestionable authority to their deeds. It's always nice to tie someone up in their own propaganda.

Slowly, reluctantly, the maelstrom subsided, the storm faded, the glittering ceiling returned and the placid serenity of the cathedral was restored.

'There is logic to Gallantry's inferences,' conceded the Celestine of Rationality, adding wryly, 'though I suppose we should have expected him to come to a lady's defence, given his name.'

Did she just wink at me?

Honestly, I'd thought it a rather mundane romantic encounter, as these things went. But I'd been pretty drunk on the Auroral Haze at the time, so maybe I'd been more memorable in bed than I thought.

'And what of this other abomination?' asked the Celestine of Temperance, the scales embroidered into her coat tilting precariously as she pointed at Alice. 'Surely we need not tolerate an Infernal in our presence?'

I'd always had a certain fondness for Temperance too. She pretty much hated me. No idea why. I suppose at some point I should consider why I'd had so many more encounters with the Celestine Presences than most Glorian Justiciars.

'Alice is—'

I was cut off unexpectedly by a voice that brooked no dissent. 'She is mine,' said the Celestine of Justice.

'A demoniac corrupted by one of your own apostates?' Chastity asked. He was looking genuinely disgusted by Alice's naked form. Perhaps it was all those ritual scars carved into her pale, leathery hide. 'Hazidan Rosh mocked you by training an Infernal in the ways of the Justiciars. Does this not offend you, Sister?'

'Actually,' I said, all too aware of the noose I was tying around my own neck by intervening, 'the fact that a demoniac could so completely embrace the teachings of the former First Paladin of the Justiciars could be evidence of a righteousness so potent as to overwhelm the foulness bred into her kind. Would this not, in turn, suggest that it is the virtue of Justice, and not force of arms, which offers the surest path to the Triumph Eternal?'

The Triumph Eternal was, of course, the supposed purpose of the Great Crusade, though by now I was fairly convinced it was utter bullshit.

'I repeat,' the Celestine of Justice intoned, her golden eyes locked on Alice's, 'this one is mine.'

I'd never seen a demoniac look as uncomfortable as Alice did in that moment, gripping the tips of her bat wings to keep them from quivering.

'If we could return to the matter at hand?' I asked, directing the question to my old boss. 'I seek only to pass into the Glorian Archives to revisit a single case during my early years as your servant.'

They say Justice never sleeps. Justice also has no sense of humour. That doesn't stop her from trying once in a while, though. 'My servant?' the Celestine asked. 'Were you ever that, Gallantry? Or was your true devotion held by Hazidan Rosh alone?'

We were on dangerous terrain now. Hazidan, despite having been the First Paladin of the Glorian Justiciars, had had a contentious relationship with the Celestines right up until the moment when they'd condemned her to live out her remaining years in the Infernal realm. Pretty dumb move on their part, all things considered.

'If I was flawed in my service to you, Celestine Justice, then we must consider the possibility that one of my verdicts was also flawed. I fear the consequences of my error may soon be suffered by us all.'

'And who was the accused sentenced under this allegedly false verdict?'

Here we'd come at last to the tricky part: imagine yourself an immortal being, the embodiment of some virtuous ideal, worshipped all over the world. Along comes a puny human who tells you that somewhere out there is another human – with a really stupid name, no less – who can kick your arse all across the schoolyard and might be working for a shadowy group of doomsday cultists whose existence you never even suspected, yet who have been manipulating your sacred Crusade behind the scenes. How would you react?

Yeah, that's pretty much how the Lords Celestine took the news.

As the fiery hail, blistering rain and pits of damnation opening up beneath our feet made our hosts' disapproval plain, Alice whispered, 'Perhaps you should leave the diplomacy to the kangaroo from now on.'

'Wanton *arrogance*,' declared the Celestine of Humility, whose voice had deepened as the flames of his displeasure coruscated around his suddenly taller and more imposing frame. Hypocrisy is a bit of a blind spot with these folks.

I was rescued by the Celestine of Rationality, who stepped down from her throne to address her compatriots directly. A bold move, I thought, since, both metaphorically and literally, it placed her beneath their gaze. 'Brethren, I implore you, let honesty have her reign.'

Honesty, in case you're wondering, also didn't qualify as one of the Twelve Virtues.

'Has not each of us secretly suspected interference in our preparations for the Great Crusade?' Rationality asked. 'Beyond, of course, that perpetrated by . . . familiar sources,' she added, briefly glancing back in my direction.

Okay, that time she definitely winked at me. On the positive side, it turns out Shame was right about the Celestines refusing to admit we were any kind of threat and thus not needing to exterminate us for having threatened them.

'Is it so high a price to afford this Fallen Justiciar a moment's return to what he readily admits was his failure and not ours?' Rationality went on, gazing up with uncharacteristic meekness to the Celestine of Justice. 'Sister, let the sanctity of our Crusade against the Infernals, if not affection for your former servant or the simple logic before you, dictate that you accede to this trifling request.'

'Why, Sister, does Rationality come begging a favour from me?' Justice asked, a hint of a smile breaking the sternness of her customary glower.

In case the innuendo wasn't obvious, Rationality traditionally considered herself the strictest of virtues, and thus did no favours for anyone.

Again, however, she looked back at me. 'A . . . small favour, perhaps.'

Was that a jab at my—?

Corrigan poked me in the back and whispered in my ear. 'Brother, remind me to give you some lessons in lovemaking. Sounds like the big lass will be expecting payment once this business is done.'

Seriously, it was only one night. I barely recall the act itself. Then again, failing to remember specific events from my time as a Glorian was what got us into this predicament in the first place.

The Celestine of Justice descended from her throne to embrace her sister. 'Let it be thus, in the name of the love between us.'

'Say,' began Corrigan, 'do you suppose the two of them ever—?'

'Shut up, shut up, *shut up!*' I hissed at him.

Justice approached us and for a moment, I feared Corrigan's lecherous tongue was finally going to be the end of us all. Instead, the Celestine opened her long brocaded coat and from inside her being a golden fog seeped out to envelop me. 'The Glorian Archives have opened to you, Gallantry. Witness what you will, but I fear whatever supposed crime you committed in my service will pale before the revelation of how far you have fallen since leaving me.'

Spurred on by those words of encouragement, I stepped inside the Auroral Haze. The gleaming armour of a Glorian Justiciar wrapped itself around me once more. I became taller, stronger and more certain of myself and the world around me than I'd felt in more than ten years.

I was Gallantry once more.

Turns out, I too had been a right prick in my day.

CHAPTER 17

The Glorian Justiciar

I'd forgotten what it felt like to wear the armour. As a boy watching Glorian Justiciars stride into the gang-ridden slum where we cowered in terror every day before whichever third-rate wonderist had been hired to shake down the poorest families for every pitiful coin we'd scraped together, those shimmering suits of golden armour looked so grand, so indomitable, that I'd assumed they must weigh almost as much as the tall, broad-shouldered men and women wearing them. Years later when, as a youth of seventeen, I was first inducted into the order, I discovered that a Glorian's armour weighs hardly anything; after all, it's nothing but rags stitched together with fraying thread. Each recruit has to wander the streets, begging strangers for scraps of cloth, until they have enough to sew those worn, filthy castoffs into shirts and trousers so ill-fitting and unseemly that the proudest warriors would have hung their heads in shame to be seen in them.

That was, of course, the point.

Any true Glorian, be they Justiciar, Ardentor, Exemplar, Pareval or any of the other orders, needed to remember that no matter how great our power over our fellow Mortals, we, too, were made of flesh and sin.

That was an easy lesson to forget when at last I'd been deemed worthy to stand before the Celestine of Justice and her blessings filled my rags with radiance, reshaping them into breastplate, pauldrons,

134

greaves and all the rest: stronger than steel, as proof against a blazing inferno or the coldest ice storm as swords, arrows and cannon-fire. A Glorian's armour was wondrous to behold, yet the rough sensation of the tatters from which it was made remained against our skin, a constant reminder that we were no better than the least among those we were called to protect, to judge and sometimes, to kill . . .

'Please!' wept the girl hiding in the cave. 'Please, I don't belong here. I didn't mean to . . .'

I couldn't hear the rest of what she said. The Auroral Song filled my ears with the serene certainty that my mission to capture this creature of deviousness, to cauterise this infection before it could poison humanity, was an act of sublime righteousness.

'Look,' she cried, holding out her arms to us. 'I'm not a demon! I don't even know what a wonderist is, or any of these other things you're—'

There was something around her arms: tattooed bands of sigils of some sort? I couldn't see them properly, because my eyes saw only the pristine beauty that was everywhere in Creation, save for where sin stained its perfect pattern.

'Abomination,' I deemed her.

'Abomination,' the eleven Glorians with me agreed.

Now was the time when a Glorian Arbitrator would be called to hear the facts of the case as we'd uncovered them and render a verdict upon the defendant. But we were far from any of our sanctuaries, which meant transporting a potentially dangerous suspect through populated areas. Under such circumstances, a senior Justiciar could be temporarily elevated to the rank of Arbitrator. The natural choice was my comrade Fidelity, a woman whose devotion made her physical beauty pale in comparison to her bright, shining spirit. It was she who turned to me unexpectedly.

'You found her, Gallantry, when her filthy spells hid her from the rest of us. You defeated her bindings when she attempted to shackle our minds. It is you who should now serve as Arbitrator and determine her sentence.'

It was an honour I'd never thought to receive so early in my tenure: barely a year since the Celestine of Justice had blessed me into her service. To be given *this sacred duty, to decide whether this Abomination should be executed or exiled back to the unnatural plane of reality from whence she'd come – to be asked this by none other than Fidelity . . . I wept, first with pride, then with shame for that same pride, and finally with joy that one so unworthy to have been born to a world where a wretched, unschooled boy called Cade Ombra should be granted such honours.*

No, I'd reminded myself, not Cade Ombra. I am Gallantry now. Gallantry!

With my comrades at my side, the twelve virtues in my heart, I spoke the charges against the accused and allowed her to give such testimony as she believed would sway the pendulum of Justice towards mercy. And yet she merely blathered and bleated, moaned of her blamelessness and menaced us with threats of her foul magics. In the end, as the others looked to me for my verdict, I proved myself unworthy of their faith. Rather than accept the burden of my office and sentence the Abomination to swift execution, I allowed my selfish, childish desire to appear tender-hearted – that conceit sometimes called altruism – to sway me away from true justice.

'Exile,' I said at last.

And so, bound by my failure of judgment, the Auroral Will cast the grotesque creature back to—

'Stop!' I shouted, shaking off the tangle of emotions shrouding my memories. All around me, the Auroral Haze billowed so thickly I could barely see the girl cowering there, frozen in terror before me. 'This wasn't what happened – it's only the story I was telling myself while the events were unfolding!'

A face appeared within the haze, golden as the fog itself. *'You asked to return to this moment, Gallantry,'* the voice of the Celestine of Justice insisted. *'This is when you encountered the woman you call "Spellslinger".'*

I tried to peer through the clouds of my younger self's remembrances to see the girl, but the vision kept blurring, my zealotry painting the world in broad strokes of gold-tinged perfection marred only by a putrid blotch surrounding the accused.

'You promised me entry into the Glorian Archives so that I could recover the memories of my eyes and ears,' I reminded her. 'If all I'd been looking to do was relive my glory days as a Justiciar, I could've holed up in a pleasure parlour for a few days and drugged myself senseless with psychedelics. Show me what *really* happened.'

Disapproving faces made up of wisps of fog are particularly good at sighing. '*As ever, you elevate the muddled perceptions of flawed flesh over the flawless precision of faith. Yet you remain my favourite among my fallen children, Gallantry, so turn away from the mirror of truth if you insist and gaze instead into the muddy pool of your base Mortal senses, blind to the deeper spiritual clarity that once guided you.*'

My old boss really knew how to pour on the guilt when it suited.

'Please!' wept the girl hiding in the cave. Her cries were like claws digging into clay, so full of anguish over what was happening to her, so terrified of . . . *me*.

'Please,' she repeated, staring up at us wide-eyed, trying to make us hear her – to make us understand. 'I don't belong here. I didn't mean to break the laws of this place. It was an accident – a spell gone wrong. Somehow, I breached the veil between my plane of reality and yours. I don't *belong* here!'

'Why would an innocent attempt so foul a spell?' asked Dignity. He was probably the only vaguely compassionate one of us, and even he tended to be – you guessed it – a right prick at times like these. 'Even now, the wickedness of your wonderism weaves itself among the strands of this realm, a foul weed seeking to take root in the garden.'

He reached down a gauntleted hand and held up a strand of her dark hair as if it were the web of a spider seeking to lure him closer. 'How could one so young rip through walls that the Auroral Sovereign himself erected around this, his most perfect creation? Unbind the lies your masters have woven around you, girl. Confess to us which of the Lords Devilish fed you this perverse magic. Testify to the plot meant to twist the souls of innocent Mortals to the Infernal cause.'

'Look at me,' she cried, sliding back the torn sleeves of the clothes she'd worn to rags fleeing from our pursuit these past weeks. 'Look – I'm not a demon! I was an initiate in the traditional magic of my people. I've never even heard of this wonderism, or these Infernals you accuse me of colluding with—'

With the Auroral Haze parted at last, I could now see what she'd actually been trying to show us: intricate bands of sigils tattooed into her skin with some sort of metallic ink. Each band had its own distinct colour and sheen: one a purplish-platinum, one burnished orange like the glow of an ember, one an iron-grey band. Sparks erupted sporadically from some of the sigils, then quickly died, dulling the tattoos once more.

'I'm only sixteen,' the girl pleaded as if that should somehow render her immune to our judgment. Even without the Auroral Haze blurring my Mortal senses, it was hard to make out her features through the matted mahogany-brown hair.

This was the Spellslinger, I knew now, though there was nothing of the wry, imperturbable mage who'd kicked our arses in this trembling, shattered girl who'd fled my fellow Glorians until she was nearly dead of thirst and her feet had been torn to bloody tatters.

'I was undergoing my mage's trials,' she said, speaking so quickly to forestall our verdict that her words were little more than stuttering sobs. 'The third test requires us to devise a spell never before recorded in the annals of Jan'Tep magic by our spellmasters. Usually, initiates only do some trivial variation of an existing spell, but I' – the tattooed sigils of three of the bands, purple, blue and grey, shimmered faintly – 'I found a way to interweave silk, breath and iron magic that I believed could create momentary breaches in the fabric of my world, allowing one to travel great distances. Instead, I found myself here.' She glanced around the cave as if every shadow hid some new terror even worse than my fellow Glorians and me. She was wrong. 'I'm sorry! I just need time to find a way home, please!'

The timbre of her voice, the rapid blinking of her tear-soaked eyes, the spasms rippling through her emaciated limbs, all spoke of the terror of being so far from safety, from all that she knew, to being surrounded by men and women in gleaming armour accusing her of being some sort of . . .

'Abomination,' I condemned her.

'Abomination,' the eleven other Glorians agreed.

Fidelity, a woman whose single-minded fanaticism for our cause led her to constantly question my loyalty, turned to me. 'You found her, Gallantry, when her filthy spells hid her from the rest of us – though the Auroral Sovereign knows it was luck and not your clumsy, banal attempts at "investigation" you seem to believe make up for your lack of spiritual insight.'

'Whereas you are as insightful as you are beautiful,' Indomitability chimed up. He never failed to leap at the opportunity to kiss up to Fidelity. I was pretty sure he was hoping to wear her down until she got so tired of his pathetic flattery that she'd finally reward him with a pity fu—

'*Is the post-facto commentary enlightening somehow?*' asked the Celestine of Justice in my mind.

'*Sorry. Forgot you were still here.*'

Take my word for it, though: Indomitability was a complete arsehole. But let's get back to Fidelity being . . . well, being Fidelity.

'. . . No doubt that same luck was at work when you defeated the nefarious bindings of the Infernal infiltrator who attempted to shackle our minds,' she said, managing to make 'luck' sound like 'unimpeachable evidence of your innate incompetence'.

'How could anyone shackle Gallantry's mind?' chortled Indomitability. 'There's so little there to bind!'

See what I mean? He just couldn't let that one pass.

A cruel smile came to Fidelity's thin lips. 'Divine Providence need not be granted only to the deserving for such omens to command our obedience.' She reached down and grabbed the Jan'Tep girl by the jaw, forcing her to her feet. 'As we are too far from the sanctuary to summon an Arbitrator, surely the Auroral Sovereign has decided that Gallantry should now serve in the role and, with his renowned wisdom, determine the wicked one's sentence.'

It was barely a year since I'd been inducted into the service of the Celestine of Justice and I wasn't nearly ready to serve as an Arbitrator. I was untrained in the eccentricities of Auroral Law, especially when it came to cases involving beings from other planes of reality who were, in some contexts, unbound by the rules and punishments meant for those of us from the Mortal realm. Yet Fidelity had foisted this dubious honour upon me, knowing I couldn't refuse for fear of confirming my inadequacy as a Justiciar and my unworthiness to stand among my fellow Glorians. It also meant she and the others were expecting me to level the severest penalty upon the foreign girl.

I wept, first with shame over my cowardice, then for failing to feel the righteousness I knew guided the others, and finally, for this sixteen-year-old looking up to me as if somehow my tears were evidence of compassion for her plight. But compassion requires courage, not 'Gallantry'.

Such a stupid fucking name. Why did I ev—?

'*Again, you drift,*' interrupted the Celestine of Justice. '*You claim to seek clarity and yet you insist on clouding those events with your present self-judgement.*'

'*No, seriously. That's exactly what I was thinking at the time. Gallantry was, is and shall ever be a fucking embarrassing name.*'

But as the trial played out before me, every word, every argument, every shameful and trivial evidentiary ruling, I finally understood why it had been so easy for those memories to become lost in the blissful delusions of righteousness offered by the Auroral Haze. When at last the trial was done, I uttered the verdict with the quavering voice of a coward who'd fooled himself into believing he was a hero.

'Execution,' I said, then stepped back and waited for the others to concur.

Fidelity laughed. Despite everything I've said about her, she had a lovely laugh, rich and rumbling. It always made you want to smile – well, except after selling out a fellow human being and your own conscience.

'I beg,' she began, drawling that second word, 'to differ.'

'What?' I asked, so shocked by this unexpected turnabout that I couldn't for the life of me figure out what Fidelity was playing at.

The others looked equally confused. Even Indomitability couldn't find a way to turn this into a good sucking-up occasion. 'You wish to appeal the Arbitrator's verdict?' he asked, then added hastily, shooting a glare at the others, 'which is the right of any of us, of course.'

Fidelity made a show of contemplating the shaking, cowering girl before us. 'Justice is more than the absence of compassion,' she said, shaking her head in apparent disappointment. 'I fear you grow too zealous in your desire to appear righteous, Gallantry.'

The others fell in line, quickly convincing themselves that my verdict – the very one they would've demanded of me had I gone the other way – betrayed me as a cruel, callous youth too soon risen to their ranks. After I then overturned my own sentence and sought redemption by offering to perform the Ritual of Exile on the defendant myself – a painful and all-around unpleasant duty, I assure you – Fidelity surprised me a second time.

'No,' she said, and took the Jan'Tep girl's hands in her own before kissing each palm. 'The child has suffered enough. Return to the Justiciars' Hall, all of you. I will perform the ceremony myself and see to it that the defendant reaches the destination called for by our esteemed Arbitrator's new-found mercy.'

The vision ended, not so much fading away as becoming shrouded ever more deeply behind the golden fog of the Auroral Haze. My gleaming armour slipped off my shoulders like rotting gossamer, my hair darkened to its natural black. Even my nose returned to being slightly crooked, a parting gift from those same Glorian comrades when I abandoned their company. I was stepping backwards through the fog, not of my own volition, as the Archives expelled me from their hallowed halls. Just as the cathedral began coming back into view, I felt a hand grab me and yank me into another part of the mists.

'You just couldn't leave it alone, could you?' asked the cowering Jan'Tep girl. I could feel her shaking through the fingers wrapped around my forearm. She looked even worse than she had moments before.

'How—?' I turned, my eyes searching through the fog that was no longer golden but a kind of sickly green. I couldn't make out the cavern I'd been in before nor the cathedral to which I should already have returned. 'What's happening?' I asked. 'Where are we?'

She took her hand away. 'It's too late now. Don't think asking questions will make it any better. Knowledge isn't justice, any more than a guilty conscience is restitution for what you didn't do.'

The girl was still young, still dressed as when last I'd seen her. I made a pre-emptive attempt to awaken my attunement, though my spells hadn't worked on her last time we met, but I felt nothing. I was trapped.

'How are you doing this to me, Spellslinger?' I asked.

She shook her head, wisps of mahogany brown hair whipping this way and that. 'I'm not her. Not yet.' She glanced around us as if she were seeing something more than just mist and fog. 'I'm still here. Still locked up.'

'Who are you at this moment, then?'

'Nobody. Not really. They call me Abomination. You did, too, so just call me that.'

'No. What's your name? Your real name?'

'Eliva,' she began, then straightened, standing a little taller. 'Eliva'ren, daughter of the House of Ren, a middling family of mages from the city of Oatas Jan'Xan, who thought she could bring honour to her name, her blood and her people.' She saw my confusion and grinned. 'Looks like I'll be somebody soon, though. Somebody dangerous.' She reached out with her fingers as if she were trying to clutch onto a wisp of air. 'Maybe not, though. Maybe I'll just rot in here until they're done experimenting on me.'

'Who?' I asked. 'Eliva, *what* experiments? Where are you?'

'Eliva'ren,' she corrected me. 'Don't talk like we're friends. Not yet, anyway.'

'Okay, fine. Eliva'ren, daughter of the House of Ren of the city of Oatas Jan'Xan, tell me where you are. Tell me how I ca—'

'No way out for me,' she said, shaking her head vigorously. 'Not unless I can draw a different destiny to me.' Again she reached out, straining so hard I could see the veins sticking out against the bronze darkness of her skin. 'It's hard to catch hold of the good ones – none of the likely ones end well, so I'll have to settle for the one they'll offer me, I guess.'

She sounded exhausted, at the end of her rope and on the verge of giving up.

'Settle for *what*, Eliva'ren? Is someone going to offer you a way out? Is that what you're trying to draw to yourself? A . . . a destiny that isn't real yet? Maybe I can help you find a better one. Tell me what to do.'

She chuckled in the way of those on the edge of losing their sanity. '*Help* me? Don't be stupid, "Gallantry". You're standing – what? Ten years from where I am? You can't change the past, you know. That's not how this works.'

I tried to grab her wrist as she'd grabbed mine when she'd pulled me here, but my fingers passed right through her arm as if I wasn't really with her, which, I suppose, I wasn't.

'You *would have* helped me, though,' she murmured, as if she were hearing my thoughts, though she seemed only dimly aware of my presence. 'That was one of my destinies – a good one.' She smiled, a whimsical, melancholic smile. 'In that destiny, you get over your fear of Fidelity just long enough to ask where she took me to perform the Ritual of Exile. She tries to put you off the scent, but that's a mistake. You're Cade-fucking-Ombra, Hazidan Rosh's finest investigator. The more Fidelity works to convince you everything was done properly, the more those instincts of yours awaken. That's my favourite destiny of all. The one where you find me before it's too late.'

'Too late for what?' I asked, kneeling, trying to make her look at me, but it was as if I were made of mist, becoming less and less real to her.

'My own fault, really. I never thought . . . it was just one night, and he was so . . . He couldn't look at anyone but me. We were celebrating because I'd figured out the spell that would change everything, make weak little Eliva'ren famous among the entire clan – famous among *all* the Jan'Tep clans. So I wasn't thinking right, and neither was he. And then the next morning, I cast the spell and . . .' Tears dripped down her cheeks, leaving streaks in the dirt and grime. 'You really want to know?'

'I do. Tell me, Eliva'ren.'

'Call me Eliva.'

'Okay, Eliva. Call me Cade. Tell me what I was too late for.'

The fog thickened between us and I found myself rising to my feet without willing to do so, my steps drawing me backwards to the cathedral. But Eliva'ren jumped up and ran to me, and though I was now as insubstantial as the mist itself, she tried to kiss me on the cheek as she whispered, 'Too late to save the baby.'

CHAPTER 18

Crimes of Dispassion

Rage clouds our vision with its own kind of haze, sometimes. Fury has a colour, after all: a deep, blood-red at once repellent, yet somehow pure: a hue that makes you want to paint the entire world to match. I've never been prone to indulging in bouts of anger, bloodlust or temper tantrums. I am a peacemaker at heart.

'May the Void take every one of you fucking morons,' I swore as the cathedral drew me back out of the Archives and returned me to the august presence of the Lords Celestine. 'You *lied* to me – you violated your own Justiciar's verdict and half a dozen of your own laws to bury the living evidence of your perfidy in an illegal secret prison! Why? So you could torture a young mage lost in our realm by accident and experiment on her in pursuit of yet more power for yourselves? The hells with ending your asinine war, I'm going to kill you all myself!'

The reason why I've made it my practice never to lose my composure is because it rarely produces the desired trembling, falling to the knees and begging for pardon in the targets of my ire.

'As ever,' intoned the Celestine of Humility to his sister Justice, his deep voice infused with the weary melancholy of one whose patience goes forever unrewarded, 'your fallen child places his own flawed judgments over those wiser not by mere years but by millennia.'

'Fury is the sister of Lust,' explained the Celestine of Chastity, the perfection of his own youthful features marred by the disgust evident in his sneer. 'Wrath is the sin by which the sinner fools themselves into believing it is others who owe them penance.'

Even Rationality, that least irritating of Celestine Virtues, felt the need to pile it on. 'Anger fuels the blaze that smothers wisdom in the smoke of rage.'

Shitty poetry aside, she was right. Personally, I would've gone with something along the lines of '*Anger is the iron with which we forge the bars of our own prisons.*' Okay, that's not much better, but it was a more accurate description of my present predicament.

'So much for "we're beneath the notice of the Celestines",' Corrigan muttered, his arms stretched behind his back where he, Shame, Alice, Galass, Aradeus and even poor Temper were shackled to ivory columns that hadn't been there when I'd left. I'd somehow managed not to notice those shackles appearing around my own wrists too.

'The Celestines cannot normally punish a supplicant for accepting their gifts,' Shame replied. 'Cade's ventures into the Archives of the Glorians must have somehow violated the terms of our agreement with them.'

'How?' Galass asked. 'Cade, what did you do?'

It would be nice if that wasn't always the first question anyone asks when things go to hell.

'We permitted you to consult the annals of your time as a Justiciar,' my old boss reminded me. 'You, however, delved beyond your own experiences and sought out those of the Abomination. Confess the nature of your misdeeds and we will, as always, be guided by mercy.'

'Her name was Eliva,' I corrected the Celestine of Justice, 'not "the Abomination".' I looked at each of the twelve Presences seated upon their grand thrones in a semi-circle around us. 'Since you're all so big on confession, how about you repent for the atrocities you committed against her?'

There were a number of 'how dare yous', threats of divine

retribution and demands for me to explain myself, but I paid little attention to any of it. I certainly wasn't going to get into specifics about their crime. When being held captive, never give your interrogators more information than necessary. I wanted to rile them, to see how much they knew about my encounter with Eliva'ren – and how involved they'd been in Fidelity's betrayal of the rules of our order.

It was Justice who spoke first, and she sought to distract me by rekindling my anger. 'Exile can have many interpretations,' she said.

'*Seriously?*' I asked. '*That's* what you're opening with?' I turned to sneer right back at Chastity, 'Does that principle apply to celibacy as well? Because sometimes when my penis gets cold, technically that makes someone else's orifice just a different interpretation of an "undergarment", right?'

Aradeus, bound to the column at my right, coughed quietly to get my attention. I'd hoped this was because he was signalling me about some cunning escape spell he was about to cast. Rat mages are good at that sort of magic. Instead, he said, 'Forgive my ignorance of the diplomatic protocols of the Glorian Justiciars, but was that comment intended to improve our situation?'

'Why? Isn't it working so far?'

Justice waved off Chastity's impending smiting of me and took control of the conversation once again. 'The decision by Justiciar Fidelity to incarcerate the Abomination rather than enact the sentence of exile as *you* happened to understand it, Gallantry, was made of her own volition and without consulting either the Glorian Hierarchy or myself.'

I noticed a pale yellowing upon one of the previously pristine columns to my right, while unsightly cracks had appeared in the ceiling above. The gleaming perfection of the cathedral was losing its lustre. This wasn't unusual – ritual magic of this type does degrade fairly quickly – but the conjuration is also a reflection of the thoughts of those summoned, all of which made me suspect the Celestines were not entirely proud of this little episode they'd kept hidden for ten years. 'Why do I have the feeling that Fidelity didn't keep you in the dark all that long?' I asked.

'She *did* come to us eventually,' Justice conceded. 'The reasons she offered for the necessity of investigating the Abomination's perverse mysticism were sound.'

'You mean, she tantalised you with the prospect of new esoteric weapons with which to one day wage the inevitable war against the Infernals.'

Justice is sometimes blind and often perverted, but she's rarely embarrassed. 'Bravo, Gallantry. You have prosecuted your case against us effectively. Do you now intend to pass sentence upon us?'

In case you needed any evidence that I'm not, in fact, an impulsive idiot who launches into lengthy speeches about honour and decency every time he's confronted with injustice, you'll note that my next move wasn't to keep chastising the Lords Celestine for their hypocrisy. After all, hypocrisy isn't one of the thirteen sins they actually attribute to the Lords Devilish. Instead, I focused my efforts on puzzling out the chain of events between one over-zealous Glorian Justiciar kidnapping a castaway from another plane of reality to the creation of a being who can literally draw an enemy's least pleasant destiny into being.

'So what was the problem?' I asked. 'You had the Glorian Ardentors experiment on the girl but nothing they tried awakened her magic?'

'Correct,' said the Celestine of Justice. Her short reply suggested she wanted me to reveal my suspicions, just as I was probing her own knowledge of the Spellslinger and this mysterious apocalyptic cult for whom she was now working.

'Then the Ardentors reported her . . . condition.'

I didn't use the word 'pregnant' because I wasn't sure the Celestines had been able to overhear my conversation with Eliva'ren. Since none of us apparently knew how her powers worked, I couldn't even be sure *when* that conversation had occurred, since it was, technically, impossible. Had it happened ten years ago when she'd first been captured, making my trip into the Archives today the fulfilment of some potential destiny she'd drawn back to herself? Or had I spoken in the present to some earlier manifestation of her?

Don't believe anyone who tries to sell you on the wonders of magic. Most of it is brutal, toxic or drives you nuts if you think about it too long.

'Indeed, her . . . condition was unexpected,' the Celestine of Justice confirmed. 'The magic of her people is drawn from six different esoteric energies which are sourced from what is called an "oasis" and then channelled through the metallic inks within the tattooed sigils of the six bands around their forearms. Neither our Glorian Ardentors nor we could have anticipated what would happen once we re-attuned those sigils to other planes of reality.'

That Justice misunderstood me suggested they still weren't aware of the Spellslinger's pregnancy, which at least meant they hadn't intentionally killed the child. *In fact, Eliva'ren never explicitly said her baby had died, only that I'd failed to help her save it, which could have any number of meanings, given how esoteric energies coursing through a mother's body can affect an unborn child.*

'Which plane of reality was the Spellslinger finally attuned to?' I asked. 'I imagine Fidelity and your Glorian Ardentors failed with the Auroral or Infernal realms, because those would have been your first two choices in searching for an edge against the Lords Devilish.'

My old boss shared a troubled look with her fellow Lords Celestine that set me wondering just how much they'd really known before today. Nonetheless, immortal beings will go to great lengths to appear all-knowing.

'I would have thought the answer were obvious, Gallantry,' she said, a tolerant if over-familiar smile on her lips.

For the record: I never once had sex with the Celestine of Justice.

I never even kissed her. Talk about dodging a crossbow bolt. Oh, and no, at no point will I be launching into a detailed explanation of the mystical and physical processes by which a manifested Presence of a so-called divine being lowers themselves into being able to have sexual relations with a Mortal. Trust me, you're not missing out on anything. It's really kind of gross.

In my head I ran through the various forms of wonderism with which I had some passing familiarity. Each type of magic is derived from momentary breaches between two planes of reality, allowing the physics of one to leak briefly into the other, which triggers the complex collision of contrary laws of nature which we in the wonderism business glibly refer to as 'spells'. As each of those sets of laws have different effects, it was easy to discard Totemic, Tempestoral, sonoral, sanguinal and most of the others for having no resemblance to the Spellslinger's powers.

That left three options, although it didn't mean I was going to start with one of them.

'Luminism?' I suggested to the Celestine of Justice. 'The Spellslinger's a jumped-up luminist, right?'

That got a chuckle from Corrigan, at least. No one else got the joke. Shame, Alice and Galass had never been mercenary wonderists, and Aradeus was too polite to mock even such a derisive target as luminists. Temper, noticing Corrigan's amusement, started to laugh, too. Here's another tip: never subject yourself to the laughter of a kangaroo, vampiric or otherwise. It's just plain unnerving.

'Thought I'd cut the tension a little,' I explained to the Lords Celestine. 'Getting down to business, abyssal magic transcends spatial boundaries, which might explain how Eliva'ren wound up in our realm?'

Rationality contradicted me. 'Logical, in principle, but still wrong. Alas, the correct answer requires adopting a less . . . *rational* premise.'

'Fortunal magic could explain it.' I was getting progressively more desperate the closer we got to the inevitable. 'The natural laws of the Fortunal realm allow for the altering of probabilities, which might suggest how the Spellslinger is able to bring forward a target's potential destinies into the pres—'

'Cease your prevarication, Gallantry,' interrupted the Celestine of Justice. 'You have already gleaned the answer, as you should have done days ago when first encountering the Abomination's new powers.' She slammed a fist on the arm of her throne. Apparently, I'd disappointed her. 'One wonders why the instincts in esoteric matters nurtured in you by your mentor should fail in this particular instance.'

Does she know about what I did? That prospect terrified me. Celestines aren't what you'd call discreet by nature. If Justice blurted out my crime, I was going to have some explaining to do – followed by some prolonged dangling from a rope around my neck when they figured out the implications of my decision.

So I put on a show of being shocked, sickened and terrified all at once. I even went so far as to utter the answer in the sort of stage whisper most often used by melodramatic stage actors.

'*Pandoralism* . . .' I breathed.

Yeah, yeah. I'm a lousy actor. So what?

I pivoted the conversation back to blaming the Lords Celestine for their hand in this disaster. 'And you call *me* reckless?' I demanded. 'Your Glorian Ardentors tortured a castaway over and over, forcing one attunement after the other on her until one of those gleaming idiots had the brilliant idea to try the *Pandoral* realm? That's *chaos magic* – those aren't physical laws that just clash with ours; they take a fucking hammer to the fabric of our reality!'

So you can see why I didn't want my only friends finding out what I'd done to myself, right? Or that I'd managed to turn a kangaroo into a vampire, but that was an accident. For now, I was taking what satisfaction I could from the discomfort evident on the faces of the twelve so-called divine beings in front of me.

'Well?' I asked. 'Anything to say for yourselves?'

'Our Glorian Ardentors have, on occasion, proved overly . . . zealous in their hearing of the Auroral Song,' the Celestine of Justice conceded.

I took advantage of that rather tepid defence to reconsider the events that had led to the opening of the portals through which the Lords Celestine and Lords Devilish had at last been able to enter this realm and begin their long-prophesied war against one another. At the time, I'd been rather busy nearly dying and being betrayed by both sides to ask too many questions.

Now, though . . .

Why had the Pandorals, those strange beings from that unknowable realm of chaos magic, suddenly decided to invade the Mortal realm? Their acolytes, the Seven Brothers, had told me it was because their own plane of reality had begun to collapse in on itself.

Okay, perfectly logical reason to decide to invade and conquer someone else's realm, but how *does* an entire plane of reality collapse?

'The Spellslinger,' I said aloud, still working through the problem. 'Her forced attunement to the Pandoral realm set off the chain of events that led to the beings who ruled it attempting to colonise ours. The combination of the magic from Eliva'ren's realm channelled through the tattooed bands on her arms, when attuned to the chaos laws of the Pandoral realm, enabled her to create an entirely new form of wonderism.'

'Destiny magic,' Aradeus said, awe-struck.

Oh, sure, sounds lovely when you dub it 'destiny magic'. The problems come when you start wrapping your head around the full implications, which no one seemed to have done.

'What if . . . ?' Corrigan began uncomfortably. 'Cade, who's to say she can only manifest or pull forward or whatever the fuck she does for a single individual? What if she's capable of triggering a destiny for an entire people? An entire *world*?'

See? Not nearly as dumb as he pretends.

'Indeed,' agreed the Celestine of Humility, leaning back on his throne as if some long-standing debate between them had now been settled. 'The Spellslinger represents an existential threat not merely to the Mortal realm, but to the Auroral Crusade itself.'

'Oh, no, not the Great Crusade!' Corrigan said mockingly. 'Go cry me a river, you self-important cock,' he added unhelpfully.

Okay, sometimes Corrigan really *is* as dumb as he looks.

'We are decided,' announced the Celestine of Justice. I suppose they took the vote silently and without us getting to observe the count. 'Justiciar Gallantry, the will of the Divine is upon you. From this place shall you venture and through your deviousness and that of your comrades shall you seek out and kill the Abomination who calls itself the Spellslinger.'

'And why would we follow your commands?' asked Galass. 'Until this revelation, *you* were the greatest threat to the Mortal realm.'

Chastity put on what I presume was meant to be his most winning smile. I'd describe it more as 'eminently punchable'.

'Alas, poor child, you fail to—'

'Don't *child* me, you insipid, pompous, gaudy halfwit from some amateur painter's banal interpretation of divinity!'

Perhaps I should have warned Chastity that former sublimes-turned-blood-mages don't take kindly to condescension ... Nah, that would have been condescending.

'Why shouldn't we conjure some Infernal temple or brothel or wherever the Lords Devilish like to appear and cut a deal with *them*?' Galass asked.

Not the worst idea, and that was precisely why I'd chosen to commune with the Celestine Presences in the first place. Not that my friends were going to see it that way once they found out.

The Celestine of Rationality broke the impasse, unsurprisingly, given her particular virtue. 'You seek answers to the wrong questions, Sanguinalist.' She stepped down from her throne and came to me. Without so much as a wave of her hand, she dismissed the seven decaying columns and the shackles binding us. 'What you are really asking is why should anyone entrust such a mission to you when far more powerful forces could be deployed in this endeavour?'

'Because the moment you divert any of your major resources to hunting down and killing the Spellslinger, the Lords Devilish will see an opportunity to initiate the first full-scale attack in the war between you,' said Alice. For once, she didn't sound annoyed at having to explain something she no doubt considered obvious.

'Ah, but there is more to it than that,' said Rationality, smiling at me, her eyes meeting mine. Yeah, okay, golden irises can, in the right light, be a *little* enticing. 'Your coven, oddly composed as it is of fallen souls, is far better suited to undertake this mission than any other we could assemble.'

'Why, fair Lady?' asked Aradeus.

Rationality walked closer, making me profoundly uncomfortable. The cathedral began to come apart in earnest, the high sculpted walls collapsing back into our rough-hewn wooden posts with the silver ribbons tied between them. The Celestine kissed me on the cheek as she said, loud enough to ensure my comrades would hear, 'You know why it must be you, Cade.'

Ah, shit, I thought. *They know. Or at least, Rationality knows.*

'She means because I'm such a competent leader,' I said quickly. Nobody looked convinced.

My one minor turn of good luck? The parting gift the Celestine of Rationality gave me was a brief kiss and the wink that followed.

'Void take us, Brother,' Corrigan said, smacking me on the back and sending me stumbling forward into what was once again a muddy field. 'Does the Celestine of Rationality really think you're going to kill the Spellslinger just to get into bed with her? Because if so, I may have to rethink my opposition to organised religion.'

I wiped off as much mud as I could and went to retrieve my clothes. I didn't keep bringing up our nakedness because I figured it would make you uncomfortable. Also, remember when I said Infernals have a weird aversion to public nudity? I guess that's why the unbelievably huge fucking contingent of Demoniac Hellions, Subjugators, Monstrosity Artillerists and a host – literally – of other troops waited until we were fully clothed before they dropped the obscurement spell and revealed that we were surrounded.

'Geez, Cade,' Tenebris said, stepping gingerly to avoid soiling the garish purple and scarlet military finery he wore over his Schemelord's armour, 'what the fuck were you thinking? Conjuring a Celestine cathedral barely five miles from an Infernal barracks? You think nobody would notice?'

'I thought you considered military service beneath you, Tenebris. Aren't you supposed to be a humble restauranteur these days?'

Corrigan nudged me. 'Ask him if he brought any of that paella.'

Tenebris gestured to the insignia of rank on his left shoulder. 'This Schemelord gig was a requirement of the deal. Strictly part-time – you know, like when some idiot summons the Lords Celestine right on our back doorstep.' He peered at my face. 'Seriously, man, you got some kind of emotional problems or something?'

I turned in a slow circle, taking in the sight of more Infernal troops than I'd ever seen assembled outside of Hell itself. 'So, what's the plan, Tenebris? This is a lot of firepower just to kill seven wonderists.'

'*Kill* you?' Tenebris chuckled, a little sorrowfully, I thought, and shook his head. 'We don't bring out this many guys just to off a bunch of losers like you.' He gave a signal, and dozens of Sorcerers and Artillerists took up position at the front. 'This is how much firepower we need to subdue your crew without giving any of you the chance to commit suicide.' He stared at me, crimson eyes narrowing. 'You must've known this was coming, Cade. All your screwing around, messing with our plans, our recruitment efforts? The bosses want a sit-down.'

'The Lords Devilish?' Alice asked, mouth agape. In the six months since Hazidan Rosh had stuck me with her, this was the first time Alice had looked like a scared teenager – and this is a teenager whose psychopathic torturer parents can hold a grudge for millennia and *really* like making examples of those who defy them.

'Tell me this is part of the plan,' Corrigan murmured, standing close behind me. 'Tell me that somehow this unbelievable screw-up that's about to put us at the mercy of the fucking Lords Devilish is, contrary to all available evidence, a brilliantly cunning ploy of yours.'

'Let's go,' Tenebris said, and a squad of Demoniac Subjugators bound us with intricate bronze shackles. The elaborate design and engraved sigils made it clear they had been custom-made for each of us – even Temper had a set, which made our capture unexpectedly unnerving.

The moment the cuffs closed around my wrists, I felt half a dozen spells suddenly incapacitating every part of my being, from my body to my spirit to my lousy sense of humour. I could see the same effect in the despair taking hold of all my friends. It hurt my soul, the way everyone looked at me like I was somehow supposed to offer words of encouragement – the looks that fill real heroes with an unyielding determination to fight back. And okay, maybe I haven't presented myself as having the most heroic heart beating in my chest, but these six lunatics weren't just some mercenary crew I'd joined; they were the best friends and the bravest people I'd ever known. And damn it, whatever the price, no gods-damned mystical shackles were going to stop me giving them my all.

As Tenebris and his army led us off in chains to wherever we were going to face the merciless Lords Devilish, I fought back against one of the spells in the subjugation cuffs long enough to call back to them, 'Hey, did I ever tell you guys about the time I had sex with the Celestine of Rationality?'

CHAPTER 19

Some Light Dinner Torture

I would have been less irritated by the gaudy surroundings in which the seven of us were being tortured had we not had to sit out in the cold half the night while the Infernals erected a Scarlet Cathedral for the coming of the Lords Devilish. The cathedral was in no way necessary.

Here's the thing about those who sit atop the Infernal Hierarchy: they're a bunch of jealous and competitive fuckwits. The Lords Celestine are twelve in number? Well, then, we better have at least thirteen Lords Devilish. Auroral armour shimmers? Let's make sure that Infernal armour positively *oozes* iridescence. Oh, and the Lords Celestine can cause an entire cathedral to appear wherever they choose so long as a group of idiots perform the right ritual? Behold as the Lords Devilish . . . sit around and wait for their servants to build the damned thing one spell at a time.

As much as the Lords Celestine and Lords Devilish might come off as near-identical groups of arseholes differentiated solely by their fashion choices, there are, in fact, a multitude of differences, one of which is that the Aurorals have *way* better shaping spells. With enough raw materials and elements nearby, an Auroral Visioneer can transmute stone, wood and even dust into a wondrous temple whose beauty would reduce even the most cynical architect to tears. Infernal magic lacks the innate sense of permanence to achieve such pompous feats. Their Artificers can, of course, twist certain debasement spells to erect vaguely similar architectural wonders, just not as quickly – or as structurally sound.

'You know, this place is kind of a dump,' I observed to the Lord Devilish who was lounging next to the bizarre apparatus holding me bound by my wrists and ankles. She was gnawing on the end of one of my intestines as it dangled between us from the open wound on my stomach. The experience was more nauseating than painful, to be honest. I mean, sure, the belly wound hurt like . . . well, like hells, but the nerves in my body had pretty much given up by then.

The rest of our coven were suffering equally grotesque indignities. Aradeus was chained to a post while demoniac seamstresses were stitching a huge, twitching rat tail onto his rear end. Given how often he protests about being a rat *mage* and not an actual rat, this was truly adding insult to injury.

Corrigan was doing an admirable job of not screaming, given he was having thin slices of an especially beloved portion of his anatomy delicately carved off and placed upon round crackers for the Lords Devilish to sample.

Shame had been taken by half a dozen malefics, each of whom had been made to look exactly like Fidick, the beatific boy who'd so deceived us, and forced Shame into committing a crime so vile that it dwarfed every indecent act she'd endured as an Angelic Emissary. The six little Fidicks were gleefully stuffing Shame into a huge metal machine of cogs and wheels, which was pumping out her pulverised bones so they could be pasted onto Alice's horns. They were getting so obscenely large that her head was weighed down, the horns slowly grinding into the floor of the cathedral.

Oh, right: the cathedral. It was, in every sense, a near-identical replica of the Celestines', except for being larger and decorated entirely in clashing shades of red. The thirteen thrones of the Lords

Devilish did have cushioned upholstery, however, so you couldn't accuse them of lacking innovation.

Temper sat nearby on his haunches, unmolested by the small army of demoniac functionaries enacting the many torments on the rest of us. The Lords Devilish must have been stumped by the kangaroo's mind, unable to squeeze from his thoughts any punishment that would crush his beastly soul. Perhaps kangaroos are just unconscionably evil fuckers who can't be grossed-out no matter what you do to them. As for Galass, well, in our little carnival of corruption, she was the carrot. Or the stick. I honestly wasn't sure how the metaphor applied in this particular context.

'Why aren't they torturing me?' she asked.

They had seated her in a comfortable chair a few feet away from my significantly less comfortable iron rack. She was unshackled, and had even been permitted to keep on her silver sublime's gown. All the while, the thirteen Lords Devilish, magnificently attired in matching iridescent scarlet robes, watched from their various thrones. What distinguished them from one another were the contrasting styles and configurations of horns which were, honestly, jaw-dropping to behold. You wouldn't expect all those elaborate bone spirals, curves, corkscrews, prongs, knobs and antlers to evoke such majesty, but damn, they sure looked cool. The effect of all this impressive regalia was, however, entirely ruined anytime one of them opened their fool mouths.

'So, Cade,' began the tallest of the Lords Devilish. His horns were like those of a gazelle protruding upwards from his broad forehead. Tiny creatures ran up and down both horns, winding around the spirals, frolicking in apparent delight. As each of the thirteen Devilish was devoted to a single experiential imperative, this must be Lord Whimsy, and he was an idiot. 'Cade Ombra. Cadey-Cadey-Cadey.' He was saying this in a way that was intended to sound ominous, like a gang boss shaking his head as if saddened by the prospect of an admired rival's impending mutilation.

'Does that arsehole have a speech impediment or something?' Corrigan asked, still staring down as that part of himself which he valued far more than his soul was becoming less impressive by the minute. The baroque process was almost fascinating. First, a three-foot-tall malefic sous-chef would shave off paper-thin slices, which a second malefic would lightly seer on a piping-hot black-iron pan. A third chef armed with a tiny spatula carefully slid the sizzling round onto a cracker, which a fourth malefic garnished with a sprig of parsley and a sprinkle of what looked like sugared almonds. Say what you will about the ethical improprieties of Infernal cuisine, but those malefics can put together one hell of a canapé.

The dubious delicacies were being served first to the Lords Devilish, then offered to the rest of us. We politely declined, of course, although Temper, licking his lips, looked tempted until he caught Corrigan's horrified look. The kangaroo turned to me, a despairing expression on his furry muzzle suggesting perhaps the price of friendship was too high and would there be any paella later on?

A less jaded observer might have wondered why the five of us – Temper and Galass having not yet been tortured – weren't screaming in agony and pleading for a merciful death. Without meaning to sound immodest, the simple answer is that former mercenary war mages aren't exactly sissies. You think funnelling mystical breaches to other realms where the laws of physics operate entirely differently from ours through entirely normal Mortal nerve endings tickles? It's *horrifyingly* painful. Human bodies aren't meant for channelling esoteric energies – your flesh, your mind, your very spirit rebels against the appalling sensations. This is why few wonderists live to old age, and none of us are quite in our right minds.

Still, torture sucks. The only relief you get from the suffering is to refuse to give the bastards the satisfaction of seeing you sweat.

Hence them needing a carrot – or no, now that I think about it, Galass was definitely the stick.

'Let's get on with this,' I told our Infernal captors as I nodded towards the confused, frightened, shivering seventeen-year-old no doubt wondering what they meant to do to her and how much worse it would be. 'Are you going to torture the shit out of her or what?'

What really pissed me off about this horror show the Lords Devilish were staging was that we all knew how the final act was meant to be played: Corrigan and I would hold out until we were no good to them. Shame and Alice, being respectively angelic and demoniac, were physically more resilient than mere Mortals. As for Aradeus, well, he was a rat mage and therefore too noble even so much as to whimper. So the real way to get to us was through Galass. Her wonderism, the only form of magic drawn from the Mortal realm itself, meant she had never experienced the discomfort usually associated with spellcasting. She was the youngest wonderist in our group, so thus far she'd not had the privilege of being captured and tortured by enemy forces – as long as you skip over her entire upbringing among the Sublimes, of course. Either way, I reckoned the Lords Devilish were counting on leveraging her suffering as the stick before they offered us a carrot. In other words, all the torments, physical and psychological, being inflicted on the rest of us right now was purely for show.

'You speak glibly of the soul-rending abuses we have in mind for the girl,' Lord Temptation said. The horns of a stag protruded from his temples, with tiny clouds nestling within the elaborate, labyrinthine points shimmering with images of all that the beholder desired, which explained why I was currently watching dozens of flickering pictures of myself choking all thirteen of these smug pricks to death with my bare hands.

Lord Ire, whose massive twin bull horns had to have their own Infernal levitation cantrips inscribed in silver around their circumference to keep him tipping forwards when he walked, offered up this sagacious philosophical argument: 'We can make such a ruin of the girl's body that you will drown in your tears, Cade Ombra.'

'I'm a *woman*, not a *girl*,' Galass corrected them both.

'Seriously?' Corrigan asked in disbelief. 'I'm getting my cock chopped off one slice at a time here and *that's* the hill you want to die on?'

Corrigan didn't understand Galass the way I did. She'd spent her childhood hiding beneath a mask of obedience and self-denial, disguising her terror and the unconscionable abuses inflicted upon her by those to whom the abbots of her order had gifted her. Now she hid those fears behind intransigence and defiance.

'Quit stalling,' I cajoled our captors. 'You, Lord Gluttony.' I noticed he was still gnawing on the end of my intestines. 'You're embarrassing yourself.' By the way, Lord Gluttony wasn't at all what you might expect. She was gorgeous – sultry, sensuous . . . Even those weirdly curving horns coming out of her jaws were oddly alluring. But, you know, currently chewing on my intestines.

'Cade, boyo,' drawled Lord Whimsy, sauntering over to where Galass sat, 'you'd best not be testing our resolve here.' He reached out a hand to stroke her jaw. 'There are so, so many ways we can have fun with this one.'

'*Boyo?*' I repeated. 'Go fuck yourself. You claim you're intending to violate and torture my comrade? Get to it, then.' I jangled my chains, which was difficult since there was only a couple of inches between them and the anchor points on the rack to which I was bound. 'It's not as if I can stop you, so if you're expecting me to get all weepy about her suffering, you clearly don't get why we named ourselves the Malevolent Seven.'

'Fucking right!' Corrigan said, then frowned at the malefic sous-chef with the carving knife. 'Hey, leave something for me to piss with, will you?'

'Such defiance,' cooed Lord Gluttony, finally letting my intestine fall from her mouth. Nobody knows how to keep a body alive better than an Infernal torturer. Gluttony rose to her feet and untied her robes. As she approached Galass, her body twisted in and around itself, as if her pale white flesh were being blown away from her skeleton by a tornado. Her aspect changed as she took on the form of a man my height, my build, my hair . . .

Okay, fair warning: this next part is gross. Really. It's the kind of thing where I'd normally recommend closing your eyes and later pretending it never happened. But since it *did* happen and was intrinsically connected to what I said next, well . . . but you have been warned.

From between the legs of the Lord Devilish who now looked otherwise identical to me rose an engorged two-foot-long phallus that reared and swayed like a snake. Bone spikes protruded from the obscene organ, while tiny crab-like creatures with snapping pincers clambered up and down its length in excited anticipation.

'Gaze into my eyes, girl,' said Lord Gluttony with my voice, my inflections and something that I dearly hoped wasn't any smile that had ever crossed my lips. 'Would you like to see what he's imagined doing to you ever since that first day whe—?'

'Galass, don't listen to this bi—'

'Shut up,' she snapped at me, then to Lord Gluttony said, 'I told you before, *don't call me girl.*'

I don't understand bravery. I don't mean, 'I fail to comprehend how mere Mortals can exhibit such unflappable courage in the face of unimaginable horror'. I mean, I don't get the things that come out of the mouths of courageous people – brave speeches, quiet songs of unyielding determination. Me, I've never been especially courageous – not when getting ugly is so much more effective.

'Go ahead,' I told Lord Gluttony as she stood there wearing my face and promising to visit untold horrors on a woman who, regardless of any other protective instincts I might've had towards her on account of how we'd first met, was a member of my coven and one of the people I admired most in the world. 'Do what you're going to do with her and then kill the rest of us.'

'*Kill* you?' Lord Whimsy asked. 'Cadey-boy, why would we do that? You're far too useful to kill.'

Yeah, no kidding, arsehole.

I tried to lean back and make a show of relaxing, which is hard to do when you're stretched out against an uncomfortably shaped steel sculpture with your guts hanging from the gaping wound in your belly. 'That's where you've got yourself a little problem. I mean, sure, there's nothing any of us can do to stop you from torturing our comrade. But any idiot can see you brought us here because there's something you need from us. Don't get me wrong, we'll probably do it anyway because there's a fucking doomsday cult out there screwing with both you and the Lords Celestine and bringing the Mortal realm closer to catastrophe with every passing minute we waste here getting jerked around by you morons.' I paused a moment, partly because I was getting perilously close to losing consciousness from blood loss and whatever happens when your internal organs spend too much time outside your body. 'Hey, fuckstick,' I called to Lord Gluttony, 'look over here. Time you gazed into *my* eyes for a second.'

I waited until she complied. Lords Devilish aren't prone to obeying the commands of their prisoners, so it took a while.

'Good,' I said when I finally had their attention. 'Hear me now, Lords Devilish, and with every ounce of wit and insight you possess, seek out the faintest trace of falsity in my words. Whosoever touches the girl— *Woman*—' Shit. It's really hard to give a good speech when you're on the verge of passing out. 'Whoever lays another hand upon her is naught but a corpse unaware that the last exhale of vital breath has already left their body. You believe this show of power will grant you an edge in your negotiations with us? Never in all the foolish gambits of a foolish species have you more cataclysmically miscalculated than you're doing right now.'

'Angry words for one whose own next breath is entirely at our discretion,' said Lord Ire.

'I don't bluff, if that's what you're hoping, shit-for-horns. You had the seven of us brought here against our will to find out what we know and to work out a deal. You have roughed us up and humiliated us to show us who's boss. That's fine. War is an ugly business. But that doesn't mean there aren't rules.'

'Oh, and whose rules are those, Cadey-Cadey-Cade?' asked Lord Whimsy.

'*My* rules, you slack-jawed halfwit. And you're on the verge of breaking the only one that matters. You wanted to smack us around and prove how tough you are? Fine. Mission accomplished. Now, unshackle us, heal our wounds and for the sake of all dignity get that tail off of Aradeus' arse so we can get to the negotiations. Because if you do any permanent damage to a member of my crew – you take one teensy step over that cliff's edge you're too stupid to see you're standing on – and I will make your worst enemies weep at the memory of what was left of you when I was finally done.'

Lord Ire started to speak, but I cut him off.

'Don't talk. Quit pretending you don't know exactly who I am, because I'm pretty sure Tenebris gave you regular reports about me back when you were using him to sell me spells. I'm Cade-fucking-Ombra, and if the next thing that happens in this feeble excuse for a back-alley brothel isn't me and my friends being released so we can work out the deal you brought us here to make, I will *end you*, motherfuckers.'

There was silence for a long while, broken only when Temper repeated, 'Motherfucker.' I don't know how, but I would swear on my own grave that the kangaroo had understood every word I'd uttered and wanted the Lords Devilish to know that what I'd just said went double for him.

But maybe not; he's just a dumb vampiric kangaroo, after all.

I'd been in plenty of stand-offs in my time, so I figured I knew all the possible ways they could end. Mayhem is common. Walking away, less so. Sadly, most belligerents usually start up again with more threats.

This was the first stand-off I'd ever been involved in that ended with applause.

CHAPTER 20

Curtain Calls

The applause showered upon us by the Lords Devilish upon the stage that was their clashing scarlet cathedral was beyond enthusiastic. This was *raucous* applause. *Ecstatic* applause. The kind of applause of which the finest minstrels, stage actors and politicians can only dream.

'Bravo!' bellowed Lord Ire.

'Wonderful, simply wonderful!' cheered Lord Temptation.

'Brought a tear to my eye,' added Lord Gluttony. 'And Infernals haven't even got tear ducts!'

Pretty soon you won't have a skull, either, you piece of shit.

Despite my show of indifference, the sight of me as the literal embodiment of cruelty and violation – that wasn't going to fade with a few weepy late-night therapy sessions around the campfire. I was pretty sure it *would* fade when I was done killing Lord Gluttony some day after we'd finished preventing eternal war from wrecking our already pretty crappy Mortal realm.

'Tenebris always said you were a good time, Cadester.' Lord Whimsy gave me a playful punch in the shoulder. It shattered the bones. 'Oops, sorry, pal.'

'No problem,' I said, grunting as I tried to keep from falling unconscious. 'You can fix it when you stick my guts back in my torso.'

'Oh, right. Here, let me help you with that.'

In a just and merciful universe, the reversal of our injuries would have happened with the snap of taloned fingers. Unfortunately, this universe is a horror show that makes the cheap theatrics of the Lords Devilish pale by comparison, so we had to sit there in silent agony while their malefic, demoniac and diabolic servants performed a variety of mystical and all-too-mundane surgeries on us. The hardest fix? Getting the tail off Aradeus. That part, admittedly, was fun to watch.

When the healing was done and we'd all established just how vicious and vile we were prepared to be, I stood on unsteady feet before the assembled Lords Devilish and asked, 'Shall we get the negotiations started, or do you want to screw around some more?'

No one applauded this renewed declaration of defiance, but none of them were laughing, either, which meant they were finally ready to get down to the haggling.

'You seek information,' said Lord Gloom. His horns, a thicket of twisted bones, grew like vines from both his temples.

I hate it when people state the obvious as if it were some profound insight, so I countered with something less obvious. 'And the thirteen of you, no doubt, seek to screw with the Aurorals but are too chicken-shit to do it yourselves.'

'Very well,' said Lord Avarice, whose glowing orange eyes were barely visible beneath the six tiny downwards-curving horns above each of his brows. 'Let us begin wi—'

'No,' I said, cutting him off. I glanced at Galass, Corrigan, Shame, Alice, Aradeus and Temper, all of whom – well, except the kangaroo – were looking as shaky as I felt after our respective torments. 'First, you pay the fine.'

'The fine?' asked Lord Ire, tendrils of angry flame like lashes whipping out from the tips of his massive bull horns to sting my cheeks. 'What "fine" would a petty Mortal wonderist levy against us?'

'You've just put us through seven hells, so before we go making any deals, I want some information up front. Prove to me that you dumb bastards know anything useful and *then* we'll talk about making a trade for the rest.'

My demand was highly unusual – you might even have called my behaviour rude and unseemly. However, we'd showed them we could take a punch, so they knew we were not to be fucked with.

'Okay, Cadey boy,' said Lord Whimsy. His chuckle told me he'd been expecting my ultimatum all along, and meant to use the proof that they did have the actual intelligence we needed on the Spellslinger's mysterious employer to further tantalise us into doing whatever they wanted. 'We'll give you a little taste for free. Call it a gesture of good faith.'

Whimsy waved his claws as if he were summoning a waiter at a restaurant. The analogy turned out to be at least somewhat apt when part of the outer wall dissolved behind us and in walked the prick who'd sworn up and down to me that he hadn't known anything about the so-called Apocalypse Eight, even after we'd freed him from a secret Auroral prison and certain torture.

'You know something, Tenebris?' I asked. 'You're starting to make me question your integrity.'

The diabolic grinned. 'It's like I told you, old buddy. I'm a patriot. Gotta think of the bigger picture.' He sauntered up to us, bowed to his superiors. 'With your permission, my Lords?'

From atop their thrones, the thirteen Devilish nodded their assent, none of them apparently noticing the note of mockery in Tenebris' words.

The diabolic turned to me and stroking the curve of one horn, said, 'So, you want to know about the Spellslinger? You want the missing piece of the puzzle the Lords Celestine are either too clueless to have found out or just decided to keep from you? Well, gather round, kiddies. Fry yourself up some leeches and eyeballs, because Uncle Tenebris has a story to tell you. Oh, and the best part, Cade, old buddy? All this mess you're trying to prevent? Turns out it's all your fault.'

CHAPTER 21

Perspective

'The problem with you Mortals,' Tenebris began, 'other than the fact that you're dumb as cows and twice as graceless, of course, is that you lack perspective. It's not that your lives are any shorter than ours. The average demoniac – like the crazy chick over there playing dress-up as a Glorian Justiciar – they rarely make it past sixty or so. Even a diabolic like me packs it in before we hit a century. The Aurorals, now, they live for centuries, millennia, sometimes. And yet they're just as stupid as you are, Cade. You know why?'

There's really nothing quite like a Diabolic Contractualist who only hours before ripped whatever fraying threads of friendship there were between you launching into a lecture about . . . whatever the hells Tenebris intended lecturing me about. I kept my mouth shut, though, and motioned for the others to stay quiet as well. My former agent wanted to rub my face in something and the best way to get him to say more than he intended was to let him revel in his cleverness.

Which he surely fucking did.

'That's right,' Tenebris went on, taking my silence as acquiescence, 'Mortals and Aurorals? You both lack perspective. You're so obsessed with the supposed righteousness of your actions that you forget everyone else thinks they're righteous, too. It's all insult and injury with you people, feuds and vendettas and—

172

'Oh, you think we Infernals are just as bad?'

I swear I hadn't said a word, though I *may* have had a tell-tale look of nausea on my face.

'Well, that's just more proof of how clueless you are, pal,' he went on. 'We Infernals are always thinking about the big picture, and we do that better than anyone else because we got the one thing the rest of you don't.

'*Perspective.*

'For instance, capturing a refugee wonderist from another plane of reality and then sticking her in some prison to experiment on her without her consent? Short-sighted, pal. *Idiotic.* They could've offered her a deal, promised to send her back to her own realm with enough power to make herself Empress or Mage Sovereign or whatever the hell they call it where she's from. But no, instead they torture her, figuring once they've learned what they can from her crazy tattooed sigil magic, they'll just execute her. It's like these guys just wipe from their collective memories all the times someone's escaped from them in the past.

'Now, those Glorian Justiciars and Ardentors discovering said refugee is also pregnant and hiding that fact from the Lords Celestine and *still* experimenting, trying to use the unborn child's innate potential for wonderism to alter the mother's attunement to the Pandoral realm? I mean, seriously . . . we Infernals may hatch from eggs but even I could tell you how fucked-up that move was. Cruelty for cruelty's sake is one thing, but cruelty for stupid's sake? That's another thing entirely.'

And I could've told him that all cruelty is inherently idiotic and this included the hours the Lords Devilish had wasted torturing us. I had the feeling he already shared my assessment.

'So, yeah, like you've probably already guessed,' he continued, placing the back of one hand over the palm of the other as he mimed the rocking of an infant in his arms, 'when the baby's attunement took hold, your genius Gloran Justiciar pals figured they could channel all those crazy Pandoral energies through the mother – they also figured they'd be able to hand the Lords Celestine an unstoppable arsenal of chaos magic with which to win the impending war against my side. Too bad they accidentally collapsed the metaphysical foundations propping up the entire Pandoral realm in the process. Suddenly, it wasn't such a nice place for the three hundred or so sentient beings occupying it. This was a few years back, of course. The Pandorals managed to attune those seven morons up north – not your morons, you understand; I mean the Seven Brothers. Can't believe those bug-faced idiots actually thought they could get away with using the brothers as a gateway for them to take over the Mortal realm,' Tenebris continued, rolling his eyes in amusement, 'but hey, *perspective*, you know? They lack it, we got it. Anyhoo, I put together the scheme that not only locked the Pandorals – I call them "Pandas" – on the other side, but also refocused those gates so that my bosses and the Lords Celestine could finally come across and fulfil the promise of the Great Crusade.'

I glanced over at Shame, who rarely displayed anything resembling human emotion. Her expression hadn't changed all the while she was being stuffed into the Infernal machine grinding her flesh and bones to paste. Now, however, humiliation and misery were etching themselves across her features.

'Son of a bitch,' I swore quietly, remembering the smug air of righteousness on Fidick's perversely innocent face as he'd forced Shame to do his bidding so the Celestines and Devilish could invade our realm, leaving her emotionally and spiritually shattered. 'One of these days, I swear I'm going to put you in the ground,' I muttered, a promise to myself, and Shame.

'What's that, Cadey-boy?' Tenebris asked, then, mistaking my meaning, whispered, 'Yeah, I know, I think this whole "Great Crusade" thing is pretty dumb, too. But someone's got to put the smackdown on the Lords Celestine once and for all, so it might as well be my team.'

He glanced back at his bosses and again I noted he wasn't exactly in awe of them; in fact it seemed to me he was barely aware of their presence. 'As for this Spellslinger chick? Well, there's a reason the Glorians kept what they'd done to her a secret from their own bosses. Instead of delivering a walking Auroral arsenal of chaos magic, those dumb fucking Ardentors turned her into the most dangerous Mortal ever to walk this realm – or any other. That destiny hoodoo of hers? It doesn't have any limits that any of us can find. One person, an army, an avocado or an entire civilisation, she can bring forth one of their three so-called "dooms" at the drop of a hat.'

And that confirmed my worst suspicions about Eliva'ren. Most magic doesn't scale up that well. Corrigan can put more and more of himself into a Tempestoral spell, but there's only so much lightning or fire or mayhem he can pull from that realm without blowing himself up. Galass can exsanguinate the blood from an entire division of soldiers if she's willing to lose her mind and soul, but there's still a limit to her abilities. So a wonderist whose spells can encompass an entire realm? That's a catastrophe just waiting to happen.

'Oh, and she's seriously pissed off,' Tenebris added.

Yeah, no shit, 'old buddy'.

The diabolic shook his head at me like this was somehow all my fault. 'Since what you wonderists call an "attunement" is really just a pattern of potential breaches between the realm you're born in and another plane of reality whose physical laws work differently, when the Glorian Ardentors forcibly attuned the Spellslinger's unborn child to the Pandoral realm—'

I guess I must've lost my cool for a moment, because I felt an Infernal quieting spell oozing inside my mouth, cutting off my ability to speak.

'Yeah, you just keep swearing your head off, Cadey,' Tenebris said dismissively. 'Outrage fixes everything, am I right?'

He came over and threw an arm around my shoulder. 'But okay, if I'm being honest here – and you know what a sentimental soul I am – even I find it tragic that instead of popping out of the girl's womb – gross way to give birth, by the way; eggs are so much more civilised – the poor kid slips into a breach and is born trapped in a realm full of Pandas.'

He removed his arm and poked me in the chest. 'Especially tragic for you Mortals, because I'm pretty sure that nutty Spellslinger chick is going to destroy this place long before my bosses or the Lords Celestine do the job. Honestly, everyone would've been so much better off if the Lords Devilish had just let me recruit her to our side when she escaped the Glorians, but no, they just let her slip through their claws. You know what? She spent nine years trying to break through to the Pandoral realm and rescue her kid, but never even came close. Ironic, right? All that power of hers and it's only good for wrecking things.'

I could see he was working up to the big reveal.

'Which is why, a few months ago, someone did finally recruit her, promising they'd bring the kid over to the Mortal realm.

'So, who are these mysterious benefactors, you ask? Ah, I do love that look on your face, Cade: so eager, so angry – kind of like a puppy who can't figure out how come he's the runt of the litter. Well, it gets worse, Buttercup, because the guys who recruited the Spellslinger are the fucking Pandas themselves.

At my look, he clarified, 'Well, okay, to be more precise, it's the cult of morons who recently rose up around the only Panda existing on this plane of reality.'

Oh, fuck me – or rather, fuck all of us . . .

'That's right, Cade: the big bad who's manipulating those dumb fucks in the Lords Celestine and others' – I wasn't sure how subtle he thought he was being when referring to his own bosses – 'to make this war even worse than what you've been imagining so adorably since beginning your own crusade against it? Yep: it's the guy *you* allowed to escape!'

Shit, fuckety-fuck-fuck, prick, bastard, shit, I thought coherently. *That damned Pandoral—*

It had never even occurred to me that both the Lords Celestine and Devilish would have left the Pandoral being to wander the Mortal realm unimpeded while they completed their own invasion. I should have known better, of course; neither side would want to risk any of their own forces – and certainly not their own precious selves – attacking a powerful adversary, because that would have given the advantage straight to their enemies.

'The Pandoral?' Galass asked. 'Cade, we never even tried to pursue it!'

Everyone was staring at me like I was to blame for this mess, which was at least partially true. '*You will serve,*' had been pretty much its only words to us – wasn't that a big clue that leaving it to the damned Celestines and Devilish to sort out would come back to bite us in the arse? Why had I never tried to hunt down that damned bipedal bug swarm?

Because you convinced yourself the Infernals and Aurorals were the bigger threat, I reminded myself. *Because, when it comes down to it, your hatred of them blinds you to everything else.*

Tenebris looked delighted by the distress I was obviously failing to keep from my expression. 'Yep, you screwed the pooch on this one, pal. Since the Pandoral's home realm is collapsing and he doesn't have the forces to subjugate this one, his new plan is to use the Spellslinger to speed up the Mortal realm's eventual doom, so all that raw ecclesiasm released by imploding an entire plane of reality will be channelled through a gate back into the Pandoral realm, preventing its collapse while leaving this place' – he glanced around as if he could see through the cathedral's scarlet walls to the entire world beyond, where there wasn't much worth saving – 'well, let's just say, you probably should've finished the fucking job and killed the Pandoral before it wandered off and gathered a lunatic doomsday cult around itself.' Tenebris held up a hand as if to forestall the obvious counter-argument. 'Sure, sure, a sentience composed of thousands of indestructible buzzing insects might look tough, but maybe if you and your band of merry morons weren't such puss—'

An Infernal quieting spell is a kind of lesser binding that requires a smidgen less esoteric energy than one binding limbs. Tenebris, being a cheap bastard, hadn't bothered with that, of course, which was why I was able to deck the smug little prick right in his three-slitted nose. I don't usually recommend punching diabolics in the face, not least because their internal bone structure is thicker and stronger than ours, to support those idiotic horns.

Totally worth it.

'*Ow!* Damn it, Cade! I was just starting to like you again!' Tenebris complained, noisily popping the bones back into place.

My brief descent into discourteous violence wasn't entirely impulsive. Tenebris had confirmed that the Lords Devilish had information we needed. His feeble attempt to goad me was just a typical diabolic's ruse to get me to reveal anything I might know without them having to pay for it. Now that we'd been through the forms, it was time to get down to business.

In the case of Infernals, this means a pact. This particular pact turned out to be less egregious than most. You might even call it amicable.

The pact began with . . .

CHAPTER 22

Be Ye Damned for All Eternity

Ye who would violate this pact, who would foreswear oaths uttered, heard and agreed this day on this hour upon this soil. Despair, weep, wail and know that clemency, like mercy or a swift death, lies forever out of reach of any who break this bond. Abandon all hope, save that thou shouldest, by fate or fortune, fulfil every article and clause herein inscribed upon this parchment in blood, upon thy spirit with the ecclesiaster of thine soul, and upon the very fabric of the Mortal realm in the eternal ink of Destiny itself.

Be it known that this pact has been forged between the Thirteen Perfections atop the Great Hierarchy of the Infernal Realm, hereafter referred to as 'the Lords Devilish', rightful inheritors of all that is, was and shall ever be, and the six feeble wonderists accompanied by a filthy beast of unknown origin, possibly some sort of large deformed rabbit, the assemblage of which shall hereafter be referred to as 'the Malevolent Seven'.

Article I: The Gift

(i)   Greatest among weapons is knowledge, and deadliest of all are secrets. In requesting such secrets as are possessed by the Lords Devilish as of the moment of the signing of this pact, the Malevolent Seven acknowledge their ignorance and impotence.

(ii)   Generosity being one of the many virtues of which the Lords Devilish are the highest exemplars, their Infernal Majesties shall impart their secret knowledge of the mage calling herself the Spellslinger, who with ease and malice did defeat the entirety of the Malevolent Seven in a manner most amusing.

(iii)   No assurances are given that said knowledge will, in fact, ensure the demise of the Spellslinger or the prevention of the destruction of the Mortal Realm by the Pandoral being as this would require the Malevolent Seven to be far more effective in their endeavours than has been demonstrated thus far.

(iv)   This magnificent gift is granted freely and without any recompense of significance, save for one trifling act of gratitude, this being:

Article II: The Auroral Banner

(i)   Be it acknowledged that the Auroral realm is a stinking pit of decrepit mundanity, that all those birthed in its rank and pus-filled womb are naught but noxious fumes emitted by a flawed design in the universe, and that those who rise highest among them are, as such, the lowest of all.

(ii)   Be it further recognised and agreed that the entire Auroral Army is as a gnat beneath the hoof of the lowliest Infernal, no more a threat than those same noxious fumes referred to in Article II Clause (i).

(iii)   Thus no weapon, treasure or flag of said army holds any worth what-soever, and holds no value nor significance to the Infinite Might of the Infernal Armies.

(iv)   That being said, and though the physical bodies of the Thirteen Perfections do not, like those imperfect forms of Mortals and, in all likelihood, the so-called 'Lords Celestine', generate waste product, still, it would be of some amusement should the Lords Devilish, by order of precedence and each in turn, wipe their arses on the most sacred symbol of the Auroral Sovereign, that being the unsightly rag sometimes referred to as 'the Glorian Banner'.

(v)   Acknowledged by all signatories to this pact is the irrefutable fact that the obtaining of the tattered cloth mentioned in Clause (iv) would be a *matter of trivial effort for the Lords Devilish or their subjects, agents and contractors.*

(vi) *Thus, for the sole purpose of giving this pact the enforceability required of a purely symbolic pretence of 'an exchange of equal value', the Lords Devilish do hereby employ and require the Malevolent Seven to secure the filthy re-purposed undergarment referred to in Clause (iv) and render it unto them forthwith.*

Article III: The Method

(i) *The methods by which the Malevolent Seven take possession of the collection of arse hairs plucked from various beasts during the act of rutting and later woven into the item discussed in Clause (iv) are to involve deception, treachery and such cunning as is attainable for beings possessed of near-identical intellectual prowess as the animals from which said hairs were taken, namely, the Malevolent Seven.*

(ii) *The Lords Devilish shall cause no interference nor offer aid in this endeavour, trusting that the task be of such scant difficulty that a drunken cow, possibly one of the suppliers of hair mentioned in Article III Clause (i), could break an ankle stepping into a pothole and, in the process of falling to the ground, successfully complete the task.*

(iii) *Nonetheless, and for the avoidance of doubt, should the Malevolent Seven fail or be captured in this mission, which is agreed to be no more difficult or complex than passing out drunk in a puddle of their own urine, the Lords Devilish will, of course, deny any knowledge of the crime.*

Article IV: The Consequences of Failure

(i) *Should the Malevolent Seven fail in their quest to secure the Auroral Banner, or should they attempt to deceive the Thirteen Lords Devilish, the following punitive retaliations shall be deemed by both parties to be so minor as to constitute a veritable waiving of rightful remuneration.*

1. *Eternal Torment: Each member of the Malevolent Seven shall be bound in chains forged from the souls of the damned and cast into a newly*

built *Abyss of Despair where they shall endure unending agony, their flesh eternally flayed by demonic whips made from the skin of the phallus of the Tempestoral wonderist known as Corrigan Blight, said whips hereby acknowledged to be of only modest proportions due to the lack of material supplied.*

2. *Arcane Disattunement: All magical attunements and abilities possessed by the Malevolent Seven shall be stripped away, leaving them as mere Mortals, powerless and forsaken.*

3. *Public Humiliation: Their failure shall be proclaimed across all Infernal realms, their names forever etched in the Annals of Infamy, to be mocked and scorned by all who hear their tale. It is hereby acknowledged by both parties that the damage done to their reputation from the spreading of this tale is likely to be negligible given their already notorious history of failures.*

Article V: The Binding Clause

Bound, are ye,
Bound are we,
That all set forth,
In this Infernal pact,
Sworn South, East, West and North,
Shall ye and we enact.

Twice signed and sealed in blood and ecclesiaster, as the beast known as Temper didst foul the first parchment with excessive licking, by all present:

The Thirteen Lords Devilish:

1. Lord Whimsy
2. Lord Mischief
3. Lord Gluttony
4. Lord Ire
5. Lord Avarice

6.   Lord Indolence

7.   Lord Gloom

8.   Lord Covetousness

9.   Lord Carnality

10. Lord Guile

11. Lord Rancour

12. Lord Vanity

13. Lord Spite

And the Malevolent Seven:

1.   Cade Ombra, Mortal mage of unknown attunement

2.   Galass, Mortal mage of Sanguinal attunement

3.   Corrigan Blight, Mortal mage of Tempestoral attunement

4.   Aradeus Mozen, Mortal (handsome) mage of Totemic attunement (rat)

5.   Shame, Auroral Angelic, Emissary Cadre

6.   Aliciaj Meharcorum, Infernal Demoniac, Justiciar Cadre (self-proclaimed)

7.   Temper, Beast of Unknown Origin and Ill-Temperament

Codicil I: Corrigan Blight

(i)   Be it hereby agreed that upon successful completion of the mission, the anatomical proportions of a specific portion of the aforementioned thunderer's anatomy shall be increased from its previously restored dimensions to one 'commensurate with the legendary beauty of this most widely beloved instrument, not for the unduly withheld accolades of its wielder by certain disreputable wonderists, but to further add to the pleasure of those upon whom its majesty is bestowed.'

(ii) No aspect of this codicil to be discussed or revealed to the unworthy and ungrateful wonderists referred to in Clause (i)

Codicil II: Cade Ombra

(i) Be it hereby agreed that the Lords Devilish shall in no way reveal, discuss, insinuate or cause to be exposed the plane of reality to which the wonderist has become attuned.

(ii) The anatomical proportions of an unnamed Tempestoral mage shall, once all previous agreements regarding said organ have been fulfilled, be returned to its merely average dimensions and distinctly unimpressive appearance.

CHAPTER 23

The Parade

Yeah, we made a deal with the Lords Devilish to steal some piece of tat called the 'Glorian Banner' from the Aurorals in exchange for information on the Spellslinger and the secret cult of apocalyptic warmongers for whom she was working. The whole arrangement reeked of Infernal scheming. No doubt it was a set-up; the Lords Devilish were almost certainly intending us to bury ourselves even deeper in the Lords Celestines' bullshit ... or as I preferred to see it, everything was going according to my brilliant, cunning and ineffable – even to me – master plan.

'This is literally the worst plan ever conceived since the first spark of ecclesiasm brought sentience to the endless darkness of the universe and ruined everything for everybody!' Corrigan was bellowing as the seven of us walked through the bustling streets of a city only recently annexed by the Aurorals.

'Is the big brute trying to get us killed, Fallen One?' Alice hissed.

I have no idea why she always directs her anger at other people towards *me*.

'No,' I replied, 'but flapping those bat wings of yours while hissing at every Glorian recruit we pass might just do the trick.'

Aradeus, despite the crowds all around us, managed to make enough space to perform an elaborate bow. 'Fear not, Brother Cade. The legendary bravery and nobility of rats leads some to forget that they are also masters of espionage. As their totemist, I am gifted with potent spells well-suited to infiltration and camouflage. Take heart in the Musk of Subterfuge I have cast upon us.'

Galass sniffed the back of her own hand then wrinkled her nose. 'Forgive me, Master Mozen, but is that why we smell so—?'

'Inconspicuous?' the rat mage suggested, explaining that his cunning camouflage spell worked by conjuring a cloud of repellent yet narcotic scents which caused those nearby to ignore us. People could still see Alice, for example, with her obvious demoniac features, lineage scars and entirely stupid bat wings, but their olfactory senses would make them turn away, confused yet eager to be somewhere else.

Look, magic is not all sparkling rainbows or whizzy lightning bolts. When a wonderist uncovers an effective spell from the bizarre physical laws of another plane of reality, they don't look the proverbial gift horse in the mouth by wondering if maybe there's a less smelly version. Frankly, I think a little stink is a small price to pay for not arousing an angry mob hungry to immolate you because of your poor choice in companions.

Shame sniffed, then transfigured herself into her customary guise of a somewhat frumpy middle-aged person of indeterminate gender, this time without nostrils.

Even Temper, periodically muttering, 'Motherfucker', was trying to keep his snout covered with his paws. I really needed to talk to Corrigan about expanding the beast's vocabulary.

'Who cares what we smell like?' Corrigan asked, spreading his arms wide and inadvertently knocking over the unwary recruits walking on either side of him, adding, 'As long as Mozen's Reek of Wretchedness tricks people into ignoring us.' Both fellows picked themselves up, stared briefly at us, then locked eyes with each other, each convinced the other had been the culprit. Ignoring the parade as it passed them by, they launched into each other.

'Fists up, moron,' Corrigan chided the one who'd allowed his opponent to punch him in the face, but the advice, no matter how good, only distracted the poor fellow, who couldn't figure out where it had come from and as a result, got punched a second time.

Galass yanked Corrigan away to stop his running commentary on the fist-fight he'd caused.

Alice was peering down the boulevard, where two entire divisions of new human recruits to the Auroral army were marching to the newly erected citadel gleaming atop the hill a mile up the road.

I wedged myself between the two tradespersons in front of me to get a peek at the oncoming soldiers. Sure enough, at their front marched a Glorian Herald.

'He is . . . he's magnificent,' Galass said quietly.

'The term you're looking for is "awe-inspiring",' I corrected.

Glorian Herald is a rank similar to Glorian Justiciar, only instead of spending years undergoing the most gruelling physical, intellectual and spiritual training imaginable to then risk life and limb investigating, pursuing and prosecuting the deadliest criminal wonderists in the entire Mortal realm, a Herald just needs to carry a twelve-foot-tall silver pole with a swathe of cloth fluttering from the top without actually falling over.

Well . . . that *and* look awe-inspiring.

I looked at Alice, who was just standing there, staring at the Glorian Herald. There was no discernible expression on her face, which is to say she was scowling as usual. Yet there wasn't a shadow of a doubt in my mind that she was feeling the same ache I always felt when seeing Glorians – Justiciars, Parevals, Ardentors or, hells, even Heralds. No matter how easily one might dismiss these shining, golden figures, they represented a mixture of kinship and righteousness that would forever be denied Alice and me – me, because of my betrayal of the order, and her, because of, well, the whole being born diabolic thing. Unfortunately, I was the only one who'd accepted that fact.

'One day,' she murmured.

'Alice, it's never—' I cut myself off even before she shot me that glare that looked one part teenager-on-the-verge-of-tears and nine parts lunatic-on-the-edge-of-mass-murder – which was ironic because that pretty much described what I had seen in every Glorian Justiciar I'd ever encountered – especially myself.

'Motherfucker,' Temper muttered, gazing at me with those soft, round, gonna-drink-your-blood-one-night-when-you-least-expect-it kangaroo eyes.

I did have to admit that the kangaroo was getting remarkably good at making that word convey a whole host of different meanings.

I could feel the entire city practically swooning at the Herald's approach. Behind him, thousands of young recruits marched awkwardly in their new Glorian armour. The thing with spiritually transforming rags into magical golden plate is that being hard as steel yet light as silk makes it really hard to march properly; you keep expecting it to be heavier than it is, so you end up bouncing like you're drunkenly skipping down the street.

'Okay,' I said, leading the way to a nearby alley where we could get to work. 'Does everybody know their part, or do I need to explain it again?'

'I have a question,' Corrigan began innocently.

'Fuck you. I don't want to hear it.' I turned to the rest of my comrades. 'Any other questions? Good. Now, Shame, you're up first.'

Corrigan glowered at me. Temper tried to glower in solidarity with Corrigan, but ended up giggling to himself. Galass frowned but said nothing, Alice muttered like she always does and Shame closed her eyes, readying herself for something neither Corrigan or I were going to enjoy.

Aradeus . . . well, he, of course, was Aradeus.

'And so commences the Great Banner Heist!' he declared proudly, turned smartly on his heel and clapped his hands twice in anticipation.

How this guy has avoided getting himself killed by every right-thinking wonderist out there really is beyond me.

'*I've* got a question,' Galass said, locking eyes with me so I'd know she wouldn't brook any casual dismissal.

'Fine,' I conceded.

'I was born into the Order of Sublimes and for my whole life I have studied Auroral theology under learned priors and prioresses.'

'What's the question?'

She pointed towards the boulevard where the Herald was marching by, golden hair fluttering in the breeze in perfect harmony with the tall banner held aloft on his twelve-foot-high silver pole. 'What, precisely, is an Auroral Banner and why do the Lords Devilish want it so badly?'

CHAPTER 24

The Glorian Banner

Wars are fought by soldiers and paid for by citizens, but they're fuelled by faith. They don't end with the death of the last soldier on either side, nor does surrender come just before inevitable defeat. Ask the infantry in most armies the night before their generals sign an armistice (that's an agreement in which both sides pretend to agree to stop fighting because of their mutual love of peace but which is actually a polite way for the losing side to say, 'Please stop stabbing us to death') and they'll swear up and down they're on the verge of a decisive victory. Weeks or months after the defeated army have laid down their weapons in exchange for generations of humiliation and poverty, they'll eventually acknowledge it was more of a coin-flip sort of situation.

Faith is what keeps soldiers fighting long after any reasoned assessment of their circumstances would have told them to drop their spears and race for the hills – faith not only in themselves or in those ordering their suicidal advance upon enemy lines, but faith in the myth that victory goes to the righteous. This is embodied not in the theatrical omens and auguries of soothsayers, but in the symbols that define what we believe about ourselves.

Don't believe me? Buy a soldier a drink some time and they'll happily talk your ear off about the idiocy of their commanders, the obvious flaws in their battle plans and the general unworthiness of the rulers for whom they fight. You'd swear that same soldier is one free beer away from defecting to the other side. Now, try pissing on the flag under which that soldier fights and you'll quickly find yourself on the wrong end of a blade. You can insult the leadership, the war itself or even the cause as much as you want. Mess with the symbols, though . . .

'So you're saying this Glorian Banner is priceless?' Corrigan asked as we ducked deeper into the alley, his interest in the mission perking up. 'Golden thread? Some sort of magic silk?' A gleeful smile lit his bearded face. 'Right, then, here's the plan. First, we let Temper here' – he patted the kangaroo companionably on the shoulder before miming what was supposed to be a kangaroo leaping high into the air but looked rather more like . . . well, we'll leave that aside for now. The rest of the plan wasn't any better – 'bound right up to snatch the banner, then land on the other side of the parade. Meanwhile, I'll—'

'Don't be a fool,' Shame interrupted. 'That's not some trivial scrap of silk you can purloin. It's the first creation of the Celestines, woven from strands of their own divinity when the twelve of them broke from the Auroral Unity to devise the Auroral Hierarchy.' She looked at the boulevard where rows upon rows of recruits were passing us by. Her features became firmer and smoother as she spoke of the banner, losing the mundane humanity in which she took such satisfaction, returning to a more angelic lustre. 'The Glorian Banner is the symbol behind which humanity is meant to unite in service to the rule of the Lords Celestine.'

Corrigan frowned, scratching at his beard. 'Not sure what a big flag woven from strands of a bunch of superior arseholes' spirits is going to be worth on the open market.'

I smacked the back of his head. 'We're not selling it, remember?'

He smacked me back hard enough to send me stumbling backwards with hazy sparks clouding my vision. 'Oh, right; I forgot. We're trading it for information about some skinny strumpet who can kill us all – and probably the entire world – with barely a thought. Any idea what you intend us to do when we find her, Cade?'

'One problem at a time. How to stop the Spellslinger and her bosses is, at best, number three in our list of problems to solve.'

'I take it our first is acquiring the banner,' Galass asked, 'but what's our second problem?'

Cheers reverberated through the alley from the boulevard. Apparently, someone had said something righteous and everyone else had agreed.

'Our second problem,' I said once the hubbub died down, 'is that we can't actually steal the Glorian Banner.'

'How can we do otherwise?' asked Aradeus, twirling the long hairs of his moustache between his gloved fingers. 'We have signed a pact with the Lords Devilish. Does not the terms of that agreement, to say nothing of our own honour, demand we fulfil the bargain?'

See? *This* is why Mortals get screwed over by Infernals all the time. It's not because diabolics are so *diabolically* clever; it's because nobody ever reads the contract properly.

'The pact said we had to *secure* the banner and then *render* it unto the Lords Devilish,' I clarified. Everyone was still looking at me like that meant the same as 'steal it ourselves'. 'Specificity is the essence of all Infernal pacts,' I explained. 'There's never a single word that doesn't mean *exactly* what they want it to mean.'

'The Fallen One is correct,' Alice said. I couldn't tell if her customary sneer was for me or for her own species. 'There is never ambiguity in any contract with the Lords Devilish.'

'But those words *are* ambiguous,' Galass insisted, scarlet tresses beginning to weave in the air as if they, too, were offended by our illogical stance. '*Secure* and *render* could mean lots of things.'

'*Exactly*,' I said. 'Which brings us to the second quality of Infernal pacts, which is that they can't involve either betrayal or breach by the Lords Devilish or their agents.'

'Except that they're constantly screwing over humans,' Corrigan pointed out, to which Temper added, 'Motherfuckers,' which made Corrigan applaud the kangaroo for having added a second word to his vocabulary since, technically, and even I would have to agree, the plural of 'motherfucker' does qualify as a separate word.

'That's the *third* aspect of an Infernal pact,' I explained. 'They're always written in such a way as to permit the Lords Devilish to double-cross the other party *without* breaking the terms of the agreement.'

'Ah!' interjected Aradeus, suddenly pleased that someone else's honour was at risk of being impugned. 'The vagueness of the words *secure* and *render* mean that the path to our betrayal lies in interpreting them as stealing the Glorian Banner ourselves and attempting to likewise deliver it ourselves to the Lords Devilish!'

'Which is precisely the mistake they want us to make,' I said definitively.

Please let that be it, I prayed silently, although, as I was on the shit-list of most major religions, I was no longer sure to whom I should be praying.

'One thing I still don't understand,' Galass began, tamping down her wilful locks as if they were as distracting to her as to the rest of us, 'if the Glorian Banner is so precious to the Aurorals, why bring it to the Mortal plane at all? Wouldn't it be better kept somewhere safe in their own realm?'

This was the part that had been confounding me ever since the Lords Devilish demanded the banner in exchange for sharing what they knew about the Spellslinger and her employers. However perverse their sense of justice, the Lords Devilish never actually rip anyone off: the more valuable the item they require, the more precious that which they offer in turn. The Glorian Banner held tremendous symbolic worth, which meant whatever the Devilish knew about the Spellslinger was equally precious. The question about the risk of bringing the banner to the Mortal realm was in itself a valuable piece of military intelligence.

'The Lords Celestine wouldn't parade the Glorian Banner about unless they needed to,' I began, feeling my way through. 'It's a show of power, of unity. Which means there must be factions within the Auroral Hierarchy who aren't as convinced of the righteousness of their plans for the Great Crusade.'

'Do you surmise that our skirmishes to discourage recruitment by humans into their armies have begun to raise doubts with the Auroral forces themselves?' Aradeus asked.

It was a perfectly reasonable conjecture, and certainly an explanation that would have pleased me a lot, not to mention making me look like an effective leader of our little seven-person resistance movement. However, it's been my experience that when dealing with Aurorals and Infernals, I rarely come out of the experience feeling particularly happy, and I never end up looking clever.

You're terrified of the Pandoral, aren't you, oh great and wise divinities? And now you expect us to see him off for you so that you can proceed with your idiot crusade against one another on your own timetable. But since you're too proud to admit your fear, you're holding back the information I need about the Spellslinger in exchange for getting us to steal the Glorian Banner because somehow that's the key to hunting down the Pandoral and his doomsday cult. So, fine, we'll steal your stupid banner, but we're damn sure not laying hands on it ourselves.

'Well?' Corrigan asked, giving me a shove. 'Are you going to explain your brilliant plan to steal the banner *without* stealing it and then handing it over to the Lords Devilish without using our *actual* hands? Or are you just going to stand there looking like you're having what I assume must be a really boring conversation with yourself until the parade's over and the banner's locked up somewhere we can't get it?'

I smiled. I didn't have a flawless plan to make all that happen, but I *did* have a plan that Corrigan would hate.

I turned to Shame, now looking much like those angelics I'd seen when I was a Glorian – which was oddly apt, given what I now needed from her. 'Would you mind lending your unique talents to the improvement of the Mortal realm by metamorphosing something mean and ugly into something majestic and beautiful?'

'What is this "ugliness" that you wish me to transform?'

I pointed to Corrigan's face. 'That.'

CHAPTER 25

Step 1: The Disguise

There's an art to disguise: expensive hair dyes, exotic pastes and paints and a great deal of technical knowledge of faces, bodies and movement – all those subtle details our eyes usually gloss over, but which arouse suspicion if they're not *exactly* right. I imagine mastering those traditions is the vocation – nay, the *passion* – of a lifetime. Fortunately, I'm a wonderist and I don't give a crap about vocation when a good spell gets the job done quicker. Also, convincing a thunderer to shave off the atrocious indigo braids of his beard would be a nigh-impossible feat for *anyone* to achieve – well, except maybe an angel.

'Stop fidgeting,' Shame said, betraying rare irritation as she batted Corrigan's hand away from his now-smooth jaw. 'I'm not used to working this quickly without threads of desire to guide me.'

'Well, I sure as hell don't desire *this*,' Corrigan complained, trying to turn his chin away from the angelic's probing fingers. 'It's uncomfortable.'

'Odd,' Aradeus observed, watching utterly entranced as his two comrades were transmogrified. 'Brother Cade didn't experience any discomfort whilst Lady Shame was sculpting his features.' He shot me an approving wink. 'I must say, Brother Cade, you cut a more dashing figure than ever with those honeyed curls and golden skin.'

I've never been clear on why thick locks of golden hair with just the right amount of curl comes with the blessings granted the Lords

196

Celestine to their Glorian servants. That shade never went well with my natural complexion, even with the sun-kissed glow that's also a by-product of said blessings. Glorians were recruited to arouse the admiration of our fellow human beings and represent the perfection the Celestines want for all humanity. We were propaganda as much as holy warriors.

Aradeus peered closer at my face. 'I do believe your jaw is squarer than before and your nose no longer broken. Was the altering of your bone structure painful?'

'Not a bit,' I lied.

Of course it hurt like hell, but complaining would've lent credence to Corrigan's whingeing and dissipated my own amusement at his current tribulations.

'It's not so much a physical pain,' he said defensively. 'That, I could handle.' He winced as Shame's forefingers passed across his forehead and the bushy hairs of his eyebrows withdrew into his skin before subsequently emerging as far more elegant golden ones. 'I'm not entirely convinced there isn't something racist about all of this.'

'Your people come from the north, do they not?' asked Galass.

'So?'

'I didn't know black skin was common there.'

'Well, it— Okay, fine, it's not especially common.'

Galass leaned in closer, watching as Shame's palms painted a sheen of gold over the ebony of his features. 'I've never seen anyone with such a pure black skin. It's almost like . . . onyx.'

Corrigan shot her a grin, which looked somewhat unnerving coming from a man whose face was changing colour as he spoke. 'The captivating skin tone comes from my attunement to the Tempestoral realm. It's actually a kind of black glass that forms *under* the skin and protects me fro—'

'So, you're saying that you don't actually look like the people on whose behalf you're offended?'

The big thunderer had a point, although not the one he was trying to make. I'd always thought there was something insidious about the Aurorals believing that righteousness had a particular 'look'. I suppose if one is obsessed with the idea of the light of the sun as the perfect representation of spiritual purity, then gold hair and skin might seem apropos. In real life, however, it looks kind of creepy.

Corrigan harrumphed while Shame finished re-sculpting his face. The process is unnerving, but it's hard to find a more effective disguise than having an angelic literally change you into whoever you're pretending to be.

'Probably won't be able to change us back,' Corrigan muttered.

Now that *was* a troubling thought. In all her own physical trans-mogrifications, I'd never seen Shame reproduce the exact same look twice. Mostly, I'd chalked this up to her not being particularly interested in how she appeared to others now that she was free of the Celestines' compulsion to fulfil the image of beauty held in the minds of those she'd been sent to. But what if she wasn't all that good at returning those she'd transformed back to their original appearance?

'Why would either of you *want* to go back to looking as you did?' Alice asked with an amused sneer. 'Neither of you were much to look at before.'

'Laugh it up, demon girl,' Corrigan said, pushing Shame away now that she had finished. 'I've always wondered what would happen to those stupid bat-wings of yours once they were struck by lightning.'

'I'm afraid you won't be able to summon any Tempestoral magic,' Shame said, standing back to appraise her handiwork. She'd done an impressive job. Other than our clothes, Corrigan and I looked remarkably like actual Glorians, right down to that ridiculous gleam in our now-golden irises.

'What do you mean, I won't be able to wield Tempestoral spells?' he demanded.

Her fingers twitching in the air between them, Galass said, 'It's true. Usually I can feel wonderism as violations of the natural laws of this realm, but right now there's an impedance in your attunement.'

'Cade, what the fuck did you let the angelic do to me?'

'Something else has changed as well,' Alice said, leaning closer to sniff at Corrigan. 'You no longer stink.'

'That wasn't strictly necessary for the disguise,' Shame admitted.

Temper hopped closer, unceremoniously shoving both Alice and Shame aside before he, too, sniffed at Corrigan. The kangaroo let out a mournful keening, then pawed at Corrigan's face.

'There, now, fella,' he said, trying to soothe Temper by patting the beast's head. 'It's still me in here. Nothing to worr— Ow!' He yanked his hand away. It was now sporting a pair of bleeding fang marks. 'You stupid oversized mutt – I should roast you with a conflagration spell and eat you for supper!'

'Can't,' I reminded him. 'Until Shame reverses the transmogrification, you're basically just a regular human with no wonderist abilities other than a pleasing glow that's barely bright enough to read by in the dark. That, and your newfound lack of body odour.' Without waiting for any further objections, I turned to Aradeus. 'Your turn.'

The rat mage proceeded to whirl his hands around in an overly elaborate series of gestures I found hard to believe were entirely necessary for the spell. Nonetheless, when he was done, Corrigan and I were dressed in suitably impressive Glorian armour.

'Let's go, big man,' I said, hauling Corrigan out of the alley and onto the street where we could surreptitiously join the back of the parade marching through the city towards the new Auroral Citadel. 'Time to steal a most worthy holy artefact.'

Corrigan grabbed my elbow and whispered, 'You were just kidding about my body odour, right, Brother?'

I was not.

CHAPTER 26

Step 2: Sneaking

Conceiving, planning and initiating the theft of a priceless religious artefact from a holy fortress protected by supernaturally blessed guards isn't the sort of undertaking one rushes into. Unless, of course, there's a parade involved.

'Worst. Fucking. Plan. Ever,' Corrigan muttered as the two of us marched alongside our Glorian brethren through the streets of Radira.

'Stop complaining. You look good as a blond.'

Sneaking into line among the Glorians hadn't been especially difficult. We'd simply appeared at the very back, among some of the shabbier human recruits, and begun berating them for various invented violations of protocol.

'Speck of dust on the right pauldron,' I said to Corrigan as we shoved past one of the proud human soldiers who'd no doubt been imagining himself about to be immediately promoted into one of the Glorian orders and blessed with any number of wondrous abilities.

'Two demerits?' Corrigan asked in an officious tone. Given his own rebellious inclinations, he's remarkably good at putting on military airs.

'Three,' I said, pointing to the recruit's open-mouthed confusion. 'Failure to maintain proper bearing.' I stuck my finger under the recruit's chin and raised it fractionally. 'Regulation angle of lower jawbone is ninety degrees from the line of the neck, recruit. As the Edicts teach us, "A true warrior of the Aurorals is neither arrogant nor submissive, but rather evokes determination and fortitude with every bone in their body".'

That's not an actual Auroral Edict, of course, but with seventeen hundred and seventy-seven of them, who's to remember?

'Scabbard clanging at the hip,' Corrigan said of another recruit as we made our way forward along the parade line. 'Are you trying to draw attention to yourself, recruit? Do you consider yourself so magnificent as to draw the eyes of our fellow Mortals away from the Sovereign and down to yourself?'

'Uh ... no, sir,' the recruit stammered, grabbing hold of his scabbard with his left hand. 'Must be a problem with the hanger straps on the belt—'

Corrigan stopped, turning to face the recruit and making those behind him stumble to a halt. 'The *hanger straps*?' he asked ominously. 'Poor equipment, is that the problem, soldier? The Lords Celestine failed to provide you with gear worthy of your stature?'

'N-no, sir! The fault's all mine!' The recruit scowled at his own hip as if discovering for the first time that it was somehow deformed.

'Four demerits,' Corrigan said, then turned away and the two of us resumed our advance through the ranks.

'Remember not to use the demerit thing on the *actual* Glorians,' I said to him.

'Why? You don't think I can come up with a suitably convincing flaw in one of your precious fellow Glorians?'

'There's no such thing as demerits among the higher orders.'

'How do you maintain discipline, then?'

I thought back to my early years among the Justiciars. 'When you get out of line, your comrades beat the shit out of you.'

We passed through the front ranks of the recruits. Ahead of us were a troop of Glorian Ardentors. 'What the fuck do we do when they challenge us?' Corrigan asked.

'Simple,' I replied with greater confidence than I felt. 'We tell them exactly who I am.'

CHAPTER 27

Step 3: Blustering

'You presume to take command of this parade?' asked the Glorian Ardentor looming over me. He was even bigger than Corrigan; however, size is of comparatively little importance among beings blessed with various lethal Auroral abilities. What matters is making an impression.

Even when I really was part of the great Auroral Song, I'd never been especially powerful. The blessings I'd received from the Lords Celestine certainly set me head and shoulders above common military men, but among my comrades, I'd always been on the weak side. They attributed this to my lack of genuine devotion, which, in retrospect, was probably spot-on. What I lacked in raw power, I made up for in what we might call the subtler Glorian arts.

A Justiciar can't just go around beating the hell out of every suspect, witness and victim who isn't sufficiently forthcoming. Nor can you apply too much esoteric pressure on their minds to get the answers out of them, as that tends to, well, burn out their brains. A proper Glorian Justiciar employs what we called the Seven Gazes: a set of glares and stares that can, without physical or mystical violence, make you actually piss your pants.

You want to know what each of the Seven Gazes is called and what it does? How about a detailed description of how it works, what the particular combination of facial expression, posture, distance, variations of vocal tone and silences apply to each one? Oh, and would you also like to know the gradations in each of the Gazes and how one learns to perform them? Well, tough shit. This isn't some poncey parlour game meant to pique idle curiosity. This is the story of how seven idiot wonderists tried to save the entire Mortal realm from eternal war. In other words, get your fucking priorities straight.

For now, I was dealing with a pair of Glorian Ardentors. These guys are kind of like Glorian Justiciars except instead of pursuing mystical fugitives and administering righteous sentences, they spend their time . . . Actually, I've never been quite sure what the hell the point is of Ardentors. It's something to do with teaching and conditioning flawed beings to become more perfect instruments of the Auroral Sovereign – who, I shouldn't have to remind you, doesn't exist.

'Well?' demanded the Ardentor. He didn't sneer at me, exactly, since that's an unseemly expression on an ostensibly perfect being. But the effect was similar. 'By what right does a fallen Justiciar seek to take control of my command?'

I hit him with the Gaze of Humility, which isn't as the name might suggest, an expression and posture in which I show how humble I am. It's more like the stare your grandmother gives you when she's caught you masturbating at her kitchen table while eating cookies. At least, that's the feeling I was instilling in the Ardentor.

'What is my name?' I asked him quietly.

Many of his fellows were passing us by on their way to the citadel.

'Y-you are the Fallen One. Cade Ombra.'

I asked him the same question. Same voice, same cadence.

The Ardentor tried to whack me with the Gaze of Vengeance. 'You are a betrayer of our order.'

'*Your* order?' I asked.

'You . . . you know what I mean.'

'I do,' I conceded, letting him experience just the tiniest hint of victory before pummelling him with the Gaze of Clarity. 'What is my rank?' I asked him.

'Y-you have no ran—' He stopped himself. When someone hits you with the Gaze of Clarity as hard as I was hitting this guy? You figure out pretty fast that everything you assumed was rock-solid about your reality might be in need of reconsideration. 'You are . . . Can you truly be the . . . ?'

I nodded without my eyes shifting from his even a fraction of an inch.

Here's the thing about rank: if you have to tell somebody you're a general or an Ascendant Prince, you've already weakened yourself. After all, anyone can put on the right clothes or insignia and *pretend* to have a high rank. That's why having to tell someone your rank inevitably makes them – at least a little bit – suspicious. Making *them* come up with your rank using nothing but the precision of the way you glare at them? That's art, motherfucker.

'The Paladin Justiciar,' the Ardentor breathed. His colleague actually gaped at me open-mouthed.

'Three demerits,' Corrigan said.

So not helpful.

I kept my eyes on the Ardentor and shifted now to the Gaze of Conciliation. This was the only one of the Seven Gazes not meant to cause someone to shit their pants, but instead to feel the warm glow not only of your approval, but of your trust in them.

'You understand now why I am here and what we must do next?' I asked him.

Want to know the difference between a thug taught to intimidate people and a Glorian Justiciar who turns such things into a fine art? Take a look at this Ardentor, who's literally concocting the entire plan all by himself using nothing but the look on my face as his guide.

'There is a hidden danger coming to the citadel,' he said, and with every word and approving look from me, he became more certain.

'The Lords Celestine sent you, the last living Glorian Justiciar – now the Paladin Justiciar himself – to eliminate the threat without these frail Mortals, whose faith is as fragile as a snowflake in summer, finding out and doubting the unyielding might of our cause.'

'And why have I come to you?' I asked, returning to the Gaze of Humility, almost as if I were mocking him, but adding flaws into my expression and tone. This had the effect of reversing the implication from one of doubt in his abilities to the exact opposite.

It should be impossible for anyone as straight-backed as a Glorian Ardentor to straighten even more, but this guy managed it. 'I am ... humbly honoured, Paladin Gallantry. I had not even known my efforts had been noticed by those above.'

I placed a finger to my lips. 'Nor have they been.'

'By the Auroral Song,' he whispered. His chin rose just above the regulation ninety-degree angle – that's a real thing, by the way. 'I will not fail you.'

'Then begin,' I said, and let the Ardentor muscle us past the other Glorians to the front, shying them away with his own Gazes as we left his comrades behind.

Corrigan sidled up next to me as we advanced to the front of the parade, the Auroral Citadel now only a few blocks ahead of us on the hill. 'So, instead of concocting our own plan for stealing the banner, we're letting this guy basically do it for us by trying to ensure it makes its way safely into our hands?'

I've never been arrogant by nature. The universe has been pretty good at reminding me of my flaws. But every once in a while ...

'Yep,' I replied.

'Wow,' Corrigan said, sounding genuinely impressed with me for once. 'You know, Cade, you're actually a much bigger arsehole than I ever suspected.'

CHAPTER 28

Step 4: Conspiracies

The Glorian Ardentor, whose name was Propriety – almost, though not quite, a stupid enough name to make me feel better about my own – turned out to be a very capable conspiracy theorist.

'For some time now, I've suspected there lurks a traitorous movement within our ranks,' he informed Corrigan and me as we walked beneath the gated arch of the massive walls surrounding the citadel and into a lush orchard whose assorted trees, heavy with fruit, defied the sandy soil and arid climate of the region. I thought of the marvels the Aurorals could bring to the lives of Mortals, if only they stuck to architecture and gardening rather than mass conversion, army recruitment and occasional torture.

'What have you gleaned about this conspiracy?' I asked in the way of one who clearly already knows the answer but is testing you to see if you're holding back.

'I . . .' Propriety's hesitation wasn't that he was unsure how much to tell me, but because he didn't actually know anything and was afraid to be caught out.

'Go on,' I told him, going so far as to give him an encouraging pat on the elbow.

He straightened his back even more, which really should've been impossible. 'I believe there is a small cadre within the ranks of the Glorians who seek the means to elevate themselves beyond their

Mortal stature. These traitors believe that should the Lords Celestine be killed in our war against the Infernals, they could ascend to the top of the Auroral Hierarchy!'

Now there's a troubling prospect, I thought. It had never occurred to me that anyone would dare betray the Celestines – mostly because no sane Glorian or even angelic would make the attempt. Nonetheless, I let Propriety think he was onto something by giving absolutely no sign of confirming his suspicions other than to ask, 'And what do you call the leader of this shadowy group of faithless Glorians?'

The trick with conspiracy theorists is never to ask them the obvious questions like *'What actual evidence do you have of a fifth column within the ranks?'* or *'What are the names of these alleged traitors?'* but instead jump ahead to the fun parts, which, for conspiracy theorists, is naming stuff.

'I call them . . . the Six Sinners,' Propriety replied with a kind of gleeful ominousness.

'Shit name,' Corrigan muttered.

'What?' asked Propriety.

'He said Shaitnahmai,' I said quickly.

'*Shaitnahmai*,' Propriety repeated in a whisper. His natural con-fusion – a suitable response when someone has just given you a completely made-up name – quickly shifted to accepting this as confirmation of his own hunches. 'Yes, that makes sense.'

'The secret name of a Lord Devilish,' I confirmed.

'Of course! Who else but one of them cou—?'

'Posing as a Lord Celestine as he paves the way for the conspirators, thus setting in motion the toppling of the entire Auroral Hierarchy without the Infernals having to lift a finger.'

The Ardentor froze, staring at me wide-eyed. Other Glorians, both ordained and new recruits, filed passed us into the massive citadel. For a moment, I'd thought perhaps I'd gone too far, but once we were alone in the great hall, the hapless Ardentor said, 'It is . . . it is as I have suspected all along.'

The magnanimity of the deception was, I thought, working far more in my favour than I would have expected. I felt oddly ashamed of myself – not for lying to an Ardentor so that I could steal a relic from under his nose, but because his gullibility left me wondering how I could ever have admired the Glorians to the point of abandoning my family, just to be counted among their number. Are people really this stupid?

'Damn,' Corrigan murmured next to me. 'Glorians orchestrating a takeover and a Lord Devilish infiltrating the Lords Celestine – it's . . . it's incredible.'

I shot him a look that I hoped he would interpret as '*Hey, idiot, I made that up, remember?*' but which he somehow took as, '*I know, right? Who would've dreamed of such villainy?*'

Fortunately for all of us, Alice and Temper hadn't forgotten the plan.

'Magnus Ardentor!' shouted a lesser Glorian Warder, running to join us in the Great Hall. 'Someone is trying to steal the Auroral Banner!'

More shouting followed, with various Infernal ranks being ascribed to Alice that would have made her exceedingly proud if only she didn't despise her own people quite so much. The confused descriptions of Temper reached such bombastic levels of zoological impossibility that I could barely keep myself from snickering. Corrigan, of course – well, Corrigan has a certain perverse sense of loyalty.

'I believe what you meant to say, *recruit*, is that the demoniac is accompanied by a daring animal of such fearsome yet majestic visage as to make one almost admire the beast-breeders of the Infernal rearing pits.'

The recruit stared back in utter befuddlement. 'Um . . . I suppose?'

More soldiers came running, and soon we had a decent-sized

contingent of Auroral troops awaiting orders. Propriety turned to me, but I demurred. 'The forces of the Auroral Song await your instruction, maestro.'

To his credit, Propriety issued a series of reasonably logical commands for pursuing the invaders. His speech on the Great Crusade being won not by the grand battles that will be recounted by history but by the small, determined actions of regular soldiers was admirably brief.

'Well spoken,' I complimented him at the end, and allowed him a second of pride before arching my left eyebrow *just* so . . .

'The demoniac and her Infernal beast aren't the true threat,' Propriety concluded quickly, waiting only briefly to see the increased furrowing of my brow before declaring, 'It's a diversion! The true thieves must already be inside the sacred vault—'

With that, the three of us dashed through the halls of an impenetrable citadel, every guard along the way ordered to let us through by their own commander, who was utterly convinced there was no one he could trust but himself . . . with a little advice from us, of course.

Look, I'm not proud of my talent for convincing people to so embrace their own paranoid delusions of grandeur that they end up doing the dirty work for me. I'm just saying . . . Ah, hells.

'I really am becoming a prick, aren't I?' I asked Corrigan as the Ardentor unsealed the seven massive locks protecting the vault.

He agreed, but was still uncertain on one point. 'How, exactly, are we going to convince him to let us take the damned thing?'

That was going to be my final trick, and if you think what's happened thus far speaks ill of humanity and faith, just wait.

CHAPTER 29

Step 5: Who's the Villain Here?

There's a lot to be learned about a nation, organisation or faith by looking around its treasure chamber. I mean, if a giant room is packed full of gold and gems, you know whoever owns it has the financial resources to do just about whatever they want. If said chamber is replete with works of art and relics, you know they've got so much damned money they're mostly using their vault for collecting curios. A vault that's entirely empty save for a single banner lovingly placed upon a block of the purest white marble, however?

'You suppose maybe the Lords Celestine are running low on cash?' Corrigan asked quietly.

Propriety was busily striding around the thirty-foot-square vault, peering into every corner, passing his hands along the walls in search of any aethereal tethers or spells that might be hiding the intruders he was convinced were there.

Corrigan's question was a reasonable one. Even immortal, god-like beings need the financial wherewithal to run a war. You can't just collapse entire human economies and hope to have any kind of weapons manufacturing – to say nothing of the recruiting efforts vital for your armies. Whatever differences the Lords Celestine and Lords Devilish might have about theology, they agreed on one thing: those doing the fighting and dying should really be human beings more than Aurorals or Infernals. The citadel was new, of course, but still, it should've been holding *some* quantity of precious metals.

'They're here,' Propriety said darkly. 'I can feel it. Why can't I find any trace of their presence?'

I said sagely, 'Perhaps if we combine our efforts?'

I proceeded to make elaborate gesticulations, humming softly with periodic outbursts which probably sounded more like hiccoughs than anything coherent. All the while, I shaped my expressions to suggest a growing sense of dread that I was attempting to hide from my Glorian comrades.

'You can't fool me,' Propriety said, coming to stand before me. 'You're trying to hide your growing dread. I can sense it.'

'I, too, am filled with dread,' Corrigan insisted. He hates being left out of things like this. If I didn't wrap this up soon, he'd end up going off on some improvised dramatic performance that would get us both killed.

Okay, I thought, *time to make Propriety a hero.*

'Perhaps I was wrong,' I conceded, shaking my head as if even saying so aloud contradicted some deeper instinct. I looked up into Propriety's soulful golden eyes with my golden soulful eyes. 'What if there is no secret threat?'

The answer to that question is: *Well, if there's no secret threat, then you're a total moron for having got so wound up in your little conspiracy theories and it turns out you're not remotely qualified for your job . . . or . . .*

'Nay,' said Propriety. You'll have noticed how the word 'no' always becomes 'nay' when a sense of pompous self-importance fills the speaker. 'Nay, brave Gallantry. That we two shou—'

'We *three*,' Corrigan corrected. He jabbed a thumb at his own chest. 'Also filled with dread, remember?'

Propriety smiled tolerantly. 'Indeed, Brother. That we three above all sense the unfolding villainy means it must be far worse than we had imagined.'

Here's the thing about conspiracy theorists: they don't really want you to agree with them; they want you to attempt to refute their claims in such a way that lets them appear both logical and brilliant.

'Nay!' I said myself, and strode over to the banner laying upon its marble altar. 'Look you here!' I demanded, gesticulating wildly over the banner. 'My revelation incantations show this to be the true banner!' I turned, swinging my arms wide, 'Here it lies, encased within the mighty walls of this fortress with only a pathetic attempt by some minor infernal and her yapping hound—'

'Noble beast,' Corrigan insisted.

There's such a thing as being too loyal to a fucking kangaroo you met only three weeks ago.

Nonetheless, I used the interruption as my excuse to walk back to Propriety and grab him by the gleaming shoulder pauldrons. 'If there is a conspiracy to steal the Auroral Banner and yet it lies here, in this vault inside this citadel, built and garrisoned by a Lord Celestine – a citadel whose construction even now confounds my ignorant mind, for it seemed an ill-considered project from the outset, yet who am I to question the wisdom of a Lord Celestine? – then, friend . . .' I laughed bitterly. 'What explanation remains other than that we three are mad?'

Removing one hand from Propriety's shoulder, I made a subtle gesture to Corrigan that it was his turn. He started approaching, clenching his fists in preparation for, I presumed, knocking out the Ardentor. I had to give him a more panicked gesture to remind him of the *actual* thing he was supposed to do now.

'Oh, right,' he muttered, then took in a deep breath and bellowed, 'By the Auroral Song!'

Propriety and I both turned to Corrigan in confusion.

'Don't you see?' he asked, then pointed maniacally at the banner upon the marble altar. 'What if the conspiracy has already worked? What if the conspirators *wanted* the banner in this vault, in this citadel precisely because . . .' He waited for Propriety to jump in, but the Ardentor still looked confused. 'Because . . .' Corrigan repeated.

Oh, hell, don't fail me now, Propriety.

'*Because* . . .' I breathed.

'Auroral Sovereign preserve us!' Propriety swore, his vehemence greatly reassuring me. Suddenly he looked positively terrified, glancing all around the empty vault as if we were surrounded by enemy forces, which was, I hoped, precisely what he did now believe. 'The very Lord Celestine who orchestrated the creation of this citadel *is* the secret Lord Devilish!' He clenched his fist so tight the knuckles turned white. 'The Celestine of Rationality is our traitor!'

'Seriously?' Corrigan asked, then elbowed me in the ribs. 'You have the worst taste in women, Brother.'

'What?' Propriety asked.

'He said, "The war's hastened this ill omen",' I tried.

'Indeed,' the Ardentor agreed heartily. He gazed around the vault as if the walls were oozing with evil worms. 'Far from being an Auroral sanctuary, this citadel is the Infernal stronghold!'

The nice thing about large square rooms with marble walls is that they're excellent for reverberations. You could almost hear the echoes of '*This citadel is the Infernal stronghold!*' repeating as the three of us stood there in silence. I swear, Propriety was so certain of his pronouncement that *I* was starting to wonder whether maybe, in fact, the creation of this alleged Auroral Citadel really had been an Infernal conspiracy all along.

'The perfect ruse,' Propriety said, walking in circles around the vault as if he were the Justiciar investigator, not I. 'To use Infernal forces to erect a citadel in the middle of Auroral territory, to have the Auroral Banner itself brought here, all with the unknowing complicity of a hundred Glorians!'

I made a show of his words filling me with patriotic urgency.

'By the Auroral Song, not while we three survive! We must get the banner to safety!'

Propriety darted to the altar, snatched it up and offered it to me. 'You must take it, Brother Gallantry! I will seek to delay the soldiers here as we cannot be sure who are faithful and who are Infernal imposters.'

The gold-fringed ivory cloth fairly gleamed in the dim light suffusing the vault, its majestic beauty suggesting a myriad supernatural powers conferred upon whosoever carried it in battle. Alas, it was just a pretty banner – a memento, if you will, of the day the twelve Lords Celestine took over the Auroral Hierarchy. The tremendous significance it held for both the Aurorals and the Infernals was entirely symbolic, a reminder that, in the eternal clash between theologies, vanity can be the most potent power of all.

'Nay, nay, Brother Propriety,' I said, refusing to take the banner. 'You know this citadel far better than we do.' I gestured to Corrigan. 'Brother . . . Impotency and I shall create a distraction so that *you* may remove the banner from this nest of vipers. Get thee from this unhallowed place into the city. Seek out the meekest of temples you can find, for surely that is where true faith is most powerful. If the Auroral Sovereign is not yet done with us, Brother Impotency and I will meet you there.' I held up a warning finger. 'But tarry not for us. If we do not arrive within the hour, flee the city and find you other trustworthy brethren.'

Propriety stared down at the banner in his hands. 'But how shall I know *whom* to trust?'

I took his other hand and placed it on my chest. 'The same way you knew to trust us, my brother, because your eyes, your hands, your *soul* is blessed with the insight to perceive the truth, no matter how unlikely or convoluted it might appear to lesser minds.'

He was so touched by my words that his glow got another glow on top of it. 'I will never forget you, Brother Gallantry, Brother Impotency.'

I couldn't quite summon a tear to my eye, but I made a show of determined resignation: a great guy who knows he's about to die but won't say it. I let it hang there a second before I shoved Propriety out the door of the vault. 'Fly, you fool!'

And with that, the Glorian Ardentor fled the citadel carrying with him the Auroral Banner to a little temple where he would, as promised, find a being he trusted instantly with this holiest of artefacts. After all, who wouldn't trust a diabolic restauranteur transmogrified to look like an Angelic Emissary after being kidnapped and threatened with exsanguination by a blood mage?

I hope Shame makes the metamorphosis hurt, Tenebris. Not sure I'll let her turn you back after, either.

'So how exactly do we get out of here alive?' Corrigan asked after our unwitting accomplice had skedaddled with the prize.

'Simple,' I replied, and stuck my head out of the vault to shout, 'The banner has been stolen! The Auroral Banner has been stolen! Assemble every Glorian, every soldier, every recruit – it *must* be found!'

And *that*, friends, is how you secure a priceless relic being kept in an impenetrable fortress and render it to your client without ever touching it. I mean, sure, it helps if the people guarding said treasure are thick-witted zealots and those paying you to obtain it are only slightly less brainless, but I think you'll find that there's always plenty of stupid to go around during wartime.

'Come on,' I said to Corrigan, pointing to the passageway that would soon be crowded with panicked soldiers. 'I could really use a decent meal.'

'Paella?' Corrigan asked hopefully, walking through the open door ahead of me.

I shook my head sadly. 'There are some miracles even I can't pull off, old friend.'

It was, as these things go, a nice moment, or it would have been had it happened that way. What actually transpired was that the moment Corrigan had stepped out of the vault, just as I was saying, 'There are some miracles even I can't pull off—' the door shut behind him, locking me inside. You see, when I suggested that war makes suckers of the unwary, I forgot to include myself among them.

CHAPTER 30

Reunions

She stood at the centre of the Glorian Vault, every inch the self–assured, almost roguish Spellslinger who'd beaten the pants off me and my friends only a week ago. And yet, something was off about her. The curls of her dark mahogany hair still gleamed with that same lustre; they still kissed the bronze skin of her high cheekbones. She wasn't quite my age; I knew that now. Perhaps twenty-four? Yet in those amber eyes I now recognised a lifetime of suffering whose tribulations began with . . . me.

'I'm sorry,' I said.

The smirk didn't change, not even a fraction. 'For what?'

I knew already that we were in dangerous territory. During our strange encounter in the Auroral Archives, when she was still the frightened young woman only recently unlawfully incarcerated by my fellow Justiciars, she'd mentioned that in the destiny she'd tried to bring forward in time, I always arrived too late to save the child. That was the key to all of this, I was sure of it: the event that had transformed Eliva'ren from terrified captive to the most dangerous wonderist I'd ever met. That also meant that if I mentioned the child too soon, I might trigger a deadly response. I'd already seen how casually she could kill, bringing forth what she called one of her victims' 'three dooms'.

So think of something else, idiot. Something that will keep her intrigued about you without awakening dangerous memories.

At first, I hadn't noticed the way the interior of the vault was changing. The alterations were subtle, like watching the world around you age ever so slowly. The gleaming walls were beginning to show stains of damp while hairline cracks were splitting the stone. Cobwebs appeared in the corners; faint odours of mould permeated the stale air. This newly erected Glorian fortress was meeting one of its dooms: abandonment and inexorable ruination. None of this was especially momentous as far as magic went, nor especially troubling. What did surprise me was that it appeared to be happening without the Spellslinger being aware of what she was doing.

Which explains why she chose this place to confront me.

'I'm sorry you had to come back here,' I said at last.

Again, her features remained unmoving, frozen in that flawless, enticing expression of mild amusement and absolute self-confidence. 'A guess?' she asked.

She's worried she gave something away. It's as important to her that she can out-think me as it is that she can out-fight me.

I began to pace around the vault, mesmerised as it slowly deteriorated before my eyes. 'The Lords Celestine don't do anything without a reason. Like the Lords Devilish, they have a particular obsession with symmetry and symbolism. This grand fortress, this testament not only to Auroral might but to its inherent righteousness, could have been built anywhere. But why waste a symbol merely elevating one's impending victories, when you can also wipe away the stain of one of your worst failures?' I reached out and brushed the now damp wall with my fingertips. 'You can't bring back the past, can you? You can't return this vault to whatever cavern or dungeon it was when the Lords Celestine had you imprisoned here to experiment on you. You can only bring the future to the present?'

'It doesn't work like that. I'm not manipulating time; not time as we know it, anyway.'

'Doom,' I said, using her word from when she'd killed the angelic Valiant. 'But what is a doom if it isn't just a depressing way of referring to future events?'

'Destiny is an ending, Cade. It's the culmination of a set of choices, ours and those of others.' She came closer, taking my hand in hers and intertwining our fingers. 'You can't take your hand away without affecting me in some way, and my reaction will affect you. It's not theoretical, it's . . .'

'Inevitable,' I finished for her – precisely as she intended, which is no doubt why she smiled approvingly. People always approve of me when I fall into their traps. 'That doesn't explain how you can make those results come to pass before any of those subsequent decisions have been made, never mind acted upon.'

She brought our hands closer to her face, smelling the back of mine with a disturbing familiarity, as if the scent were somehow comforting to her. Her voice deepened even as it quieted, lending intimacy to her words. 'Each decision we make adds momentum to the sequence of events leading to our respective destinies.' She looked up, blinking as our gazes met. 'This choice I made just now? It puts us on a path to a kiss neither of us will ever forget.' Even before I tried to pull away, she'd clenched tighter to my fingers, laughing. 'Oh, I know, that's not your way. Wouldn't be – how shall we say? – gallant?'

'I never was that,' I reminded her. 'Gallantry was just a name they gave me. It never suited me.'

She shook her head slowly. 'Ah, ah, ah. No lies between us, Cade. Whether or not you wanted to be gallant, once they gave you the name, you tried to live up to its meaning. That's what brought you to me when I needed you most.'

I didn't sense any alteration in the magic already at work around us slowly turning the Glorian vault to rubble, and yet, my vision filled with the memories of that cavern where my fellow Justiciars and I had found the frightened sixteen-year-old trapped in a realm far from her own. 'Except that I failed you. I didn't stand up to Fidelity. Had it been up to me, I would've executed you just to avoid her disdain.'

She let go of my hand and turned away. 'I never said you did me any good, Cade. Only that all the steps along the way that made you Gallantry, Glorian Justiciar of the Aurorals, brought you to me at the moment when I needed someone truly gallant.'

Given all the lousy things I've done in my life, it takes a lot for someone to make me feel like crap. 'Eliva, what am I going to find out when I meet up with Tenebris after the Glorian Banner has been handed off to him?'

'Don't call me Eliva,' she snapped, still facing away from me. 'You haven't the right.'

'Wrong.' I took a chance, striding up to her and turning her around to face me. 'You *gave* me the right, remember? When you pulled me back from the Auroral Archives into this place when it was still your prison.'

There were no tears in her eyes, no physical admissions of sentiment, yet I was almost sure I could feel the connection between us. 'Did I do that? Really?'

I nodded. 'You said you were trying to pull forward a better destiny and that I—'

'You were in all the good ones,' she admitted, speaking barely over a whisper. 'I remember that now.' I caught the flash of coloured lights from the tattooed bands around her forearms before they settled into a softer iridescence. 'The experiments they performed on me failed, all of them. The magic of my people is tied to the oases from which our spells are drawn.' A tightening around her eyes and mouth spoke of remembered agonies. 'They kept trying to force me to attune myself to other esoteric planes of reality, dozens of them, but I couldn't. Not until . . .'

'Not until those morons attuned you to the Pandoral realm and caused the slow collapse of that plane of reality, which then caused its rulers to seek to invade ours.'

She said nothing at first, keeping that near-perfect poker face that only gave something away because it was so inscrutable.

She's trying to decide whether to correct me, which means her attunement isn't to the Pandoral realm at all!

'You're so unlike the rest of them,' she said at last. 'The way you not only see through the lies, but into the truths that we all leave unspoken.'

'I was an investigator,' I reminded her.

She shook her head. 'No, it's not that.' She reached up with the palm of her hand and held it to my cheek. The sensation was softer than I expected – probably because that particular gesture usually precedes me being slapped in the face. 'I think you love the world, Cade Ombra. I think you love all of it, even the ugly parts. That's why you were such a skilled Justiciar. As much as you might rail against your fellow human beings, as much as you might denigrate yourself, you never shy away from seeing all of our contours, like a lover.' The corners of her mouth rose, but this smile was different from the others. 'Even when you look at me as though I'm some nemesis you're contemplating how best to kill, you make me feel so . . . beloved.'

'Is this the part where we kiss?' I asked. 'Because the Lords Celestine expect me to murder you, and I generally prefer to do these things in the right order.'

She laughed, a light, airy sound that brought with it the rumbling of stone collapsing beneath its own weight. The walls were coming down, and soon the roof would follow, leaving us both trapped beneath the rubble. 'See what I mean about our choices becoming heavier and heavier?' she asked. 'That's the magic that came from the torture your former Glorian comrades put me through. That's the next part of the secret the Lords Devilish will reveal to you in exchange for that silly piece of gold and ivory cloth you've so cleverly convinced one of the Celestines' own disciples to steal on your behalf.'

I glanced around us, watching the odd languor with which the vault was slowly coming apart, a sleepy, almost lazy kind of self-destruction. 'You transform the momentum of someone's decisions, the collapsing of all the possible outcomes of their actions, to warp reality to conform with that inevitability – that particular doom.' A thought occurred to me then. 'You said each of us has three dooms?'

She nodded. 'This is one of yours. You allow your guilt over past failures to lead you into the traps the Celestines, the Devilish and even my employers keep setting for you.' She stood up higher on her toes and whispered in my ear. 'This isn't even the worst of your three dooms, Cade. Are you sure you want to risk the other two?' I felt her lips brush my cheek before she added, 'Although, there is one in which you and I make love, so perhaps that will serve as some small consolation for what happens after?'

At the sound of a heavy crack, I looked up and saw the chunks of stone from the ceiling about to rain down on us. 'I don't believe in destiny,' I said, too late realising that those would've made rather ironic last words.

The rubble froze in mid-air, teetering there as if unsure which way was up and which way was down any more. Then, as slowly as they'd fallen, the chunks of ceiling floated upwards, sliding into place next to one another, the smaller shards of rock and dust filling the seams perfectly. Soon, whatever invisible force had kept us sealed inside disappeared, and Corrigan came thundering – literally – through the door.

'By every bolt of Tempestoral fury, I'm going to—' He stopped, seeing the Spellslinger. 'Oh, it's her. Of course. Come to kill us all, sweetheart?'

'Not yet,' she replied, still looking at me. 'But soon, Cade. We can only meet once more after this before my employers will demand I bring you to your final doom. You've got to give this ridiculous rebellion of yours up. No one can prevent the Great Crusade. No one can stop the doom that the Lords Celestine and Lords Devilish must bring upon each other and upon this entire realm.'

I shot her my best wry grin – the one that's meant to stop people from noticing how badly I'm shaking. 'Darling, if the war was truly inevitable, your bosses wouldn't be trying so hard to keep me from preventing it.'

I expected more threats, or some new display of power, or maybe just a disappointed sigh. Instead, she reached a hand behind my neck and pulled me into a kiss.

That kiss . . .

I didn't even try to push her away. Why would I? Even if I could've drawn a blade unnoticed and slipped it between her ribs, I . . . Well, no, I would've killed her for sure. Much as I'd convinced myself I was the last person who should take up the mantle of a hero, recent events had taught me that waiting for the good guys to get their shit together and get the job done was a recipe for utter fucking calamity. One thing about us irredeemable, morally compromised arseholes? We don't throw away an opportunity at a quick and easy victory for the taste of another's lips and, if I'm being honest, a pleasingly adept tongue. No, sir. I'm all business when it comes to saving the world.

But, since I didn't have a hidden blade . . . Seriously, that kiss was something else.

'See?' she told me when she finally let go, the heaviness in her breathing telling me I wasn't the only one who'd come close to forgetting the mission comes first. 'I told you, some things are inevita—'

'Hey, Cade, take a look at this fancy Auroral torch I found in the armoury next door,' Corrigan said, holding up a two-foot-long brass cylinder with a shorter, thicker gold cylinder at the top whose circumference was inscribed with blessings in the Celestine language. 'Can't figure out how to light it.' He pointed to the single pink opal embedded in the shaft. 'Do you suppose pressing this will do the trick?'

'Corrigan, that's not a torch, it's a—'

He grinned. 'Just kidding. I know what it's for.'

Aiming the centre of the larger cylinder at Eliva'ren, Corrigan jammed his thumb down on the opal, depressing it into the shaft. A brief grinding sound, almost as if teeth inside the shaft were crunching the gemstone into powder, was immediately followed by a blast of pinkish-gold light that struck the Spellslinger dead centre in the chest. Clothes, flesh and bone provided only the briefest resistance before the Auroral blast shot out her back, only to then curve on itself and strike again. More bolts erupted, cascading into a blinding storm of eldritch energies that would have consumed an entire island.

'It's not proper Tempestoral magic,' Corrigan decided, dropping the now spent Auroral weapon to clatter along the floor before the incandescent brass shaft could burn his hand. 'But it's not bad.'

The retribution lance Corrigan had casually used up was worth more than a dozen cannon, along with the crews, carts and horses needed to transport them and ready them for battle. Glorian Parevals competed for years to be given the privilege of being among the few entitled to wield a retribution lance in battle. The Spellslinger walked away from its Auroral fury without a scratch, her body having reformed faster than the spells could attack her.

She patted Corrigan on the shoulder as she passed him by. When she reached the doorway, she paused, turning to give me a look at once reproving and somehow sad. 'Can't you feel the weight of your actions yet, Cade? You're bringing your doom closer and closer with every bad decision. I'm not sure how long I can hold it at bay.'

'Who are you working for?' I asked, reasoning this was likely the only chance I'd get to ask before she disappeared again. 'If you're not working for the Pandoral, then wh—?'

'They are as Heaven to the Heavens, and Hell to all Hells. They are the end of all things from which all things once sprang. They are the doom that awaits you all . . . and they will wait patiently no longer.'

And then, she was gone, leaving Corrigan and me alone in the vault, and the sounds of shouts and pounding boot heels filling the passages outside.

'Shit poetry,' Corrigan observed.

'*The doom that awaits you all*,' I repeated silently to myself. *Not 'us all', just 'you all'. Which means whoever her bosses might be, her deal with them gets her away from this realm before it's too late.*

'Come on,' Corrigan urged me, hauling on my arm. 'We'll have to kill a few nice guys on our way out if we don't want to end up imprisoned in this fortress until the war's over – not that that isn't an appealing idea right about now.' I followed him out, and somewhere between the first and fifth brawl we found ourselves in during our escape, Corrigan asked, 'So, that kiss . . . how was it?'

I shrugged. 'I've had better.'

Not all lies are meant to deceive others. Sometimes the most important lies are the ones we tell ourselves.

CHAPTER 31

Payment

Corrigan and I rejoined Galass, Shame, Aradeus, Alice and Temper at an old crossroads temple some seven miles south of the Auroral citadel. My plan to abscond with the Glorian Banner without any of us actually laying our hands on it had for once gone off without a hitch. When I first walked inside the ruins of that temple, I thought I must have had something on my face – other than the transmogrified golden features, of course – because the looks of my friends were entirely unfamiliar to me. I believe the technical term for their expressions was 'confused admiration'.

'Don't get a big head,' Corrigan said, slapping me on the back of my skull yet again. 'We still have to figure out how to stop your girlfriend from dooming the entire Mortal realm and all the ecclesiasm keeping it together from being sucked through some portal to prop up the Pandoral realm.'

We'd come to this abandoned church, consecrated to some god no one could remember, to collect our payment from the chosen representative of the Lords Devilish. We were prepared for the fact that we'd probably have to torture him a bit first.

Despite their relative hardiness and affinity for intense sensations – and not just pain – there are any number of ways to torture a demon. I've performed many of them, mostly on Tenebris. In all our irritating interactions, however, it had never previously occurred to me that there is *one* method for tormenting a diabolic that is so devious, so cruel, so immoral as to make all other abuses little more than the gentle caresses of a butterfly's wings.

'You gotta change me back, Cade. You *gotta!*' whined Tenebris.

My former agent in Infernal spells was leaning over a large shard of glass from one of the arched windows, staring despondently at his own reflection whilst plucking at curls of golden hair and prodding his gilded cheekbones. Shame really had gone a bit overboard with the diabolic's transfiguration.

'What exactly did you say to her?' I asked.

'Me? *Nothing!* I showed up here for the hand-off and all of a sudden your dopey crew put the boot to me, bound me up and then ...' He was leaning so close to the glass the tip of his perfect nose was touching it, his breath beginning to fog it over. 'To do *this* to a guy? To a pal? Practically *a brother*?'

'How long has he been like this?' I asked Shame.

She gestured to the Glorian Banner lying in a heap among the dust and debris. 'The diabolic did pause briefly in his whingeing when the Glorian Ardentor came to bestow the banner upon him, then immediately fell back into some sort of repetitious quasi-poetic lament about the loneliness of being the only sane being in the universe.

'Then I recalled that it was he who set the child Fidick in my path.'

'I was just following orders!' Tenebris insisted. 'You know how it is, Cade. Business is bus—'

Shame interrupted him. 'I contemplated re-transfiguring his face to no longer require a mouth.' Her eyes flickered briefly to Aradeus. 'Then I was ... reminded that whatever pleasure such an act brought me would be at the cost of slowing down your subsequent questioning.'

'Thank you,' I said, but Shame only looked away. I turned my attention back to Tenebris, having noticed a flicker of something wistful in the diabolic's expression when she'd mentioned the Ardentor. 'Did something happen with Propriety?' I asked him. 'Did he suspect we were pulling a con?'

Tenebris tore himself away from his reflection to sneer, 'Nah, the moron bought it hook, line and sinker.' The sneer faded, leaving behind a kind of melancholic confusion. 'It's just . . . I mean, here he was, handing over one of his side's most sacred relics, and instead of having qualms about it, he was—'

'Are you coming to a point any time soon? I'm not really equipped for hand-holding Diabolic Contractualists through what's starting to sound like a severe emotional crisis.'

'You're an arsehole, you know that, Cade?' Tenebris held up a hand to forestall any further interruptions. 'Listen, I've met plenty of Aurorals in my time and they're always smug, self-righteous arseholes – kind of like you, actually. But this guy, it was like . . . like that whole secret conspiracy you'd invented made him feel . . . I don't know. *Special?* I swear, this guy was the happiest Auroral I've ever seen. *Happy*, Cade. Imagine that: a *happy* Auroral.'

I'd never heard Tenebris sound so philosophical about anyone, let alone an Auroral – it was as if his whole universe had been flipped upside down and sideways.

I turned to Shame. 'Any chance your transfiguration magic might've rattled his brains somehow?'

'I say leave him that way,' Corrigan commented from the narrow archway into the temple. 'Me, on the other hand, you need to change back *right away*.' He scratched at his smoothly shaven jaw. 'How you managed to make my skin itch *without* my beard is beyond me.'

'Best start on Corrigan first,' I suggested to Shame, 'otherwise he'll be competing with Tenebris to see who can whine longest and loudest.'

'Me, obviously,' they said in unison.

Temper, peering down from the gaping hole in the ceiling where the temple's stone-tiled roof had lost the battle with time and gravity, helpfully added, 'Motherfuckers.'

'Hah,' Corrigan chortled. 'Good one, buddy!'

'What did he say?' Tenebris asked, eyeing the kangaroo's grinning muzzle. 'Did that giant rabbit just insult me or something?'

'Oh, he burned you but good!' Corrigan informed him.

'Ignore them both,' I told the diabolic who, despite looking every bit a Glorian, managed both petulance and affront. 'Corrigan likes to pretend that he can understand Temper even though Temper doesn't speak our language – or any other language, as far as we can tell.'

'Really?' Tenebris asked, one golden eyebrow arching magnificently as he stared at Corrigan. 'Isn't that kind of immature for a guy his age? I mean, even for a thunderer?'

'Corrigan seeks to convince the rest of us that he has formed a deep bond with the otherworldly beast as a way to mask his insecurities over the diminishment of his relationship with Cade,' Shame explained. Her manifest disinterest in the subject only made her assessment more embarrassing for Corrigan and me.

'That's not—'

'It's true,' Galass said, coming to place a hand on my arm, a gesture which I'd noticed always preceded a troubling pronouncement. 'We can all see it, Cade. Ever since the seven of us began this mission to stop the war between the Infernals and the Aurorals, you've been distant, more a general trying to keep his troops in line than a proper friend.'

A headache was forming behind my eyes. I was about ready to compose my very own poetic lament to being the sole sane being in the universe. Most people assume semi-deranged, morally bankrupt mercenary mages don't suffer from stress – in truth, usually they see us grinning like psychopaths as we're hurling lethal incantations at them – but beneath our jovial exteriors, we are walking masses of anxieties and tension headaches. Oh, and apparently, we're *really* fucking sensitive when our feelings are hurt.

'Corrigan?' I asked quietly.

'Yeah?'

'Would you be so kind as to open up a rift to the Tempestoral realm and blast me out of existence? I'd hate to go on living thinking I'd in any way diminished the genuine affection between us.'

He grinned. 'I was saving that for later.'

Our brotherly bond restored, I turned back to Tenebris. 'Time to pay up. We "rendered unto you" the Glorian Banner, and in exchange, your bosses promised us information on how to stop the Spellslinger and the Pandoral from ruining the Mortal realm even faster than your arsehole bosses and the Celestines are intent on doing. So cough it up.'

'Hey!' the diabolic snapped at me, feigning outrage, 'you don't get to talk to me that way. I'm an important guy in the Infernal Hierarchy these days and I don't take shit from penny-ante wonderists who get an attack of conscience and decide to save the world all by themselves. The way this works is' – he jabbed a finger at Shame – 'you tell the bitch angelic to restore my beautiful countenance and then *maybe* I'll toss you a few scraps of intel regarding the skinny psycho girl you're all so hot for.'

With my left hand, I grabbed my former agent by the neck. Despite the impressive physique Shame had given him, he was still a snivelling, preening con artist at heart. 'Listen, you little—' With my free hand I snapped my fingers at Temper, who was watching from the hole in the roof.

'Motherfucker,' the kangaroo said gleefully.

And another relationship restored to its normal emotional balance.

'You're going to start coughing up the details on the Spellslinger's employer,' I continued, giving Tenebris' neck a squeeze, 'and for each piece of genuine intelligence that I actually believe, Shame will restore *one* part of your physiognomy.' I gave the diabolic a shake. 'Try to bullshit us even once and I'll have her transform you into a fucking Mortal.'

'You wouldn't!' Tenebris cried out. He really is a bigot when it comes to Mortals.

I yanked him closer so he could see my smile. 'The Lords Devilish and every other Infernal infesting this realm will think you're my slightly dumber-looking cousin.'

'Fine, fine,' he said, prising my fingers from his neck, then dusting himself off. 'I suppose we should start with the Spellslinger . . .'

'Who he kissed!' Corrigan announced, excitedly poking me with his still-golden finger. 'Seriously! First, he bedded the Celestine of Rationality and now he's putting moves on a gods-damned lunatic Pandoral mage who's planning to destroy the entire Mortal realm! *That's* whose judgement you prefer over mine for who should run this coven!'

'How long have you been holding this in?' I asked Corrigan quietly.

He shrugged. 'It's been building up a while, I guess. Maybe if you'd let me give the speech back in that town where your little friend's fellow demons were killing those Angelic Valiants—?'

'Would the two of you please focus on the matter at hand?' Galass asked. Her scarlet tresses were beginning to writhe and twist in the air again. We were all stressed, I suppose, but a blood mage having a panic attack invariably leads to the construction of a whole new graveyard.

'She's right,' I said, and turned back to Tenebris. 'I presume the Pandoral has promised Eliva'ren that once he's opened a gate between this realm and his own, he'll free her son and somehow get the two of them back to their own plane of existence before this one collapses completely?'

'Aw, see?' the diabolic asked, dripping with sarcasm. 'I don't know why people say you're so slow, Cade. You figured out that a crazy woman obsessed with losing her child is willing to sacrifice an entire world just to get her mewling little brat back into her loving arms. I mean, the batty chick's motives were positively inscrutable until you worked it all out. You're a real fucking geni—'

I'd like to believe that it was his crass indifference to a mother's suffering and the calamity it was going to cause all of humanity and every other species that lived on this plane of reality that led me to punch Tenebris in the face for the second time in a week. But the great scholars of philosophy and spirituality argue that ignorance of ourselves is the lock that bars the door to enlightenment and truth the key that turns only when we are willing to accept what it reveals.

So, yeah. I punched him because I was scared of what might soon befall my world, and because I was terrified it might well be my fault.

Also, I think I might have mommy issues.

Turns out, I wasn't alone in that.

CHAPTER 32

Mothers

I rubbed at my knuckles, trying to take the sting away; I hadn't considered that Shame might have made the bones in Tenebris' nose stronger than human. Then again, back when I'd served as a Glorian Justiciar, my nose had been pretty much unbreakable, so I suppose I should take some satisfaction in the crunching sound when my fist collided with the diabolic's proboscis.

'You can change him back now,' I told Shame.

'All the way?' she asked, which was unusual for her. She turned to Alice. 'A diabolic has no particular need for actual horns when living upon the Mortal plane, do they?'

Alice's shrug admirably conveyed her utter lack of concern either way. 'Such powers a diabolic can wield upon this realm will not be affected. However, horns are not mere physical appendages on the Infernal plane. Their growth and unique designs develop with our particular affinities and achievements. The loss of those horns would considerably diminish his status among other Infernals.'

'Hah!' Corrigan laughed. 'Give him little wiggly ones like pig-tails.'

My personal preference would have been for Tenebris to be stuck for the rest of his existence looking like a Glorian, only with significantly less bone density. Unfortunately, I'd made a deal with the Lords Devilish and even I wasn't reckless enough to go back on it now.

'Shame, turn Tenebris back the way he was.'

'Knew you wouldn't let me down, buddy.' Somehow, his smirk managed to spoil even the perfection of his Glorian features.

'Maybe make the horns a teensy bit smaller,' I suggested.

I went to examine a defaced frieze that had long ago lost whatever magnificence it had once conveyed. The carvings were so obscured that I couldn't even make out which god or goddess had once graced the curved stone wall. We used to have all sorts of gods in the Mortal realm, but those religions fell out of favour as our native folk magic evolved into a more sophisticated understanding of wonderism and we started encountering actual divine beings.

And may the Void take every one of those pompous, smug arseholes. Why should any of us worship gods who allow a baby to be stolen from its mother before she's even held it in her arms?

'It's a terrible thing, taking a child from her mother,' Galass said quietly, standing beside me. I had noticed she often did this when I was veering too close to introspection. She was watching my face, looking up at me with that empathy of hers that bordered on cunning, reminding me that one of the reasons blood mages become so dangerous when they lose their minds is that they are so damnably good at sensing the emotions of others.

I'd never understood why she insisted on wearing that silver sublime's gown of hers. Why cling to the very symbol of perverse servitude into which she'd been born? Anyone else would've set the garment on fire – Corrigan had offered to on numerous occasions, although his motives were somewhat suspect. But Galass had never tried to escape her past, or hide from the world who and what she was. Maybe that's why she was able to hold onto her sanity despite the sanguinalist magic coursing through her veins.

I used to be terrified that one day Galass would lose herself and it would fall to me to end her before she became the mass murderer she worked every day to prove wasn't the inevitable destiny of all blood mages. Suddenly, a different terror chilled me.

If my time comes, if I lose control of this damned magic I've kept hidden from my friends, I hope it's not you who has to put me down, kid.

'Cade?' she asked, detecting the change in me, though thankfully unable to actually read my thoughts.

I tried to form a reassuring smile, but some conjurations are beyond any of us. Fortunately, Corrigan came to my rescue.

'Let's not get all judgemental about removing children from the care of their mothers,' he declared. 'My own dear mamma tried to murder me in my crib.' Tempestoral sparks bloomed between the knuckles of his right hand. 'It's not like I meant to keep blowing holes in the roof every time I wanted to be fed.'

There was a darker and even sadder story to his childhood, I knew, that he'd never told me, though I'd caught a glimpse of it months ago when I'd had to cast a nightmare bloom to keep him from killing Galass. The spell had forced him to relive the death of his wife when their unborn baby's attunement to the Tempestoral plane had awakened too soon.

'My mother also tried to kill me,' Alice said, then looked away as if embarrassed that she might've been on the verge of sharing something personal with the rest of us. 'That was more recent, however.'

'Angelics have no parents,' Shame informed us, her fingertips passing across Tenebris' face as she finished re-sculpting his features and turned to restoring his skin to its original ivory colour and leathery texture. 'The social customs arising from such affiliations among Mortals always struck me as awkward. Are your progenitors meant to be your masters or your servants?'

'It's more complicated than that,' I replied, although given my own mother had quite happily abandoned me when I was still a boy, I didn't have much experience on which to base that assertion either.

'Well, I had a wonderful mother,' Aradeus chimed in enthusiastically. 'An absolute delight.' He was twirling his whiskers, but then paused. 'Ironically, she was a rat-catcher by profession.' His fiddling with his facial hair resumed in earnest. 'A wonderful woman, nonetheless!'

'How so?' Galass asked, adding, 'I was born in the abbey. I never knew my mother.'

'A pity,' Aradeus said, drawing his rapier to cut and thrust at an imaginary opponent, all performed with a great many graceful flourishes. 'Mine taught me to fence, to dance, and – most vital of all – how to comport myself in the company of a lady.'

I was desperately trying to come up with something rude to say about that, but Temper beat me to it. The kangaroo poked his head down through the hole in the ceiling and declared, 'Motherfuckers.'

'Okay, *that* was pretty funny,' I admitted to Corrigan. 'Maybe he really does have a sense of— What's wrong?'

I'd expected him to start roaring with laughter, but he was dead silent save for the sparks erupting with even greater force from his fists.

'Ah, I understand,' Shame said, finishing the last of the four horns before turning to point at Aradeus. 'The kangaroo chose to interpret the rat mage's statement regarding his mother training him on how to behave around women in a sexual context, thus insinuating that Aradeus practised his erotic skills on his own moth—'

'Shut the hells up!' Corrigan shouted, heading for the archway that led out of the temple. 'Are you all deaf or something? Temper wasn't saying "motherfuckers" as in, "I'd like a nice bowl of paella" or "I need to take a shit, can I use Cade's tent again?" or even "Aradeus had carnal relations with his mummy". He said *motherfuckers* as in "There are *motherfuckers* sneaking up on us!"'

Whatever doubts I'd had about Corrigan's special relationship with the kangaroo were banished when Galass' hair started doing its excellent imitation of dancing scarlet snakes. 'Corrigan's right. There are several beings approaching this temple. The flow of life within them is intermixed with the otherworldly qualities of wonderists.'

I spun on Tenebris, fully prepared to re-sculpt his face again without the benefit of Shame's transfiguration magic. 'If you've screwed us agai—'

The diabolic was admiring his reflection in the glass shard again. 'Relax, Cade. These are our guys.'

'We're *not* on the same side, arsehole,' I reminded him. 'There's no such thing as *our* guys. There's only *my* guys or *your* guys, and if *your* guys come any closer, there's going to be a lot fewer of them.'

My crew were already in position for a fight. Alice had her whip-sword drawn and a nasty demoniac curse on her lips; Corrigan was one wrong move or an accidental sneeze from blowing up half the countryside; Aradeus was kissing the blade of his rapier, which . . . Well, I had no idea what that was supposed to do, but let's assume it would be devastatingly effective in battle because the alternative was weirder than his story about his mother. Shame was in the midst of transforming herself into something that looked like a four-hundred-pound wrestler with three otter heads sprouting from her neck and shoulders. One day I'll have to ask her why angelics apparently think otters are the most frightening creatures on the Mortal plane. As for Temper, I wasn't sure what his preparations had involved, but the droplet of drool that fell through the hole in the ceiling to land on my cheek suggested he was anticipating a tasty meal.

'Seriously,' Tenebris said, retrieving the Glorian Banner before stepping past me to the open archway, 'you got your crew wound way too tight, Cade.'

Outside, eight figures had assembled. Though none were yet casting any spells, I knew every one of the bastards was a wonderist.

Aradeus, his keen eyes darting from one mage to the next,

enumerated our potential opponents. 'Two totemists. The slender beauty with the cat ears is a felinist; the hefty youth with the curved tusks implanted either side of his lower jaw is likely a borinist. The tall fellow with the mahogany bark skin is obviously a florinist, and that delightful blossom of womanliness with the bandolier of keys across her chest is surely a practitioner of portalist magic. Her long-haired companion with the poor sense of personal hygiene and those dozens of shackles dangling from his scrawny arms is clearly an incarcerationist. Equally obvious is the androgynous one who looks like a walking void and must therefore be a cosmist. This leaves only the unassuming chap whose attunement I can't yet discer—'

'Infernalist,' I told him. Those who follow my former vocation prefer to remain inconspicuous: it helps make sure your comrades are the ones who get shot first.

'Ah, quite right,' Aradeus agreed. 'That's seven, which leaves only the heavy-set *bon vivant* with the elaborate moustashios and forked beard commonly found among—'

'A fucking *luminist*?' Corrigan groaned. 'I *refuse* to fight one of those losers. It's *embarrassing*.' He shoved past Aradeus to peer outside. 'At least this guy's not wearing one of those ridiculous multi-coloured coats. In fact . . .' His eyes narrowed in suspicion, quickly becoming a glare which he aimed squarely at me. 'What. Are. Those. Guys. Wearing?'

All eight wonderists were dressed in tailored black leather calf-length coats over equally tailored and equally black leather trousers. To top them off were half-cloaks, fluttering majestically in the breeze.

'Those appear to be uniforms,' I conceded.

One of the totemists – the young borinist with the idiot tusks mounted into his lower jaw – gave a curt bow and in a reedy voice quite at odds with his presumably intentionally brutish appearance said, 'We find it useful to make an impression now and then.'

Corrigan's righteous wrath was a wonder to behold, although I would've preferred it had it not been directed at me. 'I *told* you we needed uniforms, Cade. I *fucking* told you. But no, you refused. "We'll look like a theatre troop," you said. "It's unprofessional." Well, now we're the ones who could pass for rejects from an under-funded carnival, while these pricks look like proper heroes!'

'You really think this is what we should be focusing on right now?'

Alice interrupted me. 'It is true.' She gestured with the tip of her whip-sword. 'The uniforms do look impressive.'

'I must side with Brother Cade here,' Aradeus said.

'*Thank* you. At least some—'

'Those leather trousers would be constraining in a duel,' the rat mage continued. 'I *do* like those cloaks, however. Perhaps we could add epaulettes?'

'Now you're talking, rat boy!' Corrigan bellowed.

This is the problem with wonderists: they're inherently emotionally unstable and utterly incapable of taking imminent death seriously. Well, except me, of course. I'm *exceptional* at taking death seriously. Despite how hard I'd been working to avoid using spells in front of the others that might give away my attunement, I prepared myself to conjure up a piece of catastrophic nastiness, just in case diplomacy didn't work. 'Those capes are a little too short to serve as shrouds,' I said to the eight wonderists. 'On the other hand, we'll be happy to chop your corpses up into little pieces to make everything fit.'

'Will you fucking relax?' Tenebris asked, his hands still probing each of his four horns to make sure Shame had put everything back exactly where it was supposed to be. 'I told you, these guys are working for us.'

'The Pandoral's doomsday cult is working for *you*?' I demanded, grabbing Tenebris by the collar of his newly restored brocaded coat. 'You told us *they* were the ones who'd captured you and turned you over to the Aurorals!'

He shrugged off my grip and handed the Glorian Banner to the felinist, who, unlike Aradeus, was the sort of totemist who went out of her way to look like her chosen symbol. 'That was part of the plan. We needed to make the Pandoral believe that these guys were part of his stupid doomsday cult – that way, he wouldn't suspect that either the Celestines or the Devilish were the ones who'd recruited eight of the toughest and most cunning wonderists in the entire Mortal realm' – he gave me a smarmy sideways glance – 'present company definitely included.'

'They don't look like much to me,' Corrigan muttered sulkily.

'Well, unlike *your* weak-arse crew,' Tenebris countered, 'my guys have not only fooled the Pandoral into elevating them to his inner circle, they've got a way to destroy that bug swarm piece of shit before he can channel the ecclesiasm of this world into his own fucked-up plane of reality.' Being an inveterate showman, the diabolic couldn't help but swing his arm out wide. 'In other words, boys and girls, the Mortal realm is about to be saved by—'

'Don't say it,' Corrigan warned. 'Don't you dare fucking say it.'

But he was too late, for Tenebris was declaring proudly, '—the Apocalypse Eight!'

CHAPTER 33

The Unfathomable Eight

There was something truly tragic about standing outside that temple listening to my rag-tag crew of misfits bickering about whether we should let the coven of far more disciplined, far more organised and – according to Corrigan, who was shouting loudest – better-dressed wonderists take on the mission to hunt down and destroy the last remaining Pandoral. Personally, I was entirely happy to let them deal with both the Pandoral and his cult of lunatic worshippers.

'What are they doing with the banner?' I asked Tenebris.

He chuckled in that way diabolics do when they're about to tell you how easily they played you for a fool. 'You thought we wanted that rag just to parade it in front of the Aurorals, didn't you, Cade?'

'Something like that.'

I find letting people convince themselves that they've got the upper hand is more productive than getting into a debate over who's cleverer. Also, the restaurant aside, it seemed to me that Tenebris had been having a rough time since his bosses brought him over to the Mortal realm. No point in ruining all the poor guy's fun, or not all at once, at least.

'The Glorian Banner itself never interested us at all,' my diabolical former agent went on, gesturing to the shrinking piece of gold and ivory fabric which the skeletal-looking incarcerationist was ritually cutting into strips. 'The fabric, though? I don't think the Lords

242

Celestine realised just how much potency they imbued into each of those gleaming threads.' He rubbed his thumb and forefinger together as if he were talking about money. 'There's more raw Auroral magic in there than any other relic they ever created.'

'So what?' I asked. 'Your goons are turning it into some sort of weapon?'

Again he graced me with that stupid 'smarter-than-thou' chuckle of his. 'Not a weapon, Cadey-boy. These guys figured out a way to transform the banner into something *way* more useful.'

The florinist – they're the ones who usually bring trees and plants to life – was now reshaping part of the banner into a cloth mask, the luminist – apparently not as useless as his vocation suggested – was imbuing tendrils of luxoral magic into the precious threads, while the incarcerationist was gleefully winding several of the strips into a pair of shackles of gold and silver, all of which was making it hard to decide which I instinctively detested more, luminists or incarcerationists.

'The mask . . .' I began, trying to imagine how intricate the spells would need to be to redirect the Auroral blessings in the threads in the way the luminist seemed to be doing. Although I was no longer attuned to the Auroral realm, I still retained a certain sensitivity to its magical effects. 'He's creating some kind of veil with optical properties, isn't he?'

Tenebris elbowed me painfully in the ribs. 'See? You're not nearly as dumb as you look.' He whispered the next part. 'And you're a freaking genius compared to your idiot crew. You want I should ask these other guys if they'll let you join their coven when this is all done?'

'You'd do that for me?'

Diabolics, despite their sarcastic nature, don't always recognise it in others. 'Sure! I mean, you'd have to pay me a finder's fee for getting you the gig, of course.'

'Isn't the finder's fee usually charged to the employer?'

'I'll charge them one, too, obviously. Anyway, yeah, Erghroth over there is using his florinist abilities to re-weave the threads of the banner into a mask that will help them track their quarry while Vestisius the Legendary—'

Yes, you heard that right. Luminists almost all give themselves names like *So-and-so the Legendary*.

'Vestisius is binding luxoral magic into the mask so that the wearer will be able to perceive otherwise invisible forces. And since sentient beings of the Pandoral realm entering this plane manifest as bipedal swarms of sentient beetles and are therefore kinda slippery, Direlock there – stupid name, even for an incarcerationist – is performing an esoteric transmutation on the strips of the banner to create a pair of handcuffs not even Bug-face can escape.'

'Or anyone else your incarcerationist chooses to put them on?' I suggested.

'Almost finished,' Direlock said.

'Our task is also complete,' said the florinist who, after a nod from the preposterously facially-haired luminist, handed the mask to the cosmist.

Tenebris rubbed his hands together. 'How long before you can track down the attuned?' he asked the cosmist.

She – I was assuming that from the curves of her otherwise nebulous physique that mostly looked like peering into an endless void lit by tiny sparkling stars – spoke with a voice so weary it reminded me that most cosmists die by their own hands before they hit thirty. There's something about being constantly aware of the vastness of space and how small and irrelevant life is compared to the void. 'It depends on how far away they are, and if there's more than one.'

'More than one?' I asked Tenebris. 'I thought you said these guys were after the Pandoral? Only one of them came through the gate inside the Seven Brothers before we destroyed them.'

'The Pandoral itself is far too dangerous to attack head-on,' the felinist informed me. The cat-eared woman kept staring at Temper, hopping around on the roof of the temple, looking like she badly wanted to hiss at him. 'It is that which the Pandoral *seeks* which we must find and imprison.'

I was starting to get a bad feeling about this, but I'd been getting bad feelings about everything lately.

That'll teach me never to ignore a bad feeling again.

'The Pandoral's intention is to create another gate between the Mortal plane and their own,' said the cosmist. I wished she'd let someone else give the explanations. Walking voids always sound disturbingly eerie when they talk. Maybe it's all those echoes. 'As with the Seven Brothers whom you faced months ago, the creation of a gate can only be accomplished using a Mortal wonderist tethered to this realm, yet attuned to theirs.'

Oh, okay. That explained the bad feeling. I should've remembered that the most common cause of constant low-level paranoia is over-exposure to being screwed by those pretending to be your allies.

'Tenebris?' I asked.

'Yeah, Cade?'

'You remember that Ardentor who delivered the Glorian Banner to you?'

'Sure. The guy with the stupid name. Promiscuity? Pornography?'

'*Propriety*,' I corrected him. 'You remember how you let slip that something about him troubled you?'

'I didn't let anything "slip",' Tenebris seethed. He never likes being caught out. 'I told you, it was how happy the moron was acting, what with his insane conspiracy theories.'

I was sweating now. 'Yeah. Only, now I'm thinking maybe what bothered you about him wasn't his mood but that maybe his whole theory about there being a secret conspiracy within the Aurorals to topple the Lords Celestine and how one of them was secretly working with the Infernals wasn't as crazy as I initially presumed it was.'

Tenebris smirked – that was the truth he couldn't hide – before saying, 'You getting paranoid in your old age, Cade?'

Shit.

When a Diabolic Contractualist accuses you of paranoia, that's when you know without a shadow of a doubt you've been well and truly conned into signing your own death warrant.

The cosmist was now wearing the mask made from the Glorian Banner. I could already see twin beams of light sweeping along the ground as she accustomed herself to the otherworldly sight it gave her.

'Corrigan?' I said quietly.

He broke off from whatever argument he was having with Alice about uniforms and how much better 'The Malevolent Seven' was as a team name than 'The Apocalypse Eight'.

'Yeah, Cade?'

'I need you to do something for me right now, and when I say *for me*, I mean, for the entire Mortal realm, and when I say *right now*, I mean, don't ask any questions and just do it, okay?'

He grinned. 'You mean because this is a job for the greatest hero of all time, which just happens to be me?'

'Exactly.'

Tempestoral lightning began swirling around his hands. He'd guessed what I needed him to do. 'Which one of these fucks do you want me to obliterate?'

'Me,' I replied. 'Corrigan, I need you to blast me out of existence *right fucking now.*'

'Whoa,' Tenebris said, putting up his hands, 'settle down, Cade. Whatever silly notions are going through that head of yours, I promise I can explain everyth—'

'Now!' I shouted at Corrigan. 'Blast me *right this fucking second!*'

To people like us, wonderist war mages who've seen more than our share of battles and bloodshed, there's an unspoken understanding that some day you're going to find yourselves in an unwinnable scenario in which death is preferable to the alternative. I'd always figured that Corrigan, whose spells are the very definition of destructive magic, would be the one person I could trust to obliterate me instantly when the time came.

Instead, he was staring at me, wide-eyed and helpless as a boy about to get into his first schoolyard fight and discovering he can't get his fists up. 'I'm ... Cade, I ... I can't—'

You might be wondering why I didn't explain to them that Tenebris had screwed us, that everything he'd told us until now had been absolutely true and yet had obscured what was really going on. But there wasn't time for explanations any more than I had time for recriminations over the secret I'd kept from them – the secret not even Tenebris had guessed, and which was about to bring all his plans to fruition far sooner than he'd expected. Right now, that missing piece in his knowledge was the only thing giving us this last chance to prevent his scheme from unfolding.

'Galass, bleed me to death – *right now* – do it!' I shouted, and when she too hesitated, I spun round to Alice. 'Whip-sword,' I implored, 'please – *now*. Slice me to pieces before it's too late! Fuck it, Temper, *rip my damned throat out!*'

Maybe this is the problem with friendships. Maybe this is why heroes always go it alone in the end. The six beings I was closer to than I'd ever imagined possible were about to let the Mortal realm fall because none of them could do what they must surely have sensed by now was vitally necessary.

'Never figured you for the type to lose his mind so young, Cade,' Tenebris said. 'Calm down – nobody's pulling a fast one on you.' He gestured to the cosmist wearing the mask made from the Auroral Banner. 'It's just like I said, we're trying to find the Mortal wonderist attuned to the . . . to—' The grin that came to his angular features was far more diabolical than I'd ever seen on his face before. 'Oh, man. This is *so* sweet!'

'It's me, you idiots!' I shouted at my friends. '*I'm* the fucking Pandoral wonderist they're looking for!' I turned to Corrigan. 'Do you get it yet, you big idiot? Blast me now – before it's too—'

At long last, he brought up his hands and finally, I could almost see the breaches manifesting between this world and the Tempestoral plane. If he'd cast the spell just a split-second sooner, I would have been dead, fried to a crisp, nothing but ashes and whatever failure and self-loathing turns into after you die. And the Mortal realm would have been safe. Well, safer.

Alas, Corrigan was too late.

The scrawny wonderist with the long greasy hair had already thrown the strips of Auroral Banner into the air so some perverse incarcerationist magic could wrap them around my wrists, binding me securely. His portalist companion had taken one of the keys from her bandolier and opened the ground beneath my feet. I had time to look down at a grassy expanse somewhere far from where my friends could ever get to me in time.

I fell, and along with me came the 'Apocalypse Eight' – I still think it's a fucking stupid name – who were indeed secretly working for Tenebris. Unfortunately, Tenebris was also working with the very enemy the Lords Devilish and Lords Celestine were too afraid to fight themselves.

That's how, in less time than it took to say, 'Well, Cade, guess you shouldn't have kept your attunement a secret from your best friends because maybe they'd've been prepared for this,' I found myself in a dank prison, surrounded by eight uniformed wonderists and a being whose entire body was made up of a swarm of gleaming insects. Tenebris had handed the Pandoral the last missing piece needed to create a gate between my world and his own, so all that was left now was to torture me until I was so broken and desperate, I'd be unable to resist my attunement being twisted to transform me into a living gate leading to a realm of pure chaos . . .

. . . but since torture's kind of a drag and we've already been through all that, let me tell you about how I brought a kangaroo from another plane of reality into this one and then accidentally turned him into a vampire.

CHAPTER 34

The Kangaroo

The most common cause of death among wonderists is not, as you might expect, violent confrontation with competing wonderists. It's not being burned at the stake by enraged mobs either, although that's not entirely uncommon. Cleverly orchestrated executions by military leaders, religious zealots and, of course, Glorian Justiciars are frequently responsible for the head of a would-be mage decorating the top of a pole, but even those account for only a fraction of the wonderist corpses out there.

No, the most pervasive cause of death for a wonderist is, quite simply, blowing themselves up. Well, it's not always an explosion; *im*plosions are actually more common. Sometimes it's burning up your own internal organs or causing one or both of your lungs to accidentally appear six feet outside your body. You'd be surprised how often that happens. Infernalists often drive themselves insane without even realising it. Cosmists cover their bodies in a thin layer of the void of space, and if they get the dimensions wrong by so much as a hair's breadth, they get swallowed up by that same void. Blind luminists are incredibly common, but they're still rather funny to watch because their magic makes them think they're still seeing the world exactly as they want it to be. Even totemists manage to kill themselves by accident, although don't ask me how. Maybe they become so convinced they're carnivorous beasts that they eat themselves to death?

Basically, every form of magic is, first and foremost, a death trap waiting to consume you two seconds after your particular attunement kicks in. If you're lucky and you happen to come from a long line of wonderists, you might have some training and – even better – someone to notice the early signs of an attunement. And not all attunements are equally lethal. Before someone attuned to the Auroral plane can manifest any actual abilities, they first have to devote years of their lives to training and prayer to the Lords Celestine, who then awaken those abilities as 'blessings'. That's what the Lords Celestine claim, anyway.

But yeah, all those legendary farm boys and milkmaids living in remote villages who suddenly discover they're incredibly powerful mages? It's a myth. Those poor fools pretty much always obliterate themselves the first time they feel that mystical itch awaken inside their minds.

The only chance any emerging wonderist has at survival is how quickly they can figure out which plane they're attuned to, and how smart they are about learning – either from books or other wonderists – how to focus and control the unnatural physical laws of the planes they're breaching when they activate their magic. It's these various focusing techniques that become what we commonly refer to as 'spells'.

Simple, right?

Or it *would* be simple if you weren't the type of idiot who, when given the one chance in a lifetime to access the Empyrean Physio-Thaumaturgical Device of Attunal Transmutation, decides not to attune himself to a cool, easily understood plane of reality like, say, the Fortunal realm, or even the Tempestoral, but instead has an attack of accidental heroism and attunes himself to the one plane of reality that might supply enough power to prevent an endless war from engulfing the Mortal realm.

That's why I'd attuned myself to the Pandoral realm: to give us an ace in the hole against the Lords Devilish and Lords Celestine.

Logical, right? Some might even say admirable.

What makes Pandoral magic so effective as a potential weapon against Devilish and Celestines alike is that neither they nor anyone else know how its magic operates, which makes it virtually impossible to counter. The problem was that I'd not only given myself an attunement which was, if you've been paying attention, both highly likely to lead to my own precipitous demise and for which there were neither books nor experts to guide me in how to use it safely.

Experimenting with booze is unwise. It's even riskier with drugs; with sex, almost always a good idea. Experimenting with a form of magic you don't understand is generally considered suicidal.

So I'd approached the problem scientifically. First, thanks to my experience with both Auroral and Infernal spells, to say nothing of my extensive studies of various forms of wonderism under the tutelage of Hazidan Rosh, I'd developed a sensitivity to magic, which basically meant that if I was, say, thinking a dirty thought or getting overly emotional and my attunement was threatening to open a breach to the Pandoral realm, I was able to cut it off quickly. My second step was to figure out what spells I *could* cast, which is where I got into trouble.

The only Pandoral wonderists I'd ever met were the Seven Brothers. I'd seen them use a form of telepathic communication, which I presumed worked only between other Pandoralists (or possibly only blood relatives, although I'll admit that was less likely). Also, I'd seen them warp reality in ways that were entirely destructive. Although I agreed it probably wasn't a good idea for me to attempt, I had taken the risk during my encounter with the Spellslinger outside Tenebris' restaurant and, other than having utterly failed to stop her, I was nonetheless proud of the unmaking spell I'd conjured. The third type of spell I'd seen the Seven Brothers use was the ability to reshape animals into semi-human servants.

Bet you're seeing where this is going, right?

A few weeks after we'd killed off the Seven Brothers and the Lords Celestine and Lords Devilish had begun their recruiting drive for armies of gullible Mortals to die in their pointless war against one another, it occurred to me that recruiting my own army of really cool-looking rhinoceros-headed spearmen and tiger-faced cavalry and salamander-tongued spies might give us an edge against both Aurorals and Infernals.

I'd escaped from the others for a couple of days and ridden out into the desert to try my hand at transforming a scorpion into one hell of an assassin. After finding a suitable subject, I began the careful process of awakening my connection to the Pandoral plane and feeling my way towards reshaping the scorpion into an effective and hopefully obedient servant. That's when it all went wrong.

The problem wasn't that I *failed to* make the scorpion subservient to my wishes. Once I'd felt my way through the attunement to the bizarre physical laws of the Pandoral realm, the thought patterns needed to produce the alteration became so clear as to be almost simple. The problem was *me*: I remembered Madrigal, the goat-headed servant of the Seven Brothers. In the brief time I'd known him, Madrigal had been polite, erudite, sometimes almost witty and, worst of all, entirely conscious of what had been done to him. The Seven Brothers had transformed him against his will into a being shaped to their needs, utterly uncaring of his own free will.

That's the thought that went through my head when I was supposed to be conjuring Knife-Butt, the perfect scorpion assassin. You wouldn't think it would be easy to empathise with a scorpion, but looking at little Knife-Butt squirming there in a circle in the sand, wiggling his lethal little tail like he was hoping this was all some kind of mistake and I was about to give him a nice treat . . .

I just couldn't do it. I kept remembering Madrigal.

Riding back to town, I realised how stupid my qualms were, given I was trying to avert a war that would last until the very last humans were slaughtered. So I climbed up into some nearby hills and found a large cavern filled with bats. Unlike scorpions, I figured bats had given me enough trouble in my life that one of them deserved to be my slave. Fangy the Aerial Assassin, I would call him, not worrying about whether I could make his wings big enough to let him fly with a human-sized body. Still, it would've been worth it just to make fun of Alice, who can't fly for shit on the Mortal plane with those too-small wings of hers.

So there I was, about to transform a bat, when that same hesitation came over me. Unfortunately, by then I'd opened too strong a breach into the Pandoral realm and now all those messed-up physical laws were about to leak through. I had to focus them into *something*, or else risk blowing myself up, which was when an ingenious and morally sound solution presented itself.

See, Pandoral magic isn't about physically reshaping living beings or warping rocks: it's chaos magic. It works by reversing the relationship between matter and sentience, causing the former to be reshaped according to the latter. If that sounds obtuse, well, I guess it kind of is, but simply put, Pandoral magic unravels and then reweaves the threads of reality. Usually, it works by trying to impose the caster's will on reality, but in my case, instead of forcibly transforming the bat into a warrior, I let my mystical awareness seek out a thread of an animal that *wanted* to become part of a bizarre war against Infernals and Aurorals: something that actively fancied going around kicking the shit out of demoniacs and angelics and generally making trouble.

Turns out, there wasn't a single living creature anywhere in the Mortal realm that, deep in its psyche, secretly wanted to be a malevolent shit-kicker like me and my friends. But notions of time and space don't apply to the physics of the Pandoral realm, so my incipient spell just went further and further, until it found a plane of reality that happened to have a nasty country that had bred an animal so mean-spirited and ill-tempered that its own psyche grabbed onto the offer of spreading chaos and bloodshed with tremendous enthusiasm. And as that beast was being pulled from its world into ours, being transformed to survive and thrive in this other realm, it also managed to twist my spell into granting it the means to be even deadlier here than in its own world . . .

. . . which is how I ended up summoning and transforming a weird-arse-looking rabbit-with-short-ears-and-a-thumpy-tail into a fucking vampire kangaroo.

First thing he did was to attempt to eat me.

'Whoa, boy,' I said, managing a Pandoral spatial chaos spell that caused the distance between his fangs and my face to keep changing. He snapped at empty air several times, then – thanks to the perversity of Pandoral chaos magic – accidentally bit *his own* muzzle.

The belligerent idiot then started punching at me with his paws, hopping around me in a circle trying to outflank me. Not being able to keep the warping spell going indefinitely, I got clipped with a lucky jab. Later, I'd come to learn that even a glancing blow would normally have taken my head off, but the beast was still disoriented from suddenly finding himself on an entirely different plane of reality. Also, since his translation had accidentally transformed him into a vampiric being and he was woefully short of other people's blood, he was severely weakened.

As a Glorian Justiciar, Hazidan Rosh had trained me not only in mystical forms of combat but also in fencing and pugilism. And since it turns out I'm also a belligerent idiot, I quickly lost my temper and ended up in a knock-down, drag-out punch-up with a kangaroo.

Keeping track of the passage of time while in combat is pretty much impossible, but it felt like we were at it for several hours, which means the fight probably lasted about five minutes. When it was done, the two of us were both flat on our backs, panting from exhaustion, neither of us able to see clearly out of our severely swollen black eyes. That's when the scavengers found us.

There are a lot of weird evil creatures in the world. Some occur naturally, like scorpions and rhinoceroses. Some are manifested through nefarious forms of magic like my own attempts. Others . . . Well, some monsters, you just don't know where the hell they came from. In this case, it was half a dozen weirdos who looked like men and women, only with distended limbs and bodies covered in a patchwork made of fur and scales. My best guess? Amateur totemists who'd never been given the training to focus their attunement to a single symbolic animal realm and had ended up driven mad by the incompatible characteristics they'd manifested within themselves.

'Truce?' I asked the kangaroo.

I wasn't sure how intelligent he was or whether he could understand me at all. Back then, he hadn't yet developed his comprehensive vocabulary of 'motherfucker', '*motherfucker*' and 'motherfuckers'. Nonetheless he offered up a grunt that I took for assent and the two of us got back on our feet and fought side by side against the grinning, drooling pack of scavengers.

Were they the most deadly foes I'd ever encountered? Probably not. But I wasn't in great shape for casting more spells and I wasn't keen to witness how the chaos of Pandoral magic would interact with already corrupted beings, so the kangaroo and I handled things the old-fashioned way. After the first few awkward moments of clumsiness, we fell into a rhythm: he'd distract our opponents by bounding over them, I'd grab one in a wrestling hold, using them as a shield against the others, letting go just in time for the kangaroo to rip out its throat. Our foes eventually grew wary – who says crazies can't learn? – which we used to our advantage, and pretty soon, they were all dead, the kangaroo had drunk enough blood to make him giddy as he hopped around farting with glee, and I had found the seventh member of our coven that Corrigan had been demanding because, as he'll happily explain to you in *exhaustive* detail, 'the Malevolent Six is a shit name.'

By my count, in the three months or so that Temper has been on this plane of reality, he's killed more than two hundred humans, angelics and demoniacs, not to mention every magical monstrosity with something akin to a neck he can bite. And the bastard's just getting started.

Care to guess why I've been reluctant to try that spell again?

This is the problem with Pandoral spells, friends: not only is chaos unpredictable, it doesn't remotely obey what we think of as the normal limitations of magic. Corrigan can produce only so much aetheric lightning and fire. Aradeus can summon only so many rats. Even Galass can mess only so much with the flow of life and blood.

But chaos magic? It doesn't operate at that level: it alters the underlying *causes* that shape reality.

I guess that's why there aren't many mages attuned to that particular plane, which was why the Pandoral needed his little cult of psychos to find a disposable human wonderist attuned to his realm, so that he could violate every law of nature to create a gate between them that would surely end up collapsing our world so that his could thrive again.

And now, without further ado, let's get back to all that torture I lied about skipping over.

CHAPTER 35

The Sublime Art
of Resisting Torture

Look, if *you'd* been captured and tormented twice in one week – *one fucking week* – wouldn't you want people to know how bravely you'd withstood all those cruel acts of barbarity?

'Oh, please, no!' I screamed, crawling along the soiled stone floor, knees and palms slipping on my own urine and faecal matter. I persevered, however, determined to kiss the buzzing swarm of insects forming my beloved lord and master's feet. 'Please, I beg you, oh mightiest of the mighty, wisest of the wise, please don't hurt me anymore! I can't take it – not another minute, not another *second*!'

Actually, I could take a *little* bit more. Like, maybe six and a half minutes more. Seven at the outside.

Most military scholars agree that there are only three real strategies for enduring extended periods of torture without viable prospects of escape or rescue. The first involves physical conditioning. Getting your body accustomed to high degrees of pain limits the degree of stress imposed on the mind and therefore reduces the possibility of breaking under pressure. While I wouldn't say I was in any way immune to the sensations of my skin being burned by a florinist's acid spells or being choked repeatedly by an incarcerationist's bindings,

I reckoned I was as conditioned to torture as one could be while still possessing actual nerve endings.

The second method, a combination of duty to one's cause, loyalty to one's leaders and smug self-righteousness, allows you to endure for a certain length of time without breaking. I was understandably ill-equipped to employ this approach.

Finally, you can attempt to form a bond of sympathy with your tormentors. Keep eye contact with them while making your reaction as if seeing a trusted friend, or perceiving a genuinely loving soul beneath their hardened exteriors. Try to use their names, tell them about yourself, noting any detail which attracts their unintentional sympathy, then weave these disparate strands into a kind of relationship, heavily suggesting that you are both trapped in this unfair situation and perhaps between you there might be a way out of it.

Me? I've never been good at relationships, as evidenced by the fact that my best friends include a lunatic thunderer who threatens to kill me on a regular basis, a blood mage who thinks *I'm* emotionally unstable and a fucking vampire kangaroo. Oh, and the last woman I kissed is probably going to destroy the entire world.

Damn, though. It was one hell of a kiss.

But I'm not without my own tactical talents, which is why I developed what I hope will one day be termed the Cade Ombra Combination Insanity and Reverse-Torture Methodology. Memorise these techniques and you too can endure extended periods of captivity, suffering horribly but having a few laughs along the way. You might think my approach glib at first glance, but its foundations are strategically fucking brilliant.

As a prisoner, stripped of any supplies, garments, weapons and dignity, you still retain certain priceless resources within your control: a mind, a body and a voice. While the entire point of incarceration is to remove the utility of the prisoner's body, the mind and voice can be honed into potent weapons for defence and attack.

The mind is a remarkable tool. It can intuit what your captors want from you and then shape itself to deny them their ultimate goal, even while appearing to be shattering exactly as the enemy intends. Suffering and despair are the measurements by which your opponent determines how close you are to breaking, which is why it's a mistake to put on a brave face at the start and then gradually reveal your weakness. I say, start screaming for mercy as early as possible. It helps if you also sound kind of insane.

'There is nothing I won't do for my beloved master!' I insisted, still crawling towards the Pandoral being under the disgusted glares of his so-called 'Apocalypse Eight'.

When begging, it's important never to let up, otherwise your captor could say something suitably clever or cruel and then walk away, leaving you to the less-than-tender mercies of his lunatic cultist mages. The trick is to yammer *on and on* until listening to you is torturous for *them* too and the last thing they want is to hear more of your screaming. This is the second aspect of the Cade Ombra method: take all the fun out of the process in the hope that some measure of basic rationality comes into the equation.

Torture is fundamentally idiotic. It's the lazy person's persuasion. There's no piece of information worth torturing someone over that you couldn't get through some other means. Want to know the secret combination to a royal treasury? Bribe someone, for fuck's sake. You really think the guy whose job it is to unlock it now and then for the convenience of the monarch is so well paid he wouldn't rather sell the information to you and then skip off to some other country to be rich? Also, what do you think happens when you kidnap a royal treasurer and torture them for days? You think the palace won't figure out they haven't shown up for work in some time and change the combination locks or the spelled wards or even the key itself? Of course they will, which means the longer you're holding the captive, the less likely the information they're withholding will do you any good.

Ignore any claims to urgency or the greater good: those who conceive, command, enact or tolerate the abuse of captives are doing so because they like it. Torture arouses them. That's why your job, my unfortunate fellow captive, is to take all the fucking fun out of the process.

'I am filth!' I squealed with a madman's glee. 'My flesh is naught but the shit excreted from my arsehole upon this very floor!' I scooped a little up in my hands and rubbed it on my face, grinning maniacally. 'My blood is naught but the piss trickling from my pathetic, flaccid manhood!' I bent my head lower and pretended to lick the floor. 'My soul is the pus oozing from my wounds, my spirit the foetid breath stinking of bile as I vomit all that I am or ever was upon my wretchedness!'

Okay, fair warning: you may want to skip this next part if you're squeamish. These fuckers had been hitting me with every kind of incarcerationist spell, tormentor hex and Infernalist nightmare they could come up with, not to mention felinist claws digging under the fingernails and good old-fashioned beatings, all to soften me up so I'd be unable to resist being turned into a Pandoral gate that would destroy my entire world. So, fuck them and fuck anyone who thinks I went too far. They started this torture, after all, and I was going to make them suffer.

'Strip the skin from my bones, master,' I begged the Pandoral. 'Sting my eyes,' I pleaded, pointing at my face. I opened my mouth wide, mumbling incoherently, 'Fill my throat with your thick swarming insects.' I made a hideous gurgling sound before adding, 'I want to taste you upon my tongue, feel you sliding down my gullet. Let my intestines be the path by which we are united for ever.'

Bipedal swarms of insects aren't good for producing facial expressions, but I was convinced the Pandoral was starting to look both disgusted and queasy. Certainly his cabal of wonderists appeared to be on the verge of vomiting.

Should I go for the butt? I wondered absently. It was a bit over the top, even for me. *Ah, what the hell. Corrigan would appreciate it.*

'Sting me here, master!' I shouted with more ardour than any desperate suitor outside his lover's window, legs in the air as I pushed my finger between my arse cheeks. 'Please, master, I long to be stung here – sting me, master – *sting me hard!*'

'By the Void, someone shut him up!' complained the cosmist. She was still wearing the mask made from the Auroral Banner over her star-speckled black face; the tiny stars also covered the rest of her skin. Cosmists, being so untethered to the physicality of their own bodies, are especially vulnerable to depression. I figured a few more hours of this and she'd be suicidal.

Advocates of torture claim everyone breaks sooner or later. I was intent on proving them right.

'It's an act,' insisted the felinist.

She really is rather cute, I thought, with that distant amusement that goes along with slowly driving oneself insane. Those desiccated cat ears sticking up from her chestnut curls were just adorable.

'Yes,' I agreed, laughing like a halfwit as I rolled around naked in my own filth, 'it's all an act! Don't be fooled by me, master – make me suffer – only through pain can you force me to unleash my Pandoral abilities inwards and turn myself into the gate to your own realm!'

'It's not an act,' said the luminist, whose eyes were glowing a pure white, not because he was somehow peering into my psyche but because he was casting an illusion for himself so he wouldn't have to watch me writhing in shit and piss. 'His mind is fracturing.'

See? The first part of the Cade Ombra method was working: I really was on the edge of completely losing my mind.

'Yyoouu . . .' said the Pandoral to the Infernalist. 'Yyoouurr sppelllls aaarrr—'

Oh, fucking get on with it, I thought. *You've had six months on this Mortal*

plane to get accustomed to speaking our language and it still takes you half
an hour to ask directions to the toilet?

Surely the Pandoral couldn't hear my thoughts? Perhaps he was
self-aware enough to realise he was becoming a real drag on the
evening. He stopped attempting to talk, the thousands of insects
making up his body shivered, then swarmed closer together, enabling
him to sound a little more coherent.

'Yyourr spells touch the Mortal mind,' he said to the Infernalist.
'Does the prisoner feign madness or have you and your colleagues
truly pushed him to breaking point?'

The Infernalist turned to me, an irritated look flashing across
his features. As wonderists go, Infernalists are pretty grounded. I'm
not saying they're all salt-of-the-earth types, but when you make
your living trading fractions of your soul for spells so that you can
be paid to do nasty things to nasty people, you don't have a lot of
time for ego or posturing. He'd been screwing with my mind pretty
badly these past several days, but he'd handled the job with a certain
professional dispassion I admired more than the whole 'look how
evil we are' approach of the rest of his lame-arse crew. He'd already
infiltrated my thoughts pretty deeply, and every time he had to
awaken another one of the Infernal sigils etched into his chest, we
both knew he was wasting yet another spell he'd have to pay to
replace later. But he was a pro: he knew you couldn't reason with
an extra-dimensional tyrant any more than you could a wanna-be
warlord, so he got down to business.

He placed two fingers upon a black sigil just below his ribcage
on the left side, a frowning mouth overlaid on a smiling one,
looking a bit like two crescent moons placed one over the other.
As he murmured the incantation, the inky black sigils floated from
his body, drifting through the air to inscribe themselves over my
mouth. This particular spell was called a Tongue-Wrester and I had
to hide a smirk when I felt it insinuate itself inside me. This guy

was clearly sick of wasting expensive spells, so he was now pulling out the cheap stuff.

'Ask him what you will,' the Infernalist told the others. 'His darkest truths will be revealed.'

The florinist decided to nominate himself as interrogator, which was unpleasant. Florinists are kind of like cosmists, only instead of mystically covering their entire bodies with nether-space, florinists cover every part of themselves – including the lining of their throats – in a kind of flexible bark. It may be durable and resilient, but they all sound like bits of wood grinding against each other.

'Have you lost your mind, Cade Ombra?' he asked.

Ah, I do love an amateur. The Tongue-Wrester is kind of like a verity potion – if they weren't just narcotics meant to make you blurt out whatever was on your mind. This spell, however, draws not only truth from you but your *darkest, most embarrassing* truths. Luckily, I'd done plenty of stupid shit in my relatively short life and I was way past embarrassment. Also, the florinist hadn't asked if my mind was lost *now*, only if I'd *ever* lost it.

'I have,' I confessed, recalling those first few weeks after I'd left the Glorian Justiciars, got the shit kicked out of me by my former comrades and been cut off from the Auroral Song. It wasn't exactly a fun memory to relive, but that didn't mean I couldn't *try*. 'I am alone,' I wailed, my tears genuine for once, 'utterly alone, unloved, unheard – I am nothing but failure made flesh – the worthless remnants of—'

'We will have to cease his torments,' warned the cosmist. 'I cannot bear any more of his madness.'

'Great,' muttered the Infernalist. 'You made me waste yet another spell for nothing.'

'Let us delve deeper, then,' said the felinist, coming closer, head tilted to one side like a curious cat.

You getting sweet on me, kitty? I wondered, then recalled that I was naked and covered in smeared faeces and urine, so probably not.

'Tell us your darkest deeds,' she demanded. 'Reveal to us the secrets you keep from even those closest to you.' She turned to the others. 'Once his mind has settled, we can use these against him.'

You could, I conceded silently, *if any of you amateurs were remotely competent at this job.*

Darkest deeds? Entirely open to interpretation. Nonetheless, I rattled off some particularly nasty things I'd had to do in my career – none of which I'm going to reveal here, obviously.

The secrets I keep from those closest to me? *Oh, baby, now you're really making this fun.*

'I once paid an entire military encampment's complement of prostitutes to pretend they couldn't feel Corrigan's cock when he was fucking them,' I declared mournfully. 'Almost half my entire fee for the campaign I spent bribing each of the women to keep saying "is it in yet?" until by the end of the fighting season he was convinced that his penis was getting smaller by the day . . . Oh, woe is me!'

'What the hell does that matter?' demanded the cosmist.

I couldn't blame her; they really can't feel much of anything so she wouldn't know what appalling behaviour this was.

'You're being too vague,' the Infernalist informed his comrades. He was looking mildly amused by all this – as I said, oddly decent folks to hang around with.

'Fine,' said the florinist. 'Reveal to us your secrets about the Lords Devilish!'

'They're all pricks,' I confessed.

That was the only secret I knew about the Lords Devilish.

'The Lords Celestine, then!' the florinist shouted. 'Tell us everything you've hidden from them and your own coven!'

Better and better. I *did* in fact, have a secret about the Lords Celestine that I hadn't shared with my closest companions: something so embarrassing that I'd almost rather die than have Corrigan ever find out.

'I claimed the night I had sex with the Celestine of Rationality was mediocre,' I admitted. 'It was a lie. That night was fabulous – it was magical!'

'Ennnnouuugh,' buzzed the Pandoral, evidently as disgusted by the thought of Mortals and Celestines engaging in carnal activities as I would be by the thought of whatever his swarm did when they were feeling randy. Alas for his prudishness, once the Tongue-Wrester has been cast and the question asked, the victim can't be stopped from giving the answer.

'I came three times that night,' I confessed loudly. 'Three times – I'd never been able to have three orgasms with *anyone*, not even as a teenager!' That, too, was sadly true.

'Shut up, shut up, shut up!' shouted the florinist, pairing each command with another wooden-palmed slap that threatened to knock me unconscious – which would've been good for me and bad for them.

'He'll keep answering the question until you ask another,' said the Infernalist, visibly hiding a chuckle at the plight of his colleagues. 'He won't stop until the spell wears off or he's no longer capable of speech.'

'Somebody ask a different question, damn it,' the luminist shouted, but they were all getting confused and flustered now, so in desperation he said, 'Reveal for us your secret tactics, Cade Ombra!'

'I masturbate thinking about her,' I told him. 'It's the only way to get her out of my mind sometimes. You wouldn't think that Rationality was sexy, but damn it all, there are nights when I can't get her breasts out of my thoughts – I'm not usually a breast person, either. I mean, I like them plenty, but not obsessively, you know? I think perhaps it's because I still associate them with my mother, who insisted I keep breast-feeding even when I was five years old and—'

'Cease!' bellowed the Pandoral with the buzzing of thousands of insect wings.

The Infernalist, who could've stopped the spell any time he'd wanted, finally banished it. I was really starting to like this guy. 'Well, what now?' he asked after I stopped unburdening myself of all the secrets I'd kept from 'those closest to me'. What a stupid thing to ask. Most people tell their worst secrets to at least one friend. The stuff we don't admit is almost always the trivial, embarrassing stuff.

'We kill him,' said the borinist mage. I always find totemists a little weird, even Aradeus and I'm used to him, but this boar-tusked guy had interrogated me about Temper several times and I was not at all sure the underlying motivation wasn't sexual in nature. 'We kill him and find another candidate.'

The cosmist's laugh was deeply unpleasant. 'Another Mortal wonderist attuned to the Pandoral realm? Exactly how many of them do you think there are? The Seven Brothers were the first in generations. We could scour the entire world and not find another.'

'Then we resume the torments,' said the luminist, finally removing the illusion covering his own eyes and looking down at me with utter disgust.

Good luck with that, pal. You kidnapped me, beat me, burned me, tried to drag me to the edge of madness. Now you're going to have to find a way to back the hell off before I push myself over the cliff for you.

The luminist reached down and grabbed my jaw, squeezing tightly – but not too tightly, on account of luminists not exactly being paragons of physical fitness to begin with. 'I will cast such illusions as to drive him to terror and despair heretofore unknown to any—'

'That's how we drove him half nuts in the first place,' the Infernalist pointed out.

'Well, what then?' asked the felinist. 'You want us to give him a warm bath and soft sheets and read him bedtime stories?'

Kitty-cat, I would seriously consider betraying the entire Mortal realm and turning myself into a gate to the Pandoral plane if you'd join me for that bath and we could recreate my night with the Celestine of Rationality.

Yes, my innermost thoughts had become rather crass – although, in my defence, I *was* a little on the crazy side after several interminable days and nights of mystical torments. My sense of internal etiquette and common decency were not faring well.

My captors argued among themselves a bit longer while their Pandoral master got more and more agitated, judging by the way his swarm kept threatening to lose cohesion. In the end, they decided maybe discussing in front of me how best to get me to do what they wanted without driving me irretrievably insane was probably not the soundest strategic approach, so they left me there for the night. Somewhat to my surprise, the Pandoral ordered the guards to clean out my cell and bring me proper food and water. They even provided towels so I could attempt to wipe myself clean.

All in all, my fifth day of captivity had been a pretty good one, since I understood a lot more about how my captors were thinking. More importantly, it revealed two important facts about what was going on behind the scenes. The first was that Tenebris was clearly planning to betray these guys. Not only was the diabolic an expert in persuasion and subversion, but he also knew me better than almost anyone except Corrigan. Had he wanted to, he could have given the Pandoral and his Apocalypse Eight a step-by-step guide on how to elegantly and efficiently break my will. Second, the absence of the only other person who might be in a position to force my hand meant the real conspiracy went deeper than I'd ever suspected.

That night, as I kicked back in my cell, I allowed my somewhat crazed mind to settle – not coming all the way back from that dark tunnel of lunacy into which it had retreated, but close enough to enjoy the prospect of seeing Corrigan's face when they finally tracked my prison down, only to find me already escaped.

CHAPTER 36

Absent Enemies

Two full days passed without my captors renewing my torments or making any attempts to use intimidation or negotiation; instead, they fed me once or twice a day and if the guards didn't bother giving me a clean bucket in which to relieve myself, neither did they complain when I emptied it out by pushing as much as I could under the small gap between the bottom of my cell door and the floor. As for the food, it was edible, and more importantly, not, so far as I could tell, poisoned. Even the beatings were perfunctory, thanks mostly to the carefully calibrated amount of craziness I demonstrated to keep them worried about shattering my mind permanently.

All this might sound terribly banal – the tedious complaints of a prisoner whose current incarceration offers nothing more noteworthy than an interlude between more significant events – but nothing could be further from the truth.

A captive's primary aim is to escape, which is accomplished mainly through the acquisition of intelligence, and while two days of apparent monotony might *sound* like an empty piss-bucket in terms of exciting details, that's only true if you're looking at those events from the perspective of the captive, not the captors.

Keeping and torturing someone is expensive and risky. First, you need a place to hold them, and since I hadn't seen or heard anything suggesting the presence of other prisoners, that meant this whole place was being used just for me. Few people own their own dungeons, and the rent on these places isn't as cheap as you might hope: guards will need paying, feeding and housing, unless you want them nattering over a flagon or two at their local about their mysterious employers and the strange wonderist they're guarding in the secret cell no one knows about.

Maybe the expense isn't exactly bankrupting, but it's not cheap. The risks, however, are exorbitant. I'm not the popular guy you might have expected, and while my few friends *are* powerful, that's not in the political or religious sense, which is what you really need. My captors didn't know that, but they certainly did know that my friends included a big brute with a reputation for violence that made other thunderers look positively lamb-like, a former sublime with a habit of accidentally draining the blood of entire troops of soldiers, and a vampire kangaroo who did the same, but far more messily and entirely intentionally, if a little more slowly. And every day they were keeping me was one more day when an army marching behind some would-be Ascendant Prince might appear to tear this place apart.

So, two days of *nothing*? Cheap for me, expensive for the Pandoral and his little cult. My hours of endless boredom and foreboding were actually two days of freaking out for the captors, wondering what the hells they should do next.

I passed the time comfortably enough, assimilating a mental picture of what was going on outside my cell. I'd been kidnapped ostensibly to use my Pandoral attunement to turn myself into a gate, much as the ill-fated Seven Brothers had done some months ago, and I was pretty sure my little performance had them worried enough about my sanity not to force the issue further. All forms of wonderism do get a bit touchy when the mage isn't of sound mind or body, but it was reassuring to know that as the Pandoral was concerned about what might happen if a gate – in this case, *me* – went nuts, the state of my thoughts really could affect any portal created inside me. If all else failed, I would drive myself fully crazy.

The initial torture had been meant to scare me into cooperating voluntarily. No one would bother with an intervening second step, since threatening my loved ones really wouldn't have got anyone anywhere. But the logical next move should have been to negotiate for my complicity. Two days is a long time to hold a potentially dangerous captive without making a genuine effort to get what you want from them, so it was odd that no one had banged on my door offering me vast riches or untold power to comply.

All of this suggested the Pandoral and his stupidly named 'Apocalypse Eight' were getting seriously bad advice, so I had to ask myself: if Tenebris didn't actually want the Pandoral opening the gate here and now, what was the ultimate aim of the diabolic's scheme?

This, unfortunately, I still couldn't answer. My two guards, whom I called Lefty and Righty because they always sat in the same places outside my cell door, were professional enough not to talk to me, no matter how many of Corrigan's dirty jokes I regaled them with. I couldn't guess how long they meant to keep me here, since the activity that usually precedes the closing of an illegal prison – namely, executing the prisoners and burying the evidence – would involve only me, which meant I could either wait for the Pandoral's pathetic cultists to start torturing me again, or I could force the issue myself.

I've never been a patient person.

If hearing a prisoner's innermost thoughts during the dull interludes between being kidnapped and either released or killed is somewhat boring, allow me to say, fuck you for your callous disregard for the suffering of a fellow sentient being, and also, here's where we get to the good part.

There are five ways a prisoner can affect their captivity: attempted escape, attempted suicide, making oneself unsuitable for the aims of one's captors (also known as the Cade Ombra Method), negotiation and finally, outright capitulation.

I'd tested means of escape both mundane and mystical upon my arrival, of course, to relieve the boredom and anxiety of my imprisonment – nobody takes a wonderist captive without first making sure they can't get away. Also, incarcerationists are thorough by nature. Attempted suicide wasn't my style – well, not unless I could take with me the pricks who'd brought me to such a pass – and in any case, incarcerationists are also experts at weaving wards to make suicide impossible. I'd played the 'going nuts' card already and it had done its job. That meant negotiation was next, right?

See, that's what someone – not my idiot captors, but someone more knowledgeable about the *actual* conspiracy – would be expecting. If there had been any conceivable scenario in which I would have agreed to be the Pandoral's portal, he would have already offered me the deal.

And – and this is the important part – someone was missing from this whole episode, and that someone's absence was making me curious.

That's why my next move was—

'I capitulate!' I called through the filthy little gap at the bottom of the door. 'I will let my attunement be used to turn me into a gate!'

'What?' Lefty asked.

'It means, "I give up",' I clarified. People who take jobs guarding tortured prisoners are rarely the brightest pigs in the sty.

'Says he's giving up,' Lefty informed Righty.

'So what?' asked his equally dim colleague.

I hadn't expected I'd have to explain the intricate permutations of surrender and its value to their employer's cause, but I can be generous. When I'd finished, I suggested that perhaps now would be a good time to fetch their boss. Lefty complained that it was late and he wasn't all that keen on waking people up, but I countered by explaining carefully that my moods could be changeable, so maybe this was one of those times when inconveniencing the boss was the right thing to do.

Once he and Righty took off (not the most professional behaviour, to leave a prisoner unguarded, even if they are locked up, but apparently Lefty wasn't willing to bear the brunt of their employer's displeasure alone), I set about working to change my destiny.

Clearly *pretending* to capitulate wasn't going to get the job done, so I needed to *really* surrender, to give my body and spirit completely over to these fucksticks so they could turn me into their gate and do dreadful things to the realm of reality I'd sworn – for reasons increasingly passing understanding – to protect at all costs.

It wasn't easy, but then, I'm a complicated guy.

So I sat there in my dark, dank cell to convince myself that the world was doomed, the Aurorals and Infernals were worse than anything any Pandoral might have in mind for the Mortal realm, so it would be better for my fellow humans to hasten the end of our existence. When that failed, I spent time contemplating how much I absolutely despised the Lords Celestine and Lords Devilish, and how ruining their plans for humanity was worth any sacrifice.

Turns out, when you've been tortured and beaten and lied to as much as I'd been, you can convince yourself of almost anything, which is why it took only fifteen minutes to work myself into an iron-hard conviction that I was going to cooperate with the Pandoral. My will was firm, my destiny set – and whatever happened afterwards would be someone else's problem.

Which was when someone else showed up.

'Hey, sweetheart,' I said, spreading my filth-covered arms to the shadows where I had no good reason to believe and yet was utterly certain I'd find her. 'Couldn't resist one last kiss?'

I couldn't see her very clearly but I was fairly sure she wasn't smiling.

CHAPTER 37

Bleak Prospects

She sat upon a throne that hadn't been there seconds before. You'd think you might hear the sound of a damn great throne of silver and bronze with a polished oak and red velvet canopy and pale purple upholstery coming into existence, but this miraculous piece of unnatural spellcraft arrived as quietly as the whisper of a shadow.

Me? All I was good for was triggering unbridled havoc and conjuring vampire kangaroos. I was really going to have to up my magic game at some point.

'In sixty years, this fortress gets overrun by the army of a would-be prince,' said the Spellslinger, leaning against the plumply cushioned back of her throne. 'The prince has a skin condition that causes blisters when he's exposed to too much sunlight, so he puts his throne room down here in the cellar.'

'Has his destiny become inevitable?' I asked, feeling suddenly even shabbier than before. 'Or is there still time for someone to teach him that dark red velvet and pale purple are a criminal combination?'

She laughed, though more out of politeness. It occurred to me that perhaps her own people, the 'Jan'Tep', might have more formal notions of polite behaviour than were common in this realm. She stepped down from the throne, allowing its destiny to return to mere potentiality. It was oddly beautiful, watching the woods, metals and fabrics coming apart and drifting away, first fragments of their elemental compositions, then tiny sparks and finally nothing.

'About fifteen minutes ago, the guards went to inform the Pandoral that I'm going to submit my attunement to his control and let him turn me into a gate into their realm,' I informed her, then gestured to the ceiling. 'So you'd better reach into some other part of this dungeon's destiny where it becomes easier to escape before they get back.'

She shook her head. The tumble of dark curls caressed her cheeks and I found myself wanting to do that myself. I was still entranced by that kiss. 'I'll admit, it was a clever piece of work, convincing yourself to do the Pandoral's bidding.' She stepped closer. 'How did you know I'd sense the change in your doom?'

I consider myself more disciplined than most when it comes to the allure of physical attraction. As a wonderist-for-hire selling my spells and services to warlords and Ascendant Princes all over the continent, offers of sexual gratification were as common as stale beer. I'm not entirely sure why I always refused – possibly because I could never be confident those offering to spend the night with me had consented of their own free will. Corrigan figures my time in the Justiciars left me with a stick up my arse. Maybe both are true. However, stuck in that dark, dank cell stinking of every kind of filth, all I could smell was the scent of her hair and the faint sheen of sweat on her neck, and all I could see was the strange mixture of mischief and misery in her eyes.

'I was a Justiciar,' I reminded her. 'I studied under Hazidan Rosh, perhaps the most brilliant investigator of wonderism there ever was. She taught me to think not only in terms of extra-planar rules of magic, but about how those rules became part of the human beings wielding them. Every time we've met, it's when I've been on the verge of making a decision that would significantly alter my course – my doom, you called it.'

Was that admiration I saw in her gaze, or merely a new obstacle in the path of her own mission?

'You knew that my own doom had become entwined with yours, so by deciding to submit to the Pandoral's designs, you triggered my mystical sensitivities to the alteration in my own destiny.'

'And the future of your child,' I reminded her.

I'd tried to say those words softly, calmly, almost submissively. Judging by the sharp sting on my cheek, I hadn't been entirely successful.

'You've done a lot of stupid things in your life, Cade Ombra. I'd wager none of them are as suicidal as playing games with my son's life.'

'I play with whatever pieces are put in front of me, Eliva'ren. You set the board as much as anyone else, so don't expect me to play by a different set of rules than everyone else. Let me guess: Tenebris figured out a way to weaken the Pandoral at the precise instant when the gate to his realm opens, thereby stealing whatever esoteric energies remain there. No doubt he's worked out a way to get your son out and the two of you returned to your own plane of existence before the Pandoral realm collapses completely. Meanwhile, the diabolic and whoever he's working with has you cleaning up any messes along the way, right?'

Crossing her arms in front of her, she looked away. It was the first time I'd seen any sign of guilt or shame. 'Thanks to your fellow Glorians, my son was born into the Pandoral realm. For nine years I've been able to communicate with him only sporadically, when some tiny twist of fate worked out in our favour. The Pandorals would have killed him instantly, had they not determined that the unique manner of his birth had entwined his existence with that of their realm. So, instead, they created a . . . a kind of facsimile of me within their realm. My son's been nursed and raised by a shadow of me that isn't even real.'

'But the fractures continued and now the Pandoral realm is on the verge of collapse,' I said.

She was still not meeting my gaze. 'When I was giving birth to Hamun, the attunement the Glorians were trying to force upon me caught him instead. Somehow my body momentarily became a gate into the Pandoral realm, my baby was taken from me and I was left trapped here, in this horrible cesspool you arrogantly refer to as the "Mortal realm" as if this was the only one. I was sixteen years old, suddenly more powerful than any mage my own world had ever produced, and completely unable to save my own baby.'

It was a heartbreaking story, but it was also a gambit. 'You can't manipulate or cajole me into changing my decision,' I told her, again trying to take the sting out of my words and again failing. 'If they come back and I'm still here, I'm going to do exactly what they want. Normally, I'd assume that would give you the chance to rescue your son, but since you're trying so very hard to weaken my resolve, I'm guessing it doesn't work that way.'

Now she was the one who looked like she'd been slapped. 'The gate spell is like all Pandoral magic: it's a warping of reality itself. It's raw chaos unleashed in a controlled fashion, reshaping the laws of physics themselves. Actually, it's more than that, because the gate becomes a layer of translation between two different sets of physical laws, which will allow beings to pass through – in one direction only. The Pandoral wants to go home, bringing as much power from this realm with him as he can. That means if he's the one controlling the gate, my son can't come here.'

'Then I guess you'd better get me out of here, Eliva'ren.'

She shook her head again. 'I'm sorry, Cade, but my employers don't want you escaping this cell. They want your body and will broken utterly, and sooner or later, the Pandoral's impatience and desperation will lead it to torment your spirit all the way down to the ecclesiasm of your soul. That's when we'll take you: that's when you'll become what we need you to be.' She held up an arm: one of the bands of metallic sigils tattooed on her skin was gleaming with purplish light. 'Among my people, this is the band for silk magic. It's not entirely unlike the Infernal spells you once used to manipulate other people's minds. I can make you think or feel whatever I desire.'

'So, no escape plan, then?'

At last she met my gaze. Any guilt or hesitation I'd seen before was gone. 'I'm not here to free you, Cade. I need only break your determination to submit to the Pandoral. Then I'm going to leave you to be tortured for weeks on end until at last you'll be ready for us.'

I considered that a moment, then said, 'You know, for a minute there I was really starting to fall for you.'

She smiled. There was nothing now but sorrow in it. 'Don't worry, Cade. In a few moments, you'll be entirely in love with me.'

I sat down cross-legged on the floor and gestured for her to do likewise. 'Well then, Eliva'ren, let's get down to business and see which of us is the bigger arsehole.'

CHAPTER 38

Commitment Issues

There's nothing more boring than mages fighting a battle of the minds: no exciting bolts of Tempestoral lightning, no fiery implosions simultaneously burning the flesh whilst asphyxiating the lungs. There isn't even the screeching and scurrying of rats or cats or bats to entertain you. A mind war is basically like watching two people in a staring contest, trying to work out who's winning based on which opponent looks most constipated. For the record, I was not at all constipated.

'You're not putting up much of a fight,' the Spellslinger said – maybe silently, possibly out loud; it was hard to tell at the time – as she meticulously tugged at the threads of my thoughts and rewove them into new and troubling patterns.

'I've always considered it bad manners to interrupt an artist at work,' I replied.

I felt rather than saw her smile. 'You think that because I can't afford to have your mind fray completely I'll be tentative in altering your thoughts?'

That was, in fact, one of the things I was counting on. All my enemies agreed that *somebody* was going to use my attunement to Pandoral magics to turn me into a living gate to that unfortunate realm, and since a wonderist's mind is a fragile thing at the best of times, shattering mine would make me useless in that noble endeavour.

'Your people's magics are rather blunt and clumsy in comparison to those of the Jan'Tep,' she informed me with what I felt was undue condescension. Meanwhile, a dozen new inclinations, beliefs and memories were being sewn inside my consciousness. It was hard to tell exactly what was changing, other than I was fairly sure that before this began I hadn't considered roast chicken to be evil. Maybe she wasn't as good at this as she thought. 'To even spark the band for silk magic first requires the initiate to envision dozens of intricate esoteric geometries all at once. What I'm doing to you now is literally child's play.'

Bragging is generally considered unattractive on this plane of reality, I thought. Maybe I said it out loud. It was really hard to tell, what with my brains being scrambled.

Best I could tell, the Spellslinger had begun with my sense of pride, simultaneously magnifying its intensity – which felt rather pleasant – while retooling it away from things like my joy in undermining other people's expectations and channelling it all into my disdain for would-be tyrants. And given the Pandoral was the very definition of a would-be tyrant . . .

'There,' Eliva'ren said, sounding satisfied with her handiwork. 'By the time they come to take you from your cell, the prospect of bowing down before the Pandoral will be so intolerable you'll . . .' Our eyes were open, so I could see her leaning closer, almost as if she were trying to peer inside my skull. 'What the hells have you done to yourself?'

'Nothing at all.'

'You're lying.' She leaned back again and through whatever pathways her silk magic had opened between us, I caught a flash of hundreds of choices and inclinations collapsing into a final decision, which in turn led to a single doom. 'You're still going to do it. You're going to give yourself over to the Pandoral.'

'I probably should've warned you, sweetheart. I'm rather stubborn.'

'Not for long,' she said, and I felt intangible fingers tracing threads of my sense of self, tugging and twisting and tying them in knots. 'And don't call me sweetheart.'

'Sorry.'

'It's all right. I know you didn't mean to sound creepy.' She continued her work and within seconds I found myself so open-minded you could've persuaded me to take up mime or improvisational dance or even to appreciate abstract art. That thought made her chuckle. 'You would have made a truly excellent mime, Cade Ombra. Unfortunately, I need you to be a—

'Spirits of my ancestors! How can you *still* be intending to give yourself to the Pandoral? I've tethered your instinct for belligerence whilst unleashing your hatred for everything he stands for!'

I shrugged. Inwardly, I think. Most likely my shoulders and neck hadn't moved at all. Possibly you don't care about that, but I found it amusing. 'I suppose my decision was less a matter of pure stubbornness and more from—'

'Perversity,' she said, getting there ahead of me. 'You're driven to transgressive impulses both from your own cynicism and learned from your old mentor, Hazidan Rosh.'

'She did enjoy obscenity in all its myriad forms,' I conceded, and imagined myself tapping a finger to my right temple. 'There's a positive garden of obscenity waiting for you in here.'

'Then a little pruning is clearly in order,' Eliva'ren said, but she couldn't hide her anxiety now. As fast as she was working her silk magic on me, she was still running out of time. Also, there was only so much terrain in my skull she could mess with before the structures she was building there would collapse on themselves and I'd go irretrievably insane.

'You're wasting your time,' I told her, even as she plucked out strands of perversity like unruly nose hairs. 'Also, you might want to leave some of those naughty thoughts where they are, just in case.'

'Just in case what?'

'Well, you know . . .'

She kept stripping obscene inclinations from me, although I could feel she was definitely becoming more hesitant. 'No, I don't know. Why should I be leaving any of these "naughty thoughts"?'

I gave her my best rendition of a shy smile – she was the one who'd opened me up to the possibility of a career as a mime, after all. 'Just in case you and I decide to have sex once you've got us out of here. I mean, I realise it's a long shot, but we're both adults, both unattached and in need of relieving some tension. I'd hate for us to jump into bed together and for me to be all out of erotic moves.'

No laughing now, no clever rejoinder. She was getting desperate. *'I'm sorry, Cade,'* she murmured before letting loose the cruellest arrow in her quiver.

When next she reached inside me, the soft, sleek tendrils of her people's silk evocations fused with her own destiny magic. No longer did she constrain or unleash my inclinations but instead infused the consequences of the choices I was making directly into my mind. I'd been prepared for this, of course; forcing the captive to envision imminent suffering can be far more effective than inflicting pain on them in the present. Humans are, after all, prone to believing the future will turn out better than the past. But it wasn't my destiny that Eliva'ren unveiled, nor was it any kind of torment. Instead, she showed me what my decisions were costing my only friends.

'Come on, you beautiful bastards! Let's show these golden-faced dandies who's boss!' Corrigan's cries are punctuated with bolts of indigo lightning striking the front lines of the Auroral troops. He's dressed in the gleaming, form-fitting coppery armour of an Infernal Schemelord and leading an entire division of Demoniac Hellions and Malefic Artillerists into battle.

I'd never seen him so happy.

Without you dragging him into your impossible quest to prevent an inevitable war, he negotiates a deal with Tenebris, the Spellslinger whispered inside me. *The new Lords Devilish will give humanity greater freedom than the Lords Celestine ever would in exchange for Corrigan helping to lead the Infernal armies.*

I wanted to believe it was a lie, but the strands of her silk magic weren't just casting images into my mind; they were showing the inexorable cause and effect of Corrigan's own choices once freed from my influence.

'*Motherfuckers!*' bellows Temper as he leaps into the fray, his muzzle covered in the blood of angelics, his entire body swelling with vampiric power until . . .

'Are those *wings*?' I asked, not able to make them out clearly amidst all the raucous, joyous chaos of battle. But Eliva'ren cut the tendril away, threading a different one into my thoughts.

'*Rest easy, Grandmother,*' Galass said, fingertips tracing the air over the body of an elderly figure shivering on a narrow cot in a temple. Tiny droplets of blood riddled with sickness rise up from a frail, heaving chest to spin in the air, the ailment burned away before they drift back down beneath the skin. The tremors calm, the breathing eases. Both women smile. A body is healed. A spirit soars. One day soon, Galass knows, blood magic will no longer be reviled, but revered.

You protected her from madness and misery, Cade. You gave her the chance to uncover the depths of her own strength. Will you now snatch away her destiny?

'You're lying. This is a—'

I've never lied to you, Cade. Not once.

It was true. The Lords Celestine, the Devilish, Tenebris and just about everyone else had been pulling one con or another on me since before the Great Crusade even began. Eliva'ren had never tried to deceive me, and now I understood why: she couldn't make this hurt unless she first banished any doubts I might have that these destinies were true.

'*Go on then,*' I said.

No, I hadn't spoken this time. I couldn't bring myself to speak.

Eliva'ren was relentless, driven by a conviction as strong as any I could muster that her path was the right one and that mine was entirely futile.

'*A blossom may pale before such beauty as yours, my lady,*' Aradeus says in a voice stripped of youth yet no less dashing. A trembling hand, withered with age, shakes so much that the flower in its grasp begins to shed its petals. '*Yet still the rose a smile demands.*'

And she does smile.

Shame, her age matching his, as it has all these years since at last she consented to marry him, doesn't take the rose from him. Instead, she wraps her hand around his, steadying him as she inhales not only the familiar scent of the flower but that of her husband. The smile that comes to her lips is made all the more brilliant by its imperfections, by its mixture of adoration and sorrow, uncertainty and gratitude, and all the fragrances of humanity the former angelic has come to embrace.

She'll never know that life, Cade. How could she, fighting alongside you in an endless failure to prevent an endless war? There is no end to the story you offer them other than death and ruin.

'Don't gild the fucking lily. Show me Alice.'

No words this time. Instead, I saw a woman, a demoniac, dressed in gleaming armour I'd never seen before yet recognised instantly by the steady, determined gazes of those following behind her as they pursue a fugitive murderer whose wonderist spells have left a trail of bodies behind him. She and her squad wear the raiments of a new order of Justiciars. No longer beholden to the Glorians, they serve the laws that Alice herself helped set right: laws which shield human beings from the foibles of the Lords Devilish, who prevailed against the Lords Celestine only to find that people like Corrigan, like Galass, like Shame, Aradeus, Alice and even that gods-damned vampire kangaroo Temper, never fail to hold them to account. Heroes, one and all. And if, admittedly, the name 'Malevolent Six' never quite had the same ring to it, still, it's a legend others will seek to reinvent generation after generation.

And all it requires is that you let the Aurorals and the Infernals have their war, Cade. You resist until the right moment so that Tenebris can betray the Pandoral and take what's left of the power of that doomed realm for himself and his co-conspirators. My son is freed, a war that might have gone on for millennia is reduced to mere decades and your friends find such happiness as people like you and I could never even imagine for ourselves.

'You're right,' I said, and I definitely heard myself speak this time. 'This is a better destiny than any I could ever give them. A just compromise between the prospect of humanity's eternal enslavement and merely losing a few generations of its children and the chance to choose their own gods. And hey, one thing about me? I don't give a shit about religion.'

Eliva'ren was so deep inside my mind now, my very spirit, that she already knew the gambit had failed. '*I don't understand,*' she murmured, unleashing wave after wave of alterations to my thoughts and instincts. The surgeries became so fast that all I saw were the flashes of images, most abstract, some literal, each representing choices I might make and the destinies to which they would lead. One after another they faded from potentiality, always leaving behind the same decision.

'How are you doing this?' she asked aloud, her tone sharp, anxious, her breathing haggard. 'Every time I alter one aspect of your personality, some other part of you becomes even more entrenched in following that path to the Pandoral. *How are you doing this?*'

Despite my affection for her, what I wanted to say was, '*Because I'm not an amateur, Princess. I'm a former Glorian Justiciar who broke away from the brainwashing righteousness of the Lords Celestine themselves. I became an Infernalist who trafficked in spells and horrors, yet eluded every attempt by the Lords Devilish to align my spirit to their intentions. I've survived enemies whose power over-matched mine a hundredfold. I'm still here and they're dead because I don't walk into a fight unless I know exactly how to win. I'm a fucking tactical genius, and the only reason I don't shout it from the rooftops is because tactical geniuses like me are too gods-damned cunning to let people know just how much better we are at this shit than they are.'*

What I did say, however, was equally true but less suicidal. 'I didn't choose to risk destroying myself and my friends out of pique, Eliva'ren. I didn't do it because I lack pride or dignity or as a gamble. You and Tenebris and the Pandoral and everyone else keeps trying to argue with me about which destiny humanity must follow, but that's because you've forgotten what it means to be human.'

'Because your Justiciars took that away from me!'

'I know, and I'm sorry for my part in it. But nobody's suffering gives them a licence to take away someone else's freedom.'

'Yet you're willing to deny the six beings you're closest to in the entire world their chance at happiness?'

That made me laugh. It wasn't a happy laugh, mind you, but then, happiness had never been the point. 'You still don't get it, do you? I can't give my friends those pretty little futures you showed me because they're not mine to give. Me, Corrigan, Galass, Shame, Aradeus, Alice and even that fucking lunatic kangaroo, we already made our choices. We swore we wouldn't let the Mortal realm become anyone's plaything, no matter what the cost. We're not wide-eyed idealists, Eliva'ren, and we sure as shit aren't the good guys. I may play the hero these days, but I'm fighting the fight *my* way.'

She leaned closer, placing her hands on either side of my face. Her fingertips pressed hard into my skin, but I didn't feel any magic passing between us. This was something else. She was trying to make sense of me.

Good luck with that, sister, I thought.

Realisation dawned on her slowly, and her brow furrowed as she wrestled with the implications of what had happened. 'With each alteration I made to your mind, some other part reshaped itself into finding a different, yet equally determined, commitment to your decision. Nothing I can do will move you without destroying you entirely.'

I took her hands away from my face. 'You asked earlier why I wasn't resisting? It's because I don't waste time fighting when the opponent has already lost.'

I felt her make one final, almost feeble attempt to invoke her silk magic, but too much intimacy makes the romance go stale. I sent a sudden, sharp jolt against the connection between us. Had she been prepared for opposition as she'd been earlier, or had she not been so exhausted, it might not have worked. But the tether between our minds snapped so hard the two of us recoiled from both the pain and the sudden loss.

I heard the sound of footsteps coming down the passageway, and something that sounded suspiciously like a swarm made up of thousands of buzzing bees. I rose to my feet, forcing myself not to immediately topple over when the dizziness hit me. 'Come on,' I said, extending a hand to her. 'Time you got me out of here.'

The Spellslinger, utterly baffled by what had happened, accepted my hand. We stood side by side and waited as the key turned in the lock of the door.

'Guess we're going to have to fight our way out,' I said. Under normal circumstances I would've left it there but, you know, people who mess with your brain should expect consequences for their ill deeds. That's why I added, 'Sweetheart.'

CHAPTER 39

A Brief Guide to Magical Battles

Violence is a misunderstood art-form. If you require proof, close your eyes and imagine a weapon – any weapon will do. There, see? You've already screwed it up. I'll bet all the money in my pockets – which is none, since my captors left me naught but filthy rags – against all the money in your pockets that you're picturing a sword or a spear or perhaps a siege cannon. I don't blame you; most people would. But what you're focusing on in your head isn't the actual weapon: it's not the cause of the damage you're about to inflict on your fellow human being, merely the conveyance. It's not the edge of the blade that cuts flesh, any more than the tip of the arrowhead pierces armour. The actual slicing or piercing or hacking is caused by an amount of force directed along a particular axis and delivered to as tiny a target as possible. Sharpening the sword blade makes it deadlier only because it means the force of the blow is distributed along a thinner line. The cannon does no damage to the castle wall; it's simply a means of sending a great deal of pressure to a relatively small area.

And the weapon's only dangerous if it's within range, correctly aimed and delivering enough force to a sufficiently small target to overwhelm whatever material it comes in contact with. The greatest fencer in the world armed with the sharpest rapier is no threat if you're standing half a mile away. The mightiest trebuchet is irrelevant if the engineers aiming it can't see you.

288

Magical violence works the same way. It's not the potency of the spell you need to worry about, but where it's directed. Direction, velocity, distribution of energy: these are the tactical considerations in surviving an assault by a coven of enemy wonderists.

'Is there a reason why you're giving a lecture on mystical battle tactics in the middle of a fight?' Eliva'ren asked.

I hadn't been aware that I was talking out loud. I locked eyes with the felinist slashing at me with the two-foot-long razor-sharp claws she'd manifested from her fingertips, who helpfully nodded to confirm that, yes, I was talking like a lunatic in the midst of a fight for our lives.

Well, not actually *my* life.

'Don't kill him, you idiot,' the Infernalist warned his cat-eared comrade. 'Kill the damned Spellslinger!'

'He's in the way,' she countered, delivering another more tentative slash at my legs in an attempt to get me to move without actually murdering me. I resisted the urge to flinch backwards and dropped low, nearly getting my head taken off in the process, which was really freaking out our opponents.

The borinist was trying to channel some kind of bludgeoning projection from his tusks, but he was young and hadn't learned to hide the timing and direction of his attack yet. Avoiding him was far easier than the felinist.

The cosmist, watching from the door, where the void surrounding her physical form was conveniently dissuading more of her colleagues from entering my cell, shouted, 'He can't serve as a gate if you've beheaded him, you stupid furry slu—'

The felinist – who, despite her cat-like way of wiggling her bottom when she moved, struck me as a perfectly chaste young lady – spun on her heel and slashed at the cosmist's non-existent face. The cosmist must've been relatively new to her attunement too, for she lurched backwards, her human instincts forgetting that nothing so banal as a set of mystical two-foot-long claws could do her any damage. On the other hand, the void surrounding her body consumed one of the guards – his scream was all too brief as he was sucked inside, swallowed up by the empty space in which he quickly became a tiny figure lost among the stars inside the cosmist.

Rest in peace, Lefty, I thought. *You were my favourite guard. No, really, I mean it. Righty kicked me way harder.*

The sounds of yet more footsteps racing down the hall suggested our time was running out. 'How much longer?' I asked Eliva'ren. I didn't bother looking back to see whether she was still struggling to draw forth whichever destiny we needed, or if she had given up and found some other means of escape just for herself.

'Another minute,' she said. Her grunt told me that magically causing the events of a person or place's doom to occur in the present rather than the future was harder work than she'd been letting on.

I kept bobbing and weaving in response to the felinist's slashing attacks. She'd added a prehensile magical tail that was currently intent on wrapping itself around my neck. My defence was to throw myself at the claws, forcing the felinist to either pull back or risk slicing my throat open, then having to explain to her master why she'd killed possibly the only Pandorally attuned Mortal in the world. Instead, she got her tail wrapped around the borinist's head and entangled with his tusks.

'Will you *do* something?' she asked the Infernalist, who'd finally undone his coat to reveal the sigils covering his chest. Many of these were charred, used up, but he started making a show of slowly awakening a Nightmare Bloom, which would certainly incapacitate my mind long enough for them to kill Eliva'ren and trap me once more.

You might be fooling your coven, I thought silently as I shot him a knowing grin, *but you're not fooling me.*

Infernalists have to buy every spell, which was how Tenebris and I became . . . well, if not friends, then certainly frenemies. If this guy used up a Nightmare Bloom or a Weeping Arrow and it didn't get the job done – like his Tongue-Wrester spell – then he'd've wasted a perfectly good – *expensive* – spell and would have to come up with the means to buy a replacement. So he was definitely slow-walking his casting, hoping someone else put me down first.

This was one of those rare occasions where thinking strategically was less useful than thinking tactically. It made perfect strategic sense for the Infernalist to keep his spells in reserve, given his comrades could cast theirs without cost. However, when you want to capture your opponent alive, mind-manipulation spells are vastly more effective than hacking or burning them into submission.

Their florinist finally appeared, tossing a handful of what looked like chestnuts on the filthy floor. Almost instantly, her magic caused them to start rooting into the stone and growing upwards into what would soon be a small forest, which would severely hamper my movements. Fortunately for me, I'm one of the few wonderists who's made a serious study of just about every form of magic out there and considered how best to fight against each. One of the chestnuts was still rolling, which meant it hadn't taken root yet. I snatched it up and hurled it at the felinist. I'd only been aiming to make her lurch backwards into the cosmist, who still hadn't figured out that a walking void just standing there isn't much use to her comrades. Oddly, the felinist hissed at me.

Among professional wonderists, it's understood that luminists are the biggest wastes of space out there. Their spells all involve bending light and conjuring illusions. This in itself wouldn't necessarily make them losers, since there's a lot you can do with illusions. The problem, as I've pointed out before, is that magic isn't particularly good for you, especially not for the mind. Every form of wonderism comes with its own form of mental illness. Tempestoral mages are all arsonists barely in control of their urges to blow things up. Aurorals are convinced everything they do is blessed by the Sovereign, so they always look surprised when they're killed by entirely predictable means. Luminists are congenital narcissists who can't stop themselves from using their abilities in unnecessarily flashy ways and – here's the really stupid part – they often get mesmerised by their own conjurations.

Totemists are attuned to a plane where the laws of physics transmute the symbolic representations of animals into magical characteristics; their spells are like a pallet of abilities or traits one might associate with that particular animal. How it works, I've never quite figured out – I mean, what do *actual* animals do in the Totemic plane? Regardless, like all other wonderists, totemists suffer from emotional issues. Aradeus, believing that rats are the most noble and elegant of creatures, is obsessed with living up to their example, thus poncing about spouting 'thees' and 'thous' wherever he goes while acting preposterously humble and honourable. The felinist? I guess her sense of being cat-like was more literal, which was why when she saw me about to hurl the chestnut she opened her mouth wide – she had lovely fangs, by the way – and hissed at me. That's how the chestnut ended up in her throat, which is where it took root and turned into a majestic little tree that happened to be covered in dead cat lady parts.

'Damn it all,' the Infernalist said – a common oath for those who share that attunement. He stopped screwing around, awoke the Nightmare Bloom on his chest and watched the black sigils oozing from his skin to drift in the air between us. There's no way to evade an Infernalist spell, since it goes wherever the caster wants it to, so I didn't bother ducking as I darted to the chestnut tree, grabbed the torn-apart arm of the dead felinist and stabbed the Infernalist through the heart with one of her magically created claws just before it faded into nothingness. He was left with an odd hole going through his chest.

'Damn it all,' he repeated.

I guess I got his heart dead on, because the stream of blood erupting from the wound practically blinded me. Two more of his fellow wonderists were coming into the cell, but as I couldn't see clearly enough to make them out, I was at a serious tactical disadvantage, since all my tricks depended on knowing what plane they were attuned to and how they were likely to use their spells.

'Eliva . . .' I warned.

'Don't call me that,' she snapped. I didn't bother reminding her that an earlier version of herself had told me I could.

I felt rather than saw the doom overcoming the dungeon cell – I suppose doom was the wrong word, though, because the destiny she'd brought forth was the one in which this fortress became a palace whose ruler had turned this part of the dungeon into a throne room. The whole place took on an eerie glow from all the gilded oak-panelled walls. A magnificent spiral staircase ascending to the main floor constructed itself out of the stone beneath our feet.

'Let's go,' she said. She took my hand and led me up the stairs, while the rest of the room was still transforming itself and my captors were getting pelted by blocks of stone that were quite keen to become a far more elegant floor. I stumbled a couple of times on the way up, but within minutes we were standing outside in a desolate field, staring at a fortress steadily becoming the palace it would one day be.

'Won't they just chase after us?' I asked.

Eliva'ren wasn't paying attention. Her brow was furrowed, sweat trickling down her forehead as she halted the fortress' magnificent destiny and drew forth a less likely and significantly worse one. 'Fifty years from now, the warlord conquering this region has a high probability of choosing to kidnap a fifteen-year-old girl from the town nearby. Apparently, he's enamoured of red hair.'

'Really? I prefer brunettes.'

She smiled weakly as she drew more and more of her strange

magic into her spell. 'The girl has a sister, several years older, who sneaks into the warlord's camp and first seduces him, then kills him.'

I gestured to the fortress that was now twitching like an old codger with a bad palsy. 'So, no palace?'

Eliva'ren reached out with one hand, fingers curled as if holding onto a doorknob or the face of a clock and twisted. 'The elder sister becomes a kind of nomadic war chief, leading an army made up almost entirely of pissed-off women determined to tear down every male-owned castle and fortress they can find.'

On cue, the upper floors of the stone fortress collapsed under their own weight, sending stone chips and mortar flying in all directions. I couldn't hear the screams of the wonderists previously known as the Unforgettable Eight, although a couple might've survived; it's pretty hard to kill a cosmist without first destroying their conscious minds. The Pandoral was probably still alive too.

'Where do you stand on taking advantage of unconscious women?' the Spellslinger asked me.

I turned and saw that she was tilting like one of the fortress towers currently in the process of falling. She blinked her eyes several times, trying to focus on me.

'I've never taken a public position on the issue, but I'm generally opposed to rape,' I replied.

'Good,' she murmured. 'That's good.'

Then she passed out and I was left standing there in filthy, stinking rags with an unconscious woman at my feet who'd made it painfully clear on a number of occasions that she was going to bring me to my inevitable doom and destroy any chance I had of protecting the Mortal realm from an endless war between the Aurorals and Infernals. One had to assume that said prophecy would be null and void if I knelt down and – gently, caringly – strangled her to death.

CHAPTER 40

Heroic Murder

Murder gets a bad rep, but if you ask me, homicide is the quintessential act of heroism. It's all right there in the sagas: how does the hero save the world? By killing the evil king, slaying the mighty dragon, defenestrating the dastardly tyrant.

Choking the unconscious young mother to death.

It's true, there are no sagas I know of with that particular ending recited to enraptured children at bedtime, but that only meant there was an opening for me to be immortalised in legend.

I know, I know: you're thinking that good guys don't murder innocent mothers doing whatever they must to rescue a child from a horrific plane of existence. But the world had plenty of good guys walking around *not* murdering people and things had still gone to shit. What the world needed now wasn't a good guy. It needed *a hero*.

'She's going to destroy us all,' I reminded my friends as I lugged the incapacitated Spellslinger over my shoulder.

They weren't there, of course. Best I could tell, the portalist working for the Pandoral had transported me a good two hundred miles from that roadside temple where I'd been kidnapped. Still, you spend enough time with crazy people and eventually you can't help but hear their voices at inopportune moments.

'*We can't know that for certain,*' Galass said disapprovingly, then twisted the knife a little deeper. '*You're the one who's always defying the*

295

inevitable, Cade. Are you saying now of all times you're becoming a believer in destiny?'

'Kill the bitch,' Corrigan said, scratching his balls. In my imaginings, he's always scratching his balls. Actually, that's not just in my imagination.

'Nay, Brother Cade, nay,' declared Aradeus. *'Such an atrocity cannot be countenanced, no matter the justification!'*

'You can't stop him, moron,' Alice reminded the rat mage. *'Cade is only imagining you. He's mostly hallucinating due to his prolonged torture. And because he's morally weak.'*

'You do appear rather unwell, child,' Shame observed in that motherly tone that suggested her notion of motherhood would totally involve smothering the baby to cure the colic. Angelics really don't understand parenthood.

Aradeus, however, followed an entirely more irritating moral compass. Drawing his imaginary rapier with a flourish he declared, *'Whether my sword arm be flesh or mere stuff of dreams, nevertheless shall my blade strike down any who would commit black bloody murder! Have at you, Cade – I say, have at you!'*

I stumbled, twisting my own ankle to avoid dropping Eliva'ren to the dusty ground. The pain was oddly refreshing, if only because it banished the annoying image of Aradeus from my mind.

'Yeah, rat mages are moralising pains in the arse sometimes,' Corrigan said sympathetically. *'Now, just gently set the woman down on the ground, straddle her, in case she wakes up, and choke the life out of her before she comes to her senses and obliterates the fucking universe!'*

It was a hazy late afternoon, the sun slowly setting behind the hills on the horizon. I could see houses up ahead, which was good because I was in dire need of proper food, a bath and a decent bed. Unfortunately, it also meant I was running out of time to either be a proper hero or a pathetic good guy who put his moral squeamishness above the lives of everyone else.

'*Don't do it,*' Galass warned. '*I'll never speak to you again if you do something this awful, Cade. It's not just me and Aradeus, either. Corrigan will despise you for doing this, no matter how tough he talks. Shame and Alice might seem distant, but they can only be that way because they trust you to keep us on the right path. There won't be a Malevolent Seven if you murder that woman, Cade, because none of us will be able to look at you ever again.*'

'You think I don't know that?' I asked, stopping to stand there with my ankle aching and my entire body ready to collapse, just like the fortress we'd left behind. Also, because there was the hallucination of a kangaroo standing in my way.

'Go on,' I told Temper, 'say "motherfucker" like it's supposed to mean something.'

The illusory vampire kangaroo opened its mouth, then coughed, bringing a paw briefly to his muzzle before trying again. '*Actually, Cade,*' the kangaroo began, '*what you're facing is a far more complex philosophical conundrum than you believe. Scholars of ethics refer to your dilemma as "The Horse and Cart Problem".*'

'Why are you talking like that?' I asked.

Temper smiled tolerantly, which is unnerving when the smile in question is formed by a mouth full of fangs belonging to a creature who drinks blood and has poor dental hygiene. '*Oh, Cade. Do you expect me to just say "motherfucker" over and over? It's quaint, but as you're imagining me for the purpose of achieving a decision on what course of action to take, isn't it more useful for us to have a proper conversation?*'

'No, I meant the accent. I've never heard it before. You sound halfway between some poncey foreign nobleman and an inebriated fishmonger.'

'*Ah, I believe the dialect to which you are referring is the one employed by humans from my native land in my own plane of reality. You must have picked up snatches of it when you cast the spell that brought me to your realm.*' Then, for reasons passing understanding, he added, '*Mate.*'

'Fine,' I said, resuming my march towards the settlement in the distance. 'You have until I reach the town gates to help me figure it out.'

'There's really nothing to figure out. The Horse and Cart problem is a simple one: you find yourself on a dirt road descending from a mountain when you see a driverless horse-cart rumbling by. You jump atop the driver's bench in an attempt to stop the cart's progress, but the horses have been spooked and are rushing headlong towards five unwitting travellers. You shout to the travellers, but they don't hear you, and even if they did, there's nowhere for them to flee because on one side of them is a steep rise and the other a cliff's edge. No matter how hard you pull on the reins, you can't get the horses to stop, but there's a slight fork in the road to the right. If you pull with all your might, you'll make the horses turn in that direction – but alas, there stands an innocent child who, unlike the oblivious travellers, sees you coming and knows her fate is in your hands.'

'I kill the child,' I said without hesitation.

'Because five lives are worth more than one, no matter that it makes you a murderer?'

'Because I don't like kids.'

The spectral kangaroo humoured me with a sympathetic chuckle, then ruined it by saying, *'Have you tried any? They're quite tasty.'*

I stopped again. From this distance, I could already hear some of the sounds of people near the town gates doing whatever people do as they return home from their labours.

'You're saying I *shouldn't* kill the kid but should let the five travellers die?' I asked Temper.

'Not at all. The Horse and Cart problem has no correct answer. It's merely a mental experiment forcing one to contend with competing philosophical premises. Either the act of allowing five to die is better because it requires no evil act on your part, or choosing to intentionally murder the child is better because it saves the most lives.'

I knelt down and set Eliva'ren on the road, wishing a runaway horse-cart were coming this way with somebody else holding the reins. 'So which choice am I supposed to make?'

I hadn't expected an answer. Temper was a kangaroo, after all, and incapable of speech other than repeating "motherfucker" relentlessly because Corrigan kept encouraging him. Also, Temper wasn't really here. That's why I was so surprised by what he said next.

'*Neither.*'

'What?'

'*You don't choose either path.*'

'What the fuck is that supposed to mean? You just told me the whole point of this mental puzzle is that the horses are going to either run down the five travellers or crush the innocent child!'

'*Who are you?*'

'What?'

'*Who are you?*'

'I'm Cade Ombra, you idiot. The guy who's imagining you, remember?'

'*And what is Cade Ombra?*' My imaginary kangaroo ethics professor held up a paw to forestall my answer. '*I phrased that poorly. Tell me instead, what does it mean to be Cade Ombra?*'

'Unlucky, possibly insane, and sick of imaginary vampire kangaroos.'

'*What does it mean to be Cade Ombra?*' he repeated. '*Not your name or lineage or profession or even your personality. If it's simpler for you to understand, what would it mean that you were no longer Cade Ombra?*'

It took me a moment to untangle those two questions in my head, but eventually I realised what Temper – or what *I*, in fact – had been trying to get myself to understand.

'Cade Ombra is a fool,' I said quietly, kneeling to place my ear close to the Spellslinger's chest. Her breathing was less ragged now, her heartbeat increasing. She would wake any moment. I lifted her back up in my arms and headed for the town gates. 'Cade Ombra is an idiot who can't stop himself from believing that no matter how bad the odds, he can figure out a way to save the travellers without killing the child. And the moment he stops believing that? That's the moment he stops being Cade Ombra.'

'*Here endeth the lesson,*' said the imaginary vampire kangaroo, who promptly hopped away, presumably to drink the blood of the five dead travellers, saving the child for dessert.

CHAPTER 41

Romantic Inclinations

The two of us sat either side of the small table with enough food to feed a platoon of soldiers heaped high on our plates. Neither of us had reached for cutlery, and for once it wasn't out of a concern that doing so might lead to accidental bloodshed.

'There need to be a few ground rules,' the Spellslinger said.

She looked rather delightful tonight, the intimate candlelight in this little restaurant in a quiet corner of town gleaming on her dark curls. She'd chosen an unpretentious ankle-length grey dress for the evening that looked utterly stunning on her. She'd purchased the dress from the same shop where I'd swapped my tattered rags for a surprisingly well-tailored brocaded coat in what's apparently called the 'baronet' style, which was similar in cut to my usual wonderist's coat. Instead of my customary azure, I'd had to settle for crimson with gold trim. Along with the inordinately puffy white shirt and narrow black trousers the shopkeeper had insisted I buy as well, I looked poncey enough to pass for a rat mage.

'You look nice tonight, by the way,' Eliva'ren said.

'You too,' I said, aiming for casual and somehow landing on fretful-seventeen-year-old-desperate-to-impress-a-pretty-girl.

She smiled, which told me she wasn't unaware of the innate awkwardness of this particular conversation. 'So . . . ground rules.'

'Right. Rules. Must have rules. I take it the first rule is no sex?'

She looked surprised by that. 'What? Of course not. I thought sex was the whole point when you propositioned me.'

'I wasn't propositioning you,' I half-stammered. 'I was merely proposing th—'

'So it was a proposal. You were proposing to me.'

'No, damn it, I was just . . .'

'*Brother Cade*,' I imagined Aradeus shooting me one of those swashbuckler grins of his, '*I believe you are falling in love.*'

No, I'm not. This is all part of a brilliant and cunning plan.

'*You are falling in love*,' Alice insisted. '*It is pathetic.*'

Then Temper started in on some philosophical dissertation about the inseparable connection between love in the mind and love of the body and whether the existence of the latter voided the possibility of the former and I stopped listening to my own imaginings.

Truth be told, I hadn't had much of a plan once I'd brought Eliva'ren to the town and she'd had a chance to recover from the exhaustion of wielding her strange form of wonderism to rescue us from the Unlucky Eight – although only because I'd forced her to, and only after she'd tried to torture me herself with her so-called silk magic. Then she'd passed out from the effort, leaving me the choice of whether to kill her or save her. Abandoning her outside the fortress would've likely produced the same effect, as I was sure *someone* working for the Pandoral had survived the collapse.

So where had that left us? Two people who'd saved each other's lives yet were on opposite sides of a conflict far bigger and more consequential than either of us. We were surely going to try to kill one another once this whole Great Crusade insanity came to its inevitable calamitous end – so what were we supposed to do? Wave goodbye and, vying for who got the last word, walk off in opposite directions? I could almost hear how that would go.

'*Farewell, beloved enemy. When next we meet, you will surely die.*'

'*Ah, but we shall not meet again, for when I kill you, I shall give you a gift, for you will never see death coming.*'

'*I need not see death, you poor fool, save in a mirror, for I am your death.*'

'*Yes, you are my death, the last one I must commit ere this bloody business be done.*'

'*Alas, it is already done, and soon your blood will . . . Wait, what was that last part? I didn't hear it all.*'

'*What's that? You're too far away now. I can't hear a thing you're—*'

You get the idea. It was pointless to walk away at that moment, but the alternative was to start fighting again, which was also kind of silly given we'd just saved each other's lives.

'Say, does that destiny hoodoo magic of yours happen to tell you how far away my crew are?' I'd asked instead, looking up at the town gates, unsure which of us would be expected to skip the comforts of town to avoid us having to deal with the obvious logic of resuming our conflict now rather than later.

Eliva'ren had closed her eyes briefly. Some shred of the connection we'd had through her silk magic before must've remained, because when I closed my own eyes, I saw images in flashes: Aradeus having a conversation with a group of rats; Alice, her eyes glowing an odd onyx, peering into the distance and apparently looking straight at me. Temper, hopping around madly shouting, 'Motherfucker! Motherfucker!'

'They've either abandoned you and gone their separate ways or they'll be here in the morning,' Eliva had said at last. 'Both destinies ultimately end the same, but the intervening steps are equally likely.'

Personally, I thought she was being cynical and that the others would, of course, be on their way. 'Tomorrow morning, you said?'

She nodded. 'Assuming they haven't given up on you.'

Ouch.

'Okay, then I have a proposal.'

She looked at me, those dark eyes narrowed in suspicion, even as a glimmer of her smirk appeared. Her kiss still lingered on my lips, even after a week of torture. 'All right, Cade, what are you proposing?'

'A date.'

'A *date*?'

I pointed to the bustling street, where lanterns were being lit against the falling dusk. 'That's likely the only civilised settlement for miles around. We're both hungry and exhausted. Instead of fighting over who gets to eat at which restaurant, why don't we share a meal and pretend to be civilised, just for one evening?'

'You're also filthy and you smell terrible,' she pointed out.

'Right. A bath is definitely in order.'

She placed her hands on her hips, though I noted one was now cocked fetchingly. 'And do you propose we also share the bath?'

'Only if you don't hog the tub. Also, I might need you to scrub my back.'

That last part earned me an actual laugh. If only because the whole idea was utterly preposterous, she eventually conceded that a single evening of civilised socialising wasn't likely to alter anyone's destiny. However . . .

'The first rule,' she said now, speaking more quickly because neither of us wanted our food to get cold, 'is that there can be no obligations on either side.'

I considered that a moment. The term 'obligation' can carry a lot of different meanings. 'So, you're saying you won't marry me after even if you get me pregnant?'

Oh, Celestines and Devilish take me. Wrong joke. Wrong joke!

I guess a pretty rough ten years since a confused young initiate mage had accidentally found herself on this plane of reality, lost and not yet aware she was pregnant and about to be hunted, tortured and then accidentally attuned to devastating magical forces had inured her to tasteless humour.

'Even if I get you pregnant with twins,' she said with just enough of a flicker of amusement to let me know I was off the hook. 'Whatever happens tonight, it won't affect our fates. The decisions you've made to this point have collapsed your destinies down to a single doom.' She reached out and took my hand briefly. 'It's not a good one, Cade.'

I had a number of short, pithy speeches for moments like this, about how wonderists face death every time they use their abilities, or that I'd been hunted by Glorian Justiciars and demoniacs galore and they'd all failed, or about that time I had sex with the Celestine of Rationality. I didn't bother with any of them, however.

'What's rule number two?'

'No questions.'

'I thought we were discussing the rules?'

'No, I mean, from now until we part in the morning, no matter what else happens between us, you can't ask me questions about your doom. What's going to be is going to be and nothing you try to do will change it. Tonight will be the last time we see each other before the end. I . . . It never occurred to me that two people in our position could ever have . . . could ever pretend things were different. I'm glad you suggested this "date" of yours, but it's nothing but a momentary aberration of our destinies. It really is just pretend, so you have to promise not to ask me any questions about what comes next.'

'No problem.'

'Really?'

'No obligations, no questions. Anything else?'

She didn't answer at first; I guessed she was wrestling with the situation. I figured for sure she was going to back out. No matter what anyone tells you about fate or inevitability, human entanglements have a way of screwing with destiny. So I was surprised when she stood up, grabbed me by the collar and pulled me upright, then kissed me like the entire world was on fire. 'Rule three,' she said, her voice barely more than a breath. 'We get the food to go.'

And that, friends, is the story of how I faced off against the Lords Celestine, the Lords Devilish, got kidnapped by a cult of weirdo mages, was beaten and tortured only to finally get over my secret obsession with the Celestine of Rationality by spending the night with the most amazing woman I'd ever met just in time for the world to end.

CHAPTER 42

Rude Awakenings

Eliva'ren turned out to be correct that it wouldn't be until morning before my crew found me. She had, however, left out three key facts.

The first was that she'd failed to specify exactly how early in the morning they'd arrive, or mention that between Galass' blood magic and Aradeus' rodent scouts, they'd come rushing up the stairs of the inn where we'd bedded down for the night and that Corrigan would smash through the oak door with a spell he quite unselfconsciously refers to as his 'thunderfist'.

So after several days of horrific torture followed by a harrowing escape and an unexpected – if admittedly pleasant – evening out, I woke to a sudden explosion and shards of wood spearing the wall about three inches above my head.

'Drop to the floor, you vile pricks! No one tortures my best friend while thunder beats within the breast of Corrigan Blight!'

Three days he'd been on the road to get here, all that time practising the lines he'd deliver on finding me, and that was the best he could come up with?

Galass, Aradeus, Shame, Alice and Temper all piled through the now ruined doorway after Corrigan. Temper, hopping around the low-ceilinged room, kept thumping his head on the wooden beams. At the foot of my bed stood a rat on its hind legs, watching me. My brain was still a little foggy, so it took a moment to figure out why I was so pissed off at the rat.

'Huzzah,' said Aradeus, somehow managing to draw his rapier in the cramped room without stabbing anyone. 'En guarde, villains, for none who dare torment our comrade shall leave this room alive!' He caught sight of me for the first time since entering the room and asked, 'Are you badly injured, Brother Cade? Did those miscreants who kidnapped you shatter your spine, thus explaining why you're still lying there in that bed?' He peered closer. 'And what vile creature lurks beneath the covers? Some sort of gigantic bone-eating slug that assails you even now?'

'Heh,' Corrigan chuckled. 'Bone-eating.'

This latest in a long career of lousy jokes prompted Temper to stop hopping and instead enact what I had to presume was a piece of performance theatre taught to him by Corrigan which involved miming a series of lewd sexual acts. A few of them were surprisingly accurate. Since I was inured by now to these types of antics, my attention remained focused on a more pernicious prankster.

'Aradeus?' I asked, still watching the rat at the foot of my bed.

'Yes, Brother Cade?'

'Can I presume that Galass used her blood magic to track me to this region and then you summoned the local rats to narrow my location down to this inn?'

'Indeed!' he replied, evidently pleased with himself.

I pointed to the rat at the end of the bed. 'This is the little fucker who informed you I was here?'

Aradeus frowned. 'A callous slight, Brother Cade, for the noble creature who risked fur and tail to find you.'

'Uh huh. Right. Only, since my rodent saviour here was capable of relaying my location to you, is there any particular reason why he didn't mention that I wasn't, in fact, held captive any longer, or that what lurks beneath the covers right now is not, in fact, a giant bone-eating slug?'

The rat, his beady eyes never leaving mine, twitched his head several times in a gesture which I distinctly understood to mean he was laughing at me.

'In addition to their daring, courage and cunning, rats do have a rather legendary sense of humour,' Aradeus confessed.

'You know I could transform you into a human-sized, rat-headed servant creature if I wanted to, right?' I asked the rat.

My future rodent valet scurried away.

Alice approached and pointed to the covers. 'If there is no giant bone-eating slug hiding there, what does lurk beneath your bedding?'

At first, I presumed this was one of those amusing moments of unexpected prudishness in which Eliva'ren was mortified at being caught in bed with the man she still intended to kill before helping to destroy my entire world. But prudishness wasn't really her style, so I worried she'd made her exit while I was sleeping and some kind of vile giant bone-eating slug really had crept under the covers with me. Possibly made from a swarm of insects. I carefully lifted the cover and discovered neither hypothesis was correct.

'Seriously?' I asked, seeing her sprawled unconscious under the covers and, now that the cacophony of Corrigan's entrance had died down, hearing she was quietly snoring. 'You slept through all that?'

Eliva'ren roused, first wiping at her lips, because it turned out she was a drooler when she slept. She smiled sleepily at me, only then finally noticing the smell of charred wood left behind by Corrigan's temporal blast. She grinned. 'Oops. I didn't mean to sleep so late.' She crawled out from beneath the covers, clearly untroubled by being naked in front of ... well, if not exactly strangers, at least people she'd once killed, even if she had brought them back to life.

She yawned, nestled herself against my shoulder and asked, 'Has the world ended yet?'

Which brought us to the second thing she hadn't warned me about.

CHAPTER 43

Even Ruder Awakenings

There are sights one really does not expect to see whilst standing around naked and looking out at the early morning sky from the second-floor window of a friendly little inn. One of those unanticipated sights is the entire fucking sky burning gold and red. Seriously, there were actual flames raging towards us, scattering clouds and filling the air with the screams of those who'd just woken up to the end of the world.

'Stop screaming,' Alice said. 'It's annoying.'

'What the fuck happened while I was being incarcerated, tortured and interrogated?' I demanded.

'How was it?' Corrigan asked, sad eyes almost soulful as he gazed down at me.

Watching what must be the cataclysmic supernatural effects of the Lords Celestine and Lords Devilish marching their armies towards this benighted little town hardly felt like the right time for unburdening my emotional trauma on my best friend. Still, it was nice of him to ask.

'Honestly? I'd place the experience somewhere between that time we got arrested by that mob of wonderist hunters and our more recent encounter with the Lords Devilish.'

'Oh, no, I don't give a shit about that.' Corrigan poked me in the ribs with his elbow and nodded not at all inconspicuously to the other side of the room where Eliva'ren was still reclining on the bed. 'I mean, how was it with *her*?'

His casual attitude was a clue to just how screwed we were. Corrigan's no fool, no matter how convincingly he plays the part. If he thought there was any action we could possibly take to prevent the apocalypse coming our way, or even for us to escape, he would've been the first person to start stomping about and shouting orders. Instead, he was making salacious jokes, which, as he's made clear many times, is one of the only two ways he wants to die. The other . . . well, that should be obvious by now too.

I glanced over at Galass, who, being younger and more idealistic than the rest of us, was less prone to fatalism. She met my gaze but said nothing. Even her hair was hanging limp and dull.

'Give me the lay of the land,' I told them anyway.

'Well, Cade,' Corrigan began, the tone of his voice suggesting he was poised to blame all this on me, 'after you got taken by the Arsehole Eight— How are they, by the way?'

'Corpses, mostly.'

'Too bad. I was thinking of recruiting one of them for your spot on the team after you're dead.'

'I think the luminist might've survived. Maybe you could invite him?'

'Better than a fucking *pandoralist*!' Corrigan swatted the back of my head hard enough to send me reeling towards the window, where I cracked my skull on the wooden frame – 'brilliant move, by the way. Fucking genius. You could've chosen *any* attunement you wanted and you picked the one that turns you into a walking catastrophe waiting to explode? Fucking well done.'

'I figured we might need an edge when fighting the Aurorals and Infernals,' I said, rubbing my forehead. 'Pandoral magic is the only kind that frightens them—'

Corrigan smacked me a second time, leaving me seriously dazed.

'That's because, unlike you, they're smart enough to know it's nothing but a disaster waiting to happen.' He jerked a thumb towards the bed. 'Especially after they turned *her* into a living, breathing agent of chaos.'

'Well, sure, in hindsight I suppose a different attunement might've worked out better. Maybe florinist. I've always wanted to learn gardening. But since I have it on good authority you can't alter your destiny, how about filling me in on the rest of it. What happened with Tenebris?'

Corrigan laughed. 'After you were taken and he'd explained this cabal of disaffected mid-level Infernals and Aurorals he'd put together to overthrow the Lords Devilish and Lords Celestine, your former agent tried to negotiate a pact with us! Can you believe it? That diabolic little prick offered each of us more than we could ever have hoped for.'

'And?'

'What?'

'Did you take the deal?'

He crossed his arms over his chest defensively. 'Well, Aradeus looked like he might give in, but naturally, I refused.'

The rat mage looked confused. 'I fear your memory may be failing you, Brother Corrigan, as I distinctly recall you asking only that in addition to the other terms of the pact they would . . .' Aradeus pointed to Corrigan's groin, then placed his hands rather close together before widening them.

'Lies!' Corrigan bellowed. 'Foul calumny—!'

'That is exactly what happened,' Alice confirmed.

'He was rather insistent,' Shame added, then, because she has neither a sense of propriety nor etiquette, lifted her skirt to manifest the appendage in question along with the proposed alterations.

Corrigan became agitated. 'It was a ruse, you idiots, I was stalling for time. And it worked, too!' He turned back to me. 'While I cunningly stalled the diabolic, Aradeus sent a message through some of his rat brethren to that Ardentor twat we duped into stealing the Glorian banner. He found an angelic to commune with the Lords Celestine, who immediately mobilised their forces. Naturally, spies for the Lords Devilish got wind of what was happening and immediately sent *their* forces, which . . . Well, you can guess the rest.' He gestured through the open window to the vivid golden and crimson fiery flourishes currently devouring the sky even before their avatars on the ground could fight over who got to attack the Pandoral first.

All of which plays right into the hands of Tenebris and his cabal, I realised, though I didn't mention that to the others. When you're already doomed, being told you also got played doesn't exactly inspire the heroic urge for one last fight.

'It's madness, Cade,' Galass said, looking flummoxed by Corrigan's glib recounting of what my inopportune kidnapping had sparked. 'Once those two armies reach the Pandoral, it's going to be absolute chaos.'

'Destiny, actually,' Eliva'ren corrected her. She rose from the bed, both more elegant in her nudity and considerably less troubled by the stares of three human wonderists, an angelic, a demoniac and a vampiric kangaroo than I was. Aradeus was naturally averting his gaze. Eliva left last night's dress on the floor and instead opened her pack to retrieve her everyday clothes, pulling on the tan trousers and sliding her shirt over her head before tightening her belt. 'That's what no one understood about the Pandoral realm before. It's not just a place where the physical laws produce chaos; they produce both chaos *and* destiny.'

'But those two things are opposites, aren't they?' Galass asked.

One of the bands of metallic sigils tattooed onto Eliva'ren's right forearm glimmered and tiny sparks of light began to dance in front of her, each one moving in wild, incomprehensible patterns. 'Chaos creates unpredictability. Unpredictability makes it impossible for us to control what follows – where each event or decision will lead. This prevents sentient beings, even those as powerful as the Celestines or the Devilish, from being able to truly direct the course of history.' Some of the manic sparks collided, altering their courses, until, gradually, their paths began to coalesce. 'No individual action or choice stands alone: they interact with other events, becoming affected by them. So over time, no matter how chaotic or unpredictable the choices, they inevitably form a pattern together. Order cannot prevent chaos, yet out of chaos always comes order.'

The sparks had now become a cosmos in miniature, orbiting around one another in mesmerising and oddly beautiful ways. Kind of like the woman who'd conjured them.

'That's . . .' I hesitated, trying to wrap my head around the concept. 'That's how your magic works, how you "bring forth" someone's destiny. You accelerate the chaos around them. You don't affect the decisions or events themselves, but instead cause the collisions between those decisions and events to intersect sooner?'

Eliva'ren slid her waistcoat on, then glanced at the dress she'd worn last night as if contemplating whether to keep it. I didn't need to predict the interactions of chaotic events to know she was going to leave it there on the floor. She came to stand before me, making me feel oddly vulnerable being naked in front of her like that. She sensed my discomfort, because she smiled and kissed me for what I presumed would be the last time. 'I don't get to decide anyone's destiny, not really,' she said, then stood up on her tiptoes and whispered in my ear, 'But I'm sorry all the same, Cade Ombra.'

She started for the door, but before she got there Corrigan said, 'Umm . . . hello? Aren't we going to kill her now?'

'No,' I replied.

'Because you've got some brilliant plan to defeat her later?' he asked.

'No.'

315

'Because you've gone soft and you're in love with this lunatic?'

Everyone was watching me, waiting for my answer. There was something amusing about the fact that they were far more enthralled by the idea that I was in love with the Spellslinger than they'd been about whether I had a plan to stop her and her bosses from bringing the world to an end. I decided to make them wait and went to the corner where my new coat, shirt and trousers lay in a heap on the floor. Before I got there, a bolt of indigo lightning obliterated them, fogging the air with charred fragments of expensive cloth.

'You expect me to save the world naked?' I asked, staring at the sooty remains of my beautiful clothes.

'Forget it, Cade,' Corrigan said angrily. 'I'm done with your idiocy. We all are. You said we were going to be a team of heroes and all you've done is lead us from one disaster to another.' I heard the sound of a pack being dropped onto the floor, the string ties being opened. 'From now on, we do things my way.'

Now that I was freed from the wards they'd put in my cell back in the fortress, I had any number of ways of taking down Corrigan – well, at least one. I couldn't, though. It wasn't just that he was my best friend in a profession that didn't lend itself to friendship, but that, truth be told, he was right. Nothing I'd done had dissuaded the Lords Celestine and Lords Devilish from their war. If anything, like Eliva'ren and her chaos magic, I'd brought our doom closer.

'Okay,' I said, 'let's try your way, Corrigan.'

I turned, half expecting him to blast me from existence, or at least to punch me hard enough in the face to do some serious damage. Instead, he was holding up a long dark leather coat in one hand, with matching trousers, a burgundy shirt and a belt in the other. Emblazoned on the breast of the coat in that same burgundy were a pair of lightning bolts forming the number seven. I could see more of the ridiculous outfits spilling out of the bag. The others picked through them to find theirs.

'*Uniforms?*' I asked. '*That's* your idea of taking control?'

He tossed me the coat and trousers, then wielding the belt like a whip, waited for me to dress. 'We're all going to die, Cade. That's what happens in the real world when you take on competing armies of supernatural morons. I don't blame you for leading me to my death. All I ask is that we look cool while dying.'

I heard light, mostly restrained laughter from near the door. Eliva'ren stood there watching us, amusement and sadness in her eyes, and a terrible longing for something she had never known and hadn't realised she had so desperately wanted. We exchanged looks for a moment as I dressed myself in Corrigan's preposterous idea of a heroic uniform, and in those silent glances an entire conversation took place: a pleading on my part that she reconsider, a steely rejoinder that, unlike me, she knew where all this was heading, and that she had long ago decided that the only fate she cared about was that of her son; a suggestion that maybe her unyielding resolve was precisely what made doom for all of us so certain. An apology, and a farewell.

We let her walk away, listening to the sound of her footsteps as she descended the stairs.

'Yes,' I said once she was gone.

'Yes, to what?' Corrigan asked, buttoning up his own dark leather coat and discovering that his was a little too tight.

'You asked a moment ago whether the reason I was letting her leave was because I'd fallen in love with her. The answer is yes. I'm positively nuts for this woman, Corrigan. I've got no plan, no strategy for how we can stop what's coming for us. Even if the Aurorals and Infernals manage not to destroy each other and half the world when they get here – which is highly unlikely – or they don't end up blowing up the other half in a witless attack on the Pandoral, it's almost certain that what happens after will trigger this "doom" the Spellslinger was hired to bring about, which is apparently also the only way she can save her son from the Pandoral realm. There's no plausible way the seven of us can prevent any of that from happening!'

I was breathing too fast, my heart was pounding and the aches and pains of my incarceration by the Pandoral's minions suddenly flared up like the torture was happening all over again. I couldn't get enough air into my lungs and I knew – knew more clearly than anything I'd ever known before – that this was entirely the wrong time to have an emotional breakdown in front of the only six people on this plane who might at least try to save the world.

It took every ounce of discipline I'd learned among the Glorians, every perverse impulse I'd ever acquired from the Infernals, and a touch of something considerably more dangerous than both – I believe decent people call it 'honesty' – to continue.

'On the positive side,' I managed between gasps, 'if by some miracle we survive this, I'm thinking of asking the Spellslinger to be my girlfriend.'

Nobody laughed, not even a quiet titter. They remained dead silent for an uncomfortably long time. Finally – and unexpectedly – it was Shame who spoke for all of them. 'This has always been a fight over whether the fate of this realm should be determined by gods or mere Mortals. To risk everything on sentiment seems a profoundly ... *human* course of action.'

'I like it,' Galass said, her jaw set in that way of hers that refused to accept that fate or circumstance could rule our lives.

'The Spellslinger better have been *really* good in bed, is all I'm saying,' Corrigan grumbled, though his grin was wide and full of that wild impulse to go out and die fighting impossible odds.

Temper thumped his foot several times, causing the whole floor to shake, which I guessed was him agreeing. Then he grinned at me, showing his fangs, and I wasn't entirely sure what he was trying to convey.

It was Alice who surprised me most, though, because she spoke so quietly, I almost hadn't heard her until I saw the tears in her eyes. That's when I understood what she'd said.

'*I would like to die for love.*'

Strangest coven of wonderists this plane of reality or any other has or will ever see, I thought.

I headed for the door. 'Come on,' I told the others. 'Let's go and kick destiny in the face and save the world.'

We were halfway down the stairs when I stopped.

'What's wrong?' Galass asked, crashing into me.

I turned and looked up at Corrigan near the back. Pinching the lapel of my leather coat, I asked, 'Did you really – while I was being held captive and tortured to enact a spell that would've destroyed the entire Mortal realm – did you *seriously* stop somewhere to get custom-tailored outfits made?'

'It only took a day,' he admitted sheepishly. 'We'd stopped for supplies anyway, and I saw this tailor's shop run by a florinist who uses her abilities to shape and weave all kinds of fabrics . . .'

A day. Most people don't last an hour under torture, never mind a day. And this hulking brute of a thunderer camped out in a tailor's shop somewhere for an entire twenty-four hours getting uniforms made instead of racing madly to rescue me.

'Why are you smiling like that?' Shame asked, trying to replicate my smile on her own face. It wasn't working too well.

I wasn't sure how to answer, because unless you understand the twisted mind of Corrigan Blight, you'll never be able to make sense of the fact that the only reason he would delay rescuing me to get these stupid uniforms made was because he hadn't harboured a single doubt – not even the slightest hesitation – that I would not only resist the Pandoral's torture but find a way to escape before he and the others got here.

Of course he was absolutely right.

Bow down ye gods and devils, for I am Cade fucking Ombra, we are the Malevolent fucking Seven, and we're here to fuck you up but good.

CHAPTER 44

Armies of Gold and Crimson

Upon the wide plain outside the ruins of the fortress in which I'd been held prisoner, two armies prepared to wage a war unlike any other – and those preparing to do the fighting had been misled, both about their enemy and about their odds of victory.

'Smaller than I was expecting,' Corrigan observed.

The seven of us had left the dubious safety of the town walls to trudge back along the same road where I'd carried Eliva'ren yesterday. We'd passed increasing numbers of other travellers, mostly farmhands and labourers, fleeing in the opposite direction. The two armies had approached the fortress from either side and looked ready to race for the ruins as if it were some giant stone flag to be captured the moment a neutral referee could be found to ring the starting bell. The Infernals had divisions of Demoniac Hellions, Malefic Artillerists, even a handful of Devilish Cavaliers mounted on hideous beasts who looked like they weren't at all meant for this world and wouldn't long survive their visit.

The Aurorals had come with a far more magnificent cavalry of Glorian Parevals mounted on silver-coated steeds whose gold-shod feet barely deigned to touch unconsecrated ground. Alongside them were contingents of Glorian Ardentors and Angelic Valiants. As with the Infernals, these elite divisions were small in number. The bulk of each army was made up of ill-trained Mortal recruits, who were being deployed far earlier than anyone had intended. I didn't expect that would make them feel much better about their imminent brutal slaughter.

I believe professional military strategists refer to these situations as 'shit-storms waiting to happen'.

'What do they hope to accomplish?' Galass asked.

The answer lay in the grim, iron-jawed expressions of the twelve Lords Celestine at the front of the Auroral army, armoured in gleaming gold and bearing silver and gold weapons so classical in design as to be archaic. They looked as if they were posing for heroic portraits rather than preparing to fight.

The thirteen Lords Devilish opposing them bore crimson-etched black armour and weapons more devious and crueller in design.

Neither side cared much for heroism.

'I never knew,' I said quietly, more to myself than anyone else. 'I never really understood.'

'Understood what, Fallen One?' asked Alice. The absence of her customary sneer when she called me 'Fallen One' unmasked her own disquiet. She and I were perhaps the only beings alive to have been shaped by both the Aurorals and Infernals.

'This is *all* they've ever wanted,' I replied staring at the expressions on the faces of the Lords Devilish. They might look ugly and gleeful compared to the glorious noble countenances of their enemies, but their expressions mirrored those of the Lords Celestine. 'They don't care about ruling over the Mortal realm or winning the contest of souls. They don't mind the prospect of losing and being eradicated for ever. That's how badly they crave this fight.'

Among wonderists, there's a kind of unspoken, tacit recognition that magic is addictive: a drug with as many intoxicating variants as there are different spells within each planar attunement. We all talk about magic as if it's a set of tools that gives us an advantage over others in getting what we want, but that's just the lie we tell ourselves. Casting spells, exerting power over others and the world around us . . . *it feels good*. It's better than liquor or sex or the admiration of the mob. When we speak of spells as breaches into other planes where the laws of physics operate differently, thus triggering a momentary violation to the natural order of this realm, we're burying the most meaningful word. That's what magic is, and what makes it so perversely pleasurable: it's the chance to *violate* nature, to *violate* other sentient beings.

There's a word for people who do that sort of thing for pleasure.

But we wonderists are still limited by our human bodies. We can handle only so much magic, which is why Tempestoralists like Corrigan often die drawing too much lighting or aethereal fire into themselves, and blood mages like Galass go mad with the rush of manipulating too much of the life force of others. Even angelics like Shame lose themselves in the twisting of their own bodies to match the desires of those around them.

The Lords Devilish and Lords Celestine aren't like us. They have made themselves into vessels with almost limitless capacities to channel magical forces. However, in their sudden urgency to destroy the Pandoral threat, they were beginning their war too soon, before they'd finished recruiting every possible Mortal soul to fuel their Auroral and Infernal magics.

From the ruins of the fortress a faint buzzing turned into a gale of beating insect wings announcing the Pandoral. He rose from the debris, the swarm of tiny, gleaming carapaced insects drawing pieces of stone and metal and whatever else they could find into the spaces between them, until the Pandoral loomed like a titan, at least a hundred feet tall, facing opponents whose eagerness to destroy him was a mere prelude to the violations they intended to commit upon one another.

'Both sides have fallen into the same trap,' Aradeus said. Rat mages always have especially good insight into the intricacies of tactical situations. 'The Celestines and Devilish will attack, but their charge will be inefficient, as they won't be working together. Nonetheless, the combined assault will, sooner or later, overwhelm the Pandoral.'

'At which point they'll begin attacking one another,' Galass said, arms outstretched, fingers weaving in the air in tandem with the scarlet tresses of her hair. 'Cade, I can feel their bloodlust. It's . . . it's all-consuming.'

'Focus on something else,' I warned her. 'Don't get locked into the flow of their life forces because pretty soon those life forces are going to get snuffed out and you won't be able to pull away.'

'What do we do?' Alice asked, her whip-sword drawn but dangling limply by her side. Neither she nor it had any idea who to fight. 'How can we prevent this from happening?'

'You can't,' said a voice. I recognised it immediately, with its irritating timbre and perpetually fabricated sincerity. A clawed hand patted my shoulder companionably. 'Best you and your pals get a move on, Cade,' said my former Infernal agent. 'What's got to be is going to be.'

I steeled myself inside, covering up a dozen competing emotions with a veneer of amiability as casually impervious to scrutiny as that of any diabolic. 'Glad you're not dead, old buddy,' I said to Tenebris as I turned to face him.

He grinned. 'Me? I'm a survivor, Cade.' He poked me in the centre of the chest with his clawed forefinger. 'Like you.'

Trumpets began to blare from either side of the looming Pandoral, the brilliant brassiness of the Auroral horns rendered discordant by the reediness of the Infernal instruments.

'Ugh,' Tenebris groaned, covering his ears momentarily. 'Why does our side always have to sound like fucking untuned clarinets?' The question was rhetorical, because he immediately answered, 'You know why our horns sound so shitty? Because a couple of the Lords Devilish like it that way and the others don't give a crap, which means the rest of us have to suffer from their lousy ear for music.'

'A metaphor, perhaps?' Aradeus asked, twirling the strands of his moustache. Unlike Alice, he'd kept his rapier in its scabbard, knowing it would serve no purpose to draw steel against what was unfolding on that ill-fated field before us.

'Exactly,' Tenebris agreed. 'That's what's screwed up both realms for millennia. Twelve Celestines and thirteen Devilish: twenty-three guys who fought their way to the top and then decided to play at being gods over everyone else.'

'Then why not rebel?' Galass asked. 'Join our cause—'

He waved away both her plea and her idealism. 'Because when the guys on top have cannons to shoot you with, you don't come at them with wooden sticks, girly.'

At last, we'd come to it: the scheme beneath all the other schemes. The reason why everything I had tried to do had been doomed from the start. In fact, we were half to blame for what was about to happen.

The other half, though?

'It was you, all along, wasn't it?' I asked Tenebris, working through the tiny, almost insignificant details of the past few weeks. Our first encounter with the Spellslinger, when she'd taken control of one of the Angelic Valiants and brought forth her doom, which had led me to seek out information from the Infernals because they were the most likely culprits. That had led us to that secret prison and the three captive diabolics, two of whom Tenebris had made sure were dead so there'd be no alternative but to free him. Shit. And when the Spellslinger had finally shown up in person, it had been at Tenebris' restaurant. From there, the meeting with the Lords Celestine, our capture by the Lords Devilish, the mission to take the Glorian Banner and my subsequent kidnapping by the Pandoral minions, who'd been tricked into thinking they were pulling one over on the Devilish . . .

But no ... Tenebris' influence had begun even earlier.

'*You're* the one who devised the plan to kill the Seven Brothers up in the Blastlands,' I continued. 'You orchestrated the ruse to turn them into gates so the Celestines and Devilish could come to the Mortal realm and begin their Great Crusade, knowing all along that they would screw it up and you'd be able to turn them against one another.'

'Why?' Shame asked Tenebris. It was unusual for her to care about such things, but I suppose with the world ending and all ... 'You sounded so committed to the plans of the Devilish – so dedicated to the Infernal cause.'

'I'm a patriot,' Tenebris said without irony as he polished his claws against his crimson brocaded coat. 'And like any patriot, I'm loyal right up to the point where my rulers turn out to be absolute fucking morons who're going to ruin everything we're supposed to stand for.' He looked at me, apparently expecting some acknowledgment of his assessment.

I didn't give him any.

'We Infernals believe in embracing experience, Cade. We're about *living* – here, now. The Aurorals, they think life is only a practice exam for some other, more perfect existence. But this Great Crusade?' He swung an arm towards the armies who were about to attack the Pandoral. 'There's nothing to *experience* here; it's just one endless slog of drudgery and misery. And thanks to those half-witted Lords Celestine with their so-called "virtues", it'll keep going on for ever – there's no end to the exam, no perfect "other existence". But no matter how many of us – on *both* sides – urged them to reconsider, those dumb fucks refused. The bosses are the betrayers, not us.'

'How many of you?' I asked.

His gaze shied away briefly. 'Let's just say, I represent a consortium of like-minded individuals in key positions within both camps. Unlike most of the Lords Celestine and Lords Devilish, these individuals are capable of envisioning a future in which the Mortal realm and all its opportunities are, if not shared, then let's say, split down the middle. Under the right leadership, of course.'

Most of the Lords Celestine, he'd said. I glanced back at the Auroral army. The Twelve Virtues stood at the very front of the line. One of them *might* have sensed my presence, as her head turned. I could've sworn she'd winked at me.

Shit, I thought ruefully, *if it turns out the traitor within the Auroral Hierarchy is the one Celestine I slept with, Corrigan will* never *let me live it down. Not that living is likely to be a concern of mine for long.*

'So, a new bunch of fucks to take the place of the old bunch of fucks,' Corrigan said. He sounded pleased that the universe was proving to be just as corrupt as he'd always claimed.

'Not as many, though,' Tenebris insisted, as if that was important. 'Twelve Celestines and Thirteen Devilish is way too many.' He grinned at me, his fangs gleaming in the early morning light. 'Can't have twenty-three gods in the pantheon, am I right?'

I probably shouldn't have slugged him. Given how well he'd been manipulating events, it was highly likely that within a matter of hours, Tenebris was going to be some sort of demi-god. But I had it on good authority that I myself was only hours away from dying. Possibly even minutes. Mostly, though, I thumped him because the banality of my former agent's ambitions pissed me off.

'You're going to regret that, Cade,' the diabolic informed me as he got back to his feet. 'I was going to go easy on you on account of us having a history together, but now—'

I slugged him again, harder this time, then turned to the others. 'Listen, I'm going to try something. All evidence suggests it's going to fail, but I can't think of a better plan and I don't intend to sit out this disaster without putting up some sort of a fight.'

I expected questions, or at least dubious looks, so I was kind of taken aback when Alice asked, 'Is this plan of yours righteous?'

I wasn't sure how to answer that. It had been a long time since justice had been any concern of mine, but I found myself nodding. 'I think . . . I think it might be the most righteous thing I've ever done.'

Her whip-sword stiffened, the segments rattling together into a gleaming blade whose hilt she held to her heart. Weirdly, on demoniacs the heart is just above the belly. 'I am Aliciaj Meharcorum Jedashaavethan Bestrezaada—' followed by a bunch of other barely intelligible parts of her demoniac lineage that were painful to hear until she got to the last part: '. . . daughter of Hazidan Rosh and a *true* Glorian Justiciar. Give me my orders, First Paladin. I will not fail you.'

Daughter? I repeated that silently to myself. Hazidan Rosh was going to have some explaining to do when next we met. If we ever met again.

'I join my . . .' Shame hesitated, then smiled distantly as if this were a private joke. 'I join my sister in this oath. Having only recently begun to appreciate humanity's foibles, I am loath for my education to end so soon.'

'Oh, shit. We're supposed to get all sentimental again?' Corrigan grumbled, but he was smiling when he punched me in the arm, hard enough to numb my shoulder, as usual. 'Tell me who to blow up and those fuckers will be most certainly obliterated.'

'And I—' began Aradeus, then Shame clamped her hand over his mouth and whispered in his ear. After she pulled away, he looked at her and asked quietly, 'Really? *That's* how I sound? I was merely trying to be—'

'Go on,' I told him. Calamity was unfolding less than a hundred yards away and time was growing short, but some things are worth the risk, you know? 'Give us the speech, Aradeus.'

He did. It was pompous, poncey and way too fucking long, and I didn't tear up even once and you can't prove otherwise.

'We're ready, Cade,' Galass said. She *was* crying her eyes out, but, you know, teenagers. Everything's either the greatest love *ever* or the *total* end of the world. 'Tell us what to do.'

I swear to whatever gods never existed, not to mention the ones I was so desperate to ensure never arose, it was Temper who broke me. He placed his paw on my shoulder, lifted it to my cheek, and said, 'Motherfucker' with such understanding for what I was about to attempt, such fondness, such . . . *love*.

Damn it.

'Okay,' I said, pulling myself together. 'Let's go and be heroes.'

CHAPTER 45

Making Friends and Enemies

I raced towards the ruins of the fortress beneath the raging Pandoral, beset by spells both Infernal and Auroral being hurled at him. Blazing globes of golden light enveloped the giant man-shaped swarm, exploding in a shower of sparks even as inky-black tendrils of Infernal magic burrowed between the myriad insects making up his gargantuan form and tore at him from the inside. In return, he smashed his right fist down upon troops of Demoniac Hellions, while with his left palm he crushed a cavalry of Glorian Parevals, their gleaming armour cracking open like the shells of crabs. All the while, cheers of imagined imminent victory rose up from both sides. I didn't need the Pandoral spell I was using to warp the distance between me and the Lords Celestine to see the sheen of almost erotic ecstasy on their faces. Rationality shot me a grin, as if the two of us were in on this wonderful joke and that later on we'd be rekindling our relationship.

Not fucking likely, sister. If I'm going to get murdered by a beautiful woman, I'm sticking with the one who at least has a decent excuse for killing me.

I stopped before we reached the rear lines, already short of breath. In my defence, that was mostly on account of being terrified.

Now, how does one attract the attention of a hundred-foot-tall extra-dimensional being without having him crush you underfoot?

I conjured up one of the few Pandoral spells I'd learned, the same one I'd used to accidentally bring Temper here. This time my target was far closer and much, much smaller.

Come on, you buzzing little bastard, I thought, feeling the resistance from my target. *Come to Uncle Cade and let me transform you into something uncomfortable and gross.*

'Deceiver!' shouted a golden-armoured figure atop an impressively large white horse. He was carrying a spear and riding in my direction. 'Now shall the foulness of thine deeds return to thy breast, carried by the sharp edge of my steel!'

Ah, crap. It was Propriety. Guess he'd finally got wise to my lunatic conspiracy theories.

'Wait!' I shouted back, struggling to hold onto my spell before the insect escaped my feeble tether. 'It's not what you think – I'm secretly working on behalf of the Auroral Sovereign! You must join me in this noble—'

I like to think that there was a look of hesitation on the Ardentor's face and that I might've managed to fool him one last time. Alas, I'll never know, because a bolt of Tempestoral thunder obliterated him into tiny bits of golden shrapnel. Charred Glorian viscera rained down on me.

'Wipe that shit off the coat!' Corrigan called out. 'Those were expensive!'

I ignored his injunction, focusing all my efforts on that one tiny beetle-like insect. He had come from another realm in hopes of conquering this one, and now, once the Aurorals and Infernals got their shit together, he was minutes from being wiped out, he and all his buzzing brothers and sisters. Finally, the bug separated from the others, its flight path staggering as if he were being tugged out of sticky oil by the sheer force of my will. As he flittered angrily towards me, resisting every inch, his body began to change, bloating on whatever bits of matter and energy my Pandoral spell could draw from the surrounding landscape, until tiny insect limbs swelled to the size of a man's arms and legs, the head reshaping itself into jaws which could form words. The head stayed bug-like, which I'd expected. I've no idea why the spell determined that he should have a substantial penis as he stood three feet from me, glaring at me with murderous intent, but the universe is perverse that way.

'Yyyoouuu . . .' he began, his voice eerily like that of the Pandoral itself.

'Quit with the fucking bug voice,' I told him, holding up a hand. 'I specifically altered your physical form so that you and I could have a conversation that wouldn't take longer than either my world or yours . . . well, I guess yours is fucked either way. So, are you ready to listen to reason, or do you want to keep screwing around while the rest of, well, *you* gets obliterated?'

Hesitation. The spell had left him his insect wings and he tried to fly away, but I'd intentionally made them just a little too small to hold him aloft, so he just floated a few inches off the ground before losing his balance and falling on his face. I don't know why I find winged creatures being unable to actually fly so funny. Maybe I once had a bad experience with a chicken as a kid.

'Well?' I asked again. I gestured to the onslaught the rest of his swarm was suffering under all those gold and crimson spells.

The bug-being rose to his feet and crossed his stick-like insect arms. 'Fine, you prick,' he said in a perfectly reasonable-sounding human voice. 'What the fuck do you want?'

I'd fashioned the spell to transform the target into something capable of proper conversation without it being able to sting me to death or suck my eyeballs out in the middle of our negotiations. Once again, I was grateful for Hazidan Rosh's incessant demands that I make a *proper* study of the elements of wonderism, rather than just get excited about blowing things up like *some* people I could name.

Another bolt of Tempestoral fury, this one more fire than lightning, erupted about fifteen feet to my left, where a couple of Demoniac Hellions had decided to break ranks to stab me with their tridents.

Tridents. I tell you, some beings have no shame.

'I'm guessing you still share sentience with the rest of your swarm,' I said to my transmogrified bug delegate, 'so I don't have to have this conversation ten thousand times. You're about to get destroyed, and once that happens, the Pandoral realm will have no guardians. I'll be forced into becoming a gate to your realm, and whatever's left of what you call a people will also be destroyed. Basically, you're fucked.'

'So are you,' the bug-being said nonchalantly. However, he uncrossed and crossed his arms defiantly, which is always a sign of anxiety.

'So, that's one thing you and I have in common. The other is that we both hate the Lords Celestine and the Lords Devilish. Unfortunately, they're far, far stronger than you or I will ever be.'

'You, perhaps,' said the bug-being, uncrossing his arms, then not sure what to do with his hands. 'We, however, are eternal. We are—'

I cut him off by reconfiguring my spell and removing his mouth. Honestly, I don't like screwing with the bodies or free will of others, but I didn't have time for this nonsense. 'Listen, arsehole, this is a simple proposition. You're on the verge of extinction. My people? Humans? We'll survive. I mean, sure, our lives will be utter shit, but we're adaptable like that. Practically unkillable – like cockroaches, which are insects in the Mortal realm that, unlike you guys, aren't about to be exterminated. So, here's my deal. You're going to do exactly what I ask, which is going to suck worse than almost anything you can imagine – the "almost" in this case being the alternative, which, I shouldn't have to remind you, is obliteration. In return, if we're both very, very lucky, at the end of this there'll still be a Pandoral realm, it won't be collapsing in on itself, and the Infernals and Aurorals will get their noses figuratively broken.'

Literally broken, too, if I have anything to say about it.

'Now,' I continued, pointing to the bug-being's face, 'I'm not wasting another spell giving you your mouth back, so just nod if we've got a deal. And before you concoct any thoughts of betraying me' – I drew on the Pandoral energies being unleashed by the swarm to cause the air around me to warp and shimmer, which is not as impressive as an Auroral glow, but it got the point across – 'I might not be able to defeat your boss or your swarm or whatever the hell you are, but I can still mess with the forces you need to draw on to fight back against the Aurorals and Infernals until you're wiped out. With that in mind, do we have a deal?"

I guess the rest of the swarm were getting pretty beaten up, because my newfound bug-faced ally didn't hesitate before nodding.

'Good,' I said, then, because I'm actually a nicer guy than I might make myself sound sometimes, I used up some of the Pandoral energies I'd summoned to return him to his natural form. He flew back to rejoin his swarm, and I caught a subtle shift in the massive head of the Pandoral as he too nodded his agreement.

I looked back at Corrigan and gave the signal. Once the Aurorals and Infernals figured out what I was attempting, all hell would break loose. My friends would have to protect me from more attacks than any gang of misfit wonderists could long hope to repel. Meanwhile, I'd have my own battle on my hands.

Closing my eyes briefly, I drove my hands into the air in front of me, using my attunement to form a breach between this realm and the source of my abilities. Once it opened, I took hold of it and pulled it into me.

Okay, Cade, I told myself in the way self-centred morons always hesitate before doing what they know can't be avoided any longer, *let's be honest. Your time on this plane of existence hasn't contributed much to humanity. You were a smug, self-righteous bastard when you joined the Glorian Justiciars and a whiny, self-righteous prick when you became a mercenary war mage. Now six of the bravest lunatics this misbegotten universe ever spawned are throwing away their lives so you can do this one thing that's probably not going to work because . . .*

Okay, I admitted to myself, *it turns out I am pretty shitty at pep talks. Maybe let Aradeus or Galass give the speeches from now on.*

I don't know why, but that thought brought a smile to my lips – maybe the last I would ever have to offer this unfortunate little world of my birth. But that smile also reminded me that whatever villain I'd been in life, in death, I was damn well going out a hero.

Right, I thought, expanding the breach within my chest, *time to unleash a little chaos.*

CHAPTER 46

Blind Spots

I hadn't made much of a study of pandoralist magic in the six months since I'd foolishly attuned myself to that realm of pure chaos rather than something less suicidal. Truth be told, I'd hoped I'd never need to draw on it, other than to one day scare the shit out of the Lords Devilish and Lords Celestine, who understood and feared its cataclysmic potential far better than I did. Oh, I'd intuited a few of the esoteric mechanics involved, most of which involved warping living beings and physical space into alternate variations of what nature had intended. In practical terms, this meant I was mostly good for tearing stuff apart in disturbing and grotesque ways. The one time I'd attempted something more sophisticated, I'd found myself in a punch-up with a seven-foot-tall not-quite-rabbit creature from another plane of existence that I'd accidentally turned into a vampire – which don't even exist on the Mortal realm any more. Well, they do now, thanks to me.

All of this made the endeavour on which I'd gambled all our lives especially precarious. I had to transform my body into a living gate between our world and the Pandoral realm, and I absolutely, unquestionably had to get it right on the first try. After that? Well, after that probably wasn't going to matter because she wasn't going to let me get that far.

'I warned you it would come to this,' Eliva'ren said, 'that it would come down to the two of us.'

I hadn't planned on opening my eyes, but the sadness in her voice took me by surprise. I'd expected a coldness between us as we reverted to the enemies our respective destinies had intended us to be before our spectacularly odd 'date'. Business was business, after all, and the Spellslinger's left little room for sentiment.

'Why did you have to be who you are?' Eliva'ren asked, tears filling her eyes. She wasn't even trying to hide the pain, which in turn, tore at my own emotional defences. 'Why couldn't you have been a proper Glorian Justiciar who didn't care about anything but following Divine Will? Or a narcissistic Infernalist who would have walked away from this mess the first time I showed you what I could do to you and your friends?'

I'm no expert on affairs of the heart, but it seems to me that it's pretty easy to fool yourself into believing you're in love when everything else around you is falling apart. Even now, the sight of her, the ache of her voice ... It was as if the colour of her skin, the shape of her eyes, the curve of her lips, even when she frowned, were all part of a language that I had never before spoken yet had known for ever. When I'd left the Justiciars and the Auroral song had been stripped from me, I'd taken it for granted that for the rest of my life there would be a hole inside me that nothing else could fill. Some observers – cynical pricks, I assume – might suggest a couple of attempts at killing one another followed by an – admittedly excellent – first date hardly qualified as a replacement for the majesty of the Auroral Song, but I was only just beginning to learn the terrible, heart-rending, reckless, wondrous truth: love really is all it's cracked up to be.

Now that love was threatening to tear me apart faster than the Pandoral energies currently transforming my flesh and bones into a portal. The experience was exactly as unpleasant as it sounds, but there's something to be said for mercenary work: I'd grown accustomed to finishing the jobs I'd agreed to take on, even the stupid ones.

'Who would you have preferred me to be?' I managed to say, expanding the Pandoral rift inside me. It was getting harder to speak and my consciousness was threatening to sever itself from my physical body.

Eliva'ren bridged the distance between us. She was drawing on her own bizarre esoteric energies, cloaking herself in the destiny magic that would enable her to hasten the doom she had, in her way, tried to keep me from. Her hand on my cheek, the warmth of her fingertips and the raw *humanity* of her touch, helped me hold on. 'I wanted you to be a knight without resolve,' she replied. 'I would have had you be a courtier who swept me off my feet and into his bed, only to abandon me at daybreak without a second thought. A priest who gave rousing sermons in the morn, only to give in to temptation at night.' Now it was she who closed her eyes as if to squeeze away the tears. 'I wish you'd been someone who could've beaten me,' she whispered.

All around us, the war raged, between four different sides now. The Celestines and Infernals were trying to direct most of their efforts against the Pandoral, but many of their troops couldn't wait and were tearing into their ancient enemies, even as their comrades fell wherever the Pandoral's gigantic fists struck. My friends were beleaguered too, fending off the attacks Tenebris directed at me – having known me a while, he wasn't taking any chances despite his confidence in my inevitable defeat.

'It's over,' Eliva'ren told me. 'Everything you've done has followed the same path to this same doom. Why can't you see that?'

I shrugged, or tried to. I wasn't sure how much of what lay beneath my skin was actually muscle and bone any more. 'I guess I've always prided myself on being unpredictable.'

'But you *aren't* – that's what I've been trying to show you, Cade! Every decision you've made – *every single one* – has brought us to this exact moment. Even this final gambit, making a last-minute deal with the Pandoral entity to give him an avenue of escape because you think once he's back in his realm he'll be able to access the full might of its chaos magic – you think the Celestines and Devilish will be forced to flee back to their own realms and be denied their war.'

'Sounds . . . like a . . . good plan,' I said. I was starting to choke, but only because my lungs weren't really lungs any more.

She slammed her fist against my chest, which hurt more than it should have, given what was happening to me. 'This is *exactly* what my employers wanted you to do all along, Cade!'

Yeah, Tenebris always has been a little too cunning for anyone's good. Can't believe the Lords Devilish never saw him coming.

My body felt as if it were coming apart, but it was only Eliva'ren shaking me, shouting in my face as if this was all my fault. 'I'm going to collapse the Pandoral realm, Cade. I'm going to bring forward its eventual demise by thousands of years so that the limitless energies there flow back into this realm while I twist your attunement first to Infernalism and then Auroralism, channelling all that power into Tenebris and his cabal. They're going to become gods!' She swung an arm to the battlefield. 'Look at what's already happening! The Celestines and Devilish are beginning to fall. The cabal will take their place, but a hundred times more powerful than they ever were, all because of you—'

'Not only me,' I reminded her.

All her anger and despair drained from her, leaving only determination behind. 'You can't imagine what it's like to have given birth to a son you've never seen, knowing his entire life is being spent in a place where he's utterly unlike any other living being that exists there. Nine years my child has lived in the Pandoral realm, raised by an illusion, wondering why his real mother never comes to rescue him.' She hit me again, a right cross to the jaw this time. I barely felt it at all. 'Damn you for making me hate myself even more than I thought possible!'

I'd worked out most of the details of how Eliva'ren's son had been kept alive all these years and how Tenebris intended to bring him back here. With the energies he'd channel through me from the Pandoral realm as it collapsed, he'd have more than enough power to transform the boy's physical body into one that could survive on the Mortal plane. He'd probably even recreate the breach to Eliva'ren's home so that mother and son could reunite with their own people. My failure to master Pandoral magic aside, I'd studied almost every other form of wonderism, and had a knack for esoteric theory. The mechanics of this scheme were intricate, almost beautiful in their way. But as flawless as they looked, there was one missing piece in the clockworks of destiny: an extra gear Eliva'ren had been incapable of seeing.

'I'd imagine it's uncomfortable for someone who can perceive the dooms of everyone and everything around them to be surprised,' I said to her. My voice was weaker, little more than a whisper. Whatever was left of my insides was held together with Pandoral energies, but I fought to make sure she could hear me over the din of battle.

'Fate is never surprised, Cade. How can you still not see that?'

I glanced back at the war being waged by the oh-so-gullible Lords Celestine and Devilish against the Pandoral. The swarm was thin now, mostly a person-shaped cloud of erratically buzzing insects that weren't long for this world, or any other.

Eliva'ren didn't hear me.

'What?' she asked. Thousands of images were appearing and disappearing all around her now in a wild dance of potentiality so strong that I could feel them tugging against the chaos of my own attunement.

'I said, Fate can't see itself.'

She stared back at me, sympathy for my impending doom giving way to resignation. 'Your consciousness is coming apart, Cade. It won't be long now.' She reached out and touched me again, but this time there was nothing human connecting us. This was power against power, chaos against inevitability. Had I been given an entire lifetime to master my attunement, still I couldn't have beaten her. Then again, I had no plans to do so.

'Ever since—' I coughed, which is a strange sensation when your throat and lungs are no longer made of flesh. 'Ever since I met you, you've shown me how easily you can see the destinies and dooms of others.' Pain assailed me; it was getting harder to make myself heard. 'But . . . but it occurred to me that you've never spoken about your own destiny, Eliva. Not once.'

She looked irritated. 'That's not how it works. I can't—'

'You can't see your own influence over the world because the power emanates *from you*. You're always in the eye of the storm. You can predict all the choices, the critical decisions that fork the destinies of others, but only the ones that don't involve you, because you're incapable of perceiving yourself as *part* of another's destiny.'

Her eyes narrowed. 'What are you talking about, Cade?'

It was becoming hard to see her now. A haze was coming over me, my perceptions losing their grip on the Mortal realm. I smiled, or tried to. 'I was never meant to be a hero. I was an angry young man who thought joining the Glorian Justiciars would make me righteous. When that failed, I became a mercenary, convinced that having fallen so far, I was absolved of ever having to care about anyone else.' I couldn't make out the shapes of my friends any more, only the swirl of colours in the eruptions of their magics. 'Then I met a bunch of idiots and too late I discovered that my destiny didn't belong to me any more.'

'It's a nice thought.' I felt sure she was smiling back at me. 'Hold onto that thought for as long as you ca—'

'You're still not getting it, Eliva. You're not seeing how I'm beating you at this game of destinies because you're not seeing yourself in mine. The Cade Ombra who hadn't met you would've done precisely what your abilities are telling you I'm doing right now: negotiated a last-ditch pact with the Pandoral to make my body into a gate so he could get back into his plane of reality and force the Aurorals and Infernals to retreat. But *this* Cade Ombra? The one who met you, who fell in . . . Well, let's just say that *that* guy's got an entirely different plan.'

'Cade, what are you . . . ?' Too late, she finally understood that because she couldn't perceive her own destiny, she was also blind to how someone might make a choice entirely foreign to their own nature because of her. 'Cade, it won't work – you don't understand how the Pandoral realm operates, never mind how to—'

Silently, I let the Pandoral know it was time. The paltry swarm of surviving insects containing what was left of his consciousness flew towards me, a gust of glittering wind. As my sentience finally lost its hold on the gate my body had become, I let it come apart in hundreds, maybe thousands of fragments of consciousness, each one finding a home inside one of the bugs as they flew into the gate inside me. I managed to utter one final message to the remarkable, dangerous and altogether entrancing woman who'd unwittingly brought us both to this moment. After all, when you're the hero, it's important to have the last word.

'Stick around, sweetheart,' I heard what had once been my mouth say. 'I'm going to bring your son back.'

CHAPTER 47

Curtains of Possibility

I entered the Pandoral demesne unencumbered by expectation – or any sort of viable plan. All I'd known about this realm was that its denizens were reputed to be small in number, no more than three hundred beings who stepped onto other planes of existence as tiny bug-like creatures. I'd assumed that swarms of glittering-carapaced flying beetles just happened to be a hardier solution for the Mortal realm than, say, dried leaves or choleric butterflies. Certainly, the evidence suggested that each Pandoral split their individual sentience across a multitude of tiny physical forms, my clearest proof being that my own consciousness was currently divided between the hundred or so bugs that had survived the recent assault.

It was kind of cool, really, fluttering about as a hundred separate pieces of oneself. Gives you an entirely different perspective on solitude. As for the esoteric environment in which I'd found myself, it was like nothing I'd experienced before. I wasn't entirely sure it even qualified as any sort of measurable physical space. I was passing through endless curtains made of shimmering strands of a silky fabric that reflected everything around it, only ... No, those *weren't* reflections. The images were erupting from the strands themselves. Each one contained myriad unfolding events, like tiny stories inscribed along the threads of silk.

The images were incomprehensible at first, until I began to

move through the tendril-like curtains and the events I was seeing became more familiar. People and places I recognised came into existence, lived and died a thousand thousand times in every way imaginable. I saw Corrigan, retired from his career as a mercenary wonderist, telling grand tales to a gaggle of grandchildren. Along the next strand, he was hurling bolts of Tempestoral fury at some sort of Infernal behemoth. In some, he was dying from Tempestoral sickness eating him up inside, despite being the age he'd been when I first met him.

The further I travelled through the curtains, the more I saw myself in those strands. My life unfolded with a multitude of different fates, different dooms. It was difficult to focus on them, although perhaps focus was the wrong word, since I wasn't sure I even had eyes. Though I'd passed through the portal of my own body as a swarm of bugs, now my consciousness persisted inside tiny motes of glittering dust. Was this how the Pandorals experienced their own existences? If so, perhaps it wasn't such a bad way to live.

'You have to pull yourself together,' said a voice behind me, which was odd, since there were so many of me you'd expect at least one of me would've been looking in that direction.

The swarm of dust motes making up my physical being spun in the air, momentarily leaving me dizzy until I was able to ignore the infinite strands of the curtains to observe a boy standing there. He was maybe eight or nine, with dark curly hair and bronze skin.

Well, at least I didn't have to hunt through the entire Pandoral realm to find him, I thought. *Then again, this entire plane might be the size of a back-alley brothel for all I know.*

'Think of hugging yourself,' the boy instructed me, and because apparently he thought I was an idiot, he mimed the gesture. 'You need to create cohesion between all the pieces of yourself, then you can take a proper shape.'

I attempted to do as he suggested. It was harder than I'd expected, because first I had to make all my dust-mote selves spin around one another to prevent them from colliding. The sensation was oddly cramped. After a few seconds – or maybe it was millennia; I had no idea how time worked here – I managed to shape myself into a somewhat formless blob with two spindly arms and one eye stalk.

'Try harder,' the boy told me, placing a hand over his mouth to stifle a giggle.

Cut me some slack, kid. It's my first time at this. I'll bet you were an ugly baby too, once.

After watching me fumble around as an awkward cross between a puddle of goo and a vampire kangaroo, the boy said, more usefully, 'Use the strands to guide you.'

I let my awareness return to the shimmering, dangling tendrils and focused on those in which I was roughly the correct age and not either dead from blood loss (must remember to keep an eye on Temper if I get out of this) or dealing with the charred remains of an arm and leg severed by lightning (thanks, Corrigan).

'We don't have a lot of time,' the boy pointed out unhelpfully.

I felt like swatting his head, but that required a working hand, so I went back to focusing on images of myself inside the strands while 'hugging' myself ever tighter. The sensations became more and more painful, like being crushed under thousands of rocks, until I felt the internal structure of skeleton, connective tissues, muscles and fat pushing back against that constriction. After a few dozen tries, I finally assembled myself into a reasonably Cade-like figure.

'Your smile is crooked,' the boy observed.

'That's the face I make before I slap impolite little snots,' I told him. 'But I make it a policy never to hit a child until I know his name. What's yours?'

'Hamun,' he replied. 'I am Hamun'ren of the House of—' Then he smiled, and damn if he didn't have his mother's smile. Without warning, he rushed over to me and threw his arms round my waist.

His face pressed into my stomach as if he were trying to breathe me in. 'I knew you'd come to find me.'

It was a strange sensation to have a child hug you as if you were really important to him. I'd given up any notions of being a parent when I'd first joined the Glorians, and nothing about my time as an Infernal wonderist had changed that conviction. 'How could you know I would come?' I asked. 'We've never met.'

He let go of me, then dangled his fingers through the shimmering strands around us. They warped and shifted, showing moments that might have been pulled from my life these past ten years, though I couldn't be sure which ones were accurate and which ones mere possibilities. 'I've known you since before I was born, Cade.' He said my name awkwardly, as if he feared being too bold. 'You met my mother when she was still pregnant with me.'

'And you remember events from *before* she gave birth to you?'

'You can find everything here,' he said, tugging on a single shimmering strand. The images trickling down its length showed the same vision I'd seen in the Glorian Archives when Eliva'ren had somehow drawn me to her in the past. 'Everything that touches one's existence, everything that *could* touch one's existence.'

'This is . . .' I was staggering under the implications – all the spells I might have been able to discover being attuned to the Pandoral realm, all futile now because even if I somehow survived the war unfolding on the Mortal realm, Eliva'ren had made it clear this plane of existence was going to be obliterated.

'Hamun,' said a woman's sternish voice: a show of authority mixed with a hint of affectionate amusement. 'What have I told you about conjuring strange men?'

Out of the coruscating curtains stepped Eliva'ren.

No, not Eliva'ren, I quickly realised, *but the manifestation of her the Pandorals conjured to raise her son.*

Aside from the unassuming robes and the basket of bread she was

346

carrying under one arm, she looked much like the woman I'd left behind in my own realm – the woman who'd sworn to bring me to my doom. Before I could ask whether she intended to do so here, someone else spoke, a voice that shook me to my core.

My voice.

'Don't badger the poor kid,' said a lean fellow wearing the sort of long azure coat I generally favoured. He was my age and height, his raven-black hair smoothed back from his forehead. We might've been reflections of one another, except that he greeted me with a patient smile my own mouth wouldn't even know how to form. 'Weird, isn't it?' He came closer, offering himself up for inspection even as he ruffled the boy's hair with fatherly familiarity.

I looked down at Hamun, who was staring back at me with a sheepish expression that couldn't hide his anxiety over how I might react to meeting myself. 'The Pandorals created a . . . a replica of *me* in their realm?'

'Hamun didn't want me to be alone,' the mystical construct of his mother said, then she playfully swatted the back of the boy's head. 'Though why he asked the Pandorals to summon an ill-bred, ill-mannered wonderist instead of any number of worthier suitors is ample proof that children shouldn't dabble in such affairs.'

'Oh, come on, sweetheart,' the other me said, throwing an arm around her shoulder. 'Have I been so bad a husband? I mean, the jokes alone—'

'Ugh,' the other Eliva'ren groaned, then she batted at the shimmering strands around us, sending images of me at all kinds of awkward moments in my life whirling around us. 'Was there not a single path in the life of Cade Ombra in which you were capable of *subtle* humour? Must your entire existence be an endless series of jokes about genitalia and vampire kangaroos?'

'To be fair, most of those are Corrigan's,' I replied, and only in the echo from the other me did I realise we'd spoken at the same time.

Aw, aren't we cute? I thought.

The Eliva'ren who'd raised the son who belonged to a different version of herself looked troubled as she reached out a hand to still the strands around us. They were vibrating at an increasing rate. 'The potentialities are beginning to intertwine. The Pandoral realm is collapsing at last.' She knelt before Hamun and hugged him fiercely. 'You know what must happen now, don't you, my darling? You know what to do?'

He hugged her back, so tightly his feet almost came off the ground. 'I do, Mother.'

'No weeping,' she said, though she herself was crying. 'Everyone has three dooms, my love, and this is the very best of mine.' She gently pulled his arms from around her, then placed his right hand in mine. 'Go with him now. He'll take you to your mother.'

The other Cade grabbed my shoulder, squeezing hard enough to remove any doubt as to the sentiment – if not the words – he was about to convey. 'Hey, shithead. Don't fuck this up, okay?'

'Daddy!' the boy said. 'You're not supposed to swear.'

Cade looked at me, a pained expression on his face. 'Nine years without swearing. Can you imagine what that was like?' Then he grinned at Eliva'ren. 'Though there were a few compensations.'

'Go,' she said to me. 'Hamun will know how to navigate the strands. The two of you must follow what will at first be the mere *potential* of the gate back to your world, through its varying probabilities until you find its inevitability. Don't look back – and whatever you do, don't let yourself be drawn into other potentialities. This realm is about to collapse.'

I felt oddly guilty for the Pandoral being who had helped me get here and was now going to witness the end of his own plane of existence. Then again, he'd known what was coming, and in that brief moment of connection I'd had to him through the bug-being I'd created from one of the insects making up his swarm, he'd reminded

348

me, '*Order is only temporary. Chaos is eternal. The Pandoral realm will arise again, and when it does, you stupid meatsack, we'll come for yours.*'

'Come on, Cade,' the boy said, tugging on my hand. Even as we slipped between glittering strands of potentiality, I paused to glance back at the other me, holding his Eliva'ren in his arms and watching existence crumbling around them.

'Hey, arsehole,' I called out to the me who'd experienced at least a few years of a life I'd never imagined for myself, 'what was it like?'

He didn't have to ask what I was referring to. For a moment, he looked starry-eyed, which was surely just the tears coming. Then he smiled, a smile I badly wished my own lips had ever had reason to shape. 'There are no words, Brother.'

And with that, Hamun and I raced through a landscape without ground or sky or direction with the jaws of oblivion snapping at our heels.

CHAPTER 48

Paths of Potentiality

It's a strange thing, to be led through a kaleidoscopic miasma of collapsing possibilities by a nine-year-old boy. I mean, all that chaos and having events that may or may not have already happened whipping me in the face like slender tree branches through a forest at once dark as midnight yet shimmering from a thousand, thousand stars was, to put it mildly, weird. But the more discomfiting sensation was simply being pulled along by someone else's hand. For all that my life had been one long string of fuck-ups ranging from the merely embarrassing to the nearly cataclysmic, I'd always been in charge of my own destiny.

That sounds laughable right about now, I know, but it's true. The choices – okay, idiot mistakes – I'd made had been mine, not someone else's. I was utterly shit at taking orders, which was at least part of the reason I'd left the Justiciars and entirely why I'd skipped over every other possible career to become a mercenary war mage. I'd even ended up leading our little band of emotionally confused wonderists. And yet here I was, being led around by some kid who seemed to think *he* was in charge.

'Stop ruminating,' Hamun said, yanking me to what I thought was the right but when I actually looked at our direction realised was more like forty-five degrees downwards on a perpendicular axis to— You know what? Let's just pretend we turned right.

'Ruminating's kind of my thing, kid.'

He shoved me back all of a sudden, which I thought was the beginnings of a temper tantrum but turned out to be just another change of direction. 'We're not just moving through space, Da— Cade, I mean.'

Awkward.

Give the kid credit: he knew how to stare; this one made it clear I'd be better off pretending not to have noticed any slip of the tongue on his part. I wondered whether maybe I'd taught him that. He pointed to the curtains of shimmering strands. Their vibrations were becoming ever more unnerving as possibilities collapsed all around us. 'This space we're moving through is made up of potential events constrained by the choices we either have or could make.'

'And we're running out of potential outcomes?'

He nodded. 'We can't go anywhere our choices couldn't lead to, which means we have to keep conceiving alternatives other than the ones that already haven't worked.'

He sounded awfully smart for a kid, but I supposed he'd had a lot of time to think about this stuff. Still, I had to make it clear who was the superior intellect here.

'So you want me to think happy thoughts?'

Hamun rolled his eyes and gave a martyr's sigh I recognised all too well as my own. 'Do you really want to find out what happens when your consciousness is snuffed out because it no longer has a universe in which to exist?'

'Fine. What do we do?'

The vibrations were speeding up but the strands were shimmering less, their odd emanations of images of various possible existences being replaced by a lifeless, formless grey.

'For there to still be a gate for us to exit through, there has to be a path beyond.'

'You mean the Mortal realm on the other side has to not have ended already? Or do you mean I have to not already be dead?'

He grabbed my wrist and pulled me sideways through strands that were shedding their potentialities so fast it was like watching the universe end over and over again. 'It's different from that. The two realms are tethered to one another by *destiny*, not time. You have to make it so the Mortal realm has a destiny that's more likely than the ones in which it falls to the Aurorals or the Infernals.'

I considered that as we ran headlong through what I could now see were an endless series of cataclysmic disasters.

'You know, kid, people accuse me of not knowing my limitations, but you are seriously out of—'

'There's no way out, otherwise!' he shouted at me, and for the first time I could see how scared he was that we wouldn't make it out of here – scared that I was going to fail him. 'There has to be a way to force a new destiny into existence,' he tried to explain. 'You need to think of a set of choices that don't end the way my mother thinks they're going to end!'

We stumbled, which was odd in a place without floor or ground. The greying strands all around us were starting to twist in on themselves now, tying into knots and crumbling into motes of ashes – the stuff of nothingness, I supposed.

'I'm ... I'm sorry, kid. There are no other choices left for me to make back on the Mortal realm. There's no cunning ruse or devious scheme left. I tried everything I could. I think maybe your mother's right, that every person, every place, inevitably arrives at one of three dooms. I've used up all of mine.'

Hamun started to cry, then fought back the tears. 'My da— The other you ... He said this might happen. He told me a secret ... A spell, he called it.'

A deafening crack split the air and I looked up to witness the ceiling of this universe shattering to pieces. Behind it was more of the seamless grey oozing through the fissures of space and even the physical laws that made it possible for space to exist.

'Okay,' I said to Hamun, 'so maybe now's a good time for that spell.'

'Kneel,' he told me.

I wasn't sure what that would do, but I obeyed. 'Now what?' I asked.

Hamun's lips were moving, but he wasn't speaking.

'Kid?'

'I'm trying to remember the words and somatic gestures.'

'Seriously? The other me taught you a spell in case everything fell apart and you couldn't be bothered to memorise it?'

He glared at me, then his eyes widened. 'I think I remember it now. He told me to say—' He slapped me across the face, suddenly, hard as he could, which turned out to be pretty hard, then he got right up in my face and shouted with all the unbridled sanctimony of a nine-year-old boy channelled through the words of a real nasty piece of work, '*Cade Ombra, get your fucking shit together, you dumb-arse motherfucker. You think I'm going to let you fail this boy because you can't figure out how to change his destiny? You found a way to defeat the Seven Brothers and keep the Pandorals from conquering our world. You've outsmarted Lords Devilish and banged*—' Hamun hesitated. 'What does that word mean?'

'Nothing, it's—'

He slapped me again. '*You banged the Presence of the Celestine of Rationality! And if that wasn't enough, you conjured a kangaroo from an entirely different plane of reality and turned him into a fucking vampire. This should be easy, you lazy prick! Now, get off your arse and save my boy, because I don't give a shit if our entire existence disappears for ever, I'll still find a way to come and beat the shit out of you!*' Hamun stopped, panting for breath, then said, 'That's it. That's all of it.'

'No, it's not,' I told him. 'You forgot the last part.'

He looked confused. 'The last part?'

I pointed to my cheek. 'Pretty sure he told you to end that speech by . . .'

Hamun smiled and slapped me upside the head a third time. Funny how you can feel pain when the universe is collapsing all around you. Funny also how a snot-nosed little kid who's just slapped you around and insulted you can be so cu—

Oh, there we go.

Hamun saw my expression. He looked around, seeing nothing at first, for all the strands had turned that same formless grey. But then one turned, just a little, and there, in that mostly-but-not-entirely dead strand, was a single gleaming flicker of possibility.

'How . . . ?' he asked.

I leaped to my feet, grabbed him up in my arms and raced between curtains of oblivion hard as stone for that one thread, that one possible destiny that we hadn't seen before because it hadn't existed.

Because I hadn't yet made it happen.

Faster and faster I ran, the curtains of this wondrous, deadly plane of existence falling all around us until at last we leaped towards that faint flicker of potentiality that I was going to have to make inevitable so that the boy in my arms could finally meet his mother.

CHAPTER 49

Inevitability

Having transformed my body into a portal to that ill-fated plane of existence, I hadn't actually expected to survive the return journey from the Pandoral realm. The only other time I'd seen anyone perform that particular spell had been the Seven Brothers, and when it was over there hadn't been anything left of them but splatters of viscera all over the walls.

But air brushed what was left of my face once more and I felt the boy, Hamun, tumble from my arms, and I heard the gasp of the mother who'd never once, not even at the moment of his birth, held him until this exact moment.

Not a bad way to go, I thought.

They say a hero is defined not by their strength or courage but by their willingness to sacrifice themselves. Actually, I may have made that up. Certainly, it was a self-serving definition of heroism in my case, since it was the only measure by which I qualified for the title. So I was okay with death. I was even okay with a particularly gruesome death. I had returned one small boy to his mother on the eve of the world's end, and if my accomplishment was meagre, didn't that make my sacrifice all the more heroic?

'Hold him together!' I heard Galass shouting, which suggested I still had ears, which was unexpectedly good news. Unfortunately, it appeared I also had nerves.

'Stop your whingeing,' Corrigan bellowed before deafening me and everyone else with a tempest of aetheric lightning bolts intended to keep at bay whoever was currently trying to kill us.

'I can't hold onto his form,' Shame murmured, close enough to my ear that I heard her despite the ringing left behind by Corrigan's Tempestoral spells. Through the agony permeating my entire body, I could feel Shame's fingers moving over my skin, reshaping flesh and bone that was apparently unwilling to be rebound into human form.

'Allow me to assist,' said a youthful voice sounding far more confident than anyone of that age had a right to be.

At first, I figured it must be Hamun – maybe the version of me he'd known in the Pandoral realm had spent these past nine years acquiring mystical insights into how to transform my steadily devolving body into something more closely resembling an adult human male with dark hair and a slightly broken nose. All very logical: a nice bookend to my having rescued him and then him returning the favour.

Then I considered – in the midst of the unspeakable agony which made my torture at the hands of the Lords Devilish and later the Apocalypse Eight feel like mere love taps by comparison – just how irritating that voice had sounded. It was the sort of voice that gave me an uncontrollable urge to punch the speaker's face in, which then reminded me that it was the voice of someone who I had, in fact, once decked, despite him being only eleven years old and more beautiful than any angelic. In my defence, he was a right little shit.

'You!' Shame practically screeched, which wasn't helping my ears recover at all. She barely registers above a long-buried corpse when it comes to emotional reactions, but even *she* had a desperate need to kill this little fucker.

'Ah, ah, ah,' warned Fidick, the boy who'd once tricked me and people far wiser than me into doing his extremely dirty work. Shame had managed to get my eyes vaguely back in their sockets, so I could just make out that beatific, punchable smile of his. 'If you attack me, there will be no one to hold Cade's body together, and Galass can't keep his life's blood flowing by herself.'

Shame looked only slightly hesitant about not ripping the kid's head off, regardless of what it meant to my survival, and I couldn't blame her. Fortunately, Alice stepped up, the segmented blade of her whip-sword twitching like a demoniac's tail. 'Forgive me, Sister, but would it be rude if *I* were to butcher the child on your behalf? I would like to start with his feet.'

I shivered a little at how casually she referred to slicing off the little brat's ankles.

'Well, somebody do something,' Corrigan said, exhaustion evident in the way he was panting. Tempestoral magic is potent, but there's only so much of it even someone as physically hardy as Corrigan can channel. 'In case no one has noticed, most of the Lords Devilish and Lords Celestine are dead, the ones who aren't are fighting off their own men, who've apparently decided that Tenebris and his cabal of careerist pricks are a better bet, and anyone not currently occupied in the battle appears intent on blaming *us* for all the trouble Cade's caused!'

'Fight on, Brother Corrigan,' Aradeus called out cheerfully. In between the blur of his rapier I could see rather a lot of rats gleefully hurling themselves at our foes. 'Temper and I shall have your back every step of the way!'

The kangaroo didn't look all that interested in anyone's back, but he certainly was intent on their throats. The psychotic beast was not only biting the necks of those opponents intent on attacking us, but pausing in between to drink the blood of those already dead.

'You're going to give yourself a tummy ache if you keep gorging like that,' I warned him.

Hey, it sounded funny in my head. But that brat had to come along and ruin even that momentary bit of solace.

'It's time, my lady,' said Fidick.

I could see him more clearly now: the slender frame, the angelic blond curls, the posture so relaxed it could only belong to someone who'd suffered the worst humanity had to offer children and somehow decided he didn't much care. When last we'd seen him, Fidick had claimed he was done with Aurorals and Infernals and wonderists like us. He was going to go off and find some nice family to adopt him. Apparently, he'd changed his mind.

'Go on,' he urged Eliva'ren, who was still holding tightly to her son. 'Kill the other wonderists so that I can reshape Cade's planar connection – that's the only way you and your son can return to your own world.'

Eliva'ren's face as she looked up at me over her son's shoulder was filled with twisted, mangled expressions of incalculable gratitude and unfathomable misery. She had warned me all along that in the end she would bring forth the dooms of my friends and the far worse one awaiting me, and despite all my attempts to fight that destiny, here we were, back at that same fork in the road. The last time – was it truly only a few minutes ago that I'd sent my consciousness into the Pandoral's insect forms to enter his realm? – I'd tried to convince her that the one part of my destiny she couldn't perceive, the one unpredictable, redeeming element of chaos, had been her own influence over me.

Turned out, I was wrong. Nothing, not even Eliva'ren herself, could make her change the course she'd set for herself nine years ago in that Glorian prison when her child had been born into an entirely different plane of reality. But of course, as the remnants of the Pandoral being had warned me before I'd fled his collapsing realm, order is only temporary, and chaos has a habit of showing up when you least expect it.

'Mamma?' said the boy.

It was a small thing to say – the kind of appeal a mother hears thousands of times a day from her child. Only, this was the very first time Eliva'ren had heard her son's plea.

Talk about a potent magic spell.

'It's the only way,' she tried to explain to him. 'This is how we get home. You have . . . you have grandparents and aunts, and an uncle who's so funny he can make you laugh in the middle of a toothache. You have a people waiting for you, and a culture. A future. A destiny.'

He smiled up at her, in that moment looking far wiser than his years should allow, and precisely as wise as one who has spent every day of his short life watching the strands of potentiality shimmer all around him with all that their possible futures could be. 'I do have a destiny, Mamma: three possible dooms, just like you always tell people. One was to die in the Pandoral realm, but Cade came to get me. Another is to return home to our realm and live out our lives with all those uncles and aunts. But the destiny I choose is' – he held onto her as he reached up on his tiptoes and whispered something in Eliva'ren's ear that I couldn't hear.

Which was when things really went nuts.

CHAPTER 50

Chaos and Order

During the seven years I spent selling my services as a mage-for-hire I'd fought in plenty of wars. Some of those armed conflicts were big, most were small, and all of them involved a fair amount of chaos. In fact, you could boil down pretty much all military strategy to the precise calibration of order among your troops and chaos in your enemy's. In all those years and battles, I had never witnessed chaos of the kind unfolding on that unremarkable field outside the ruins of a fortress whose name I doubt anyone fighting that day had even bothered to learn.

Even before Hamun's fateful words to the mother he'd just touched for the first time in either of their lives, the scene had been something of a shitshow.

'The Celestines are trying to rally their troops,' Alice warned, peering at the Auroral army some two hundred yards away. She really does have remarkable vision, even for a demoniac.

'Which ones?' I asked.

The vertical slits of her eyes narrowed even further. 'There appear to be three left alive. The Celestine in command is the one with whom you claim to have fornicated.'

Like that's something I'd brag about. Still, if the Celestine of Rationality came out on top, that might be good news for us.

'What about the Devilish?'

'Dead.'

'All of them?'

'Their corpses are being dismembered and eaten as we speak.' She didn't sound too broken up about that. 'Most of their surviving forces have sided with Tenebris and his cabal. All diabolics, naturally.'

Well, they are the best schemers in the Infernal realm, I thought, though I had more pressing matters to contend with than what the new Infernal Hierarchy would look like. I felt like someone had pulverised every bone and sinew in my body to a fine paste, then sculpted it back into a semblance of me, only to have forgotten to let the clay set properly. Shame was barely able to stand and Galass had collapsed into the arm of Aradeus, who was still somehow managing to keep wielding his rapier to fend off some over-eager Demoniac Hellions. Corrigan's Tempestoral bolts were getting feebler, while a squad of Angelic Valiants and Glorian Ardentors was growing bigger as more of them were deciding killing us was the best opportunity to gain favour with the Auroral Sovereign – who still was only a bullshit story the Celestines invented to keep everyone in line.

I hadn't seen Temper get struck by any weapon or spell, but the kangaroo looked as if he wasn't long for this life. He was moving weakly, stumbling over his own feet, still trying to guzzle blood from every single body he could find. Perhaps he thought the blood would cure him of whatever sickness had likely been killing him ever since I'd brought him to this realm.

Sorry, buddy. I should've cast that Pandoral spell on some unwilling bat rather than seeking out a willing spirit. I guess your species just aren't that bright.

Meanwhile, on the patch of dusty field where I was trying to keep myself from vomiting for fear my still-unstable internal organs would come out my mouth, things were getting tense.

'You know what will happen to him,' said Fidick. Eleven-year-old kids really shouldn't be able to sound so ominous, but I could see his words were having an effect on Eliva'ren. 'Look around you, Jan'Tep. This entire plane of existence is doomed. It was poorly made, the walls between it and other realms too frail.' He pointed to me. 'The very phenomenon that allows wonderists to garner spells from those other planes of reality has brought this one to the brink of collapse. You think the Aurorals and Infernals are the only ones seeking to dominate this realm, to harvest the ecclesiasm of sentience so abundant and so wasted on the conscious beings who infest it? You will raise your child in a place where war is never-ending, because consciousness engenders separateness, and from that separation comes conflict. You will die, leaving your son to suffer for your mistake.'

There really wasn't much fault I could find in Fidick's argument. Despite everything I'd gone through to try and prevent an eternal war between the Celestines and Aurorals, all I'd really accomplished was to make it easier for Tenebris and his merry band of plotters to replace them. Would the new lords send countless generations of human beings to war against one another like an endless line of toy soldiers? Maybe not; I recalled what he'd said about winning the battle for souls through seduction and sensation rather than combat. Perhaps the entire world would be split down the middle, with brothels and paella restaurants on one side and pristine marble cathedrals on the other. Either way, people like us, wonderists who had just enough power to defy both sides, would become nothing more than targets to be eliminated so we couldn't interfere in the future.

'There's still time,' Fidick continued, his youthful voice growing more confident as he sensed Eliva'ren wavering. 'Bring forth the doom of the other wonderists and I will refocus the gate within Cade to lead back to your world, your people, your family.' He shot me an impressively innocent smile. 'Alas, with the angelic dead, we'll have to crack open his chest cavity to make room for you both to pass through, but no one said going home was going to be easy.'

I really wanted to punch that little prick in the face again, just once, but I was so weak it would only have embarrassed us both.

'Mamma, please,' Hamun repeated, tugging at his mother's hand. 'It doesn't have to be like he says. We can help make things better here.'

Shouldn't have added that last part, kid, I thought. *Your mamma's seen too much of this world to believe that.*

Still Eliva'ren hesitated. She was watching me now, searching for some sign that maybe her son was right. I could have lied to her – hells, I pretty much had a sacred duty to do so, all things considered.

For once, my talent for deception eluded me. 'It's an awful place,' I said. 'I've travelled the length and breadth of this continent and two others, and everywhere I go, the powerful few find ways to oppress the many. Maybe on your world there are spiritual forces that reward decency and kindness and punish venality and cruelty. Not here, though. Whatever magic comes into this realm is wielded by guys like me – worse than me, for the most part.'

Corrigan fell back, a nasty gash glowing gold on his left shoulder where an angelic's halberd had sliced him. 'I really think you should leave the speeches to me from now on.'

'Now,' Fidick told Eliva'ren, a command, not an appeal. 'Cade's little crew are failing already. The angelic is too weak to fight, the blood mage can't stand on her own. Their Tempestoralist can no longer summon so much as a spark. Their demoniac and totemist are reduced to fighting off their opponents with swords. The other creature—' He made a sour face as he glanced at Temper, who was panting and swaying on his feet, no longer able to bend down even to lap the blood from an open wound. He was struggling to breathe, even as he growled his only word over and over again – and perhaps it really was the most apt word for this screwed-up existence in which he'd found himself.

'Their doom is already unfolding, Eliva'ren,' Fidick went on. 'Your choice is merely to quicken it – wait too long and you will lose your chance to get home with your son.'

'Cade . . .' Her voice was gravelly, as if misery had become stones and broken teeth in her mouth. 'I'm sorry.'

The field around us began to change, grass and weeds withering away. Shadows appeared on the ground in the shapes of the six people – well, five and one kangaroo – I loved more than I'd ever thought possible. The shadow beneath my own feet wasn't even human-shaped. I guessed it was going to be a bad death for me.

I forced a smile to my lips, which only made me more nauseous. I decided that Corrigan had been right, that if this was the end of my existence, I was going out with a better speech. 'Hey, it's okay. I got to live longer than I had any right to. I've cast spells from three different planes of existence – three different forms of magic – and witnessed wonders most people can only dream of. I got to fight alongside the best and most ridiculously screwed-up band of mages this world has and will ever see. And I got to make love with the most remarkable person on this plane of reality or any other . . .'

'Cade,' she repeated, a lament this time for all the potentialities collapsing between us.

'. . . the Celestine of Rationality,' I finished. 'I mean, don't get me wrong, you were great. That thing with the one leg up in the air and— But I guess I shouldn't get into that with children present.'

Of all the inappropriate jokes I've told in my life, and there have been a great many of them, I really thought this one had landed flatter than any other. All of them were staring at me – Eliva'ren, Fidick, Galass, Shame, Aradeus . . . Even Corrigan looked mildly horrified, and he was bleeding out from a golden wound on his shoulder.

Then an odd kind of miracle happened.

'Motherfucker,' Temper said.

As that was the only word he knew, I couldn't be sure he meant it the way it had come out, but the best jokes are those you don't see coming.

Eliva'ren's first laugh came out as a perfunctory chuckle, as if she felt politeness demanded recognition of the irreverent way we were facing our doom. Then that laughter became genuine, and because it turns out that jokes are their own kind of spell, with a power to heal, to change and to make us reconsider our fates that may well be limitless, inevitability began to collapse under its own weight, certainty cracked at the seams, the cold grey stone fragmented into probabilities which shed the dust and mortar to float above us as those most beautiful of living things, possibilities.

'No!' Fidick screamed, petulant in his outrage. To be fair, he was only eleven, and he'd experienced a lot of trauma in his young life. Also, he was evil to his rotten fucking core. 'Kill them!' he shouted to the Aurorals and Infernals now encircling us. '*Kill them all!*'

I'm not sure why the angelics and demoniacs appeared willing to follow the orders of a little boy, however beautiful – I suppose he was part of Tenebris' cabal, so maybe they figured he was destined for big things.

Too bad destiny doesn't always work out like you hope.

Shame overcame her exhaustion from maintaining my body's cohesion long enough to grab Fidick by his pretty face and quickly mangle it. Alice shouted something in her own language. I didn't recognise it, but presumably it meant, 'Hey, you promised I could cut off his feet first!' I'm fairly confident in my translation because even as Shame was holding Fidick up by his mutilated face, Alice had whipped out her sword and sliced him off at the ankles. Fidick screamed, but it wasn't especially loud since he no longer had a mouth.

Not content with that, she began to—

You know what? Given our recent conversion to gallant heroism, maybe I shouldn't describe the death and dismemberment of a beautiful young boy. Suffice it to say, he deserved it, and it went on for a while.

You never want to believe that brutal murder can be a balm for the soul, but I swear, when it was done, I saw something deep inside Shame unclench. It was as if Fidick had kept her in a binding spell all this time, and only now was she free of him – and free to perceive humanity as something more than unconscionably cruel. Aradeus took the despicable little prick's remains from her and, with remarkable gentleness, set the pieces down in a dip in the field as if he intended to bury him, should we survive the next few minutes. I would have expected Shame to rage at this act of undeserved compassion for so foul an enemy as Fidick had proven himself. Instead, the former Angelic Emissary looked with curiosity at Aradeus, as if he were a puzzle that she was only just beginning to solve. I think that might be what it looks like when a person is starting to realise they're in love.

Alas, the numbers of Aurorals and Infernals who'd decided to focus all their attention on killing us had swelled to more than a hundred. Eliva'ren shoved Hamun behind her even as she began unleashing her destiny-summoning abilities on a massive scale. The grass that had been dead only seconds ago was coming back to life, while behind us, the ruined fortress reassembled itself into what I suspect might have become a rather lovely palace had not one of the Valiants got in a lucky shot with a golden arrow.

Eliva'ren screamed. Her son screamed louder.

That had always been the problem with her abilities: although she was unimaginably powerful, her powers were still contained within a human body with all its innate frailties. She'd always been clever about when and how to show herself, always preparing in advance to ensure she couldn't be taken unawares. She'd never before exposed herself to this many opponents.

'No!' I shouted, fighting against my own weakness to draw on my Pandoral attunement. It was too late, though. If that chaotic realm still existed, it was completely cut off from this one. I was, for the first time since I was a teenager, just a regular human being without any magic at all.

Eliva'ren fell to her knees and Hamun, brave boy, tried to shield her with his own body. You'd think the gods-damned Angelic Valiants would've been moved by such righteous bravery in a child, but they just kept coming, content to murder innocents alongside the same Infernals they'd come to this plane of reality to exterminate.

Corrigan did his best, managing a trickle of Tempestoral magic that was just about enough to give the same Valiant who'd shot Eliva'ren a nasty burn on his cheek. Alice and Aradeus were both caught in Infernal man-catchers, the long poles with spiked levers that wrap around the victim's neck, digging into their throats the more they try to resist. Shame was unconscious, having wasted the last of her strength on me. Well, also on murdering Fidick, but you can't blame her for that. Galass, usually loath to unleash her blood magic on living beings, was so weakened by helping Shame to keep me alive that she barely managed to bring a pink blush to the cheeks of the enemies she was trying to exsanguinate.

'Sorry, buddy,' Tenebris said, approaching the ring of soldiers surrounding us. 'I would've tried to warn you off, but you never did listen to reason . . . Or Rationality.'

Void take me, how many deaths will I need to suffer to live that one down? The answer turned out to be at least one more.

Tenebris was accompanied by his two fellow diabolics, a pair of Glorians who I guessed were also part of his cabal, and a brand new convert to his cause.

'Oh, he listens once in a while,' said the Celestine of Rationality in a rather naughty tone of voice. I suppose with both the Celestines of Chastity and Humility dead, she could afford to be a little risqué. 'But he never did learn to heed what he hears.'

I saw something then, just a strange jerking motion in the corner of my eye. I knew it might be nothing, but some small part of me, the part that trusts in the perversity of the universe and the unexpected redeeming power of unusual friendships, decided to go out believing that I was due for a second miracle.

'What did you say?' the Celestine asked, stepping through the soldiers, both Auroral and Infernal, who made way for her. 'Come, Cade. There's something tragically disappointing in the only Mortal I've ever taken to my bed making his last words a vulgar insult.'

'Just one word,' I corrected her, then I looked to Corrigan, who was only barely conscious, but not even impending death could keep the grin from his face as we said together, louder and prouder than any battle cry, 'Motherfucker!'

And because the universe is just as perfectly perverse and wondrously insane as I've always believed, that's when the kangaroo exploded.

CHAPTER 51

All that Blood
Had to Go Somewhere

I'd never understood why Temper had been so determined to drink the blood of his newfound home dry. I'd assumed there must be something addictive about it, or perhaps that wherever he'd come from, kangaroos happened to be the most bloodthirsty creatures imaginable. I suppose I should've given more thought to the particularities of the Pandoral spell I'd used to summon him here, seeking out a creature who for some reason wanted to be transformed into something other than what nature had intended. 'Blood-sucking kangaroo' had seemed a poor choice to me, but out there on that field, surrounded by far too many enemies, my only friends vastly outnumbered, I finally learned that *blood* hadn't been Temper's desire, but rather what blood could give him on this realm that it couldn't in his own.

Blood magic, as I may have mentioned, is the only form of wonderism native to the Mortal realm. Everything else draws on the physics of other planes of reality. Galass had been hampered in her training both from a lack of available mentors in the art as well as rather too benign a nature. Temper, as it turned out, did not suffer from the latter. Turns out, there's a lot you can do once you've ingested enough blood from humans, Aurorals and Infernals.

'By the Void,' Corrigan swore, fighting to stay conscious long enough to witness this particular . . . well, *miracle* doesn't quite feel like the right word.

'Are those—?' Galass stopped herself, realising that if anyone was going to keep Corrigan alive it would have to be her.

'Magnificent,' said Alice with far less jealousy than I would've expected under the circumstances.

What had first appeared to be Temper exploding had been only the first part of his transformation. A fine mist of blood had sprayed from his every pore, clouding the air in a scarlet haze. Only when we felt the first aftershock, like the gust of a hurricane so powerful it not only banished the blood-mist, but knocked the nearest ranks of attackers off their feet, did we see what he'd become. Temper leaped into the air, far higher than should be possible, even with his formidable hind legs. Then came a second gust as the massive wings that had *bloomed* from his back beat once more, sending him even higher.

'The wings,' Aradeus began, as mystified as we all were, 'are they made of—?'

'Blood,' Alice finished for him. 'Not even among the Infernal beasts has such a thing been witnessed in millennia. The artform for manifesting bloodwings was lost long ago, as was that of conjuring bloodfire.'

'Bloodfire?' Hamun asked, standing next to his mother and not looking nearly terrified enough for a small boy. 'What's that?'

He was answered a moment later when the Auroral forces tried to attack Temper. Their arrogant trumpets were answered by a crimson gout of flaming droplets of blood that disintegrated everything they touched. Angelics and Glorians screamed as they died, some trying with their last breaths to turn and attack the Infernals, who'd had the sense to step back from that fight.

We stayed like that a while, watching Temper obliterate our

enemies, sounding his traditional battle cry between each blast of bloodfire. I could already tell it wouldn't be long before all the blood he'd ingested to create this rather foul and clearly evil form of wonderism would be used up, but he was a smart kangaroo, so I was pretty sure he'd keep enough in reserve that we'd still have a rather nasty rejoinder to make when Tenebris inevitably came over to try to threaten us into submission.

That's when negotiations would begin in earnest.

CHAPTER 52

Real Heroes Settle for a Draw

You couldn't call it a peace treaty, but what Shame and Alice managed to negotiate with Tenebris and his cabal ended up being . . . well, a tolerable armistice. It would probably last about a week.

Our lives are plagued by absolutes. The Lords Celestine – up until they got their arses roasted by a faction of their fellow Aurorals – had insisted there was both absolute good and absolute evil. The Lords Devilish, stupid pricks, had gone out of their way to prove them right. A philosopher once speculated that fire was the absolute of heat and ice the absolute of cold. I've never visited the sun, but I'm going to take a wild guess that it's significantly hotter than a campfire.

Human beings are prone to thinking in absolutes, it's true, but we're sure not built for them. There's never one *absolutely* right choice, or even an *absolutely* wrong one. We never win an absolute victory, nor can we ever truly lose everything, even though it does sometimes feel that way.

'What the fuck's your problem?' Corrigan asked. He reached up to swat me across the head, then groaned and slumped back on the mossy knoll where Galass had told him to rest after stitching the still sizzling golden wound.

'What's my problem?' I repeated. 'Oh, nothing much.' I pointed to the ruins of the fortress, where Tenebris and his cabal of disaffected

Aurorals and Infernals were already using some of the power they'd taken from the Celestines and Devilish to erect a grand palace. The Pantheon, they were calling themselves, those six arseholes. 'We risked everything, killed who knows how many angelics and diabolics and malefics and all the rest, to prevent a war from turning the Mortal realm into one giant game board, and humanity into an endless supply of pieces for the Celestines and Devilish to play with.'

'And we did,' Corrigan insisted. 'Those pricks are mostly dead or captive or whatever Tenebris and his merry band of idiots are doing with them.'

'Yeah, only now that merry band of idiots are setting up shop as the gods of the Mortal realm.'

'So? We'll fuck them up, too.' He laughed, groaned from the pain of aggravating his wound, then chuckled more cautiously. 'It's kind of our motto now.'

I tugged at the tatters of my coat. 'Sorry I wrecked the uniform.'

Corrigan shrugged. 'Ah, we'll buy new ones. Aradeus says he's got some more colourful designs in mind. I've decided I'm open to the suggestion ... With your approval, of course, oh great and wise coven leader.'

'Seriously?' I asked. 'You expect me to lead anyone after this mess?' I held up my hand, which served no purpose, I supposed, but was meant to illustrate my current incapacity. 'There's no longer a Pandoral realm, Corrigan, which means I have no attunement. I'm not a wonderist any more.'

'You weren't much of one before, but we still followed you.'

That admission caught me off guard. 'But why? Corrigan, you second-guess me at every turn – and you're right to do so! My entire peace plan fell apart, our enemies played us for fools right up until the end, we barely came out of this ali—'

'Don't forget, you slept with a crazy doom-witch.'

'That too,' I acknowledged.

Undeterred by pain or the promise of worsening his injuries, Corrigan forced himself to his feet, grabbed me by the collar and hauled me up to standing. 'You're a fucking idiot, Cade Ombra. The worst tactical commander I've ever met – despite being the most brilliant tactical *mind* I've ever encountered. You've got no sense of proportion, no ability to recognise when the odds against us are too great. You'll risk sending six of us to our deaths just on the off-chance you might save one of us. You're a self-righteous, belligerent martyr. A closet idealist. You claim to be a cynic but you can't stop yourself from rushing headlong into every mad quest to save the world even when you know – *you know* – you can't possibly succeed.'

'Then why do you keep helping me?' I asked.

He grinned. 'Because I fucking love watching you try.'

Then he pulled back his right fist and punched me in the face so hard I passed out.

I couldn't have been out for long, because the pain in my jaw felt all too fresh when Eliva'ren came and sat beside me. Whatever claim she'd thought she had to being a potentially good mother was rendered untenable by the fact that not ten yards away, Hamun was hanging onto Temper's back as the kangaroo repeatedly hopped twenty feet in the air before spinning around in circles and landing again. All the while, beast and boy chanted a word that should never come out of the mouths of children. Or kangaroos.

'What do you suppose we should call his species?' Eliva'ren asked. 'Flying vampire kangaroo? It's a bit long-winded.'

'Kangadragon?' I asked.

She nestled against my shoulder. 'Misses out on the whole blood-drinking thing, doesn't it?'

Hamun must've heard us because he called out, 'He's a vampidragaroo!'

'Stupid kid,' I said.

I felt the blush in Eliva'ren's cheeks as she smiled against my chest. 'Yeah. I'm thinking of putting him up for adoption.'

'I heard that!' the boy said, then came running to us, flopping against my other side. 'You are the *worst parents ever!*'

I sat there, frozen for a moment, not sure what the hell I was supposed to do now. So I followed my instincts and did the stupidest thing imaginable: I held Eliva'ren tighter and reached around with my other arm and laid it across the boy's shoulder, knowing full well that such gestures are not only questions, but promises.

'Eliva'ren of the House of Ren?' I asked.

'Yes, Cade Ombra of the Malevolent Seven.'

'If I somehow, despite having no magic left in me, no army other than five very emotionally challenged wonderists and one—'

'—vampidragaroo,' Hamun put in, helpfully.

'Yeah, that. If I can somehow stop the Mortal realm from falling to pieces in the next year or so, what are the odds you'll be so impressed that you agree to marry me?'

She nestled deeper into my chest. 'Pretty slim. I've never seen myself as destined for marriage.'

'That's what I figured.'

Hamun leaned in closer and whispered in my ear, 'Don't worry, Cade. I'll work on her.'

I sat there, those two unexpected and wonderful weights pressed up against me, and watched as Tenebris and his pantheon erected a palace so grand one could only describe it as befitting the gods themselves.

I was definitely going to start by blowing that piece of shit up.

ACKNOWLEDGEMENTS

A Litany of Sinners

The Infernal travesty that this book has inflicted upon innocent readers of fantasy everywhere might well have been avoided had it not been for an unholy cabal of malefactors collectively known as 'my publishers, colleagues and friends'. United in their sinful enthusiasm for profanity, these literary reprobates gleefully unleashed upon an unsuspecting world a vampire kangaroo whose only spoken dialogue (uttered no fewer than nineteen times in the manuscript) is the word '*motherfucker*'. *[We asked for more, but Sebastien worried that overuse might 'distract from the blood-wings thing', so we let it drop. -AP]*

Truly, the fantasy genre has entered a downwards spiral from which it may never escape.

On the other hand, you'll never convince me that The Lord of the Rings films wouldn't have been even better if only Peter Jackson had enhanced Tolkien's original text with a few carefully chosen '*motherfuckers*'.

Alas, I was informed by our crack legal team that any such quotes might get us in trouble with the Tolkien estate. Instead, I have offered the following timestamps for the standard DVD edition of the movies so you can skip to those points and, at the appropriate moment, add in the necessary textual amendment to heighten your friends' enjoyment of the film. Best not to warn them in advance . . .

1. Begin playing at 00:08:06, then, after the word 'late', calmly add 'motherfucker.'

2. Begin playing at 02:08:27, then, at 02:08:32, shout 'motherfucker!' at the top of your lungs.

*Note: You may be tempted to substitute the word 'fools' for 'motherfuckers' at 02:09:11. However, I advise against this as it would be in poor taste. Let's keep this classy.

3. Instead, wait until you get to 02:34:36, then, at 02:34:40, substitute 'very' for 'motherfucking.' Your friends will thank you.

Such inarguable examples of sublime prose aside, those seeking to assign blame for the artistic atrocity you hold in your hands will find below the many sinners and their sins who have contributed to our shared cultural downfall.

Purveyors of Pathological Publishing Purulence

First and foremost, let us condemn those who inflicted upon the fantasy genre not only this unholy author but encouraged him to unleash this blasphemous manuscript upon an unwary publishing industry.

Jon Wood of RCW Literary surely takes the lion's share of the blame, since I warned him that *The Malevolent Seven* was written for fun, without any intention of publication. He foolishly insisted on showing it to my publisher. It was the fastest sale I've ever made.

Heather Adams and Mike Bryan of HMA Literary took an unpublished, idealistic Canadian writer and proceeded to mould him into the hack whose name appears on this and seventeen other fantasy novels published in sixteen languages around the world.

Jo Fletcher, formerly publisher of Jo Fletcher Books, an imprint of Quercus, a division of John Murray Press, a Hachette UK company, has one of the most discerning eyes in the industry. Apparently, she stared into an eclipse too long the day Jon handed her the manuscript for *The Malevolent Seven*.

Anne Perry, Publishing Director of Arcadia Books, formerly Jo

Fletcher Books, an imprint of Quercus, a division of . . . you get the idea. Anyway, despite my many generous attempts to irritate her to the point of striking me from her new list, she not only went ahead with the publication of *The Malevolent Seven*, but bought two – *two!* – sequels. I now suspect she only agreed to this so that she could punish me by insisting the sequels be named *The Malevolent Eight* and *The Malevolent Nine*, condemning booksellers to a lifetime of readers asking where they can find Malevolents One through Six. *[This is true. – AP]*

Effusive Enthusiasts of Execrable Epics
While some of the above at least have the excuse that they were being paid somewhere along the line, the following individuals discussed the various plot points and themes of The Malevolent Eight *as a favour. I hope one day they can learn to live with what they've done.*

Jim Hull of NarrativeFirst.com is an expert in story structure who was kind enough to chat with me about the dramatic implications of a band of mercenary mages trying to prevent a war by killing as many people involved as possible.

Andy Peloquin, famed author of the popular Darkblade books, read the first finished draft and provided several helpful insights. I believe one of them was, 'Maybe you could make the murdering of the angels even more violent and disgusting.' *[Thank you, Andy. -AP]*

Instigators of Inordinate Scriptural Scrutiny
Every time you come across a line in this book and think, 'Why the hell would anyone write a sentence that offensive?', you should know that the answer is I was testing my editors, of which there were several, and not one of them asked me to strike the line.

Jo Fletcher – you remember, the aforementioned malefactor who bought the first book? Well, she edited every word of this manuscript *and left in all the naughty parts.* For shame, Jo. For shame.

Lauren Campbell was once a truly excellent author's assistant.

Then some strange curse befell her and she met me, resulting in her having to read each chapter of this book as I wrote it and, through what I can only assume was some sort of necromantic binding spell, not once suggesting I tone it down.

Anne Perry – yes, her again. I begged Anne – *begged* her – to tell me that the torture scenes and innuendo were over the top. She instead suggested I read a couple of mainstream romantasy books, whereupon I discovered that my stuff is positively tame by comparison. [*Also true. -AP*]

Gaby Puleston-Vaudrey, Assistant Editor at Arcadia, *could've* reported her boss to the authorities. Instead, she carefully ensured the entire process flowed smoothly and the publication dates were met.

Tania Wilde was the Managing Editor for this book and so is equally condemned for not ripping up the manuscript.

The proofreader of this book has wisely requested that their identity not be revealed. Actually, it's more that the proofreader wasn't yet chosen when I was writing these acknowledgments, but I'm sure they would've asked to be kept anonymous anyway.

Perpetrators of Prideful Production Pandemonium

Our prosecution of the sinful can't be limited to those responsible for the text itself. Surely many innocent souls were jeopardised by the seductive production values of the finished book.

Andrew Smith is to blame for the outstanding art direction of the cover, but surely the resulting excellence could've been avoided were it not for Keith Bambury managing the exceptional team of David Grogan and Justinia Baird-Murray at Headdesign.

Tara Hodgson oversaw the production of the book. It's my belief that she had actual angel blood mixed into the ink and the pages you're holding were made from puppy skin.

Ben Galley of Anicovers.com took the original artwork and brought it to life through animation. Kind of like how an evil wizard takes a corpse and reanimates it into a flesh-eating monster.

Joe Jameson narrated the audiobook. He'll deny this, but he told me in secret that he prepared for the recording session by acting out the parts – *all* the parts.

Carrie Hutchinson edited the audio and didn't bleep anything out. How could you, Carrie?

Cacophonous Conveyors of Consumer Calumnies

Let us turn our pitchforks upon those who, with an unbroken chain of malicious temptations inflicted on bookstores, reviewers and everyone involved in the purveying of fine fantasy books around the world, seduced you, the rightful judge, jury and executioner of this trial, to purchase (or possibly steal from a friend's bookshelf), this tome of torments.

Alex Haywood, who marketed the novel in the UK and abroad, was aided in her criminal endeavours by the diabolically cunning Laura Beard in executing her campaigns of terror.

Morgan Amer holds the title of Sales, Marketing & PR Director for Mobius in the United States and Canada. What does it tell you that someone would agree to have not one, not two, but *three* deadly sins in their job title?

Ella Patel, Beth Wright, Amanda Harkness and the infamous Mickey Mickelson committed numerous public relations sins, such as getting publications to review this book, tricking bookstores and conventions into having me speak and generally spreading lies about this book being 'fun' and 'irreverent', rather than 'unholy' and 'irredeemable'. Actually, it's still early in the process, so it's entirely possible those last two will show up in any number of reviews.

Aimee Ravichandran hurled a multitude of mind-warping spells (or, as she calls them, 'uplifting and informative posts') into the maelstrom of confusion that is the social media landscape.

Megan Schaffer, Kyla Dean, Sinead White and Jess Dryburgh, along with Imogen Bird, their counterpart in North America, placed this book into countless bookstores. Law enforcement suspects this was achieved through a process called 'reverse-shoplifting', in which the perpetrators sneak into bookstores wearing giant overcoats to mask the bags of books strapped to their bodies and then proceed to stick these on shelves without being caught by the bookstore clerks. I'm still not sure how this results in me getting paid any royalties, but okay.

Indemnified Innocents of Inscrutability

Christina de Castell, my darling wife, offered at several points to read the manuscript. Hers is that rare, discerning eye that only librarians possess which allows them to judge books not by their own tastes but with an understanding of how broad swathes of prospective readers will appreciate the story.

I made sure never to get around to giving the manuscript to Christina.

She is, therefore, blameless for the contents of this book. Everyone else heretofore mentioned is guilty as sin.

Malefic Messengers of Mystical Chicanery

A special exemption is made by the Lords Devilish and the Lords Celestine for those readers who, despite all the warnings offered here, choose nonetheless to provide expansive five-star reviews on Goodreads and elsewhere, share their love of my emotionally compromised, homicidal mercenary mages online and in person, or purchase dozens of copies for friends and family. This dispensation was difficult to obtain from the Auroral and Infernal judges, so please, make extensive use of it.

Also, don't hesitate to get in touch through my website at www.decastell.com/contact. I'm always happy to hear from readers and I reply (eventually) to every letter I receive.

Sebastien de Castell
January, 2025
Vancouver, Canada